SEEKER

SEEKER

BY NICHOLAS TAYLOR

Seeker

Somnium Press, LLC
PO Box 621458
Littleton, CO 80162

ISBN-10: 1938387074
ISBN-13: 978-1-938387-07-4

www.NicholasTaylor.co

Dedication

This book is dedicated to all of the friends, family and readers in my life who read and encourage my writing. Without your love and support none of what I do would be possible.

Other Titles by This Author

The Legon Series
Legon Awakening
Legon Ascension
Legon Restoration

The Contractor Series
Pactum
Seeker

CONTENTS

PROLOGUE

BRYAN HARLEY stood quietly in the night air, observing the house before him. It wasn't terribly late at night, but still many of the nearby windows were dark. Bryan was a Shape Shifter. At the moment, he was naked, kneeling behind a bush. The evening air was getting crisp as fall came into its own. Bryan didn't care to be cold, but it was necessary; after all, he needed to hide. Bryan was exceptionally skilled at hiding. Shape Shifters or Shifters as they are called, are rather adept at not being spotted. Bryan could not turn himself into a couch or any nonsense like that, but he could change his skin tone to whatever he liked. He changed his skin, rippling his flesh and breaking up the pattern of his body, defusing his form. Bryan couldn't become a couch, but he could turn himself into any other human shape he wanted, even changing his voice to that of the human he copied.

The downstairs lights went off in the house. Bryan paused for a moment before creeping to the front door. He had a key given to him by Angelica Vies, his employer. He looked around before slipping the key into the lock, and then turned it with a soft click. Carefully, he opened the door and stepped inside. A bristly welcome mat brushed the soles of his feet, tickling them. He looked around the entryway. Above him, the sound of a shower started.

Good, he thought. *That should keep him from hearing me.*

Bryan made his way up a narrow staircase, the narrow carpet runner making his approach even quieter. He turned his skin off-white to match the stairwell walls, just in case his quarry wasn't in the shower. Bryan only held a small syringe clasped in his hand, hidden from view. The staircase wound up to the second floor. Bryan padded down the upstairs halls and peeked through the gap of a bedroom door. The room was bright, making his eyes water for a moment. Bryan moved around a queen-sized bed and pressed himself against the wall next to the bathroom door. This is where he would wait.

While the movies made it seem like shower ambushes were the best, Bryan disagreed. It was one thing if you were planning on shooting the mark, but didn't work so well when you wanted them alive. No, he couldn't kill the mark -- he would need information for months to come -- and he didn't fancy wrestling a slippery, soapy man to the ground while also trying to stick him with a needle. Instead, Bryan waited and thought back to when he'd started all this Shifter stuff.

1972 was when Bryan figured out what he was. He was in junior high at the time. He'd just been caught taking a candy bar from a gas station. Bryan was an accomplished thief but had been caught this time, so he bolted, hiding under some trash behind the station as the clerk ran out back looking for him. Bryan had heard of the clerk, some guy who did some time for breaking into houses. Bryan figured that's how he'd been caught. Thieves know their own. He also knew this guy was going to kick his ass. The clerk had been clear about that, yelling it at the top of his voice and thirteen-year-old Bryan was on the verge of pissing himself. He just wanted to not be found, he wanted to blend in with the trash. The clerk searched for a solid ten minutes before giving up, passing Bryan by several times. It wasn't until Bryan stood and looked down at his hands that he saw why he hadn't been seen. His hands were black and shiny like the trash bags.

Bryan stood against the wall smirking, thinking back on the memory. After freeing himself from the trash, he'd had to spend a day getting his hands back to normal.

Bryan didn't truly start to come into his abilities until he was seventeen. He sighed, remembering the year. Britney Wamble had shot him down when he asked her out. She wasn't rude about her rejection in any way, but Bryan was still pissed as hell. Who had she been to say no? He'd gotten her back and that cocky little prick Richard Hicks, too. Richard was one of those good-at-everything, never-made-a-mistake kind of guys. Bryan hated that type. He remembered the night well. He'd discovered if he concentrated when he touched someone, he could mimic their appearance perfectly. Later he'd learn to find scars and learn a mark's personality, but in 1976, Bryan hadn't progressed that far yet. Still he thought he'd made a pretty decent Richard.

He'd tracked Britney to a small shop where she worked and followed her home. Bryan closed his eyes, relishing the memory. Oh, the lesson he'd taught her. Bryan smiled at the thought; she was one of many. Bryan hadn't done his homework and when she told the authorities it was Richard Hicks who had raped her, Richard was able to alibi out. He'd apparently spent the week with his family in Portland.

Bryan shrugged. *You were young and dumb.* He didn't make mistakes like that anymore. Now he knew what he was doing, knew how to mimic people to a T. After his failed attempt with Richard, Bryan had doubled his effort at mastering his craft. He caught his reflection in the glass of a picture on the wall. It was a picture of the mark and his wife. Bryan was currently taking on the appearance of someone he'd run into at the airport. Bryan couldn't even guess what his own appearance was anymore; it had been decades since he'd been himself. He reached out to get a closer look at the picture, looking at the mark and his wife. She wasn't anything to write home about, but from his recon, he'd only have to screw her once every few weeks.

Families were the quickest thing to blow a job. Pulling one over on someone's co-workers was hard enough, but convincing a mark's spouse that you were their loved one was something else. Bryan spent weeks watching people, seeing how they worked together and how they played off each other. He'd also have to get little details from the mark, things like family trips and the like, things that kept someone's mind at ease when a loved one didn't seem right. In this regard, it was easier to be a woman; men rarely picked up on the little things.

The shower stopped. Bryan focused, gripping the syringe tightly in his hand. He held his breath as the bathroom door opened and a figure came out in a towel. Bryan rushed forward, wrapped his arm under the mark's chin, and pulled back as he jammed the needle in the guy's throat. The man jabbed an elbow into Bryan, but Bryan held fast and waited for the tranquilizer to take effect. As it did, the man's body went limp in his arms. Bryan lowered him to the bed and pulled off the towel. He placed his hand on the man's chest, his own flesh rippling as it took on its new appearance. Bryan began methodically inspecting the mark's body for tattoos or scars, finding only a few. The wife wouldn't be home for two days. Bryan made the skin on his belly split open, revealing a plastic bag with a phone inside. He turned on the phone and dialed Angelica.

"Did you get him?" she asked, not even bothering with a greeting.

"Yeah, I've got him. Where do you want to store him until we're done?" Bryan asked.

ONE

ALISON KAUR walked up to the police station at a fast clip, her shoes scraping loudly on the wet sidewalk. She held her coffee cup before her like a shield from the drizzly cold October morning. Dim light filtered through the overcast sky, making the police station appear dark, dull and uninviting. Alison was a homicide detective for the Denver Police Department, though she currently found herself on loan to the FBI, a bi-product of her contract (called a Pactum) with a team of Mages. Magic, or Vis, as it is called, had only been out in the open for a few years, and it had already changed the world Alison had grown up in. Gone were the days of thinking that things that went bump in the night were just fairytales. She knew better now; she knew that the fairytale was real.

She stepped into the elevator with cops and city workers, filling the small space with a wet musk from the morning rain. She rode the elevator to her floor watching the little numbers above the door light up with each floor the elevator passed. The door opened, and Alison made her way into the controlled chaos that was a police station. Rows of desks with piles of paperwork lined her path. Alison wove her way through the mass of people as she approached her desk, trying not to spill her precious cup of coffee. Sean Hughes, her partner, turned to greet her.

"Morning, Kaur," he mumbled, sounding not quite awake. He ran a hand through disheveled sandy hair, his gray-blue eyes tired, "we've got a meeting in ten," he said.

"Did you give Vis this morning?" Alison asked.

Sean gave a half smile and nodded "yeah, Mandy only gets enough from Heidi to last a week," he yawned. "I figure taking a few days' worth from me should give her a spring to her step, ya know, and it's the least I can do."

Alison wasn't going to argue that. Not long ago Sean had forced a Succubus escort by the name of Mandy Stafford to spy for him. He hadn't given her the information she needed or the supplies she needed for the job. As a result, Mandy and Sean both had all but been killed by a group of Trolls. To top it off, Mandy wasn't Sean's informant, she was Gabriel Decor's informant, and Gabriel was one of their partner Mages. Sean's dumb move cracked the case they were working wide open and confirmed just how dangerous of people they were dealing with. Later Sean had learned that Mandy did what she did to survive; that she -- as well as most other Succubi -- were for all essential purposes forced prostitutes. Now he gave her some of his Vis, his life force, to help her live. Doing so made him tired, and he had to be careful how often he did it, or he would run the risk of getting sick or even dying. Alison respected him for sacrificing the way he did as penance for endangering Mandy.

"How is Mandy?" Alison asked.

Sean's face darkened, his voice concerned, "Still shaken up pretty badly … she killed three men and a Troll. That's gotta have an effect on her, ya know?"

He was referring to a raid on a Trinity location Mandy had helped with. Mandy had gotten into trouble during the raid, and Alison knew Mandy was lucky to be alive. For her part, Alison could still see the raid in her head; hear the sound of men screaming, the smell of gunpowder. It was a terrifying memory that made her remember just how dangerous Vis users could be.

Alison set her purse under her desk and enjoyed sipping her coffee before the meeting. When it was time, she walked into a special conference room that had been made bug-proof by the Mages. Inside the room were a group of familiar faces. The first was Faith Penn, a Mage Seeker. She was small with deep green eyes, a stunning figure, and short dark hair. Next to her was her brother Gabriel Decor, a Paladin, the warrior elite of the Mage world. As a former Ark, Gabriel was very high-ranking. He stood leaning against a wall in a black overcoat, the grip of his sword Iram protruding. Gabriel was handsome, his jawline firm, his eyes dark beneath his wavy black hair. Next to him stood Maddison Beldame, the Paladin for the FBI. Her long silver hair framed a delicate face with ruby eyes. While Gabriel and Faith wore heavy coats, Maddison wore a skintight black leather outfit, her blade a Katana like Gabriel's named Vindictam. The Beldames believed that the way a warrior looked and the statement their appearance made was as important as fighting skill. Maddison was the perfect blend of beauty and horror.

The conference table was littered with notepads and sticky notes detailing the Trinity case up to this point and most important of all, the recent raids on Trinity locations. Alison was sure she'd never forget when she and the team of SWAT, Mutari, and Mages had to take an abandoned train yard that Trinity had been using for a headquarters in Denver. At the same time, the FBI had hit several safe houses with Maddison and her team. In the three weeks following, the FBI and DPD were still collating and collecting information and evidence from the raids. The case was still getting far too much media attention for Alison's liking. Early in the case, Gabriel had cut a car in half, and then tore up a Trinity safe house. These actions garnered a lot of attention but nothing that didn't blow over in a week or so. Now however, the media was talking about the biggest "collaboration of Vis and non-Vis users in history," combined with the largest organized crime bust in decades. The case was also doing a fantastic job of making for political buzz. Pundits on both sides of the aisle were quick to make uneducated comments on the case. Those who embraced Vis users in the world were calling the raids a sign of how far society had progressed and calling the event a miracle. Those opposed to Vis were calling for tougher laws and in many cases military action. Groups on all sides of the lines of law enforcement policy had opinions, and it was making Alison's inbox all but explode. It wouldn't be long until the truth about the case would be bent and twisted into an animal all in itself.

Just thinking about it made Alison's gut hurt, and she wondered if she'd have an ulcer before long. The Mages didn't seem all that affected by the media circus. Alison figured if she were as powerful as they were, she wouldn't care either. Another part of her wondered if they didn't understand or care about the impact the media could have on people. Either way, none of them showed any interest when Alison or Sean showed them news reports or articles.

Agent Cedric Alesbury with the FBI cleared his throat as he sat, the cheap conference room chair creaking, "Hughes, can you give us a wrap-up."

"Right," Sean started looking at his notes, "we've busted a total of ten Trinity locations in the Denver area. One prior to involving the FBI, and nine since. Teams have finished cataloging evidence from the train yard we took, along with the other smaller locations. As far as arrests go," he turned a few pages of his notes, "we have made a total of fifty arrests, ten of those being Succubi that we have separated from the regular prison population."

"What's the condition of the Succubi?" Sergeant Montoya asked.

Sean frowned in concern "not great. We have had people coming in to give them Vis, and the State has paid for several Mages to give Vis to the Succubi, but it's starting to get expensive … we just can't hold these girls much longer, sir." Sean finished.

Alesbury glanced down at the table. Alison knew he was thinking the same thing all of those in the room had. Succubi were for all intents and purposes forced into prostitution; however the law didn't see it that way. Also, all of the women in question had not only solicited sex, but also sold drugs, and or guns along with Vis-enchanted objects; though the latter wasn't illegal.

Other Succubi had been arrested in the raids of other Trinity locations, but most of those were just hookers. In light of their situation and the expense of detaining Succubi, the D.A. let the other Succubi off with community service in exchange for information about their time in Trinity.

"What's the cost per week in Vis?" Drew Brent, the D.A. asked.

Sean read his notes again "Fifty thousand a week."

Hearing the number, Alison groaned on the inside. Even with the FBI chipping in a large amount of funds, the case was costing the taxpayers a small fortune, and that was before having to house a group of Succubi who without Vis would either die or go on a killing rampage. She watched Brent, waiting to hear what he was thinking.

Brent was in his late fifties – possibly sixty, his black hair starting to thin and gray. He took his glasses off and cleaned them with his tie, contemplative; an expression of deep concern on his face. "We are in a bit of a bind on this one. On one hand, I can't afford to spend two point six million dollars a year keeping a group of drug dealing hookers off the street." He sighed. "At the same time, I can't very well justify letting said drug dealing, gun running hookers back on the street." He put his glasses back on, looking at Maddison, Gabriel and Faith, "I don't suppose the three of you have any suggestions?"

Maddison was matter of fact, "Unless you want to kill them or force other inmates to give them Vis, paying to feed and house them is the only option I see."

"Gabriel, Faith do you have any input?" Brent asked.

"I have to agree with Maddison; those are our choices and letting the girls die or forcing other people to give their Vis isn't truly much of an option." Gabriel said.

"They are all but dead anyway," Faith muttered in a far-off voice.

"Excuse me?" Alesbury asked.

Faith looked at him, holding his gaze, "They are all but dead as is. If they get released, those Troll clubs affected by this will want answers and want to know when their members behind bars are going to be let out. In some cases, I would think the clubs will blame the Succubi, so either way they are dead. Your best bet is to move them to another city and give them protection."

Brent sighed, "It's a pickle either way; we can't force someone into witness protection, but I will see what I can do. In any case, we need to get those girls out of prison before the media gets wind of the cost the city is incurring."

Brent looked to Alesbury, "What can you tell us about Trinity?" his tone that of someone asking a mechanic how much a costly repair was going to be.

Maddison was the one to speak, "We first got wind of them back in a small town in Utah, but since then we've found them in other cities, though we've had a hard time confirming which cites and to what extent they are playing in local affairs."

"Trinity is a different kind of animal," Alesbury explained. "They don't care about territory; in fact they seem to not even have one of their own. Denver is one of the first cities we've seen where they have such a defined presence. We aren't sure why that is."

"Defined?" Alison asked.

"Yes. The operation they were running with McLoughlin was far more complex than those in other places we've seen. Here in Denver, there were several safe houses along with a well-run network of Mutari and humans working side-by-side. They were running the show here more seamlessly than the government does with its Pactums. In other cities, Trinity was more of a middleman-type group. Those types would run guns and drugs along with a little human trafficking, but that was the extent."

Maddison spoke, "We think they were using Denver as a proving ground for a new branch of their organization. Before they were a middleman; but with Corey McLoughlin they became a partner, which suggests that Trinity is growing into a whole different kind of organization."

Alison didn't like what she was hearing. She could see what Maddison was talking about. Trinity was becoming a franchiser. Work with them, and you get all of the drugs and guns you want but also you now have Vis-enchanted objects to sell and use along with Vis users to work with. She could see where local crime lords would find Trinity to be both attractive, and a threat at the same time.

"So why use Denver then?" Alison asked.

Gabriel chimed in, "Simple. There are more Mages and Mutari per capita in Colorado than the rest of the country, and from a Mage point of view, it makes sense. We don't actually view the world in countries like Humans do; to us North America is just a large land mass, and here we have a large group of potential recruits right in the middle of that continent. If I were Trinity, I would start here too. Denver is connected to the rest of the continent and also has the Human and Mutari resources needed."

"I don't think that's entirely it," Faith said.

Everyone in the room eyed the quiet girl.

"We've found a lot of gold and silver from outside the US. Mutari aren't going to work for foreign coin," she pointed out, "but Mages will."

"But why would they need foreign Gold for Mages? Couldn't they use what's local?" Maddison asked out.

Faith shook her head, "Not if they are foreign Mages - they would have coin from other parts of the world on them, and …"

"Mutari staff," Gabriel spoke softly, "they would bring some of their own staff, so they didn't have to find new people …"

"That or they are expanding their operations from other parts of the world into the US or maybe even using services outside the US," Faith observed.

Alison was having a bit of a hard time following the Mages but from what she could gather, they were thinking that Trinity wasn't just in the good old USA. They were a global organization which if true; would be a huge problem for the FBI.

"What does this mean in the short term?" Brent asked, trying to bring the room to a manageable perspective. "If I'm in North America and I'm Trinity, what do I do?"

"There are going to be more locations," Gabriel said, "they won't give up that easily. Plus we know they have to have gun and drug depots; the safe houses we cracked weren't well stocked and the main headquarters had a good amount of inventory, but we didn't find any signs that Trinity was doing any production of Vis objects or even packaging drugs there."

Montoya nodded, "Right. So for now, we need to find the other locations and stop those."

"Do you think we should be considering the bigger picture here?" Faith asked.

"Yes I do," Alesbury said, "but for the time being we can hinder Trinity if they keep large amounts of inventory here in Denver. It's not a win, but it will slow them down and give us more time. What can the Seekers do?" he asked her.

"We will search for anything we can find. I will have to work closely with Maddison's Seeker and any others you have on staff," Faith explained.

"So am I to take it that you will be in charge of that?" Alesbury asked.

Faith nodded, "Yes, as Gabriel is the Paladin in charge, that makes his Seeker – me – in charge of any Seekers."

"And if Gabriel were not in charge?" Alesbury asked.

Maddison cocked an eyebrow, "Who would you have running the Mages?"

"You," Alesbury offered.

Maddison shook her head with a kind smile, "I take my orders from Gabriel," she said. "You will find that most Mages from Paladin families will feel the same. Until otherwise stated, Gabriel would be the head of the Arks and therefore our leader," she said simply and kindly.

Alesbury didn't argue with Maddison and Alison assumed the man had known that would be her answer. With that the meeting was at an end, and Alison went back to her day.

As Alison was wrapping up for the day, she tapped Faith's arm, "What are you doing tonight?" she asked.

Faith was about to answer when Alison said, "Oh, you're coming over to my place for dinner and wine? That sounds great, Faith! I'll see you at seven," Alison said cheerily, hoping Faith wouldn't fight her.

Faith looked at her dryly and then with the hint of a smile, "Fine."

FAITH PENN walked up to the door of Alison's condo, the gloomy day matching her mood. She stared at the door, not wanting to go in. She wanted to go back home and hide from the world. *Hiding things – there's a novel thought Faith,* thought Faith. Her arm stretched out, she rapped on the forest green door three times. Faith plastered a smile on her face that she didn't think Alison would see through.

The door swung open to reveal Alison in an apron that did not fit her personality in the least bit. Faith cocked an eyebrow.

Alison glanced down at herself in confusion and then made a face, "It was a gift from my mother … the next time she visits she'll be happy to see that it's been used. Come in," Alison said brightly.

Faith walked in the condo. To the left was a study with a small desk and off-white walls. In front of her was a staircase leading to the second level. She followed Alison up the stairs, noting a stain on the carpet.

"What's that?" Faith asked.

"What's what?" Alison turned, then following Faith's gaze said, "Oh that's blood I haven't been able to get up." She sounded irritated, "That night you saved Sean and Mandy, Gabriel came and got me. There were a couple of Vampires outside. Gabriel said that he would protect my house as best he could, but one of them made it inside. He must not have gotten hurt too badly though; I didn't find a body." Alison said.

"Was anything else amiss?" Faith asked. *How had she not heard about this? What else had she missed?*

Alison shook her head, "Not really. I think once they knew that I wasn't here anymore, they didn't bother with the house. I just need to talk to some of the crime scene clean-up guys; you wouldn't believe what kind of stains they know how to get out."

Alison kept moving up the stairs with Faith behind her. The condo smelled of what she thought was pizza. This was clearly the main floor – it was a large, open great room, functioning as kitchen, dining area, and living room all in one space making the condo feel bigger than it was. The wall was lined with large windows, allowing what little was left of the sun's setting light to find its way in through the clouds. Faith made her way across Alison's polished wood floors and saw the pizza on the counter. It appeared homemade.

"Who are you?" Faith asked Alison.

"Yeah I know, it's amazing I can cook," Alison said rolling her eyes, "if you can believe it. when I still had a life, all of my friends used to come over, and I cooked for them."

"Why don't you cook anymore?" Faith asked curiously.

Alison shrugged, "Honestly, it's not even that I mind only cooking for one; it's just that by the time I get home from work, I've either already eaten or I just don't feel like putting in the effort. Have a seat," she offered a chair.

Faith took the offered seat. Alison placed a plate in front of her with a slice of pizza on it, "Let me know if you want more."

"What's on it?" Faith asked.

"Basically sausage with a balsamic reduction. You'll like it; trust me," Alison said.

Faith took a bite and found that she did like it, "Where did you learn to make it?"

Alison blushed slightly "I kind of reverse-engineered it from a local restaurant. Theirs is better," she shrugged, "but mine has more love in it." Alison held up a bottle "I'm thinking we start with Cabernet."

Faith didn't argue about the wine; she figured if Alison's choice of wine was half as good as her cooking, she was in for a treat.

Her hunch was correct, and the Cabernet tasted incredible. It had a rich, robust flavor and just the right amount of bite. Faith was shocked when she felt a slight buzz hit her. She looked at Alison who hadn't spoken much, "Is there something in this?" she accused, holding up her wine glass.

Alison nodded, "Yep, grapes."

Faith's expression flattened "Mages don't feel alcohol, Alison."

Alison bobbed her head, "Sure they do, if you get a little something from their sister-in-law that makes it so they can't fight the effects of booze." Alison smiled, "Heck, and since you've never really had to deal with alcohol affecting you, I bet that glass of wine is doing the trick."

Faith put her glass down and looked at the bottle. She'd watched Alison uncork it, so the wine couldn't have anything in it. Then Faith looked at the pizza with accusation and back to Alison, who wore a smug impression.

"And why are you trying to get me drunk?" Faith asked coolly, feeling the wine more and more. Alison was right, Faith had never felt the effects of any substance before in her life and her tolerance would be near-nonexistent.

"Something's bothering you and I knew you wouldn't talk about it unless your inhibitions took a bit of a break," Alison said without a hint of remorse.

"And what did you give Erin in exchange for this?" Faith asked.

"She told me if you didn't see it coming, I didn't owe her anything."

Faith deflated. She should have seen this coming. Not that she could read what people were thinking, but rather that she had been munching on a Vis-laden pizza and hadn't even sensed it.

"So, do you want to tell me what's going on?" Alison asked. "You're kind of my only friend Faith, so you're all I have to worry about."

Faith looked at Alison, knowing she hadn't fooled the woman at all. She sighed, not knowing where to start. How did she explain what a disappointment she was to herself?

"Is it Angelica?" Alison prodded and then seeing Faith's face nodded sagely, "yep."

"You're worse than a Contractor," Faith accused, "you can read me like a book."

"What's got you so worked up about her?" Alison asked, not letting Faith change the subject.

Faith gazed down at the table, thinking for a moment and then said, "I can't best her," she admitted with shame. "She's too good; I've been looking for her for years now …"

Alison made a confused face, "Really?"

Faith nodded, "Yeah. I didn't tell anyone I was looking for her … I thought that if I was able to find Angelica, I would feel like I belonged at my brother's side, like I deserved the place I was given."

"Why don't you feel like you've earned your place?"

"I became Gabriel's Seeker because Patrick died and I was Gabriel's sister." She said, honest.

Alison was firm in her reply, "I don't buy that."

Faith eyed her.

"Think about it," Alison gestured animatedly, "Gabriel is unreal! I know I don't know what all he can do, but honestly the guy is scary good. Even that Maddison chick thinks he's the cat's meow."

"And how is this supposed to make me feel like I should be his Seeker?" Faith asked.

Alison looked her in the eye, "Because people who are that skilled don't make the mistake of dragging their kid sisters along for the ride. Sure, he may have taken you on at first because you were his sister, but trust me; if Gabriel didn't think you were up to the task, he would have found a way a long time ago to give you the slip. Think about it Faith, he not only trusts his life with you but also yours, do you think he's the kind of person to put his own sister in danger if she can't handle it?"

It was hard to argue with Alison. Faith knew how talented and disciplined Gabriel was.

"I know, and he believes in me, but I just can't help but feel inferior compared to him … and my mother for that matter."

Alison laughed, "Now *that* I can understand." She shook her head. "My mom can be a piece of work," she winced.

Faith perked up at that. She remembered not too long ago when Alison had confided her own feelings of self-doubt.

"My mother isn't unkind to me," Faith said, worried she'd given the wrong impression.

"I know; she's a nice lady. But she's also supposed to be like what, the best Seeker there is? And didn't she train Angelica?"

"Once again, how does this make me feel better?" Faith asked, "Though you're right on all counts."

Alison shrugged, "It just seems to me that Melinda would put a whole lot more effort into her daughter than she would someone else. And I would think with her being able to work with someone since birth …"

"I should be better …" Faith was defeated again.

"NO!" Alison exclaimed, "You aren't getting the point. You have the same training as Angelica, if not better. You have your brother who believes in you and most of the Denver Police Department, by the way. But your mother and Angelica have been doing this for years; you can't beat them at their own game, not yet at least."

"So what?" Faith asked, "Give up?"

Alison smiled, "No, never that. If you can't beat them at their game then make a game that you can beat them at." She held up a hand to keep Faith from talking, "Look, there's lots of ways to the top of the mountain."

Faith hadn't looked at it like that before.

"Angelica is using the same set of tools you have. You know their weak points, don't you?" Alison asked.

Faith sat back in her chair thinking. *Could I find my own path up the mountain?*

She must have been thinking for a while because she jumped at a pop when Alison uncorked another bottle. "Alright. Enough of that for tonight, just think about it, Faith," she said, pouring another glass.

TWO

FAITH PENN strolled through the gate of a train yard that not long ago had been the Denver headquarters for Trinity. The train yard was a vast expanse of mud, metal, and debris with plants growing in surprising little patches of life. Thick air carried the scent of dirt, oil, and chemicals, making Faith wrinkle her nose. All around her, things were cordoned off in yellow police tape. Faith found the tape odd. Humans put it all around crime scenes like it was a ward against intruders. If anything, Faith thought that it drew attention to a crime scene. *I suppose they wouldn't use it if it didn't work* she thought.

The top few buttons of her shirt were undone, exposing her skin to a crisp October breeze. She slipped her hands into the pockets of her overcoat and tapped into her Vis to warm herself.

Next to Faith was Maddison's Seeker, Amy Calamus. Amy was just a little taller than Faith with a similar figure, but where Faith had short dark hair, Amy's was long flowing blonde, her eyes an electric blue. Faith knew that her looks and the way she dressed made her stick out in a crowd. That was the Decor way, just as Maddison had turned her eyes red in accordance with her family's tradition. Amy was quite different from the other two women. She was from a family of Contractors and Enchanters.

Amy seemed to strive to blend in to her surroundings in every way. She wore jeans and a sweater. She looked good but utterly normal. Added to that, she used Vis to make it so people didn't notice her, which meant in a very real sense Amy was all but invisible.

Amy's blue eyes swept the train yard and came to rest on Faith. "What?" she asked.

"Nothing … it's just … you're very different from Maddison," Faith observed, and then added quickly, "Not in a bad way, it's just …"

"That Maddison does everything she can to draw attention to herself, and I'm not even a blip on the radar?" Amy said knowingly.

"Yeah," Faith said, "sorry," she added as an afterthought.

Amy went back to looking around "there's no need to apologize; that's what I go for. I don't want to be noticed, and Maddison does. It's how she works and how I work." She paused for a moment, "I also find that when no one notices me, I am able to observe the world more easily without being bothered."

Faith thought about that for a moment "I can see how that would be helpful." Then her tone became businesslike, "I want us to look for anything we can find today that might give us a lead."

Amy looked confused, "Wasn't the area already scrubbed by DPD, and you?" she asked.

Faith nodded, "Yes it was, in fact I did a very thorough job of looking for anything I could find." And then thinking back on her dinner with Alison added, "But Angelica and I were taught by the same person, so Angelica isn't just fighting me, she's fighting Melinda Decor."

"And I had a very different Vis training," Amy said catching on quickly, "but I don't see how I can do anything you can't …"

Faith nodded, "True, but if Maddison chose you to be her Seeker, then you must be exceptional. You have a different background than I do and will look at things differently. I want a new set of eyes on this place." Faith swept her hand in front of her, "Also, I want to see how you work, so I know how to best work with you. Even if we don't find anything today, we will be better equipped to work together in the future."

Amy nodded her agreement and started to walk around. She picked up a stick from the ground and held it in her right hand, poking things. When she came to boxes, she opened them and looked inside. Faith was happy Alison had told her to try new things. Amy didn't have her eyes closed and wasn't muttering spells. She turned up the lid of a can with the end of the stick and made a face.

"What are you doing and what's with the stick?" Faith asked with the hint of amusement.

Amy looked at her, "I'm using my eyes," she went back to looking around, "it's something Mages don't seem too big on. And the stick ..." she gestured around them, "is because we are in the realm of nastiness here and I don't want to touch anything," she finished with a shiver.

Faith was curious about how Amy worked, so she asked a follow-up question, "Do you always look around with your eyes first?"

Amy shrugged, "I don't know ... sometimes ... it depends, really. I figure you used Vis to take a gander at the place and if Angelica doesn't want us to find something, she'd have destroyed it or done a good job hiding it. There's too much Vis in the area from all the Mages and Mutari, and let's not forget the fight you had here. So something small could go unnoticed." She leaned over and picked up a plastic lighter. Holding it up to her eyes, she said, "Videre," softly. The lighter glowed a light peach.

Amy looked at Faith, continuing what she was saying, "And unless you use your eyes you miss things that Mutari and Humans drop. Things like enchanted lighters." She tossed the lighter to Faith who put it in a bag. Amy was kneeling down again in the area she found the lighter, "I spent years studying how humans investigate things, ya know," she said, "my hope was to combine my Seeker training with that of Humans."

Faith was intrigued, this girl was extremely observant.

AMY CALAMUS felt a twinge of self-consciousness as she explained her views. Faith Penn, along with her whole family, were legends in the Seeker world. Amy knew that Faith had been defeated by Angelica. Maddison told her as much, and said that Faith was shaken up by it. This made Amy feel uncomfortable. If Faith had been defeated, how on earth would Amy be able to do anything against Angelica?

Amy, like all Seekers, had passive spells that were always working; she could tell if anyone around her was a Mage, for example. Seekers tried to hide their Vis flow, but Amy had never met anyone who could hide their Vis flow completely from her. Indeed it was one of her most prized skills. Whenever Maddison had to deal with another group of Mages, it took Amy little in the way of effort to find other Seekers, but as far as reading Faith's Vis flow went ... well, from what Amy could tell, the woman was Human.

Amy focused back on her work while answering Faith's questions. She liked Faith and was looking forward to working with her in a way, but at the same time, one thing Amy disliked more than anything was being the center of attention. It was this trait that led her to become a Seeker in the first place. Not that she wanted to see combat or even that she wanted the money that came with the trade, but rather that she was able to make herself invisible to the world. She was fine when she was one-on-one with someone, but get her in a group, and Amy felt her heart rate go up.

"How do you go about working?" Amy asked Faith.

"Have you heard of layering?" Faith asked.

Amy shook her head, "I'm not sure I have."

"It's when you start with a simple spell that looks for Vis, and from there you keep adding new spells looking for different things. Each spell is a layer, and you bounce between layers, giving them more power or less. It in effect exposes the kinks in concealment spells and overwhelms most wards."

"I think I may have heard of that before," Amy said. "How many layers do you add?" she asked.

"It depends, but around fifty," Faith said casually.

Amy looked down at a can of paint, trying to hide the expression on her face. *Fifty? I can't even think of that many spells that test and break down concealment Vis; let alone use them all at one time.* Amy was in slight awe of Faith; she couldn't imagine the concentration it would take to keep fifty active spells working at the same time. *And Angelica beat her?* Amy wondered in horror.

"That's amazing, Faith. I don't think I could ever do that," Amy admitted.

Faith smiled at her warmly, "You can; trust me, it just takes some practice. The key is learning how to weave spells that work together."

They continued to talk about Seeking as Amy walked around looking for anything she could find. She knew they only needed a small lead to break the case. She found a handful of other Vis objects but otherwise they didn't have much to show for a day's work.

"So what now?" Amy asked Faith as the sun set.

"We will take these to the station to check in and then to my husband to find out more and maybe to Paul, he's a Goblin we work with. He might be able to tell us who made the objects." Faith said.

FAITH PENN walked into the police station with Amy by her side. Again Faith was reminded of the subtlety of Amy's Vis use as people only said hi to Faith, their eyes passing over Amy. The girl even seemed to weave around people as they walked; they could see her and avoid her, but they really didn't pay her any other attention. Faith wondered what types of spells she was using and tapped her own Vis, reading her surroundings. Amy wasn't using much in the way of Vis, and her spell didn't seem to stretch all that far around her.

Faith stopped, "How are you blending in so well?" She asked flat out, "You are using almost no Vis."

Amy smiled "it's in the way I carry myself mostly. I've learned to blend in to groups without using Vis at all, so the spells I use are minor."

"Can you hide your Vis use?" Faith asked.

Amy made a face, "Not like you can; it's something I need to work on."

Faith thought for a moment and then said, "I'll make you a deal. You teach me some of your techniques, and I'll teach you some of mine."

Amy's face lit up, "Really?" And then less animated said, "I mean if you want to; I would be fine with that."

Faith smiled, "I think it would do us both some good."

Part of Faith reeled at the idea of teaching anyone tradecraft. Seekers were not huge on divulging their secrets, but if Amy could give her an edge on Angelica, it was worth it. They walked into the conference room that Faith and Gabriel had cleaned and protected at the beginning of the investigation. Sean was the only one in the room working at a computer.

"What's up?" he asked as they entered.

Faith turned to Amy, who took a plastic bag from an oversized purse and set in on the table. Sean held it up, looking at the lighter inside.

"Good work," he said, without the hint of sarcasm.

"I would have thought you would make a comment about us just bringing back a lighter," Faith said.

Sean chuckled, "In the human world, cases have been won and lost over hairs found at crime scenes. What do you think it does?" And then he added, "And good job using a plastic bag, Penn, I think this is the first time I've seen you try to handle evidence properly. We might make a cop out of you yet," he said with his usual sarcasm.

Faith scowled and nodded to Amy, "the bag was her idea; not mine. But don't worry, I touched it without gloves before we put it in the bag."

Sean shook his head and looked at Amy, "Well, good try, Amy. So what is this thing? I assume it's not a normal lighter."

Amy spoke, "It's not. It's enchanted, but we don't know with what."

Sean looked serious, "So this is a James question, I take it."

"Yes it is," Faith said, "I sent him a message to come in."

At least he wasn't fighting them on using Vis anymore, nor did he seem to discount the roles that others played in Mage teams.

James came into the conference room not long later, smiling brightly. Faith loved this about her husband; he was always in a good mood.

"So, what do you have for me?" he asked after greeting everyone.

Faith handed him the lighter. James held it up to his face inspecting it, his wedding ring glowing red with Vis. He clicked the lighter on and smiled.

"It's a concealer," he said, "when you click the flame on it will make it so people around you won't pay any attention to you. In fact, you could use this to get away from the cops if you needed."

"So you think this was something the humans or Mutari were using?" Sean asked.

"I would suspect whoever needed it. I know a lot of Trolls have them when they deal Vis objects on street corners. But they would be great for anyone doing anything they didn't want to be noticed," James explained.

"Would it work on video surveillance?" Sean asked.

James shook his head, "No; this one would only make it so people didn't notice you. You would still need to be out of the line of sight of video cameras."

Sean smiled. "Thanks, James," and he went back to his work.

"Why does that make you happy?" Amy asked.

Sean explained, "This is a good thing. If a camera can pick up what the owner was doing, that could mean that a traffic or ATM cam would catch people. It's a nifty little tool, but most people would be overly confident with it. When you know everyone around can see and hear you, you check to make sure the coast is clear before you do something you want hidden."

"But with this, people won't think to do that," Amy said.

"Where would you get something like that James?" Sean asked.

"I wouldn't know, to be honest with you. I make a lot of Enchanted objects for sale, but those are all sold through Goblin Guilds, I never deal with vendors. Also, with this being for more of an illegal purpose, I would be surprised if Trinity got them from a standard Guild."

"We could talk to Paul about it; he'll know who'd sell this." Faith said.

"Paul's that Goblin, right?" Sean asked.

"He is. Do you want to come with us when we talk to him?" she asked.

Sean thought for a moment and then said, "Yeah I do, but I need to take care of some stuff first, would it be possible to go this afternoon?"

"Sure thing."

SEAN HUGHES walked up to a storefront on Broadway and stopped at the door, thinking this wasn't the place he was looking for. He turned to leave when Faith took his arm, "This is the place."

She opened the door, which dinged, and as soon as he was inside, the feeling that he was in the wrong place left him and he looked back at the door. He noticed that while the store's windows had shown shelves of books, there was a wall where the window should be. Around him were objects of every kind, many of them not resembling anything Sean had ever seen. Rows of shelves filled the space and he caught the scent of lavender air freshener.

"That won't happen again," a familiar voice said.

Sean turned to see Paul Labus standing behind a counter. He wore thick black-framed glasses, his face round and scruffy with a beard. His hair was a brownish red puff of tight curls.

"Yeah sorry, that's to keep humans from coming in here. But now that you've entered once, you can again," Paul said.

"Why don't you want people in here?" Sean asked suspiciously.

Paul laughed, pointing at all of the odd things in the shop, "What, and show them this freak fest? No thanks. I sell Vis objects and change out a little gold and silver. Only Vis users can enter this place without feeling the way you did."

Amy was looking at something on a shelf. Sean looked at it closely, "What is that?" he asked.

It looked like a little glass disc in a frame of silver. "It's a cooking thermometer," Amy said.

"What's wrong with the kind we use?" Sean asked.

"That one will tell you the temperature of everything you're cooking and it will let you know when each dish reaches the temperature you want," Paul said.

Sean made a face. "I guess that's kind of handy," he admitted.

"Oh, and did I tell you it has a one hundred yard radius, and will go find you to tell you something's done?" Paul added proudly.

Sean looked at the timer again. How many times had he burned something because he didn't hear the timer?

"You want one, don't ya," Paul said, "come on man, that's cool -- don't try and act all not impressed on me."

Paul was the type of nerd Sean liked. Paul reminded him of his father, who spent every Saturday watching info commercials buying stuff. That made Sean smile.

"Can a human use it?" he asked.

"Sure can," Paul said.

"How much?" Sean hedged.

"2SE should cover it."

Sean did the math in his head. *Dang, that thing is like sixty bucks.*

"Yeah ok, my old man will love this thing. I have to get it," Sean said.

Sean paid Paul with cash, giving him the amount two ounces of silver was worth for the day. Paul wrapped up the thermometer and then said, "So what's the real reason you are here today?"

Faith spoke this time, handing Paul the lighter, "We found this at the train yard."

FAITH PENN watched as Paul held the lighter in his hand and examined it closely. She saw his Vis flow as his liver lit up. Most types of Mutari only have one organ that produced excess Vis. This was the case for Goblins. Their livers would produce extra Vis, which allowed them to use their abilities. Paul would be able to tell the purity of the materials used in the lighter. Goblins weren't supposed to be able to tell what enchantments an object had, but with their ability to examine the purity of an object, they were able to tell when it was Vis-altered, and in many cases they could figure out what the enchantments were on it.

"Hmmm .. a concealer, huh," Paul said.

"How do you know that?" Sean asked.

Paul looked at him like he was a moron, "I'm a Goblin, dude." He looked back at the lighter, "What do you guys want to know? I'm sure you had James check it out, and he can tell you a lot more about it than I can."

"We're wondering who might sell them, or who might have made it … do you think they have an enchanter on staff?" Amy asked.

Paul looked up from the lighter, "Things like this are pretty common, to be honest with you, but …" he said, holding up a finger and walking behind a counter, "if it's a local Goblin that sold it, I might be able to give you an idea."

He held a magnifying glass up to the bottom of the lighter, "Good, that's what I was hoping for," he said, "a lot of things like this are made in bulk by enchanters and then sold to Goblin Guild distribution arms. That's the case for this one."

"Do you know the guild?" Sean asked.

Paul nodded, "Sure do; it's the Ex Conspectu Goblin Trading Guild, do you want to know more about them?"

Sean just gave him a look.

"Right, you're a cop. Ok, well Ex Conspectu means out of sight in English, and that's how the guild likes to be. They keep a pretty low profile and deal mostly in fringe objects like the one you see here."

"Fringe?" Sean asked.

"Yeah mostly in things that aren't common. Concealers are popular; a lot of Mutari had them when Vis wasn't out in the open. Now that Vis is public, people aren't buying them as much. But the guild sells a lot of other things and does good business. They will sell anything to do with security or concealment. They specialize in selling items for keeping things hidden or safe."

"Do you know who belongs to this guild?" Sean asked.

Paul smiled, "You're in luck. There are only a few Goblins in Colorado that are members of Ex Conspectu."

Paul wrote down the name and address and handed the piece of paper to Sean, "There's two guys in Denver that are in that guild and only one that would be able to equip an organization like Trinity."

Sean looked at the paper, "Samuel Bellows, will he be a problem?"

Paul thought for a moment, "I don't know, but you may want to bring a Paladin to be on the safe side."

"Maddison and I can do it," Amy said.

"We are just talking to him, remember," Sean said.

"I know, but you'll want a Paladin around in case he has a Troll guard or something," Amy said.

Faith agreed with Amy, telling Sean he needed a Paladin with him. Sean didn't argue with her about it. They thanked Paul before leaving.

MADDISON BELDAME sat in the DPD's conference room that was fast starting to feel like a jail cell to her. The room wasn't small, and when it was just Detectives Hughes and Kaur plus Gabriel and Faith, the room would have been fine. But now that it was also home to Maddison and her Seeker, along with the occasional staff member from the FBI, the room was starting to feel cramped. Next to her were Gabriel and Alison, the prior holding her attention. She shifted uncomfortably in her seat. There were so many reasons to feel uncomfortable around Gabriel. It wasn't enough that she'd had a crush on him since she was twelve. No; he also had to be one of the most talented and powerful Paladins she'd met, was from another prominent family, and oh yeah, was in charge of her at the moment.

He wasn't saying much, just reading a book, but Maddison's noticed his eyes flick in her direction from time to time. She was seated in a way that she could watch him without seeming creepy … she hoped. She also had a view of the door. *Always look for an attack,* Gabriel had taught her years ago. It was a lesson that had served her well. Gabriel was seated in a way to watch the windows. In effect, they were watching each other's backs. When they came into a room, it wasn't a conversation they needed to have; it was a habit. You watched the place where an attack was most likely to happen and if your partner is watching that spot, then you find a place where you can watch for danger they can't see.

Maddison figured that's why she liked to work with agent Alesbury. He, like so many members of law enforcement lived in a near-constant state of readiness and distrust. He too assessed the possible threat of everyone in a room. Maddison liked to work with people like that, the untrusting. It was something that she understood.

Sean, Faith, and Amy came into the room.

"We've got a lead; we're going to go talk to someone," Sean announced.

"What did you find?" Alison asked.

"We got a line on a Samuel Bellows who might be supplying Trinity here in Denver. I just want to talk to him and see what I can find out," Sean explained to Alison.

Alison nodded, "Right, let me know what you find out."

Gabriel started to stand, but Faith waved at him, "Maddison and Amy are going."

Gabriel sat back down and inclined his head to Maddison, "Have fun."

Maddison felt a moment of indecision. Sean and Alison were Gabriel and Faith's charges per the Pactum they had with the DPD.

"Are you sure?" Maddison asked.

Gabriel smiled warmly, "Yeah, I think we all need to have a working relationship together."

"Unless you find Sean that unpleasant, in which case we understand," Faith said sarcastically.

Sean gave Faith a cocky smile, "Don't be like that Faith; I know you love me." Sean said. Then he directed his attention to Maddison, "Ok let's go; I want to catch this guy before he closes."

THREE

MADDISON BELDAME sat down in Sean's car. She looked over at the man, trying to figure him out. Faith had told her that Sean changed when he learned about Succubi, that he had become a better person. Maddison could see flashes of what she figured was the old Sean. She looked around the car. The interior was all black with leather and power everything. He wore trendy clothes and looked like he agonized over the placement of every hair on his head. But his eyes were not that of a cocky prick; they were that of concern and determination.

Sean looked over at her, "What?"

Maddison looked forward, "Nothing," then changing the subject added, "I don't think the Goblin will be a problem."

"Why is that? Every other Mutari -- and Mage, for that matter -- has tried to kill us."

Maddison looked at him so she could read his expressions. "Those were Trolls and Wolves; they are different." Sean's head went up and down slightly "Most of the other Mutari aren't dangerous," she said.

"What about Vampires?" he contradicted, "Two of those were sent to Alison's house. And what about Banshees and Wraiths?"

Maddison paused, "And what about humans?" she asked.

That brought him up short. "Yeah ok, I see what you mean," he relented, "so what's different about Trolls and Wolves? Why are they so much more aggressive?"

"And Wraiths," she added. Maddison had only dealt with a handful of them in her time as a Paladin, but those that she had were terrible. "Most Trolls are fine, but they tend to be more on the aggressive side. As for Wolves that's just what they are, they are all aggressive."

They were pulling up to the street where Paul told them Samuel Bellows owned a shop. Sean parked the car on the street and got out. Maddison focused. Amy got out of the car and sat down on a bench as she pulled a book from her purse. Sean gave Maddison a quizzical look.

"Just because there shouldn't be any problems doesn't mean there won't be," Maddison said.

They walked up to the door of the shop, Maddison opening the door for Sean and pushing him in by the small of his back. He looked back outside, concerned, and then once in the shop shook his head.

"I hate that," he said, referring to the shop's spells that kept humans out.

The inside of the shop was brightly lit, Seeking objects lining the walls and stacked on the shelves. In the corner of the room, a Troll sat pretending to read a book. A tall man with thick brown hair walked out from a back room of the shop. Maddison could read the Vis pulsing from his liver. He was the Goblin. His blue eyes looked Sean and then Maddison over, resting on her eyes. She caught the hint of fear flash on his visage before he spoke.

"To what do I owe the honor of a Beldame visiting my humble shop?" He asked, his voice warm and deep.

The Beldames were the only family that changed the color of their eyes and since her sister had been an Ark, Maddison wasn't surprised that Samuel knew who she was. It wasn't lost on her that the Troll perked up when Samuel spoke. She eyed him, her hand almost twitching to Vindictam her sword. Just to be safe, she flexed the wards she had on herself and Sean.

Sean spoke confidently, "Yes, that is Maddison Beldame and I'm Detective Sean Hughes with the Denver Police Department, are you Samuel Bellow?"

Samuel looked at Sean, a slight hint of disdain on his face, "Yes I am, and humans don't patronize my shop."

Sean smiled, not letting Samuel's jab affect him, "I'm not here to buy anything, I am here to ask you some questions about some of your clients."

Samuel shook his head dismissively, "I am sorry Detective, but I do not divulge information about my clients," he gestured to the door, "so if you are not here to buy anything, then I must ask you to leave."

Sean looked at the door and then back to Samuel, a look of mock confusion on his face, "I'm sorry Sam, are you a doctor, priest, therapist, attorney, or anything like that?"

Samuel shook his head, "No, I'm not; I'm a simple shop owner."

Sean nodded, "Ah … see then, you do have to talk about your clients. OR …" Sean said, holding up a finger, "I can arrest you for obstruction." Sean smiled, walking forward, "You see Samuel, I think you've been selling to some very bad people. People who we, meaning the DPD and the FBI, are looking for."

Samuel backed away a bit, his bravado faltering. Maddison saw that the Troll's hand was out of sight.

"Sean!" she called, reaching forward.

She yanked Sean toward her as the Troll threw a paperweight at him.

SEAN HUGHES lurched back, falling as Maddison tugged on him. Something flew past his head and Maddison sprung toward the Troll. Sean hit the floor, landing hard on his backside. Samuel turned and ran toward the back of the shop. Sean picked himself up and sprinted at the Goblin.

Sean chased him into the back of the shop, Samuel spilling out the back door and into an alley. Sean followed him, yelling for the man to stop. Samuel ran down the alley, looking over his shoulder at Sean who was gaining ground quickly. Samuel looked worried, and Sean ran faster. When he was close enough, Sean reached out, grabbing the man's belt. Samuel fell to the ground, and Sean let go. He jumped onto the man, driving his knee into Samuel's back. He twisted his arm behind him and pulled out his cuffs.

"I didn't do anything wrong!" Samuel yelled.

Sean finished wrestling Samuel into the handcuffs, "That's why you ran, right?"

Sean read him his rights and told him to stay on the ground. A moment later Amy came into the alley.

"Are you ok?" she asked.

"Yeah, Maddison didn't kill the Troll, did she?" Sean asked. He didn't want to have to deal with another dead suspect.

Amy shook her head, "No she didn't, she has him in the shop."

Sean sighed in relief, pulling out his mobile phone to call dispatch. Once he was on with them, he told them they needed to send a car to pick up the Troll, along with something to suppress his Vis.

ALISON KAUR looked at the folder of information on Samuel Bellows, who was sitting in an interrogation room. Alison picked up a pad of paper and the folder and made her way to the room. Inside, Samuel sat at a table, his cuffed hands on its smooth metal surface. Maddison Beldame leaned against a wall, eyeing Samuel coolly. Alison set her pad on the table and pulled out a chair opposite Samuel.

His eyes were cold blue as he looked at her, his body language telling her he didn't look at her as an equal. Alison was used to this. As a woman, most suspects didn't give her any respect. At one time that would have offended her, but now she saw it as an edge. Whenever someone dismissed you for no good reason, you could use that against them. In this case, Alison doubted that Samuel Bellows cared that she was a woman. No, he likely thought he was better than she was because he was a Mutari. He gave Maddison a similar look, but instead of it being colored with a sense of superiority, it was tinged with disdain for a member of a higher class.

"Would you like to tell me why you had one of your employees attack members of law enforcement while you ran?" Alison asked calmly.

Samuel looked at her, his skin flushing with anger, "You can't keep me here, you're just a Human."

Alison smiled, "That would be true if you were a Troll, but you aren't." Alison pointed out, "Unless I'm misinformed, the best you could do would be to tell me how pure the steel of prison bars are."

"Your laws don't apply to me," he tried.

Alison actually chuckled at that. She leaned in, not wanting to waste time with him, "Look despite what you may think, our laws do apply to you. And I have you assaulting an officer, along with aiding an organized crime syndicate," she read the look of disbelief on his face, and she added "I know I don't have hard evidence on you yet. But we are scrubbing your shop. We have two Seekers and an Enchanter there right now, along with our own forensics team." Alison leaned back in her chair, "Trust me; they'll find evidence and based on what people's opinion of Vis users are right now, I don't think the DA is gonna have a hard time getting a conviction." Alison looked at Samuel, curious, "Tell me: do you think the other inmates are going to be afraid of a Goblin?"

Samuel looked uncomfortable. Alison knew she had him. Samuel Bellows was hot air, and she doubted that he even remotely had a spine to speak of.

"Look Samuel," Alison said with more warmth, "I get it, you don't like me or any Human … that's fine; really it is. But right now you have a choice. You can be civil with me and not see a courtroom … or I can charge you with the aforementioned crimes. Either way I win."

Alison sat quietly for a moment, letting Samuel make up his mind.

"What do you want?" he asked after a moment.

Alison tried not to let herself smile, "Information. That is, unless you are running Trinity."

Samuel chuckled without humor, shaking his head, "Shoulda known not to deal with them." He said, and then looking at Alison, "What do you want to know?"

"Everything you do," she said simply.

"How do I know you aren't playing me? That you aren't going to charge me with anything?" he asked.

"Neither Detective Hughes nor I have even filed an arrest report yet. You can walk out of here like nothing ever happened; I promise," she said.

He laughed, "Yeah, Human law enforcement not lying." He looked at Maddison, "I want a promise from her."

Maddison inclined her head.

Samuel looked back to Alison, satisfied, "I don't know much about Trinity and frankly, I don't care about them. I do supply them with enchanted objects, though."

Alison was surprised at how much Maddison's word meant to Samuel and not for the first time she wondered about the differences between the Vis and non-Vis community.

"Objects made en masse?" Alison asked, remembering a conversation from earlier in the day.

Samuel shook his head, "Yes, and no. Masse in the Vis world isn't what it is in the Human. One hundred items that have been enchanted is a large order. I take care of anything Trinity needs for bottom level people. It's mostly concealers and things of that nature. I'm sure your Seekers have found my ledger, it's all in there."

"Are they a big client?" Alison asked.

Samuel winced, "Nah; not really. Like I said, they buy a lot of little things, stuff that I don't make much on. Plus, on most of the stuff I give them, they have a deal with someone else in my guild. For those orders, I'm just a middle man." He shook his head, not looking at Alison, "Had I known working with Trinity would have caused me problems; I wouldn't have been willing to be a middle man and I definitely would have charged them more," he lamented.

Alison was shocked to hear how frank Samuel was being. "How do they pick up the merchandise?"

"They don't," Samuel was matter of fact, "I drop everything off at a self-storage unit, and they pay me."

Samuel really was just another middleman. "Ok, thank you for your time. I need you to wait here for awhile before we let you go," Alison said, and then pulled out the cuff keys and uncuffed him.

She walked out of the room with Maddison, turning and walking into a room on the other side of the one-way glass. "McLoughlin was in essence a middle man, all of the Human and Mutari we have encountered so far have been them, and now so is Samuel Bellows ..." Alison complained.

Gabriel was looking into the room at Samuel, "That's Marcus," he said softly.

"How do you know?" Montoya asked.

Gabriel shrugged, "It's his style. During the war, he kept people on a need-to-know basis unless they were high ranking. If you keep your front line assets in the dark, they can't shed light on you when they get caught. But if we can find someone high up, that will be different."

"How so?" Sean asked.

Gabriel looked at him, "You keep your high ups in the light. They are leaders, after all, and leaders can't lead without proper information." Gabriel said.

"So what's our move," Maddison asked.

Alison answered, "Simple; we raid the self-storage unit and see what we can find."

Montoya spoke, "Fine, get me an address and I'll get your warrant."

FAITH PENN stood behind her brother as he walked up a line of self-storage units. The sun had set, and the air began to take on the cold bite of fall. Faith spared a slight amount of Vis to keep herself warm and focused on the area around them. She could feel spells trying to block up her head. Faith thought about attacking the concealment spells, but decided to take a page out of Amy's book instead. She looked around her with her other senses, not using Vis at all.

The storage units were in rows separated by a drive. The lights from the city and moon cast the space between the units in deep shadows, making it hard to see anything. Faith breathed in deeply through her nose to see if she could smell anything. Gabriel was walking in front of her, so the only scent she caught was his cologne. *That didn't work* she thought. The only sounds were that of the team walking forward … she paused, hearing something creak. The sound came from a little ways ahead of them and from above. They were almost to the storage unit Samuel made drops at, when the sound led her gaze to a figure. Faith enhanced her eyes with Vis, cutting through the darkness.

She grabbed Gabriel's shoulder. On the roof of the units across from them, almost out of sight, was a man. Whoever it was hadn't seen them yet, she didn't think. Faith was happy she hadn't yet tried to break the concealment spells she'd found.

Gabriel put his finger to his ear and spoke softly to Maddison. Then he paused, telling Alison and Sean to wait. A moment later there was a clang from the roof and the sound of a small scuffle. Maddison poked her head over the edge of the roof and mouthed "Banshee."

"Why was he waiting for us?" Sean asked, "You could take him out easily; why not run? Or do you think that guy is always up there waiting for trouble?"

Gabriel looked back at the roof, not happy, "No, he knew we were coming and he shouldn't have. Maybe Angelica sensed us in the area. At any rate, a Banshee could have killed us, they are very powerful, and while Mages are much stronger, if we hadn't seen him …"

Sean nodded, "Doesn't matter how good your defense is if you don't see your opponent stab you in the back. Got it."

Gabriel looked at Faith and added softly, "Good catch."

Faith made a mental note to thank Amy later and focused up ahead of them, "Three units down to your left. It's being protected. Do you want me to crack it?" she asked.

"No," Gabriel said placing his finger to his ear, "Amy, can you block any Vis communication out of here?"

Faith heard Amy's voice buzz in her ear, "I'm on it."

Faith waited until the other Seeker had the area locked down before she focused her attention on all the concealment spells in the area. Faith let Vis well up in her and pulse out in broad waves. There was a slight gasp from Alison and Sean. Ruby Vis shown around them as Amber waves from Faith touched them. Faith felt resistance and poured more energy into her spells. Around them, there were pops and snaps as wards buckled. Faith pushed harder, feeling the last of Angelica's spells break. She opened her eyes, satisfied. *Maybe I can beat her* she thought.

ALISON KAUR stood behind Gabriel, her gun drawn and ready. As soon as Faith was done Gabriel rushed forward, a flash of lavender Vis hitting the door of a large storage unit. The door flew open as Alison, Sean, and Gabriel rushed inside. Alison leveled her gun, sweeping the open space. Boxes were lined up in neat rows and in the back of the room with an exceptionally startled expression on his face stood a man in his early thirties with dark brown hair. He jumped upon their entrance.

"Denver Police, hands up!" Alison yelled at the man.

She half expected him to turn into some monster, but he didn't. He just raised his hands high in the air.

"Ok, ok, I'm not armed, please don't hurt me," he was terrified.

"Goblin," Gabriel said.

Alison walked quickly up to the man, turning him around and slapping cuffs on him. Sean opened one of the boxes, "Looks like some more of those lighter things," he said.

Gabriel opened another, pulling out a bag with white powder, "What is this?"

Sean laughed, "That, my friend, is some good old fashioned blow," he turned to the Goblin, "and you are very much under arrest."

Alison read the Goblin his rights before Sean fished his wallet out of his back pocket.

"So, Mr … Christian Biesczat, do you want to tell me why you have boxes of drugs in here?" Sean asked.

"I want an attorney," Christian said.

"Oh come on now," Sean started.

"Enough Hughes, he wants council." Alison said, cutting off Sean. Trash or not, Alison wasn't about to violate Christian's civil rights nor mess up her case.

Alison called in the arrest to the station and asked for CSIs to be sent over. Amy and Maddison joined them in the unit.

"Wow," Amy said, looking around the unit.

Alison didn't know much about the girl, but Faith seemed to like her.

"Maddison," Alison said, getting the woman's attention, "I want to have a Seeker here to help for a few hours if possible."

Maddison agreed, "Ok," she turned to Amy, "Amy, you want to head up the team sweeping for evidence?"

Amy's face reddened a bit. "Umm … I don't know how good of a leader I would be," she said softly.

"Don't worry about it -- they know the drill; can you just search for anything you think could be useful?" Alison said.

"Sure," Amy agreed.

"I'm going to stick around too, in case any Trinity members come back here," Gabriel added.

"Right. Thanks, Gabriel," Alison said.

MADDISON BELDAME winced slightly as her wards were tested. The Banshee she'd taken in, a Mr. Vasco Trejo, was in interrogation room three. Or what was left of interrogation room three. He was screaming at the top of his lungs, using Vis as he did. The room was in a near constant glow of blue from Maddison's wards. She'd thought to protect the walls, floor and ceiling with Vis but didn't take into account any objects in the room, like chairs and a table; all of which were now crumpled metal heaps being tossed about on the waves of Vis blasting from Trejo. Maddison watched from one-way glass as the air rippled from his mouth, crashing into the table and slamming it against the glass. The glass flashed blue and Maddison shook her head.

"You almost look like you're in awe," Agent Alesbury said.

"I am," she admitted, "I've never seen Banshees as more than a minor threat. And I guess I don't see Trejo as a threat, but wow, I've never seen anyone go at a room like that," she said.

"How long has he been in there?"

Maddison looked at him. He was looking intently into the room, "Two hours," she said.

"Two hours!" Alesbury was amazed, "Has anyone gone in and talked to him?"

Maddison shook her head, "Nope, it wasn't safe, and to be honest, I don't think Vasco is in the talking kind of mood. I may have to knock him out," she added as an afterthought.

"Where's the Goblin?" Alesbury asked.

"Room one," Maddison said, mesmerized as Trejo ripped off his shirt. He was in his fifties with long black hair and mustache, his face pock-marked with age and a hard life. His chest was covered in fading tattoos. He looked at the one-way glass and screamed, running forward. Maddison couldn't see him in the room as her wards flashed brightly, but she heard him pounding on the glass.

"Man, wouldn't the anti-Vis movement love to see this guy," Alesbury said.

It was true. A video of a Banshee losing it in a police station would be terrific ammo for those that opposed Vis users. "Seriously," she said.

Sean came in the room with Alison. They both looked at Vasco. Sean shook his head, getting out his wallet, and handing Alison a twenty.

"I really thought he'd be done by now," Sean said.

"You took bets on how long Trejo was going to be freaking out?" Maddison asked, shocked.

"Yep," Alison said, not sounding ashamed at all.

Sean looked at Alison, "Yeah, this one has a gift when it comes to figuring out how long the crazy ones are going to throw crap."

Then suddenly, Sean hit the window, "HEY!" he said, pushing an intercom button.

In their lapse of attention, Vasco had decided to urinate on the glass, "That's what I think of you PIG!"

"Dammit!" Sean said, "can someone Taser him?"

Maddison sighed, "Don't we need to talk to him?"

"No," Alison said, "Not now; we got Biesczat to flip."

"How did you do that?" Alesbury asked.

Sean shrugged, "He had a lawyer, but once we told him that Trejo had been in interrogation for two hours and that we suspected he was on top of that roof to kill him, Biesczat spilled his guts." Sean said, "We didn't lie," he pointed at Vasco, "he's been in there for two hours."

Maddison smirked, "Do we have a safe house?"

Sean smiled widely, "That we do. Montoya is working on a warrant."

She looked back at the Banshee, "Well in that case. Somnus," she said. Trejo slowed and then collapsed to the floor, unconscious.

FAITH PENN flew in the air, cloaked in a bubble of Vis. She circled the area over the safe house; Amy also in the area. The lesson from that night with Vasco Trejo waiting for them was fresh in their minds. Faith scouted the area for anything she could find, but there were no signs of Vis in the area. All she could find was the safe house with its wards.

"I can't sense any Mutari in the area," Amy said, concerned.

"That means they are all inside or gone," Faith replied.

"Gone?" Amy asked.

"Anything is possible."

Maddison and Gabriel were approaching the safe house, which was in a run-down part of town. Maddison in the back, Gabriel taking the front. DPD and FBI were in the area, but holding back.

Gabriel moved in on the house, Iram slashing with a bright band of purple. Faith and Amy assaulted the house's wards, which popped.

"That was too easy," Faith noted as Maddison went inside.

“Nothing!” Gabriel’s voice sounded.

“Me either,” Maddison said.

Faith landed and went inside before they allowed the Humans in. Amy stayed in the sky, watching for an attack.

“What do you mean?” Faith asked the two Paladins who stood confused.

The house was trashed in a way that said whoever was here left in a hurry. Faith ran her hand along a sofa.

“There were Trolls here not more than thirty minutes ago,” she said.

Gabriel came out of an office, “The lock box is open and empty.”

He pushed his finger to his ear, talking to Alison and Sean, “This place is empty they knew we were coming.”

FOUR

ALISON KAUR turned on the TV in her bedroom as she got ready for the day. The news was on, and she turned it up so she could hear it in the bathroom.

"There is now more speculation around Denver's investigation into an alleged crime ring that specializes in Magic." The anchor said.

Alison stepped from the bathroom to watch. The word "magic" caught her attention. It was the word the media used when they were about to run a smear piece. Alison sat down on her bed as images of protesters at the state capital came into view. *When did that start up?* she wondered.

The camera panned to a female reporter, "Today, many worried citizens have come to the capital to show their concern for recent events," she said.

She held the mic to one of the protesters, "We've had enough of witches and wizards being the lapdogs of the government and corporations!" The interviewer pulled the mic away, adding what she thought were the general complaints about Vis users. Her summary of protesters' complaints was wide and varied. Many people thought there needed to be tighter control on Vis users by the government. Other protesters were claiming that Vis users were in the pockets of giant corporations and still others were blaming Vis users for topics ranging from the country's poor economy to an increase in childhood allergies. Alison was happy to see that there wasn't a consistent theme to the protesters' cause. If those picketing ever managed to get on the same page as one another, they could potentially rally others to their cause and turn into a huge thorn in Alison's side.

The reporter gave the mic to another woman who talked about the failed raid the night before, saying that now police were attacking whoever they wanted. Alison's face flushed as mentions of the train yard raid came up with people insinuating that the police had been wrong to go after Trinity there. Then the news started running video clips of Gabriel taking down the Guardian from the first safe house they'd cracked. On the bottom of the screen, estimated death tolls ran along. Alison gritted her teeth. Anyone watching the news would see the first raid on a Trinity location, but they would also see what the news thought was the total death count for the whole case. But the news wasn't saying the count was for the whole case. The average home viewer would believe the careful half-truths that made Gabriel look like a mass killer. Alison looked at the number of supposed dead and rolled her eyes. The DPD had not revealed the amount of dead or even arrested in the case thus far. The news as per usual was pulling numbers out of their asses.

Alison turned off the TV, irritated. Her phone rang, and Alison looked to see a number from the police station.

"Hello," Alison said.

"Hey, this is Pam," a voice on the other end replied.

Alison figured she'd be getting a call from public relations after seeing the news.

"The news?" Alison asked.

"Yeah we need to get this under control," Pam said, not referring to the case but rather the media.

"Why are they running this?" she asked.

Pam laughed, "Ratings. I checked this morning and running Vis-friendly pieces isn't getting the attention they were a week ago. I sent an intern down to the capital. He only counted thirty protesters and some of them are homeless people the other protesters gave signs to."

Alison rubbed her temples. It was common practice, the media loved to sensationalize everything. All they had to do was interview a small group of people, make sure the camera never showed how small the group of protesters was, and add in a few clips of video with biased voiceovers. Then boom, you had public concern. The other stations would jump on the bandwagon within a day or two.

"What can I do?" Alison asked.

"Give me something to use. It doesn't have to be much," Pam said.

Alison thought for a moment and then told Pam about Vasco Trejo, telling her that he assaulted two police officers who were saved by Mages. She didn't want to talk about evidence, but Alison mentioned that large amounts of cocaine were found.

"Will that be enough?" Alison asked.

Pam sounded happy, "Yep, I'm looking this guy up, and he is a piece of work! And finding a stash of dope! Don't worry, honey, the other stations will jump on this. I've got your back."

Alison hung up and breathed out. *It would be so nice not to have to worry about the media* she thought but also remembered that the media cracked a lot of cases wide open. Like with most things, there was both good and bad about the media. Though in the last few years, she'd found the media to be more of a hindrance than a help.

Alison finished getting ready for her day after popping off an email to the team to say that she'd dealt with the media. On her way to the station, she drove by where the protest was happening. Sure enough, not many people were there. She stopped for a moment. It was starting to rain. She pulled up the forecast and was happy to see that the rain could turn to sleet. In

Alison's experience, the best way to test a protester's resolve was to watch them in the rain and cold. Some of the people became more adamant as they got soaked, but for the most part, people jogged to convenience stores to wait out the rain. Alison smiled to herself. Pam would be able to handle this no problem.

She found Gabriel as she was walking into the office, "Morning," she said.

He looked down at his phone, "What's wrong with your news organizations?" he asked.

Alison shook her head, "They are running a bit about how Vis users are the enemy. Well, they aren't saying that verbatim, but that's the gist of the piece. PR is working on putting a positive spin on the case."

"Taking drug dealers, pimps, and gunrunners off the streets isn't positive enough for people?" Gabriel sounded legitimately confused.

Alison was brought up short. She agreed with Gabriel, but how did she explain that facts were not always what swayed people's thinking?

"We've kept most of our findings out of the public; most people only know what the news has told them," she hedged.

"I see," he said, not pushing the subject anymore.

FAITH PENN sat and listened to the others discuss how the investigation should go now that they'd hit a dead end with Trinity. Samuel Bellows had been released and didn't have any more information for them as he had only been a merchant; not a member of Trinity. Vasco Trejo wasn't talking and would be charged with his crimes. This left them with a whole lot of nothing, but from Faith's perspective, Sean and Alison were pros at turning nothing into something.

"We have all these safe houses, right? Maybe we can figure out who owns them all," Sean said.

"We've tried that, and each house was owned by a person …" Alison said, "no shell companies or anything." She huffed, "In fact, each of the houses was owned by a dead person whose identity had been stolen."

The whole identity theft thing was a bit of a mystery to Faith since Vis society didn't have anything like it, but she thought she understood the basics of it. You just say you were someone else so you could buy stuff. It seemed pretty straightforward to her.

"Couldn't you just do that phone GPL thingy again?" Faith blurted out.

"GPL?" Sean asked.

"Yeah isn't that what it's called? You know, it tells your location," she explained.

Sean nodded, "Right, GPS you mean; honestly Faith, when it comes to technology you're like my mother."

"Only Human technology," Faith said coolly. "And at least I know what a thermometer is," she jabbed.

"How was I supposed to know what a Vis thermometer looked like?" Sean asked, indignantly.

"And how am I supposed to know what GPS is?" Faith retorted.

Sean looked like he was going to argue more, but Alison spoke, "How can GPS help us?"

"Well," Faith started, "you arrested all of those people at the other safe houses and the train yard. I know they were let go, but couldn't you still get access to their phone records and GPS? That's how you found Davison and the first safe house, right?"

"We still have all of their phones in evidence, but I don't know Faith," Alison said, trying to make it sound like she didn't think it was a terrible idea.

But Sean perked up, "Faith I knew you were more than a hot piece of tail! We can pull all the data from the phones and put it on a map to look for common spots," he said, animated.

Faith decided not to comment on him calling her a "hot piece of tail" as he was agreeing with her.

"And I can talk to Alexander Fop, he's a Vampire who is willing to help us," Gabriel said.

For her part, Faith was going to be using as much Vis as she could as she and Amy tried to find Trinity. Part of her was excited about this prospect. She'd be working like the Seekers of old with broad spells that covered hundreds of miles.

After the meeting, Amy came up to her, "What are your orders?" she asked.

"How much broad work have you done?" Faith asked.

Amy looked sheepish, "None, really. I've had a little theoretical training on it."

Faith was hoping that she had at least some experience, but tried not to let her disappointment show, "That's fine; I'll help you."

Amy looked uncomfortable.

"You really don't do a lot of looking with Vis, do you?" Faith asked.

Amy looked ashamed, "No I haven't. I'm sorry."

"Don't be sorry; most of us never have a need for broad Seeking, at least not since the war," Faith said and then added, "but it's something you should learn. I have no doubt that if there was a need for Arks today, that Maddison would be one."

Faith didn't want to make Amy feel ashamed. In many ways, Faith saw Amy as a better Seeker, but now she could tell that while Amy was extraordinarily gifted, her training had been incomplete. Faith excused them from the rest of the team and took Amy to the roof of the station.

Before them was the city. Buildings towered overhead, but they still had a good view from the rooftop. The sky was dark with light rain helping to dampen the smell of smog and trash. The breeze blew slightly, rustling Faith's overcoat. The breeze didn't drown out the sounds of the busy city below them, so she had to raise her voice a bit when she spoke.

"What do you know about broad seeking?" Faith asked.

"Just that you are looking over large distances. I know it's a lot different than cloaking things or finding them at close range. I also know that Paladins have similar techniques," Amy said.

It was true Paladins could use spells miles away from where they were. It was hard to use Vis in this manner, and you had to be extremely powerful to do so. The same applied to broad seeking; not everyone could do it.

"It's not easy. I'm not surprised you didn't learn it; very few Seekers learn broad seeking. Sadly, many Seekers never develop their skills enough to be strong enough to use it. That's not the case for you," Faith assured her.

Faith looked out over the city. Broad Vis use was what most oftentimes made it into Human fairy tales. She wondered if Alison and Sean would be frightened to know it was real.

Faith let massive amounts of Vis well inside of her. She focused her attention and her Vis on the nearby park, "Veni me," she said, calling all of the pigeons and birds in the park. The air over the park turned with birds taking flight, startling a few nearby people. The birds flew toward Faith. Amy was just in-front of her, and Faith saw goosebumps cover the other Seeker's arms. The birds came swirling around the top of the station.

"We infuse them with Vis -- they will not need food so long as the spell lasts, but they will search with their eyes which we will also enhance. They will look for what we want. When they find it, they will stay in the area, and we will be able to see with their eyes. These are our spies, and they will look for pockets of Mutari," Faith said. She told Amy the spells to use and gave her a few hundred birds.

Amy looked scared, obviously never having used Vis like this before. Faith closed her eyes and began to weave her spells. A low, rhythmic script flowed from her almost as a song, "Mutair volitare in circulos petere, quaerere tota die, si quid me quaeritis ...." she gave the birds direction and focus. She enhanced their bodies and eyes; she gave them the ability to fly in poor weather and took away their hunger. Faith's concentration was great, and the spell took her half an hour to complete. When she was done, the birds flew away in flocks as they searched.

AMY CALAMUS watched as Faith worked, birds swirling around them like something from a horror movie. She couldn't help but feel awed and fearful. Faith's eyes were closed as she spoke in Latin, her voice low and smooth, with a rhythmic flow. She opened her eyes which glowed a bright yellow. The birds flew away from them, and Faith stretched her arms out in front of her, the crystal ball she used as an amplifier glowing almost as brightly as her eyes. She spoke with a loud voice that boomed in Amy's ears as the ball became blinding. Amy knew that Faith would have used Vis so no one could see her working, but she still wondered how the rest of the world didn't see and feel what she could. The woman before her was both great and terrible at the same time, and while Amy knew Faith didn't see it in herself, Amy was certain she was standing before one of the most gifted and powerful Seekers in history. Faith was wrapped in Vis that danced around her like angry flames, her eyes as bright as the sun. So bright was her Vis that Amy noticed the rest of the light around them dim. *Who is this woman?* she thought with a shiver. After what seemed like hours, Faith's hands came down to her sides and her Vis faded.

Faith looked like she was about to collapse.

"Are you alright?" Amy asked.

Faith smiled weakly, "Yes, just very tired. I will not be able to use more than the most minor of spells for the rest of the day." She said, "In this is the risk of broad seeking; after you use it, you are weak and vulnerable to attack from foes that could normally never hurt you. For this reason, you must prepare to use broad Vis by first ensuring all of your defenses are strong and ready for attack," she explained.

Amy was in awe; she'd never pushed herself that hard.

"Your turn," Faith said.

ALISON KAUR drove down Colfax away from the station, Gabriel next to her looking out the window calmly. The trees were losing their leaves; swirls of brown, yellow, and red floated behind the car as they drove. They were on their way to meet with Alexander Fop, one of Gabriel's informants. Alexander was a Vampire. Alison didn't know why she was nervous; none of the other types of Mutari worried her, but Vampires did. Maybe it was that she'd read too many horror novels as a kid, or that two of them were coming to kill her the night Sean kicked the hornets' nest. Whatever the reason, she was feeling tense.

Turning on Downing, houses rushed by along the tree-lined street as they entered an upscale part of town. Gabriel pointed to a house with old red brick and a pointy roof, "There."

She parked on the street in-front of the house and got out of the car. She walked next to Gabriel as they made it up the short walk to the front door. Gabriel rang the bell. A short man in his early sixties with jet black hair and dark eyes opened the door. He was dressed in nice clothes and Alison assumed he was fairly wealthy.

"Come in," he said, with the slightest of Italian accents.

They entered the house, Alison's nerves becoming more and more on edge. The decor was warm; the house entryway made of wood, a staircase curving to the second floor.

Alexander held out his hand to Alison. She took it, surprised by how warm it was, "Alexander Fop," he said, "you must be Alison Kaur."

"Yes," she said.

Alexander led them to a study and sat behind a large desk. Next to the desk, a grandfather clock ticked soothingly. Gabriel pulled a dark bottle of wine from his coat and set it on the desk. Alexander picked up the bottle, reading the label, "You shouldn't have, Gabriel," he said, and then nodded, "I read something about this one in a magazine recently. I've been meaning to get a bottle, but you know me and American wine," he sighed.

Gabriel chuckled, "Most of the rest of the world is on board with it."

Alexander waved a dismissive hand, "Well, shall we try it?" he asked, pulling out a corkscrew.

He opened the bottle and poured three glasses. Alison was wondering if this was just going to be a social call or if Gabriel hoped to talk about the case. Alison turned down her glass, saying she was on duty.

Alexander smiled warmly, "As are we my dear, as are we," he said, placing the glass down in front of her.

Gabriel gave her a look, and guiltily she took a sip. The wine was good, full of body and with lots of bite. Alison watched as Gabriel and Alexander sipped at their glasses, the latter closing his eyes and swishing the liquid in his mouth, "Perhaps the Americans are starting to learn how to make a decent bottle of wine," he said, opening his eyes. He looked at Alison, "You look like you are in a hurry, my dear."

"Sorry, but I have a job to do; a very important one at that," she added, feeling a bit more confident.

Alexander nodded solemnly. "You haven't the slightest idea just how important your work is," he said without malice, "what is it you think we are doing here?" he asked her.

"Getting information about Trinity," she said, matter of fact.

"Yes, but what kind of information? Surely judging on where I live, you don't think I'm running drugs or pimping whores, do you?"

She was brought up short at that.

He looked at her intently, "I am nearly one hundred years old."

Alison felt her mouth plop open.

"We vampires live as long as Mages. My father was almost one hundred and sixty when he passed away," he said.

Alison sat for a moment, taking that in. She'd heard that Mages and Vampires lived longer than Humans, but she had no idea they lived twice as long.

"Alexander is here to give us insight," Gabriel said.

"Mine and the other Vampire houses must think in terms of lifetimes and how the things we do today will affect us years from now. As such, we rarely touch the world around us directly," he said.

She understood; Goblins were the merchant class of the Mutari, and Vampires were the elite. They had a hand in everything but not directly.

"What have you heard?" Gabriel asked.

"I haven't been able to find much on Trinity or what they are up to, but that is to be expected. However, among my kind, those houses that sided with the Nobilis have been acting rather oddly," he said, looking at Gabriel. "Tell me, how are the Arks?"

Gabriel looked down, "Disbanded. Do you think Nobilis sympathizers are hoping for the Nobilis to return?"

Alexander took another sip of wine as Alison felt more and more out of her depth with the conversation.

"I doubt they think the Nobilis will return. For one, the Nobilis are all dead, and traitor or not, Marcus Vies is no Nobilis. No; I think they hope that a new regime is coming. They have been pulling out of deals as of late. Gabriel, they are battening down for a storm. Are you sure the Arks aren't still in existence?" He asked.

Alison didn't like what she was hearing. Alexander didn't seem to see Trinity as some crime ring; he saw them as something much more dangerous. Gabriel didn't look happy, but he also didn't look surprised.

"We have been in contact," he said. And Alexander looked relieved.

Alison was taken off guard, "You have been in contact with the other Arks?" she asked without thinking.

"Yes," Gabriel admitted, "when we found Angelica, I contacted them, and ever since they have been keeping their eyes open for anything dangerous."

Alexander looked more comforted, "That is good to hear. I am sorry, but I do not have much in the way of information for you." Then he added, "But know that most of us still side with the Arks." This was said as a consolation.

Alison felt extremely confused as they left the house.

SEAN HUGHES clacked away at his computer. He'd been working for two days, trying to track and analyze the habits of the hookers, pimps, drug dealers, and enforcers they'd already busted from Trinity. It was a long, arduous task, but would give them a solid shot on finding more Trinity locations. Sean didn't lie to himself; their current plan of finding and busting safe houses was merely a Band-Aid. Until they got a real lead on where the heads of the organization were hiding, and what their plans were, all the DPD and FBI could do was slow Trinity down. In the meantime, Denver had a little less trash floating around on the street.

Sean pulled up a map of the city, surrounding towns, and counties. Working with the FBI gave Sean a lot more freedom than he'd had before, and also a significantly higher amount of resources. Amy came into the conference room and sat down behind Sean. He wasn't sure what he thought of her. She kept to herself, didn't want to be noticed, and she was sharp but choked in large groups of people. On the bright side, she was in shape and nice on the eyes, something that Gabriel said was common among Seekers and Paladins.

"What is that?" Amy asked.

"A map of the city. When we arrested all of those people, we took their phones. I had the tech guys pull all the info they could off them and have been getting phone records. The FBI's tech people were so kind as to provide this map for me." Sean pointed, "Each red dot is a cell tower that had five or more of the arrested people visit its area multiple times and stay in that location for more than an hour."

There were a lot of dots. It'd taken Sean some time, but he was able to weed out homes and restaurants. On the screen were five green dots. These were the towers in the areas where he suspected safe houses were.

"When we started this investigation, Angelica wasn't protecting against human technology. Faith tells me there are ways to make it so we can't track cell phones. There were a handful of Humans we knew were involved that got away. Since the arrests, we haven't been able to track their phones," he explained.

"But these records were from before Angelica was trying to cover those tracks," Amy said.

Sharp he noted. "Yep, at least one of those towers marked with a green dot has a safe house." He looked at her, "How do you suggest we search now?"

She looked at the screen for a moment, "Look for buildings big enough to be a safe house, and see if the owners are dead."

Sean smiled, he hadn't thought of that. He patted Amy's shoulder, "I like the way you think."

Only three of the towers had buildings that could hold a safe house, and of those three, only one of those buildings was registered to a deceased man.

"We have our safe house," Sean announced, walking into sergeant Montoya's office.

Sergeant Montoya looked up at him, "Let's hear it." Sean explained how he'd found the safe- house, being sure to give Amy credit where it was due. The Sergeant looked down for a moment, "Very well I'll get you a warrant."

MADDISON BELDAME looked at the front door of the safe house. Her gut told her something was off. She kicked the door, breaking the lock and doorjamb. She stepped inside, her blade drawn but not needed. The space looked ransacked. Papers and debris were strewn about; the house's former occupants had been in a rush when they left. She got on the radio, "It's empty."

"WHAT!?" Sean demanded.

"Sorry Hughes, this place has been cleared out," she explained.

Gabriel came in the house followed by Alison and Sean. Gabriel knelt down, whispering a spell.

"There were Mutari in here not more than an hour ago," he said.

"You mean we just missed them?" Alison asked.

Maddison clenched her jaw, "They were tipped off." She stated, matter of fact.

"How can that be?" Sean asked, "I thought we were safe from bugs?"

"From bugs in your office yes; from moles, no," Gabriel said, and then looking at Sean's angry expression added, "we never found out who gave Javier Davison the antidote that allowed him to escape from lock up." Gabriel referred to an incident that occurred before Maddison's involvement.

Maddison agreed with him; the mole could be anybody, for all they knew.

"Perhaps this is something for Heidi to investigate," Maddison offered.

Alison looked at her, confused.

Maddison explained, "She is a Contractor, she uses Vis to read emotions. It is nearly impossible to lie to an experienced Contractor. And Heidi is very experienced."

"What, have her question everyone in the office?" Sean asked angrily.

Maddison had noticed that Sean seemed to use anger as his standard approach to anything besting him. She could understand his distaste for having every cop questioned. In-fact, she even thought it could be counterproductive.

"No; we shouldn't be that blatant about it. We don't want officers of either agency thinking they are not trusted. But we need to find this leak or Trinity will continue to stay several steps ahead of us," Maddison stated.

"She's right," Gabriel said, "we have to find out who the mole is. I don't like to think that we can't trust our own, Sean, but we can't have our secrets out."

Maddison felt a flutter in her stomach as Gabriel defended her idea. *This is not the time to think like that,* she chided herself. But still it was nice.

* * *

Sean Hughes sat in a diner with Alison, Gabriel, and Faith, lamenting their failure for the evening. The door dinged and Mandy came walking in. She was in a pair of jeans and a sweatshirt. Sean saw her nearly every day now; they'd talk about how the case was going and how her life was going. Mandy sat down next to Sean.

"Rough night?" she asked, taking one of his fries.

"You could say that," Alison said, "we tried to hit a safe house that was tipped off."

Mandy frowned, "You've got another leak?"

Sean winced, "Yeah, or maybe the same one as before -- whoever slipped Davison something to help him escape. We never caught the guy."

"They aren't using Vis to relay messages, that's for sure," Faith said, "Amy and I have that place locked down tight."

"As do Maddison and I," Gabriel said.

Sean looked at his burger, irritated, "We've never had problems like this before. I don't think it's someone who's been at the station for years; we'd have noticed them acting funny, and none of the new people seem off to me," he said more to himself.

"Heidi will find them," Gabriel assured him. "So Mandy, what have you been up to?" he asked, effectively changing the subject.

Mandy smiled, "Looking at schools, actually. I haven't decided on what I want to go into, but I've been looking at schools around town," she said, happily.

Sean smiled at her, "That's not all you have going on, though."

The others looked at her questioningly. Mandy beamed, "I contacted my family," she said, "I told them what I was … I totally thought they'd tell me I was a monster, but my dad said he didn't care and neither did my mom. They don't really want to know what I've been up to for the last few years which is good; I don't want them to know. But I'm flying home at the end of the week to visit them for a few days."

Seeing her happy lifted Sean's mood. It didn't matter that they hadn't caught anyone tonight; his work on this case had resulted in Mandy being freed from a life she hated. If that was the best he got out of this case, it was worth it in his eyes; everything else was just gravy. Everyone congratulated Mandy, and the conversation turned to her for the rest of the night. He and Alison left together; she was his ride back to the station.

Once they were in the car, Sean said, "We'll find the mole." He was convinced.

Alison looked at him as she turned on the car, her smile turning into resolve, "I know we will."

Seeing a victim who was doing better was good for a cop. It gave you the drive you needed to keep going, even when things seemed like they weren't going to work. Mandy had done that for Sean, Alison, Gabriel, and Faith. They would hit the ground running in the morning, and they wouldn't stop running until they took down Trinity.

FIVE

Heidi Decor left the team's house, prepping herself for a jump to the police station. It would be her job to find the mole who was tipping off Trinity. It wouldn't be the first time Heidi had been tasked with doing this type of work. When Vis came out into the open, many companies and government organizations were keen to rid themselves of spies. As a result, Contractors for a time were the most-requested Mages to work Pactums. Soon though, governments decided they looked weak if they needed Mages to find internal leaks. As for corporate espionage, there was still a decent market for Contractors. On the downside, only extremely large corporations had the money or the need for Mages to root out their competitors' agents. Now there was a market for Vis lie detectors, and conversely lie detector countermeasures, which allowed companies to screen their own employees. Heidi worked closely with James on several such projects. The upfront money wasn't overly good, but in the long run, having a line of lie detection products was turning the team a tidy profit.

She focused on the jump anchor Gabriel had placed at the police station, and jumped. She flashed into existence, startling a group of homeless men and women by a bench. She walked briskly to the building, noting that few people were in at the early hour. She put on her spectacles and pushed Vis into them. All of the emotions of those around her came into view. She didn't need to use an amplifier to read emotions, but using one made things easier for her, and brought people's emotions into better focus. She altered the Vis in the glasses. The tricky part of reading emotions wasn't reading what someone was feeling, but rather why they were feeling what they were. Rooting out a mole was a long process, and a lot of work.

This had been one of the major problems in developing lie detectors. Like the Human polygraph machine, early detectors could only tell when someone was feeling a strong emotion; not what the emotion was, or why they were feeling it. For most Human law enforcement, polygraph machines were not of use for that reason. If a man was being asked if he killed his wife, and he said, "No," in many cases a polygraph would say he was lying. This didn't mean that he was lying; if an innocent man was asked if he killed his spouse, he would likely feel anger at the question, which the machine would pick up as a lie. Conversely, if a man was asked if he'd killed his wife and he had, then his fear would also show the same response. Even the emotion itself couldn't always be accurate, as an innocent man might feel fear that he's being blamed for a crime he didn't commit, and a guilty man could feel anger towards his victim. Sifting truth from fiction was a complex task.

Heidi was part of a group of pioneering Mages who had developed techniques that allowed them to use Vis to see what parts of someone's brain was working, thus allowing them to not only see the person's emotions, but also if their brain was working from memory or making a lie. This was fine and dandy for Humans, but Heidi was finding that there were an increasing amount of lie detector countermeasures on the market, and if someone had a Pactum with a Seeker, Heidi's tricks could be blocked. It was even possible for a skilled Seeker to make it all but impossible for a Contractor to read people's emotions correctly. Heidi feared this was going to be the case for the DPD mole. Faith and Gabriel had the station locked down tightly, which would block the average Seeker, but Angelica was far from average. From Heidi's days with Patrick, she knew that if Angelica put her mind to it, should could probably not only get Vis objects into the station but possibly even Mutari. The question that faced them was: was it worth it for Angelica to put in so much work? It was more likely that Trinity had a Human on the inside they were prepared to burn.

"Good morning Sean," Heidi said, walking to the man's desk. He was one of the few people in.

"Hey," he said, and then yawned. "You ready to trap a rat?" he asked.

She smiled tightly, "They'll know I'm looking."

"You think so?" Sean asked.

"Yes, they have blatantly thwarted two raids. Trinity will have to know that we are looking for a spy now."

Sean didn't look happy with her response. She could read his uncertainty.

"Does that bother you?" she asked.

"It does actually, from what I've seen these people aren't dumb. So either they are really confident their spy won't get found, or they have some reason for burning them," he said.

When Sergeant Montoya came in, Heidi joined him in his office.

"So, Hughes tells me you're to smoke out a rat," he said, matter of fact.

"That I am," she said, reading disquiet in his emotions.

He was silent for a long time, and then said, "What do you need to do? I would prefer you not interrogate my people."

"That's fine," Heidi assured him, "I've done a lot of this type of work, and I don't need to interrogate people … well, not right away. I will find people who I think are likely suspects, and from there we will have to talk to some of them."

"Is it faster when you just interview people?" Montoya asked.

Heidi nodded, "Yes, it is very difficult to lie to a Contractor. In a one-on-one conversation, only a very skilled liar would be able to fool me."

Montoya considered that for a moment, "Very well. I want you to interview everyone who knows about the mole first, including me."

Heidi was shocked when he said that he wanted to be checked out. Her emotions must have been fairly apparent on her face.

The Sergeant chuckled, "What Decor, did that surprise you? I have nothing to hide, but more than that, if I can say we are doing everything possible to find the snitch; Internal Affairs might just keep their noses out of this. Where do you want to talk?"

If that is what Montoya wanted, then so be it. She launched into a set of questions. Some were just to get a base of his emotions, but others were to figure out if he was the mole. A few minutes later, Heidi relaxed the Vis in her glasses.

"I do not think you are the mole," she said.

"You don't think?" Montoya prodded.

Heidi shrugged, "Like I said; I'm very good, but nobody is foolproof."

"I can live with that," he said, and then excused her.

Heidi found it unlikely that the Sergeant was the mole, but she wasn't about to tell him that her interview was only part of her test. It was possible to trick a Contractor with the help of a skilled Seeker after all, but even then you would have to be exceptional at deception. It was for this reason that Heidi did not cross anyone off the list. It was possible the mole wasn't helping Trinity willingly. Heidi had seen there were lots of ways to turn someone into a spy for you. Everyone had a trigger; you just had to know how to find it.

Heidi's thoughts turned to both Marcus and Angelica Vies, and when they betrayed the other Arks. What had been their trigger? She'd never been able to figure out why the Vieses had done what they had, and she doubted that she would ever know.

She came to Sean and Alison's desks to see the latter just setting her stuff down. This was going to be the uncomfortable part.

"I am to interview everyone who knows about the mole," she said calmly.

She'd grown to see Alison as a friend, and to an extent Sean, too. She didn't want to offend them. However neither one showed any sign of being annoyed.

"Obviously," Alison said, "do you want to talk to me or Sean first?"

"You," Heidi said, relief coloring her tone.

"Conference room?" Alison confirmed.

"Yes, please."

Heidi didn't find any trace of deceit with Alison or Sean, nor did she with agent Alesbury. Heidi didn't interview the Mages. She couldn't objectively interview any of them but Amy, and since Amy was a Seeker, she'd easily be able to pass any interview. The same would have been true for Faith, Gabriel, and Maddison, even had Heidi not known them for years.

MADDISON BELDAME left the station with Gabriel to get lunch. As they walked, both of them were stared at. Maddison drew attention because of her appearance, and Gabriel because he'd become something of a legend in the police ranks. Most people had a look of mixed awe, disbelief, and distrust, with a healthy dose of curiosity. Gabriel somehow seemed softer since the days he'd been her teacher. To most, he seemed a happy-go-lucky kind of person, but Maddison could see hints of hardness etched into his character. He moved with confidence and purpose with everything he did.

"What is it?" he asked her.

Maddison looked forward, embarrassed that he'd noticed her scrutiny.

"Nothing," she said, and then said almost unwillingly, "I am comparing the Gabriel Decor from when I was young to that of today is all."

Gabriel seemed amused, "And what does the comparison tell you?" he asked.

As they walked the streets in the nippy autumn day. Around them, people moved about and traffic rushed by, the movement of it picking up colored leaves and making them dance in the air. Maddison breathed in before answering.

"I'm not sure," she admitted, "I have never known what to make of you. On one hand, you are my teacher, but on the other, you were one of my sister's dearest friends." The last part stung to say. Maddison didn't care to think about her sister; it still hurt to think about her being gone.

A silence spread that felt like an age to Maddison, though it was probably only a short time.

"She would be proud of you," Gabriel said with confidence.

"Thanks," Maddison said. What else was he going to say?

"I mean that. As your teacher, I am proud of you. I knew your sister well, and even during the war, she talked about how proud she was of her little sister." Gabriel gave a dry laugh, "She'd talk about how you'd pass her someday, and that she'd never hear the end of it." Gabriel looked at Maddison, holding her gaze. His eyes were honest, and Maddison looked away, feeling uncomfortable.

She was on the verge of showing emotion. Of showing how much what he said meant to her. Maddison wanted to be strong. She wanted to be like her sister, like an Ark; she would not show any weakness.

"Does this place work?" Maddison asked, pointing to a restaurant and effectively changing the conversation.

They entered with more people looking at them like they were freaks, but in the moment people saw them, wards made it so the Humans didn't notice them anymore or think about them. A college-aged man came to the table to take their drink order.

"Hello my name is …." he trailed off.

Maddison rather enjoyed the reactions of people. The young man looked her up and down. Maddison was in incredible shape, and she knew the effect her appearance had on men. The young man's eyes traced her body in its tight leather suit. His gaze rested longingly on her cleavage, but then it moved up her long silver hair, and stopped on her crimson eyes. Then he showed the first hints of fear, as instantly his mind and emotions became at war with each-other.

Maddison read his name tag, "Hello, Rob. I'll have a glass of water, please," she said, as if nothing were out of place.

"And I'll have a glass of iced tea," Gabriel said.

"Umm, ok right ah … I'll get right on that, er … do you know what you'd like to eat?" he asked.

"Give us a minute," Gabriel said, and Rob tottered off.

Maddison looked over at Gabriel.

"What?" she asked innocently.

A wry smile was playing on his face, "What? You know what. Do all Beldames enjoy making people squirm?"

Maddison tried not to let her face flush, "I have no idea what you are talking about."

Gabriel laughed, and looked at his menu.

Rob came back moments later with their drinks. They ordered lunch, and Maddison contented herself making small talk with Gabriel. She found herself relaxing in her seat, and straightened up. When she was with Gabriel, she felt no need to keep on her guard. Life was just easy and natural. Again, this made her feel slightly weak.

"Why so tense?" Gabriel asked.

Maddison looked down. "Just the case," she lied.

Gabriel sighed, "Yes, it has that effect."

"You seem chipper," she pointed out.

Gabriel shrugged, “I’m always more relaxed around you. I noticed that even when you were my student.”

She cursed herself for not saying the reason she was tense earlier was due to how natural it was being around him. *Coward.*

“I’m still your student,” she said, almost protective of the title.

He smiled, “Thank you. I’ve been meaning to ask; how did you and Amy hook up? Faith tells me she is very talented.”

This was a topic that Maddison was much more comfortable with.

“Paris, actually,” she said.

“Romantic,” Gabriel joked.

Maddison laughed, “Well you know me; why go to Paris to find a man when you can come back with a Seeker? Anyway, I was out there to see an old family friend. He taught at one of the Vis schools in the states, but was on a retreat with students. Amy was no longer one of his students, but she was on the trip helping him out,” Maddison smiled thinking back on the day she’d met Amy. “She didn’t flinch at how I look or who my family is. And even more noticeable, I didn’t notice her when I first met my friend.”

“She is rather good at not being found, isn’t she?” Gabriel said.

Maddison nodded, “The best I’ve seen. She doesn’t even need Vis to be out of sight. At any rate, I could tell she was gifted, and dedicated. Plus that she was different …”

“And you had to partner with her,” Gabriel smiled.

Maddison didn’t argue with him. It was true. “We have become best friends; there are only a handful of people I trust as much as Amy.”

“That is wonderful. It is so important to have a strong bond with your Seeker. It will save both your lives someday if it already hasn’t.”

“I’m sure it will,” Maddison said before going back to her lunch.

FAITH PENN'S eyes were closed, her body relaxed, seated on a soft pillow. She was in a small space surrounded by Vis to ensure that none could find her. Her mind reached out for miles, riding the seeking spells she'd placed the other day. She could feel them being fought. Angelica was doing her best to block Faith, but sooner or later Angelica would fail. Faith didn't have any new confidence that she could beat the woman. No; she knew Angelica was better than she was, but Angelica had to keep dozens, if not hundreds of people and Mutari hidden, as well as any buildings they were using. Faith wasn't hiding anyone, at least not at the moment. If Angelica wasn't being pulled in so many directions, Faith might not be able to beat her; but as it was, she knew that given time and pressure, Angelica would break.

She focused on the birds under her control. They were moving about the city, ever watchful. She could see with their eyes. Faith didn't care to view the world through the eyes of birds. It always gave her a sense of vertigo. She closed the connection with them, and continued to feel around the city for anything she could find.

ALISON KAUR sat with Heidi as she watched the office.

"What are you looking for?" Alison asked?

Heidi took her eyes from the room, "Right now, just the general feel of the office. People feel a whole range of emotions all day long. If you don't know what a person is normally feeling, it's harder to tell when they lie to you."

Alison nodded, and then asked, "What's it like being able to see what people are feeling?"

Heidi shrugged, "I've been doing this for so long that it's pretty normal for me. But I suspect it's like it is for you. You see everything around you, don't you detective?"

Alison smiled, that she did. "I do, but you seem so much less jaded than I am," Alison joked.

Heidi gave an easy smile, "It's all about subject matter."

Alison gave her a quizzical look.

"You are only looking for the bad, and so that is what you see. I do not see the world that way; there is both good and bad in the world. When you look for both, you will find that despite what you may think, there is more good in the world than bad," Heidi explained.

Alison snorted, "You don't work where I do; trust me, there is only bad."

Heidi looked serious, "I disagree," she looked out over the office, "I see many people here who are happy about one thing or another. If you look, you can see it," Heidi said that last part like a challenge.

Alison thought she'd humor the woman, and looked at the room trying to ignore the bad she saw. There was so much bad around her even in the station. She trusted the people in the office, but she still knew them to be human. Some people were just in sour moods, others showed the telltale signs of lying when they were on the phone or talking to others. She pushed these thoughts from her mind, and looked for only the good. It took her a moment, but there it was. People were happy all around her. A man a few desks down from her was grinning as he talked on the phone. She focused on his face, his smile slightly stupid, his eyes gooey. *Talking to his girlfriend* Alison realized. There were scenes like this playing out all over the office.

"I take it you see," Heidi said.

"How can you tell that?" Alison asked.

"Your emotions are getting brighter." Heidi became ever more serious, "Alison, I have been around true despair and evil, and even there you can find happiness, and joy. Perhaps, if you try to see the world as it truly is, and not as a place filled with evil, you will not be so jaded."

Alison laughed uncomfortably, "I'll see what I can do."

FAITH PENN was about to call it quits for the day when one of her flocks became excited. She sighed. The group of birds had been giving her a hard time all day long. She reached out to the excited animals, and paused to see what they were freaking out about.

They were following a balding man in his forties. He was in the north part of town exiting a convenience store. Faith watched the man for a moment as he turned around. As his face came into view the birds became more excited, and Faith felt a hint of Vis protecting the man. She steadied the birds so she could look at him.

Her eyes flew open. He was Norman Cross, and he was one of Corey McLoughlin's inner circle. Faith made sure the birds would follow him as she contacted Sean and Alison.

"Hughes," Sean said, answering his phone.

"I've found Norman Cross," she said.

Sean perked up on the phone, "Where is he?"

Faith relayed Norman's location to Sean, who told her to keep an eye on him. Faith did as she was asked, keeping careful note of where Norman went, in hopes of finding more members of Trinity.

By the next day, it was obvious that Cross had gone to ground after the train yard raid. Faith hadn't seen him make contact with anyone they were looking for, nor did he seem to be doing anything that would be considered suspicious. She guessed that Cross had left Trinity, and that Angelica was no longer protecting him, as the few wards he had were waning hour by hour.

"He's still a good catch," Alison pointed out as they sat in the conference room strategizing.

"Is he?" Alesbury asked. "Based on what we've seen from Trinity, they aren't going to let anyone who knows anything out of their sight."

"Trinity was scattered after our raids," Sean said, "it's possible that they just haven't gotten around to tracking down any threats there may be to their organization yet."

What Sean was saying was a definite possibility. With all of the pressure Faith had been putting on Angelica, it was likely that she was prioritizing those she wanted kept safe. Faith let her attention slip from the meeting. At the end of the day, what they did next wasn't her decision. It was up to her, and Amy, to find, and hide; that was their place in all this.

Faith closed her eyes, checking on all of the many spells she had running. She was disappointed to see that the vast majority were being blocked or not finding anything. A few spells found things that Faith quickly dismissed as false positives. Angelica was starting to fight back, and Faith knew that she would soon be finding a bunch of phantom leads designed to confuse her or lead her people into danger. Faith had wondered why it had taken Angelica so long to start fighting back. *Did she just not see me as a threat?* Faith wondered. Worry crept into her as she began to realize that up to this point Angelica hadn't been putting in her full effort. Faith knew deep down inside that this was no longer the case. Angelica Vies was going to put all her effort into fighting Faith.

SIX

SEAN HUGHES sat at his desk thinking about what their next move was going to be. They'd sat on bringing Cross in for two days in hopes that Trinity would make some move. *We need to bring him in,* Sean thought. It was obvious now that Trinity didn't consider Cross to be a threat, but Sean and the others knew that Cross could shed light on Trinity.

"Let's do it," he said to Alison.

She nodded her head knowing what he meant; getting up to tell Montoya that they were going to bring Cross in.

"Penn, is there anything that we should know?" he asked Faith.

She looked thoughtful, "No. Angelica is busy trying to block me and fight me in other areas."

Sean inspected Faith. The last few days she'd been looking more and more tired. Gabriel told him that it was because Angelica was actually fighting back now, and that Faith was being pushed to her limit. According to Gabriel, Faith had yet to meet someone who was her equal or better than she. Up to this point in Faith's career she'd out classed her adversaries so soundly that she rarely needed to put in much in the way of effort. Angelica was different. Not only was Angelica older than

Faith, but she was better. Sean could see it in Faith's eyes. She was going toe to toe with someone stronger than herself. But more than that, Faith was trying to find new ways of besting Angelica. Sean wondered about the strain Faith was putting on herself.

"How goes the fight?" Sean asked her.

Faith looked at him flatly, "Fine," she said tartly.

Sean smirked *that one is a fighter* then he added, "It's a pain, isn't it?" he asked, then reading the look on her face, "you have to fight as hard as you can in the way your enemy expects you too so they don't suspect you're trying something new. At the same time, you have to come up with, and try something new. It isn't easy."

Faith sighed, "You're telling me."

Sean laughed in earnest, "Trust me Penn I understand, welcome to my world."

ALISON KAUR stood in Montoya's office as the sergeant looked over her documentation for going after Cross.

He breathed out in a whoosh, "So you don't think he can lead us anywhere." He said as more of a statement than a question.

Alison shook her head, "No; we've been watching him for a few days. We are worried that Angelica is going to figure out we are watching him and have him killed. Norman Cross might not have any information on what Trinity is up to right now, but he should be able to give us some insight into how the group runs."

"Right, right, ok, Kaur bring him in."

Alison left Montoya's office at a fast clip, motioning to Faith, Gabriel, and Sean. They all followed her as she left the station.

Faith's birds were tracking Cross in the Highlands, at one of the many restaurants in the area. The four of them made their way to the Highlands and found Cross at Trattoria Stella's. He was sitting outside at a table by himself. Alison thought about moving in, but Sean cautioned her.

"Cross isn't to be underestimated," Sean said, "when he was with McLoughlin, he was in charge of enforcement. He'll be armed, and it's a Friday night."

Alison understood what Sean was getting at and agreed. It had been an unseasonably warm day, and as a result, the restaurants lining 32nd were packed with patrons. If Cross put up a fight, a lot of innocent people could be hurt. Not to mention, the event would make the news, tipping off Trinity and making for a PR nightmare for the department. So Alison sat on a bench and waited for Norman Cross to have his last meal as a free man.

The air became chilly as the sun set, and Alison was getting anxious for Cross to leave Stella's. Finally, he paid his bill and left the restaurant to head east on 32nd. Alison and her group followed Cross at a safe distance, watching as he turned right on Lowell, then left into a parking lot behind a strip mall.

Alison quickened her pace and the others followed. She didn't want Cross to get in a car before she could arrest him. As she came into the parking lot, she saw Cross walking to a car.

"Denver Police!" Alison yelled.

Cross spun to look at her though he didn't seem surprised.

"FUOCO!" a voice called.

Alison felt a flash of heat from her left. A wave of hot air slammed into her, sending her to the ground as her vision flashed lavender.

FAITH PENN felt wards flex as they absorbed the fire spell. Alison and Sean were both on the ground. Confused, Faith turned to see Keith Spencer and Tracy Hope materialize from the side of a building and attack Gabriel. They had been led into a trap. Faith spun to help Alison and Sean, but she was assaulted with a bolt of ruby Vis. Faith was knocked back, but caught herself.

"Vista," she said cloaking herself in an orb of amber Vis. At once she felt spells assault her, the air around her cloak tinged red. *Angelica is here,* she realized. Faith was hit again by Vis, and her cloak broke. She fell to the pavement, scraping her hands. Angelica Vies appeared and barked, "Pena!"

Vis rushed at Faith. Her defenses gone, she held up her hands in a pathetic attempt to shield herself. The spell hit her, and pain tore through her entire body. Her throat tore as she screamed.

"Who are you to challenge me, girl!" Angelica called in an angry growl.

Faith looked through the pain to see Angelica standing over her with a knife. She lunged at Faith who was totally crippled with pain. Her vision blurred as a figure stepped in front of her. The pain vanished, and with it came clarity. Sean had tackled Angelica, and was on the ground with her trying to wrestle the knife from her hands. Faith stood to aid Sean, who looked incensed with rage. He kneed Angelica in the gut, making her drop the knife. Faith rushed forward, hand outstretched. Vis flew from Angelica, and Sean was tossed several feet in the air, blood spraying from him in a great arc. Faith's face was splashed in crimson as Sean hit the pavement.

"Sean!" Alison cried out.

Faith had never felt so angry. Vis poured from her, at Angelica who vanished in a flash of red Vis. Faith felt herself being attacked by Angelica, but fought back as hard as she could. Across the lot, Gabriel was dealing with Tracy and Keith. Faith turned an eye to Sean's still and bloody form on the ground before saying, "Vista." She focused all of her energy into helping Gabriel. While Faith had been incapacitated and unable to use Vis to help Gabriel, Angelica had been able to help Tracy and Keith. Faith threw herself into the fight, doing her best to mask Gabriel's movements while trying to find, and fight, Angelica. *This is what it is to be a Seeker, Faith!*

ALISON KAUR blew into Sean's mouth and resumed chest compressions. He lay in a pool of blood, his abdomen and chest ripped open by a cut. Alison's whole body was shaking, and she didn't know where her phone was to call for help. All around her Vis flashed as the Mages fought.

"Come on, Sean!" she yelled, and puffed more air in his lungs.

"Alison, look out!" Gabriel called.

Alison turned to see a man enter the parking lot, his skin tinted green.

"Shit!" she said, pulling her gun.

TAT! TAT! TAT! She fired off three rounds standing and moving back away from Sean, drawing the Troll. It flinched back as each round hit it. It rushed forward at her. Alison moved left, turning to avoid the Troll's hand. It swung its arm, catching her and sending her careening in the air. She landed on her arm, feeling it buckle with a wet snap. She cried out, rolling off her broken arm. The Troll was coming again. Alison still gripped the gun in her hand, and gritted her teeth against the pain, taking aim. Again she fired, this time hitting the Troll in the leg. It yelped and fell to the ground. Alison stood up, moving away and firing at its head. She didn't think the bullets would be able to punch through his Vis-strengthened skull, but she was hoping it would knock him out … it didn't. He rose and Alison fired her remaining shots.

She stumbled back against a car as the Troll came at her.

There was a brilliant flash of blue, and Maddison Beldame came into existence before Alison, her silver hair flowing in the air around her, her sword Vindictam gripped in her hand. She didn't spare a look for Alison as she slashed Vindictam. The nearby cars were coated in scarlet as she halved the Troll.

GABRIEL DECOR walked into the parking lot, resting his hand on Iram's grip. Alison yelled at Cross who was about to get into a car, and he turned to look at them. There was a flash of orange and then lavender as Gabriel's wards blocked a fire spell. In a fluid motion, Gabriel reacted to the unexpected attack, drawing Iram, moving to avoid any unseen attacks. He was right to move as a broad sword cut through the space he was just occupying.

Gabriel twisted his wrist, bringing Iram up to block Dolor, Tracy Hope's sword. There was a clang of metal on metal as the two Vis-infused swords met. Gabriel pushed Vis into his body and mind slowing his perception of time, and increasing his speed and strength. He twirled, blocking attacks from Keith, and then another by Tracy. *Spostare.* He moved back away from the two Mages, and then sent out a wave of light followed by a series of small spells. Keith's wards flashed as he blocked Gabriel's harmless light, and then Keith was struck with several other spells that knocked him off balance. Tracy just rushed forward, not reacting to any of Gabriel's Vis. *She's gotten more confident,* he noted.

Tracy and Keith blurred, shifting in and out of focus. Gabriel was having a hard time finding them. He moved quickly, blocking what attacks he could, using Vis to increase his speed and reaction time even more. Faith was in trouble. Gabriel's wards flared as they were pounded with spells from both Tracy and Keith. Things were getting out of hand in a hurry. Gabriel was worried he wouldn't be able to contain the fight to the parking lot much longer. He spared a moment to place his finger to his ear.

"Maddison we need you!" he said urgently.

There was no reply. Angelica was blocking communication out of the lot. Gabriel turned as Faith screamed. The sight of his sister writhing on the ground in agony gave him pause. In that moment, Tracy attacked. Gabriel felt his arm burn as Dolor cut into him. With it came pain in the form of a spell from the edge of the blade. Gabriel snapped his attention back to the fight. The Vies family were fans of using pain on an opponent, a technique that Angelica was using on Faith at the moment. Unlike Faith, Gabriel was no stranger to pain. He didn't give the burning in his arm a second thought as he attacked Tracy. She backed away in surprise, blocking several attacks before being joined by Keith.

Gabriel had to fight smart. For all intents and purposes, Faith was out of the fight, and Angelica was still assisting Tracy and Keith. Gabriel had power and skill on his side, and he used them, drawing on the deep well of energy inside him. He threw himself into the fight with the other Mages, using sheer force to hold them at bay. Again he tried to contact Maddison, this time getting the hint of a reply.

Tracy and Keith became more difficult to find and attack. *Dammit, Angelica is focusing on the Paladins.* In the next moment, Gabriel saw an attack coming, and lashed out at Keith.

"Good to have you back," he said.

"Sorry," Faith replied, her voice hoarse from screaming.

Gabriel hadn't been doing all that well thus far, but with Faith dealing with Angelica, he could now go on the offensive, and he did, attacking Tracy. He slammed the palm of his hand into her chest. Her body shone emerald with her own Vis, and she flew back into a car, caving in its side.

Gabriel lashed out at Keith, intending to kill the man before Tracy was back to him. Blue light filled the parking lot, and Gabriel saw Maddison out of the corner of his eye.

MADDISON BELDAME jumped into pandemonium. Next to her was a Troll rushing at Alison. Sean looked like he was dead on the ground. Faith was cloaked, and Gabriel was fighting two other Mages. Maddison moved in front of the Troll and slashed, sending power into Vindictam and slicing the

Troll at his mid-section. His upper and lower halves separated, falling to the earth. The air in the corner of the lot flashed yellow, red, and peach, as Amy and Faith battled Angelica Vies.

Maddison ran to Gabriel's side, bringing up Vindictam to meet the edge of a broad sword held by a blonde girl. *Tracy Hope,* Maddison thought. Tracy gritted her teeth and attacked. Angelica was no longer able to assist her Paladins now that she was dealing with two skilled Seekers. Tracy hadn't a hope against Maddison. Tracy's attack was blocked with ease, and Maddison lunged forward, stabbing at the girl. Next to her, Gabriel stood in a cocoon of lavender. It felt incredible to fight alongside him. Maddison smiled, relishing the experience. So this was what it was like fighting side-by-side with an Ark.

Keith went down with a scream.

"Jump!" a voice called.

Tracy vanished in a flash of green Vis. Next to Gabriel, Keith lay on the ground clutching his thigh. Angelica Vies came into view, and Maddison felt her gut clinch. Angelica grabbed Keith, and they vanished in a ball of ruby light.

"Amy," Maddison said.

"The area is clear … I think," Amy said, materializing next to Maddison.

Gabriel swore next to her. Maddison turned as he ran over to Sean, who was still on the ground. Faith appeared.

"Faith, take care of Alison," Gabriel ordered.

Faith complied, going to tend to Alison, who sat on the pavement holding her arm.

What happened here? Maddison wondered.

She moved over to Sean, who looked dead.

"Is he alive?" she asked.

Gabriel was over Sean, Lavender Vis running from him. "Yes, but just barely," Gabriel said. Sean looked awful with a cut running up his body gushing blood. His skin was a sickly gray. Maddison fought back a twang of emotion, seeing someone she knew injured.

"What are your orders?" she asked.

"Secure the area," Gabriel said.

Faith was helping a hysterical Alison over to Sean.

"Sean! What happened?" Alison asked, terror in her eyes.

"He's alive. I stopped the bleeding, and almost have him stabilized." Gabriel said quickly.

Alison pulled a phone from her pocket, dialing a number "This is Detective Alison Kaur, we have an officer down. I need an ambulance!" she said.

Maddison turned from the scene to secure their soundings. People were starting to come to investigate what had happened. Maddison nodded to Amy who began to weave a spell that made people leave the area and stop thinking about what they had seen and heard. Maddison reached out with Vis, feeling for danger in the area.

FAITH PENN moved in a mental fuzz. Not only had Angelica beaten her, but she had utterly dominated her. As a result, Sean was near death, and Alison's arm was broken. She looked at her brother. Any injuries he'd sustained during the fight were gone now, but his white shirt had blood on it. Faith didn't know if it was his own or someone else's. He knelt over Sean, using spells to keep him alive until Erin could take care of him.

Erin jumped into the parking lot looking pale, her expression worried. She saw Sean and ran over to him, gently moving Gabriel out of the way. Erin pulled out her wand, and began muttering spells that would close Sean's wounds and start his body growing more blood. "He'll be fine," she said. "He needs to stay the night in a hospital, though. I can only re-grow so much blood," Erin continued her work.

In Faith's mind, she could see Sean tackling Angelica Vies again and again. Her memories moved in slow motion. She watched a man she generally found to be a jerk run in-front of her to save her life. He'd done so without any hint of fear or reservation. He had to know he couldn't beat Angelica, but he took her on anyway. *Moron,* Faith thought, fighting back tears.

The ambulance showed up; the paramedics loaded Sean on a gurney with Erin ordering them about the whole time. Before the ambulance left, Erin turned to Gabriel and pointed at Alison, "Set that arm; I'll check you and Faith out later." She vanished in the ambulance.

"I'll take care of her arm," Faith said.

Faith walked over to Alison.

"Are you alright?" Alison asked, concern and pain etched on her face.

Faith didn't answer.

"Are you alright?" Gabriel asked Faith. His voice held concern and a tone of command.

Was Faith fine? No; she wasn't. Her body hurt from Angelica's attack, and from hitting the ground, but physical pain was something that could be ignored. Faith was hurt in a far worse way. Her spirit felt crushed at the realization that she was to blame for their current situation.

"I'm fine," she said.

Gabriel nodded, and left to check the area with Maddison. Faith reached out to Alison, "Let me see your arm."

Alison proffered her arm. It was twisted and turning in the wrong direction. "Pena," Faith said, uttering the same words Angelica had used to inflict pain earlier. The intent behind Faith's spell was not to cause pain, but rather to dull it.

Alison relaxed, her face becoming soft. "Thank you," she said, "wow did that ever hurt. I've never broken anything before."

Faith smiled weakly, "I'm going to set your arm and use Vis to hold the bone in place. Erin will be able to completely heal it."

"Can you completely heal it?" Alison asked.

Faith shrugged, "yes, but Erin is better than I am at healing bones."

Alison nodded, "You do it." She said, "I want you to do it."

Faith looked in Alison's eyes, trying to figure out why Alison wanted her to heal the bone. Faith decided not to argue with Alison as it was Faith's fault Alison was hurt. Instead, she felt with Vis, finding the break in Alison's arm. Faith tried not to wince as she found the damage. Alison's arm was broken in several spots. If she were being treated by Humans, Faith was sure she'd need surgery. Faith set the bone with Vis, and then wove a spell to mend the bone.

"There you go," Faith said, "try moving your arm."

Alison moved her arm around looking at it, "Good work, Faith." Then she added, "What happened today?"

Faith looked down, her face flushing with shame, "Angelica was setting us up."

Alison looked serious.

"Alison, I'm so sorry …" Faith started.

Alison waved her off, "No one's dead, and sometimes you get hurt on a job like this."

"But Sean is your partner!" Faith protested.

Alison looked at her seriously, "Sean made a decision, and he made the right decision at that. I saw Angelica about to kill you. You and Gabriel are as much my partners as he is, and you do what it takes to keep your partner alive. Would you have done anything differently?"

Faith shook her head, "No."

Alison looked satisfied with that answer, "Good."

"You aren't mad at me for failing?" Faith asked, perplexed.

Alison laughed without humor, "I'm not happy you got beaten, but it happens. You aren't the only one to blame here, Faith. I've made a lot of arrests in my day, and should have been suspicious of how easy it was to track down Cross. Not to mention, this all smells funny to me."

"I agree," Gabriel said, coming up to them with Maddison and Amy, "this trap was too perfect."

"The mole?" Amy asked.

Gabriel nodded, "I think so. Alison, can DPD take care of this area? We need to go to the hospital."

Just prior to the ambulance's arrival, several squad cars had shown up. Alison started giving the cops orders.

While Alison did that, Gabriel pulled Faith off to the side. "Good work," he said.

She gave him an angry look. "I know I screwed up, don't be a dick about it!" she spat.

Gabriel rolled his eyes, "I'm being honest."

Faith looked at him, concerned, "Did you get a head injury?"

Gabriel laughed softly, "No. You're getting to Angelica. I've only seen her attack someone outright on one other occasion, and it was during the war. It was another Seeker who had been giving her a hard time. Did you see how mad she was? And trying to use a knife? That's something you do when you're not thinking straight, same as using the pain spell. She had you from the moment you walked into this parking lot. Had she been using her head and not her emotions, she would have just killed you with Vis," Gabriel said with a smile, patting Faith on the shoulder. "Angelica is extremely good at what she does until she gets mad, and then she makes mistakes. She failed today to kill you, which will make her even more aggravated."

"To kill me? She was after everyone," Faith said.

Gabriel smiled proudly, "No, she wasn't. The Troll was just to keep Sean and Alison busy, and Keith and Tracy were to do the same with me. No, Faith; you were the target today," he laughed in earnest, "and that she didn't even see Sean before he took her down -- that one's going to have her fuming." He became serious again, "Push harder Faith, keep Angelica angry."

"Ok …," Faith said, unsure of how to respond to Gabriel.

Deep inside, Faith relaxed a bit. Gabriel wouldn't lie to her; and from everything she'd been told about Angelica Vies, it seemed that once the Seeker lost her composure, she had a hard time working as effectively. Part of Faith was happy to have been one of a remarkably small group of people to have done this to Angelica.

A question popped into her mind, "Whatever happened to the other Seeker who made her mad?" Faith asked.

Gabriel's smile faded, and he mumbled, "Oh … yeah, well, Angelica killed the other Seeker's spouse, and then tortured the Seeker into insanity in front of her children before killing her." Gabriel looked awkward, "We didn't learn about the whole kids seeing their mother tortured and killed in front of their eyes thing until after the war."

Faith's slight feeling of happiness vanished, "Fantastic," she said.

Gabriel patted her on the shoulder again, "Don't worry though; that Seeker's Paladin was dead. I'm sure next time Angelica will just try to kill you." And then realizing that what he said wasn't comforting, added, "Not that she'll kill you … I mean, I'm not going to die, so …"

"Let's go to the hospital," Faith said, ending the conversation.

ALISON KAUR walked down one of the halls of Denver General Hospital. Sean had been unconscious for several hours, and despite Erin's assurances that he was going to be alright, Alison was worried about her partner. She put money in a vending machine, staring at the buttons. Memories of the evening played in her head like a movie on repeat. This was one of the ways Alison learned. She would play events over and over in her head, taking them apart and analyzing them. Visions of flashing light played in her head. She jumped slightly as she heard a ga-dunk next to her.

A man in a doctor's coat and scrubs was at the machine next to her, getting a soda. Alison focused on her machine and pushed a button. She made her way back to Sean's room, sipping on the drink; its carbonation biting at her tongue.

Sean wasn't awake when she got back, but Mandy Stafford had arrived. The woman stood over Sean, wringing her hands in worry. Even though Sean had a room to himself, the air of the place still had the odd scent that only existed in hospitals. The window outside his room was dark with only the moon shining in. Heart monitors beeped with a steady rhythm next to his bed and an IV dripped. Mandy looked up at Alison.

"He's going to be ok," Alison said to Mandy.

Mandy nodded, and then asked, "Are you going to be ok?"

Alison thought for a moment, "Yeah ... I broke my arm, but Faith fixed that pretty quick." She looked down at Sean from the end of his bed, "To be honest, I thought Sean was dead."

Mandy looked at him, "Gabriel told me he lost a lot of blood. Where are Faith and Gabriel now?" Mandy asked, looking up from Sean.

"Talking with the Sergeant," Alison said.

Mandy looked back at Sean, shaking her head.

"What are you thinking?" Alison asked.

"About if it was a good idea for Vis to come out in the open," Mandy said. "My life is better now, but I have to wonder about the world as a whole." She shook her head again, and said to herself, "Mages attacking in plain view of the public."

"Don't you wish that things could go back to how they were four years ago?" Mandy said looking at Alison.

Alison was about to say yes when she realized that she didn't, "No. Oddly enough, I'd rather know what all is out there. Don't get me wrong; things were more simple back before Vis ... but we were living in the dark. I would rather know about what's really going on around me."

"I can see that," Mandy said.

They stopped talking, and both watched Sean as he lay in the hospital bed, unconscious.

SEVEN

FAITH PENN was lying on the ground, Angelica Vies standing above her; knife drawn. Faith was held down by fear and pain; she had lost her will to fight, and knew at any moment her life would end. Angelica smiled wickedly, looking over at her knife which started to glow hot with Vis.

"No," Faith begged pitifully.

Angelica drove the knife into Faith's abdomen. Faith screamed in pain as the fiery knife cut into her. Faith's vision clouded with tears. From where the knife dug into her, Faith felt burning tendrils of pain extend from the wound to fill her body with agony. Her breath hitched in her chest, her body shuddered with sobs. *I want to die,* Faith thought.

"You were never good enough to beat me," Angelica said, her voice dripping with cruelty.

"I know," Faith said, between sobs.

Angelica's form turned into Alison's, "You let all of us down, Faith!" Then it was Sean, "All you are is a piece of tail, and that's all you will ever be." Sean's form melded into Amy Calamus, her blonde hair glowing. "I can't believe I ever thought you were someone to look up to," she sneered. Amy morphed into Faith's mother, "You are no daughter of mine," and in an instant, Gabriel took form, telling her that picking her to be his Seeker was a mistake. Then, worst of all, Gabriel melted into the gaunt and bloody form of her cousin Patrick Decor, Gabriel's former Seeker. His clothes were soaked with blood, his body covered in wounds that oozed a thick, dark liquid. His lifeless face looked down on her, "You will never replace me."

Faith woke with a start covered in sweat, her body trembling. Frantically, she looked around her dark bedroom for Angelica Vies. She wasn't there. The only other person in the room was her husband James, who was sound asleep next to her. She lay back down in bed. The sheets were damp with sweat, the bed hot. She wanted to toss the blankets off, but held to the fabric like a shield. *It was only a dream Faith; it's ok,* she thought to herself again and again. The house creaked, making Faith tense for a moment. She tried to close her eyes, but as soon as her lids fell, she could see the fight, with Sean on the ground in a pool of blood. Faith got a drink, trying to calm herself. This time when she closed her eyes, she could see Patrick's dead face.

She couldn't stay in bed anymore; she wasn't afraid of Angelica attacking at any moment, so she decided to take a walk around the gardens. She got out of bed, not worrying about waking James. He slept like the dead. She put on her robe and slippers, and left her room. Faith and James had their own wing of the team's expansive house, making it feel like they had a house of their own. Faith went down a set of stairs, making her way to a large set of French doors that opened out onto a stone patio.

It was late, and while there wasn't any snow on the ground, the air was cold, biting at her face and arms. "Tepido," she said softly, infusing the words with Vis. Her body glowed slightly for a moment as heat filled her. Now, the frosty night air felt good as she walked down a cobble path to the gardens.

She approached rows of waist-high hedges that formed paths through the garden. She entered the hedgerows and walked among them. All of the plants were dead or dormant for winter, which seemed to match how Faith felt at the moment. She too felt like she was dead or dormant on the inside. She stopped, looking at a rose bush. Its branches were like brown skeletons, the flowers blackened and dead. *Fitting,* she thought.

Faith sat down on a stone bench, surrounding herself in lifeless rose bushes. She breathed out with a huff, her breath coming out in a billow of fog. It was a cloudless night. The moon was full, shining down on the garden and lighting everything in a bright blue light that threw everything into contrast. Again this was fitting. Not too long ago, Faith had been starting to feel confident again. She had been feeling like she could actually stand against Angelica, and that maybe she could beat the woman. That confidence had proven to be false. Not only had Faith been thoroughly beaten, but Sean and Alison both had been hurt. Gabriel had done a good job holding off the other Paladins, but Faith wasn't able to get an upper hand on Angelica until Amy showed up.

"You are so weak," she said aloud.

There was a slight breeze as she said this, as if even the garden was telling her it agreed. In the back of her mind, she felt wards she placed around Denver and the detectives being tested. They weren't being pushed hard, and were in no danger of failing, but it was a little reminder that Angelica was out there. Faith felt a shiver as she felt one of the house's spells flex. *She is looking for me,* Faith realized.

Gabriel had told her this would happen. He told her that Angelica was angry, and therefore going to go for Faith directly. Gabriel seemed to be happy about the development; he told her it meant that Angelica was going to start making mistakes. For Faith's part, she remembered the pain spell Angelica had used on her. Faith had never known pain like that before. She couldn't even move, it was so strong. Faith knew spells like that, but she'd never used them on anyone in anything other than training, and even in those cases she'd only used a little power. Angelica, on the other hand; had used her full strength behind her attack. She'd wanted to show Faith just how much she could hurt her. *And if she can, she'll do far worse to you if she finds you,* a voice in her mind said. Furthermore, the pain spell had told Faith something else. All spells took time and effort to master. Faith's pain had been excruciating, but not so strong that she didn't see Angelica raising a knife to kill her. In that, Angelica showed that not only had she mastered pain spells, but in mastering them, she had used them many, many times.

There was a step behind her and Faith jumped, getting to her feet and turning to the sound in a moment, ready to defend herself. She paused, her heart thudding hard in her chest; her hands outstretched and bright with amber Vis. James stood a few feet away, his hands up in front of him. Faith lowered her hands, her face flushing in embarrassment.

"Sorry," she said feeling horrible, "you startled me," she explained.

James lowered his hands, "I gathered. Are you ok?" he asked, concerned.

She turned, sitting back down the on the bench, "Yeah, I'm fine."

James sat down next to her, "That's a lie if I've ever heard one."

Faith looked at him.

"Baby, I don't think I've ever snuck up on a Seeker, let alone a Decor Seeker," he said.

This twisted inside Faith. James wasn't trying to make a jab at her, but she couldn't help but take it that way. "So now I'm not even as good as every other Seeker on the planet."

"I didn't say that," James said, "you're a very good Seeker; why would you say something like that?"

She looked at him, his face showing worry.

Faith sighed, "I don't feel like a good Seeker right now. I had to be bailed out by Amy today."

"I know, but why would that make you a bad Seeker?" he questioned.

"Because Angelica Vies played me," she said, dejected.

"Yeah, but isn't she like the best Seeker in the world or something?" he asked. Then, sensing he'd said something wrong added, "Well, one of the best."

Faith looked at him, "No, you were right. My mom trained her, but that was years ago." She breathed out, "Now Angelica is probably the best there is."

"So why are you beating yourself up for losing to her?" James asked, his voice honest.

Why was Faith beating herself up over this? Was it because she was scared for her own safety? No; if she was being honest, she wasn't even that concerned for James or her brother's safety. James was at the house almost all of the time, and Gabriel was an Ark. Faith knew that while Angelica was trying to find their house, she wouldn't have a chance. The property had spells on it that had been in place for generations. Mage team houses were some of the most secure places there were. Angelica was just trying to find the house to mess with Faith, and it was working. What really had Faith so bothered by this whole thing?

"I don't know why it's bothering me so much," she admitted.

"I get being scared of her; is that how you feel?" James asked.

Faith shrugged, "I am scared of Angelica, but that isn't what's bothering me. I think it's that I feel like I'm a failure. I know that Angelica is amazing, and that I am better than most Seekers out there. I get that on a logical level, but for some reason, on an emotional level, I can't quite come to terms with it. You know what I mean?"

James nodded, "I can see that. If it helps, we all have faith in you, Faith," he said with a smirk.

James found it endlessly entertaining to tell Faith that she needed faith. She smiled despite herself at his corny joke. She loved this about her husband. He could always make her smile, and he was one of the best listeners she knew. He wrapped one of his arms around her, filling her with warmth that had little to do with the heat of his body.

"Come back to bed," he said softly.

Faith complied, walking with him back to the house.

GABRIEL DECOR breathed out slowly, controlling the speed of his breath. His eyes were closed as he sat in meditation, his mind like a calm lake. This was part of his morning routine; a routine he'd gotten out of after he started working with Alison and Sean. Gabriel still found time to train each day, but he wasn't able to spend the time in meditation that he would have preferred. He wasn't upset about it; he'd become spoiled since the end of the war. During the war, his time was at such a premium that he barely had time to sleep, let alone take the time training that he wanted to. Today was going to be different, however; because today was Saturday and he didn't have to work. The only things he had on his to-do list for the day were to visit Sean if he woke up, and Maddison was coming over in the evening to train with him.

He concentrated on his Vis, letting it build in his body. He focused it in different areas of his body, paying attention to how the energy moved inside him. Vis control was at the center of Gabriel's training. Many Paladins spent their time working on fighting and technique which was valuable, but not as valuable as learning to control one's Vis. Focusing on Vis while meditating was extremely helpful in learning how to control the Vis you could use. Along with that, Gabriel spent time each day with basic Vis control techniques and exercises. It was in this way that he was able to develop the power that he had, and this was true for every powerful Mage. It didn't matter how skilled you were with a blade or how much drive you had if you didn't have any power to use. Once you could control your

Vis, and had learned how to increase your Vis output, learning new spells was easy.

Gabriel thought back to when he was young. His father would make him spend time each day in meditation and in exercise. When the day came that Gabriel was to learn how to use the Vis he'd built up, he was able to learn spells and master them at a rate that made him seem a prodigy. The same was also the case for Faith and Maddison. Gabriel suspected that Amy had also spent years training herself.

When he was done meditating, he rose from the floor where he was sitting, making his way out of his wing of the house and headed for the training area. The training area of the house was almost a wing in and of itself. The room had tall, vaulted ceilings with large windows providing plenty of light. The room was cast in orange and pinks from the rising sun. Faith was in the center of the room already working on her yoga routine. Gabriel moved next to her and started a routine of his own. As he moved into different positions, he relished the feeling of his muscles stretching. He progressed on to more advanced poses pushing himself. When he was done, he was covered in sweat and felt incredible. Faith was also done, waiting for him.

"Shall we?" he asked, choosing not to comment on the bags under her eyes.

"Sure," she said.

They stood opposite each other, squaring off, holding their palms in front of themselves.

"Vis," they both said.

Lavender Vis shot from Gabriel's palms, meeting with Faith's amber Vis. They weren't using a lot of Vis as they began to push on one another's energy. The idea of the exercise was to push on one another like resistance training. They would take turns changing their Vis, making the other person match them; then pushing harder and softer. It was a straightforward task, but one that helped someone learn how to control how much

Vis they were using so they didn't push themselves harder than needed. It had the added effect of helping to build one's stamina and power. Faith didn't have near the power of Gabriel, but he still found the exercise helpful. When they were done with that, they moved onto other training tasks.

Gabriel kept noticing that Faith wasn't keeping her focus; which resulted in their training not going overly well. Gabriel called a stop to their current task.

"What's wrong?" he asked, trying not to sound irritated.

Faith gave him a flat look, "I'm fine."

"You sure?" he asked.

Faith looked angry, "You know what, Gabriel, I'm not fine!"

"Do you want to talk about it?" he asked.

"No," she snapped, "that would take time away from training, and we all know how important that is to you!"

Gabriel flinched away from her hostility, "Look, Faith, if you don't want to train, we don't have to. What's gotten into you?"

She gave him a deadly look, "I don't know -- maybe getting my ass kicked by Angelica Vies … when was that? … oh yeah, yesterday!"

"You're pissed that I asked if you wanted to train after you were defeated? I thought that would make you want to train," he said, being honest. He couldn't understand her reaction. Every time he'd lost, he found himself wanting to train, wanting to become stronger lest he lose again. Admittedly, he could say the same for when he won a fight. When he defeated another, he trained to ensure that he could defeat the person again. Faith needed to train to make sure she didn't get killed by Angelica. His patience with his sister was starting to wane.

"Really? That was what you thought? Are you sure you were thinking, Gabriel? Do you even care that Angelica tortured me yesterday? Does that even factor in with you? Or how about how Sean almost got killed, does that matter to you either?" she roared.

"ENOUGH!" Gabriel barked, her jabs about him not caring pushing him over the edge.

Faith went silent in an instant.

Gabriel had moved from concerned and slightly irritated to just irritated. "Faith, I am tired of the 'poor me' garbage! We all get beaten, and there is always someone better. If you spend your time dwelling on that, you will never grow!"

"That's easy for you to say," Faith countered, "you're the best Paladin in the world!"

Gabriel laughed without humor, "No Faith; I was the third best in the world. Gregory Arnold was the second best in the world, and he was killed by the best Paladin in the world who is Marcus Vies!" Faith looked down at the floor as Gabriel went on, "I doubt in the last ten years Marcus hasn't been getting stronger, and the reality of it is; he is still probably better than I am! Furthermore, I have been defeated countless times in one-on-one combat, and in large scale battles costing the lives of thousands," he reminded her. Gabriel knew it was easy for her to forget when they were young, before Gabriel was what he was now. She also didn't remember the war. She hadn't been in it. She hadn't seen the horrors he had. Done what he'd done. "Marcus not only destroyed the Nobilis, but in his act of betrayal shattered the Arks. No, I am not the strongest Paladin in the world … I never was … it was always him," he ended, his voice soft, his frustration spent.

Faith looked at him; anger and confusion on her face, "So what? You have no hope of beating him?" she demanded.

"I didn't say I didn't have a hope. I do have a hope, but chances are, the next time I fight Marcus Vies I will be defeated and likely killed," he said, holding her gaze, his voice not cold with anger or sorrow, but with the cold that could only come with grim truth.

Gabriel was being honest with her. He knew that he would likely perish if … no; when, he fought Marcus again. Gabriel could still remember the first time he'd fought the man. By the end, he was on the ground in a pool of his own blood, barely clinging to life, his arm severed. Had the other Arks not come to his aid, Gabriel would have died that day.

Faith looked like she didn't know what to say. Her expression fluctuated between anger, sorrow, and confusion. Instead of responding to him, she stalked past him and left the room. Gabriel called after her, but she didn't turn around. *Fool,* he thought, *now you pushed her away.* He'd hoped that honesty would galvanize her into action, but it had the opposite effect. He looked down at the floor, defeated and concerned. Gabriel wasn't sure what to do next. Faith had the skill to hold her own against Angelica, but if she never gained the confidence and resolve she needed to, Angelica would continue to defeat her again and again. If that happened, then Gabriel would die for sure the next time he fought Marcus.

SEAN HUGHES' eyes fluttered open. He was in a soft bed. Above him, off-white ceiling tiles came into focus, and then the beeping sound of a heart monitor. He moved his fingers, restoring feeling back to his body. He could remember flashes of a fight. He knew he'd been hurt pretty badly, but his body didn't hurt. All he could feel was a headache like he'd been drinking. He moved his arm, feeling a pinch from an IV. He looked at the tubes coming out of his arm.

Next to his bed was a sleeping woman. Her hair was long blonde, her skin cream. She wore a sweater and a pair of jeans. Sean looked at Mandy Stafford, and not for the first time thought of how beautiful the woman was. He smiled, happy to see her. He turned his head to the window, the sky holding hints of pink. He wasn't sure if it was morning or evening, but he thought it was morning as there was little in the way of sound outside his room.

He sat up in the bed looking for a clock. He found one on the wall, the digital read out saying it was six am. He tilted his head to the side with a resounding series of cracks, making Mandy stir.

She looked at him, relief coloring her expression, "You're awake! I've been worried sick."

"Don't worry, I wouldn't leave you hanging for Vis," he said, smirking.

She scowled at him, "That's not what I was worried about. How do you feel?"

"Fine. I have a bit of a headache, but that's it," Sean said.

There was a knock at the door, and a man in a white lab coat came in the room, accompanied by Erin.

"How are you feeling, Mr. Hughes?" the doctor asked.

"I'm alright," he answered and then spoke to Erin, "I take it I'm alive because of you?" he asked.

The doctor shot a distrusting look in Erin's direction as she answered, "Yes, and you might want to be a bit more careful the next time you attack a Mage," she cautioned. "But thank you for saving Faith's life. I am rather fond of my sister in-law."

Sean was surprised. He could only remember bits and pieces of the fight. "I saved her life?" he asked. Erin nodded.

The doctor spoke, "The bulk of your injuries were healed by the time you got here, but you were running pretty low on blood. In fact, by all accounts you should have been dead. You didn't have enough blood in you to survive," The doctor said, matter of fact.

Sean felt cold. He'd been hurt before; he'd even been in a serious car wreck, but he'd never been close to death before.

"How am I still alive?" Sean asked.

The doctor glanced over to Erin, who smiled, "You were rather low on blood, but thankfully you weren't so low that I couldn't use Vis to keep you alive long enough for your body to make more."

"That's something else your Mage friend helped you with; you shouldn't have been able to grow back enough blood to live or even wake up as quickly as you have," the doctor, said shooting Erin another look.

Sean understood the doctor's apprehension of Erin now. She was doing things that Human medicine couldn't even imagine doing. Sean suspected that the doctor was wondering what else Erin was capable of; a sentiment that Sean shared with him. The doctor checked a few of Sean's vitals and said that if he was still doing well the next day, he could go home. Then he left, leaving Sean with Mandy and Erin.

"That guy doesn't seem too fond of you, Penn," Sean said to Erin.

She looked at the door, a frown on her face, "That he doesn't."

"So how much is this going to cost?" Sean asked her.

Erin looked back at him with a scowl and flicked his forehead, "Nothing; you saved my sister in-law's life. Besides you got hurt due to a fight you shouldn't have been in, which is in our Pactum with you," she added.

"What do you mean?" Sean asked.

Alison's voice came from the door, "Meaning Faith was bested by Angelica; had she not been, we would have been fine. How are you feeling?"

"Fine. How was Faith beaten? And is everyone ok?" Sean asked, concerned. He may not have acted like it all the time, but he liked all the Mages a lot. At first he hadn't; but now he saw them as friends and partners.

Alison greeted Erin and Mandy and then stood next to Sean's bed.

"She's not hurt," Erin said, "but she's pretty upset about everything. You might not want to give her a hard time about it."

"I wouldn't do that. I know I pick on you guys a lot, but I wouldn't do that about a fight we lost. Will she be ok?" he asked.

Erin didn't look optimistic, "I don't know, to be honest with you. She has been stressing about Angelica a lot lately … I really don't know how much longer she can last. Don't worry though; if Faith cannot perform her duties, Gabriel will find a Seeker to help him," Erin added, trying to comfort everyone.

Sean wasn't sure what to say. Faith always came off so feisty, it was hard to think of her quitting.

"She'll come around; don't worry," Mandy said.

"How can you be sure?" Erin asked her.

Mandy looked confident, "Because she's a Decor; they don't know how to quit."

Erin smiled a bit, "When you put it that way, I don't think I've ever seen Gabriel or Faith quit anything they've started." Erin said this looking slightly awed, and added, "You're right, Mandy; I was wrong to think that Faith would quit."

After that, Alison brought Sean up to speed with everything that had happened, giving him an account of the fight. As she talked, everything started coming back to him. An image flashed into his head: Faith on the ground screaming with Angelica standing over her with a knife. Sean heard the heart monitor's beeping pick up as he thought about it.

"You alright, Hughes?" Alison asked.

"I remember now," he said with clenched teeth. "How dare that bitch think she could attack one of my partners," he growled.

Alison smiled coldly, "That's how I feel about it."

"You might want to think about using a little excessive force bringing that one in, Kaur," Sean said.

"Hey you can't be too careful with a suspect that's dangerous," Alison said, smirking.

Erin laughed, making the detectives look at her, "You aren't going to get the chance. He isn't letting his sister see it, but I've never seen Gabriel so mad. You won't be bringing the Vieses into custody. Aside from the fact that there is no way to imprison them, Gabriel is going to kill them," she said.

Sean didn't argue that with her. He knew it was true. Even if there was a way to imprison the Vieses, Sean knew that Gabriel was going to kill them. The thought didn't genuinely bother him; in truth, he was comforted knowing that Gabriel was going to do it. The Vieses were some of the worst kinds of filth there was in the world. Killing them would be a service to all.

Later on in the day, Sergeant Montoya came in to see him. Sean was happy he didn't get yelled at by the man, but was a little surprised at how uncaring Montoya seemed about the whole situation.

"You'll have to be cleared before you can go into the field," Montoya said.

"Yeah, I kind of figured," Sean said.

"Are you going to need to take any time off?"

"No; I feel fine, and I want to get back to hunting these people down. The doctors said I can leave tomorrow, so I can come in Tuesday morning," Sean said.

Montoya nodded. "Fine, make sure you get approved for duty," he said, and then left.

That left Sean alone with Mandy. She told him she didn't have anything to do for the day so she stayed with him until it was time for him to go to sleep. He was sad to see her go, but happy to know that she'd spent the night at the hospital watching over him. She'd even taken it upon herself to call his parents, keeping them in the loop. When he'd talked to his mother, she'd said she couldn't wait to meet Mandy. *I hope you get to meet her, mom,* he thought, and then fell asleep.

EIGHT

FAITH PENN was finishing her lunch when Amy and Maddison arrived at the team's house. Faith closed her eyes for a moment, trying to clear her mind, trying to put herself in a better mood. She was still mad at Gabriel, but she couldn't let that affect her training with Amy; after all Amy had done nothing wrong, and neither had Maddison. A small voice in her head told her that she had overreacted with Gabriel, but Faith wasn't paying attention to that voice at the moment.

Faith put her plate in the sink, and then made her way to the entryway. Gabriel was already there, talking with Amy and Maddison. Both of the women wore workout clothes that looked comfortable. Maddison looked out of place with her silver hair and red eyes, dressed in yoga pants and a comfy shirt. Faith's thoughts must have been plain on her face.

"You don't know what to make of her without the S&M get up, right?" Amy said brightly.

Gabriel stifled a laugh, while Maddison rolled her eyes, "Amy honestly, it's not an S&M outfit."

"Right," Amy said sarcastically, then greeted Faith, "how are you today?"

Faith smiled, finding it hard to be in a bad mood around Maddison and Amy, "I'm fine; are you ready to train?"

Amy said she was. Faith led her away from Maddison and Gabriel, taking her to the gardens. Faith liked to work outside whenever she could; she also found that having extra space was handy as well. Amy followed her, smiling slightly as she took in the vast garden.

"Does your builder do all this?" Amy asked.

"Yeah, he's pretty handy to have around. So, is there anything specific that you wanted to work on today?" Faith asked.

Amy looked sheepish, "Well … I was wondering if we could talk about the fight yesterday, and see what we need to work on …"

Faith's good mood vanished.

Amy noticed Faith's shift in mood, "We don't have to though," she said quickly, "I just thought it might be a good idea."

"No; you're right," Faith said, "we should go over that."

Faith didn't want to make Amy feel guilty about bringing up the fight. Amy was right to want to go over the fight with Angelica; it was something that Faith should want to do herself.

Amy looked serious. "I've never fought anyone like that before … it felt like the first time I ever sparred with my teachers when I was learning how to be a Seeker," Amy admitted.

"Angelica Vies is extremely talented, but she also has years of experience and has mastered nearly every Seeking technique. Can you tell me what felt good, and what didn't?" Faith asked, finding that as she comforted Amy, she found herself feeling better about her own performance.

Amy nodded, "My offensive spells felt pretty good, and the ones I had on Maddison; though I don't think they had anything to do with me, but rather that Angelica was busy with you. My cloaking wards felt pathetic; the only one that wasn't being tested was my invisibility cloak."

"She didn't need to see you," Faith said, "Angelica has learned not to trust her eyes; she wanted to find you with Vis. Once she did that, she could attack you. As for your offensive spells, those would be the ones I'd be most worried about," Faith said.

"Why is that?" Amy asked, looking confused.

Faith smiled tightly, "Your cloak was being tested because Angelica had to put in effort. If your offensive spells felt strong, that is likely because they were being diverted." Reading Amy's deepening look of confusion, Faith added, "Have you ever fought a high level Seeker before?"

"No," Amy said honestly, "I had a teacher; he was good, but he wasn't anything like you and Angelica."

Faith was flattered that Amy saw Faith and Angelica in the same class.

"That makes sense. When you are fighting someone like Angelica, you should always feel like you are having to put a lot of effort into an attack. If you don't, then you are being diverted; that or you've broken down your opponent's defenses. It takes a lot of work to divert someone's Vis, but once you master the technique, it is very useful as most Seekers don't even know it's possible," Faith explained.

"Ok … so how do I know if I'm being diverted or if I'm winning?" Amy asked.

Faith thought for a moment, "Here, let me show you the differences."

AMY CALAMUS felt self-conscious as Faith explained the principles of Vis deflection. Amy had never even heard of the technique before. From what she could gather from Faith, it was something that only the highest level Seekers knew about or trained on. In one aspect, this made her feel uncomfortable. Amy was aware she wasn't the best Seeker in the world, but by virtue of Maddison wanting to partner with her, Amy had to be one of the best in the world. But here she was learning about something she'd never even heard of! So how could she be one of the top Seekers in the world? Amy couldn't help but wonder what else she didn't know. On the other hand, Amy was honored that Faith was willing to teach her something that was so secret. Amy realized that by teaching her how to deflect Vis, Faith was sharing techniques that the Decor family had been guarding for generations; sharing the information with only those they found worthy.

Faith stood across from her, "I want you to feel the difference when I deflect your Vis, and when I don't. I'll make sure that you can hear me the whole time, so you don't need to use any audio detection spells."

With that, Faith vanished in a flash of amber. Her voice called out, "I am right in front of you; I won't move, and you don't have to cloak yourself. I won't be fighting back."

Alright, you can do this, Amy. She closed her eyes, Vis infusing her body, enveloping her in a cocoon of peach light. A crystal ball levitated before her, pulsing with energy. Amy spoke a spell that was focused to the area right in-front of her. The spell rippled out before her.

"Not deflecting," Faith said.

Amy felt resistance on her spell at once. She resisted the urge to put more power into the spell, telling herself the point of the exercise wasn't to beat Faith; but to learn what it felt like to have her Vis deflected. *Like you could fight her anyway,* a voice in her head said. Amy felt her spell crashing against Faith like surf on a rocky cliff. And like the surf on stone, her spell had no effect on Faith's cloak.

"Now deflected," Faith said.

Amy stepped back. Her spell wasn't being fought hardly at all. The only reason she knew her spell wasn't working was because she couldn't see Faith.

"How are you doing that?" Amy asked, awe coloring her voice, along with a healthy dose of concern.

Faith appeared in-front of Amy again, "Pretty cool, isn't it? Can you see what an advantage that could be?"

Amy could, "Yes, you could totally throw off your opponent if you wanted to; they would think they were winning, and not try as hard."

"I don't think you're seeing the whole picture yet. Attack my cloak again, but this time act like you don't know where I am." Faith instructed.

Amy did as she was asked, and felt Faith fighting her directly. Amy felt Faith's wards buckling, and Amy, thinking this was part of the training, put more effort into fighting. Her wards buckled, and Faith appeared next to her.

"I thought you were going to show me deflected Vis?" Amy asked, looking at Faith in confusion.

Faith smiled, but her voice came from behind Amy, "I did."

Amy spun to see Faith mere inches away from Amy's back. The Faith Amy had thought she had found was just an illusion. Amy felt her gut clinch in fear.

"When a Seeker tries to kill another Seeker, they generally have to reveal their location. If you use deflected Vis properly you can get your opponent to show themselves, and they will never see your attack coming." Faith said soberly, "Angelica was trying to do this to you."

Amy felt cold, "She was?"

Faith nodded, "I was already blocking her from making phantom images of herself. At the time, I wondered why she was trying so hard to make them, but I understand now." Faith looked thoughtful, "Did your teacher know Angelica?"

Amy tried to clear her head from the knowledge that Angelica Vies was almost able to hurt her, "Ummm yes, he fought her on a few occasions, I think. He said in the Tournament Potestatis?"

Faith nodded, "The Tournament of Power. I'm sure the Vieses have been keeping as up to date as they can on upper level Paladins, so she'll know who Maddison's Seeker is, and who you trained with. If she's fought your old teacher, Angelica should have a pretty good idea of what you are capable of." Faith shook her head. "I swear those tournaments did more harm than good," she lamented. "Who was your teacher?"

"Peter Leaky," Amy said.

"Leaky huh? That isn't a name I know; he's not from a prominent family is he?" Faith asked.

Amy was a little irritated, "Why would that matter?"

Faith's expression softened, "I don't mean to sound elitist; it's just that Vis deflection is a closely guarded technique by a few prominent families. The teachers of Seeking don't divulge their tradecraft. Your teacher may have been very skilled at what he did, but if I've never heard of him, he's not Ark level, which means that unless he's from a prominent family, he wouldn't likely know deflected Vis. If Angelica has fought him, she'll know that."

"So she knew I didn't know the technique?" Amy asked, worried.

Faith looked at her kindly, "I am sorry Amy, but yes. I think we best find out what you haven't mastered or heard of yet. I'm not trying to be mean, but we need to know where Angelica is likely to hit you."

FAITH PENN felt sorry for frightening Amy. The woman was one of the most talented Seekers Faith had ever seen, and in many ways she saw Amy as being far better than herself; but if Amy was missing pieces in her training, Angelica would be at an even greater advantage. As an aside, Faith noticed that helping Amy made her feel better about herself. Not that she was more advanced than Amy, but rather that it showed Faith that no matter how good you thought someone was; there was always room for improvement. Also, Faith liked Amy; she wanted her to be able to defend herself from anyone at Ark level. A voice in her head added, *and if the Arks are needed again, Maddison will most certainly be one. Amy must be ready.* Faith tried not to think about that, though.

Faith spent the next few hours testing Amy, finding holes in her training. When she was done, she was happy to find that there weren't many things that Amy hadn't used or heard of. What did worry Faith was that while Amy was extremely skilled when it came to cloaking herself, finding objects, and doing basic Seeking work, she wasn't as skilled as she needed to be when it came to fighting other Seekers in conventional battle. This was something that Amy was going to have to work on if she wanted to hold her own against any high level Seeker.

They had gone back into the house, Faith deciding they were done for the day. Amy was sipping at a drink looking thoughtful, "Faith, what was the Tournament Potestis? And why isn't it around anymore? I am sorry for my lack of knowledge. When I was growing up, my family kept themselves separated from anything to do with Seeking or Paladin arts."

Faith put down her own drink, "The Tournament Potestis was held before the war. Every year, Paladin and Seeker teams would compete in different events. There were events just for Seekers, Paladins, and then team events. No one was allowed to use deadly force, and it was more of a community-building event. Anyone could enter the tournament, but in general, prominent families would have their own mini tournaments prior to the main tournament. "

"Why was that?" Amy asked.

"Well, prominent families have a group of branch families that are composed of brothers, sisters, and cousins. Generally a family would only enter one or two teams into the Tournament Potestis. For example, the Decor family has sixteen Paladin Seeker teams that belong to the branch families.

"The tournament also had another purpose. It allowed families, schools, and teachers to prove just how powerful they were, and it allowed potential Seekers and Paladins the opportunity to see who was out there to train them. For those who entered the tournament, they got the chance to prove themselves."

"But why isn't it around anymore?" Amy asked.

Faith sighed, "The war. The tournament proved who the most powerful Paladins were, we thought. When the war started, our side chose the top Paladins to become the Arks. Later, we learned that those Mages that composed the Nobilis had withheld themselves from the tournament or allowed themselves to be defeated so they could learn the strength of their future enemies," Faith explained, remembering back to when she was young. "Do you know how the rankings for Arks work?"

Amy shook her head.

"The top three Arks are ranked by their skill and power; after that an Ark's number doesn't mean anything. Gabriel, for example, was the third seat. He'd placed third in the last tournament which took place two years before the war."

"But he had to be only ten or eleven when he was in the tournament then …" Amy said.

AMY CALAMUS watched Faith smile before she spoke, "Yes, Gabriel was the youngest to ever place that high. For the most part, Paladins and Seekers under eighteen weren't allowed to enter."

Amy let that sink in. She'd been training for years to be a Seeker, but when she was eleven, she couldn't even control Vis enough to lift a book off a shelf; let alone fight against the best Mages of the time.

Faith went on with bitterness, "Marcus Vies won the tournament, and therefore was the Ark Captain. Gregory Arnold won second place, and was the Ark Lieutenant. It was a bit of a shock, really. With Gabriel being so young, he shouldn't have even been in the tournament, and as for Marcus and Arnold, they were a rarity because Marcus was not from a prominent family, and Gregory was born in a Human family.

"It was a big win for my family," Faith added, "our family entered two teams that year. My mother took the top spot for Seekers, with Angelica coming in a far second. My father didn't rank in the top twelve, so my parents were never made Arks. But my father won in the way that mattered to him. He'd trained the top six Paladins, and my mother trained Angelica. For the Decors, it was a huge win. It was a message to the whole of the Vis world that the Decor technique was superior to that of others, and that the Decor line was strong. My father even trained Maddison's sister," Faith said, looking over at Amy.

"Edward trained Stella?" Amy asked.

Faith nodded, "Yes."

Amy breathed out. She knew the Decors were influential, but she never knew just how influential. Maddison's sister Stella had been wildly famous in her time, and her legend still captivated young Paladins. The same could be said for Gabriel, but Amy never knew that Edward Decor was behind them.

Faith continued, "After the war, it became apparent that it wasn't wise to let your potential enemies know your fighting prowess, and as a result there has been no tournaments since. Some think that had the tournaments not taken place, the Nobilis would have never been confident enough to start the war; or even if they had, our side wouldn't have taken as many casualties."

"How big was the gap between Gabriel and the fourth place winner?" Amy asked.

Faith laughed dryly, "There was a substantial gap between the top three Arks and the rest of the Arks. That's not to say that the others aren't powerful in the extreme; it's just that Gabriel, Marcus, and Gregory were completely in a class of their own. I know that Gabriel misses Gregory a lot. The three of them used to train together. Gabriel would push himself to keep up with his elders, and I think Marcus and Gregory pushed themselves so they didn't get passed up by a teenager," Faith laughed again with real humor.

"I can see why you're taking losing to Angelica so hard now," Amy said. "You are from a family of greatness. You aren't like me. I grew up being amazed by average Seekers, but for you; you grew up with legends. Now you are among their ranks, but you didn't have the years of time your mother and Angelica had. Nor were you surrounded by other students like Gabriel was to push him. How are you supposed to compare? And how are you supposed to fit in with those people."

Faith's eyes were glistening as she started to speak, "I've spent my whole life being just out of reach of my family's coattails … My mother was like Gabriel growing up, you know. She was a prodigy, and still is." Faith wiped at her eyes, "I mastered things faster than any other Seeker in the branch families, but I wasn't praised for it. I was supposed to far exceed them. If anything, the branch Seekers seemed underwhelmed by my progression even though I blew them out of the water. And then Patrick was killed, and Gabriel chose me to be his Seeker."

"You were the best choice," Amy tried to comfort her.

"No, I wasn't actually. My father and mother talked it out, and before Gabriel asked me to be his Seeker, my mother said that she would no longer be my father's Seeker, but Gabriel's." Faith said, "But Gabriel said no. He wanted me; his kid sister to do it. He said he saw something in me." Faith looked into Amy's eyes, "He chose not to have the best Seeker in the world; the one person who could beat Angelica Vies. No; he chose me. Amy, you have no idea how powerful Gabriel became in the war, and since then. He is by far more powerful than Gregory was, and if he isn't more powerful than Marcus, then they are at least equals."

"And had he chosen your mother instead of you, his team would be stronger than Marcus' team," Amy noted flatly.

Amy sat back in her chair breathing out "how do you live with that kind of pressure?" she said more to herself than to Faith. Then she added, "I don't envy you, Faith. I used to. When we met, I knew your reputation … and that of your brother, and family. I thought, 'what I wouldn't give to be her,' but not anymore."

Faith laughed, "Thanks, Amy."

"Sorry," Amy said, "you've got to stop comparing yourself to your mother and Angelica. Faith, I know you don't see it, but you and Gabriel are the strongest team in the world." Faith gave her a disbelieving look. "It's true. Maddison tells me all the time. So does her whole family. Even my old teacher told me 'Faith Penn is the best Seeker there is right now'. And think about it: Marcus and Angelica have been hiding for what, like ten years now? Even if Angelica can't beat your mom; if Marcus is as powerful as you say he is, the Vieses don't need to hide. But they do hide because they know that not only can you and your mother find them, but if you ever did, Gabriel would defeat Marcus."

"Do you think so?" Faith asked sounding incredulous.

"Heck yeah, I do," Amy said, and she meant it, "no wonder Angelica hates you so much, and why she's working her hardest to beat you." She read Faith's expression, "Come on Faith, she has more motivation than you."

"How so? I thought you said you saw the pressure I'm under," Faith said defensively.

"If you don't live up to your mother's reputation, what happens to you? Nothing, right? You're still a top-rated Seeker with a good life and loving family, but if Angelica fails, what happens to her and her husband?"

"They die," Faith said softly.

"Right, Angelica is fighting with the rage and fear of a lifetime of hiding, and she's fighting for her life. I don't know what the Vieses are up to, but don't think for a moment that

Angelica doesn't see a sword hanging over her head every second of every day. And be honest, Faith; are you fighting like your life and the lives of those around you are at stake?"

FAITH PENN let Amy's words sink in before she answered, "No, I'm not fighting like my life and the lives of my family are on the line." She was silent for a moment. How had she not seen this before? Of course Angelica was beating her … she had to. Angelica was in a corner, and therefore would do whatever she had to in order to survive. In many ways, this would make Angelica more dangerous, but it also meant that she was desperate, and desperate people made mistakes. Something inside of Faith started to build. It wasn't the flimsy confidence she'd had before. It was something deeper and more profound … it was what Gabriel had; it was resolve. It was the resolve to hold nothing back, to fight for her life, and if need be, to give her life. If she wanted to beat Angelica, she needed the same resolve. Faith's depression evaporated, her feelings of self-loathing and doubt replaced with purpose. The same purpose she saw in her brother's eyes every day. *Is this what it is to be an Ark, Gabriel?* she wondered.

She looked back at Amy, the other Seeker looking like she was worried she'd said something wrong. Faith would be eternally grateful to Amy for what she'd done. She wouldn't let Amy go unpaid for the perspective she'd given Faith. Maddison was up to Ark level, and Amy was so close. She would not let Amy go into another battle without being at the level she was capable of. Faith needed to speak with her mother. Faith was already feeling guilty about teaching Amy what she had. Vis deflection was a coveted secret, but Amy needed to know. Faith needed to get her mother's blessing to teach Amy everything she knew.

"Thank you so much, Amy," Faith said. She looked out at the dark sky, "I don't want to be rude, but I need to speak with my mother. Would you mind coming with me?"

Amy looked confused, but said she would go with Faith after she told Maddison where she was going.

GABRIEL DECOR stepped back, raising Iram up to meet Maddison's attack with Vindictam. The Katanas clanged together, sending a vibration up Gabriel's arm. He pushed Vis into his body, augmenting its natural abilities.

"Your use of augmented Vis has improved," Gabriel noted, "even from the last time we trained."

Maddison took a few steps back, assuming a defensive pose, "After our fight with the other Paladins, I thought it might be a good idea to work on it. Tracy and Keith may not be their top Paladins."

Gabriel lashed out with Iram in a quick set of attacks. Maddison blocked them, but not without considerable effort. Gabriel circled around the training room, "Yes, and Tracy has been getting better. The first time I fought her I could tell she had potential."

"And Keith?" Maddison asked, eyeing Gabriel with caution.

He shook his head, "Perhaps he could be powerful someday, but until he gets his head in the game and focuses, he'll be worthless."

Gabriel swung Iram, letting Vis pour out from the blade in a broad, sweeping arc across the room. Maddison raised Vindictam, its edge burning a bright blue. There was a bright flash as Gabriel's attack hit Maddison, and a crash as she flew back, hitting the floor.

"It would have been better to avoid that attack," Gabriel pointed out.

Maddison sighed from the ground, "Yeah, I can see that." She huffed and stood up, "I forget I can't use brute force with you."

Gabriel smiled. "You should use pure force only when absolutely needed," he countered. It was easy for Gabriel to slip into a teacher-student role with Maddison, "Please forgive me Maddison, I'm not your teacher anymore."

She waved off his comment, "Of course you are. Besides, you're right. I haven't had to fight anyone who was anywhere near a match for me up to this point … but with this case? There's a real chance I will have to defend myself from other Mages who are Ark caliber, or even Marcus Vies himself."

Gabriel didn't want to agree with her, but she was right. "You did excellent work the other day," he said honestly, "I have no doubt that if the Arks were reestablished today you would be one of us."

Maddison blushed, "Do you think so?"

Gabriel nodded, "Yes, of course I do …" he paused before making his next statement, "I think that you are very close to your sister's skill level, and you may even have passed it. It's been so long since the last time I fought alongside her," Gabriel said, remembering the past.

"Thank you," Maddison said solemnly. "I never got to see her fight," she admitted.

"Watch yourself in the mirror sometime, and you'll have an idea of what Stella Beldame was like in battle," Gabriel said warmly.

The door to the training room opened, Faith coming in with Amy.

"I am going over to Mom and Dad's, and I'm taking Amy with me," Faith announced.

"Is that alright?" Amy asked Maddison.

Maddison shrugged, "Go for it."

Faith turned, taking Amy with her as she left the room.

"That was odd," Maddison noted.

"Yes it was. Faith got mad at me today. She was feeling down about her fight with Angelica, but she seems to be better now," Gabriel noted.

"Something is different about her," Maddison pointed out.

Gabriel thought about that for a moment. What was different about his sister? It was the air about her, the way she was carrying herself. Gabriel smiled, *you found your resolve, didn't you?* He turned back to Maddison, beaming. "Guard yourself!" he said, attacking.

MELINDA DECOR sat at her kitchen table, her husband Edward rubbing her feet from the chair opposite her. Their front door opened, and Faith came in the kitchen with Maddison Beldame's Seeker, Amy. Faith looked tense.

"What is it?" Edward asked, concerned.

"Everything is fine," she told her father, and then spoke to her mother, "Can I speak with you?"

Melinda examined her daughter for a moment before responding, "Sure, sweetie." She thought about telling Faith and Amy to wait for a moment, her massage felt so good; but something told Melinda that Faith wasn't going to wait.

Faith told Amy to make herself at home.

Melinda walked with Faith to her office. Faith was carrying herself with something more than confidence … she was walking with purpose. *What has happened to you?* Melinda wondered. They entered her office. Melinda sat behind her desk and Faith took a seat opposite her.

"So what's up?" Melinda asked.

"I want to take Amy on as a student," Faith announced.

Before Melinda could say anything, Faith launched into an explanation of her day. Melinda listened as her daughter spoke, her gut clenched. She'd always known the struggle that Faith had being around so many powerful Mages. It wasn't fair, and in many ways Melinda blamed herself for letting Faith become a Seeker. Faith didn't seem to be suffering from any of her past issues, though. As she spoke, she was matter of fact, and she laid out her reasons with an air of conviction. Melinda was relieved to see Faith coming into her own. This made Melinda want to jump out of her seat with joy; she'd hoped for it for so long. She refrained from expressing her joy, focusing on keeping her expression from showing her excitement.

"So I want to train Amy because Maddison will need the best Seeker she can get. I also think it will sharpen my skills, which I need, and Amy could be a huge asset in tracking down the Vieses," Faith said.

"And she's already done you a great service," Melinda pointed out.

Faith nodded once, "So may I train her?"

Melinda was going to say yes if for no other reason than that it would help her daughter, but she didn't want Faith to think that was the reason she was agreeing to her request.

"Let me talk to her first," Melinda said.

Faith smiled faintly, "I'll get her."

A few moments later, Amy Calamus sat alone with Melinda in her office. Amy looked uncomfortable.

"My daughter has found some potential weak points in your skillset," Melinda said.

"Yes," Amy admitted, "they were not pieces I knew I was missing."

"Have you ever worked with any of the Beldame Seekers? Maddison's father Matthew is extremely skilled," Melinda asked.

Amy said she hadn't, that she and Maddison were kept so busy that Maddison didn't make it home often. Melinda sat back in her chair, "This makes sense then."

"What does?" Amy asked.

"The Decors and Beldames use virtually the same techniques as each other. Our teaching style varies from teacher to teacher, but we cover the same things. Maddison was wise to find someone with a different background than her own. In time, the Beldames would likely teach you what you needed to know, but in light of recent events, I agree with Faith; you need to be trained. I will allow my daughter to train you on Decor secrets, but keep in mind, Amy, this is tradecraft that our family has guarded jealously for generations. You must agree not to divulge what my daughter teaches you to anyone -- including your own children someday -- unless you get permission."

Amy looked shocked, "Faith wants to teach me?"

Melinda smiled, "She didn't tell you, I take it. I suppose that figures; she didn't know if I would agree to this or not. Like I said, at some point I'm sure the Beldames will teach you. If you would like to wait for them to do it, that is fine. So I suppose the question then is: do you want to be trained by us?"

Amy looked overwhelmed, "Yes please, it would be an honor; and I would never tell anyone what I've learned. But what do you mean by 'us'?"

"Faith has never trained anyone before, so I will be dropping in from time to time," Melinda said and then called Faith into the room.

"You can train her," Melinda said to Faith.

Faith looked happy, "Thank you."

AMY CALAMUS couldn't believe her luck as she left the Decor's house with Faith. She was going to be trained in the Decor style of Seeking, and by the daughter of Melinda Decor, no less. The thought of Melinda herself dropping in to work with Amy to make sure Faith was teaching correctly made Amy feel giddy. Maddison would be thrilled; she'd wanted to see if Melinda would be willing to tutor Amy a bit, but to have Faith dedicate herself to teaching her everything she knew …

"We won't have the time that I'd like, Amy," Faith said, "we still have this case we are working on, but I will try to teach you things here and there, and when we get time we can work together."

"Of course," Amy said, "and if there is anything you want to learn from me ..." she offered, not sure what Faith could ever learn from her.

Faith smiled, "I would like that. From what I've seen, we have both learned two very different styles of Seeking. With our combined knowledge, I'm confident we will be able to overcome Angelica."

Amy was excited to tell Maddison about her day, and couldn't wait to start working with Faith.

NINE

MANDY STAFFORD returned home from running errands and plopped down on her couch. She'd spent so much time with Sean at the hospital over the last few days, she was running behind in the rest of her life. She pulled her phone out of her purse to look at her to-do list. *Relax Mandy,* she told herself, *you don't need to work so hard anymore.* One of the biggest adjustments she'd had to make since Heidi started giving her Vis was that Mandy no longer had to rush. Before, she always had to focus on finding clients, which left her little time for the rest of life. That was no longer the case. Now she had time to think and live. She closed out of her to-do list instead, letting her mind wander. *What to do?* she wondered. She had the entire afternoon and evening to herself.

She thought of calling a friend, but realized she couldn't. All of her friends were Succubi like she was, and they were working the streets. This made her feel sad for them. She'd worried that her old friends would resent her now that she didn't have to hook, but so far that hadn't been the case. They all seemed happy that she was able to escape the fate of most Succubi. She suspected that many of them also were thankful that it was she and not they who had incurred the wrath of Angelica Vies.

A memory popped in her head from her short stint with Trinity. The image of Leslie Wormald flashed in her mind. With it came a twinge of guilt. Leslie had welcomed Mandy into Trinity with open arms, showing her around, and unknowingly helping Mandy to expose the Vieses. She wondered how Leslie was, or even if she was still alive. Mandy knew there was a good chance the girl had been killed for being friends with Mandy. *Did you get her killed?* Mandy wondered, her guilt flaring stronger. What if she had? How could Mandy live with herself knowing she was the cause of someone else dying?

Mandy got up from where she was sitting and grabbed her purse and keys. She left her apartment, determined to find Leslie. She wanted; no needed, to make sure she was ok. Mandy had tried to tell herself that Leslie would be fine. That Trinity wouldn't have held her responsible for Mandy's betrayal.

Mandy walked the streets of downtown Denver, looking for Leslie. In a way, it was easy for Mandy to track down another Mutari. She could read the Vis flow of all those around her, which saved her the trouble of having to pay attention to Humans and Mutari other than Succubi. That said, it was several hours before Mandy caught a glimpse of a Succubus who looked like Leslie. The girl had her back to Mandy, and she rushed up and tapped her shoulder. The Succubus turned around, her eyes showing recognition of another of her kind. She wasn't Leslie.

"Sorry, you aren't who I was looking for," Mandy said.

The other woman didn't seem bothered by Mandy mistaking her. "Sorry, who are ya lookin for?" the woman asked.

"Her name is Leslie; she's got long blonde hair and blue eyes. She keeps herself looking around nineteen," Mandy explained.

The other Succubus nodded, "Ya ya, I know her. There's a diner about two blocks south of here that she works a lot."

"Thanks," Mandy said before she left.

Mandy walked with a bit of bounce in her step. Leslie was alright. If she was working, then that meant that Trinity hadn't killed her. Another thought entered Mandy's mind *what if she's still working with Trinity?* Was it safe for Mandy to find Leslie? *You have to confirm for yourself that she is ok.*

Mandy found a diner that matched the woman's description, and walked in. The diner wasn't dingy, but it wasn't overly nice either. Mandy scanned around the room until her gaze landed on a girl sitting at the counter. Her long blonde hair covered half of her face; she wore a miniskirt and a tight top. Mandy walked over to her and sat down on the bench next to her.

Leslie turned to look at Mandy, a look of shock crossing on her face, "You're alive!" Leslie said, surprised.

"I'm glad to see you are too," Mandy said.

Leslie's expression turned from shock to annoyance. She huffed. "No thanks to you," she accused, "thanks for using me."

"Leslie …" Mandy started. What could she say? She had used Leslie. Mandy never wanted her to get hurt, but at the end of the day Mandy had still used her. "I'm sorry."

Leslie looked at her for a moment, reading the look of shame on Mandy's face. "Yeah, you look sorry," she finally said, "why did you do it?"

Mandy paused, thinking, "Maybe we should sit someplace a bit more private," and then added, "unless you need to work."

Leslie got off the stool she was on and walked over to a booth, plopping down, "Nah I'm good for a while … you taught me how to manage my Vis better so I don't have to work as much."

Mandy felt a flick of pride hearing Leslie say that. Mandy was no moron; she knew there was no way to get Leslie out of her lifestyle. Mandy was a rarity not having to hook. Moreover, Mandy knew that even if Leslie ever found a steady source of Vis, the girl would still be a hooker. Even knowing that, Mandy was happy she'd helped Leslie to not need to take on as many clients.

"So why did ya do it?" Leslie asked again.

"I didn't have a choice … had it been up to me, I'd have never joined Trinity," she said, launching into her story of how Sean had forced her to do what she had. She told Leslie about how she'd gone back to the safe house after being there with Leslie, and what all happened.

"No way; Angelica wants you dead?" Leslie said.

"Yeah … well I don't know if she does so much now," Mandy said.

Leslie shook her head, "That cop sounds like a real prick, but I'm glad to hear that he's come around." She said, "Dang Mandy, I'm sorry for being mad at you. Had I known you didn't have a choice and all …"

"It's ok; how would you know something like that? It's not like I told you," Mandy said.

"Yeah, but still, that sucks." Her expression got playful, "But it sounds like now you have a little bit of a crush on this cop. I suppose someone sayin they'll dedicate their life to you could do that to a girl."

Mandy blushed.

"Does he know?" Leslie asked.

Mandy shook her head, "No, I didn't even know until a few days ago." She sighed, "He got real hurt, and was in the hospital … and it was then that I realized I have feelings for him … I think. I'm still not sure, ya know what I mean?"

"Sure do. Better to make sure your feelings are real before you tell him about it; men are dumb," Leslie said.

"Amen to that," Mandy chuckled.

Leslie looked thoughtful for a moment, "Hey, when you were with Trinity you told me not to work for free … I was just wondering what else I need to know about being a Succubus? Trinity didn't tell us anything, and I'm starting to see that they treated us like products; not people."

"So I take it you don't work for them anymore?" Mandy asked.

Leslie shook her head, "Nah, I didn't think it would be safe after everything that went down at the train yard. All the girls I know who were working there left. They said something about Trinity not honoring Pactums or something like that."

Mandy nodded, "That they did not."

"I've heard of Pactums a bit, but I don't know anything about them."

"A Pactum is a contract," Mandy explained, "Trinity should have had one with each Mutari they employed. I'm going to guess they didn't have one with you, or with any other new Succubi."

Leslie said she didn't have one.

"You can make a Pactum with a Troll club, and they will run security for you. They will escort you to Goblin Guilds to change out money, and all that. Trolls have been security for us for hundreds of years," Mandy said.

"Really?" Leslie asked, surprised.

"Yeah," Mandy said, "at one point in time Succubi and Incubi had their own government, and the whole nine."

"What happened?" Leslie asked.

"Vampires," Mandy said, and then started to explain, "there was a time when we were very powerful. We didn't have to work for Vis like we do now. You see, Trolls all but worshiped us. Many of them gave us Vis on a regular basis. With the Vis they produce, they can support us with ease. Like now, we kept ourselves looking young; but we didn't have to deal with worrying about running out of Vis, we were kept in a constant supply. Since we can keep ourselves in whatever physical condition we like, we have always been some of the most beautiful people alive. Even Humans sought us out." Mandy thought for a moment, going over what she knew of the histories. Leslie looked wide-eyed at her, and Mandy knew she was trying to think of a life where she was the top of society, and not the bottom.

There was so much more to that time in history, though. Mandy explained that the Succubi were immensely wealthy, and had a lot of power. She explained to her the downsides of using high amounts of Vis. Mandy explained that it warped your mind and made you unstable. She explained that was one of the biggest problems for the ancient Succubi.

"So why did the Vampires overthrow us?" Leslie asked, "And is that why we hate them?"

"They over threw us because we were a threat to them. They also can affect how the world sees them, and while they live a lot longer than we do, they cannot control how old they look … we had the loyalty of the Trolls, and even many of the Elementals of the time. The Vampires on the other hand, had Werewolves and Goblins. Even today, Goblins are under the control of Vampires."

"I thought Goblins were the most powerful Mutari these days," Leslie said.

Mandy shook her head, "They'd have you think that. The Vampires don't control them like they used to, but most Goblin Guilds are backed by Vampires. Anyway, the Vampires saw the threat we were to them, and so they attacked us, killing off our leaders; turning everyone they could against us.

"If I'm being honest, we were tyrants by that point in time … I suspect that's why Mages didn't step in to help us."

Mandy explained that over the course of several decades, the Succubi were destroyed, and once they lost their power, they moved to the bottom of society. Trolls still ran guard duty for Succubi, but they no longer saw them as near gods and goddesses; now they were just people who would do anything for Vis.

Leslie was looking down at the table, "So it's the Vampires that force us to be this, then?"

Mandy nodded, "Even now they make sure we aren't able to climb the social ladder. Though the threat isn't that Mutari will follow us anymore; now they worry that Humanity will."

Leslie looked confused, and Mandy explained, "If Humans wanted to, they could easily restore us to where we once were. It would only take ten or fifteen Humans to be willing to donate Vis to a Succubus on a regular basis, and you would never run low on Vis. You could keep yourself young, beautiful, and strong with ease."

Mandy could almost see the wheels in Leslie's head turn, and she wondered what the girl was thinking. Leslie changed the subject, asking how the rest of Mandy's life was, and after a few hours Mandy left the diner. The whole time she drove home, she thought about how Leslie had changed once Mandy had said that Humans could raise Succubi back up. *Mandy, she's not as clueless as you thought.*

SEAN HUGHES rolled out of bed, stretching as he made his way to the bathroom. He looked at himself in the mirror. Despite the fact that he hadn't been at work since the fight with Trinity, he was looking tired. He inspected dark bags under his eyes. *Not looking so good, Sean,* he thought. Today was to be his first day back at work. Sean was looking forward to being back on the job. He had never been one for taking more than a few days off. He was one of those people who had to be working in order to keep from going mad with boredom.

He took off his shirt, revealing smooth skin. There was no sign that he had been mortally wounded. When Erin healed his wounds, she'd done so without leaving scars. Sean knew that for many, seeing the scar of an injury could bring back unwelcome memories or even make it hard for them to feel comfortable in their own skin. Sean had no scars from his fight, but he his body still didn't feel quite right. When Angelica attacked him, she'd cut through a scar he'd had since he was five. Sean couldn't remember what had happened or he'd been doing to get that scar as a child, but the scar had been part of him his whole life. Erin hadn't restored Sean's flesh to how it had been prior to the attack; she'd simply healed his wound without leaving a scar. Now the absence of that childhood scar confused him.

He shook off the feeling and got ready for his day. While he was looking forward to getting back to work, he still hated traffic, and was in a slightly irritable mood when he parked his car. He rode the elevator up to his floor and his sour mood vanished. As he exited the elevator, the officers in the room started clapping. Sean beamed at them as he made his way to his desk. People he'd never talked to before clapped his shoulder and told him they were happy he was back at work.

"It's good to be back," he said loudly.

Sean knew the feeling of seeing someone come back to work. Tension in a station grew when someone was seriously hurt, and seeing them come back broke that tension.

Alison and the Mages were by his desk, Maddison and Amy standing back a bit. Alison stepped forward and gave him a hug, "It's good to have you back, Hughes."

"I didn't know you felt that way about me, Kaur," he said suggestively.

She smiled. "I do; I was so worried I was going to have to do your paperwork if you didn't come back soon," she said sweetly, pointing to stacks of paper on his desk.

Sean groaned, deciding he could use a few more days to recover.

Gabriel shook his hand. "Glad to see that scratch didn't keep you down too long," he said sarcastically.

"Scratch? Nah, it was more of a paper cut really; honestly I'm sure I'll suffer worse doing this paperwork." He looked over at Faith who seemed almost timid.

"Thank you for saving my life Sean," she said genuinely.

Sean smiled, patting her shoulder, "Don't mention it; there was no way I was gonna let a piece of ass like you get killed or torn up."

Faith rolled her eyes, but looked like herself again, "I'll have to tell Erin that her de-pricking operation didn't work."

Sean laughed, "You can't remove that! I was born a jerk and will die one." Then seriously, "But really, Faith; I'm glad you're ok. And don't you worry; we'll find Angelica, and next time she won't get away."

She looked serious, "That she won't."

There was a fire in Faith's eyes that hadn't been there before. He didn't think normal people would recognize what it was, but Sean did. He'd seen combat in every form. From the battlefield to working his first beat as a cop. The look in Faith's eyes was determination. It was the same as her brother's.

"She doesn't know what she's started does she?" Sean asked her.

Faith shook her head tightly, "She really doesn't. Thank you, Sean, for saving me. If you ever need anything …"

Sean waved her comment off, "We are a team, and this is what being in a team is about." Then looking in her eyes, "You've changed -- I can see it in your eyes. If me getting torn up was part of what it took to put that look there, then I'm glad it happened. Besides, I owed you."

"You're happy you got hurt?" Amy asked, confused.

"Of course he is," Gabriel said, "if he were a Mage, he'd be a Paladin; no questions asked."

"A good one at that, I dare say," Maddison added.

"Thank you," he said to the Mages.

Before he could say more, he heard Montoya yell at him from his office "Hughes, if you're done being the center of attention, come to my office."

Sean smiled, "And if I'm not done?"

"Don't be a prick, get in here!"

"It's good to be back," Sean said to Alison.

Sean walked into Montoya's office and sat on the chair across from the Sergeant. There was something off about the man.

Montoya acted like he didn't care, but the truth was a far different thing. Montoya had only been to see Sean once since he'd been hurt, and hadn't called. Now he looked at paperwork like he was put out to have to deal with Sean. *I wonder what's up.*

"How do you feel?" Montoya asked.

"Good, sir; I'm ready to get back to it."

Montoya nodded, "Good. You have to be cleared by a shrink to re-enter field duty."

Sean wasn't surprised to hear this. Normally this would be an irritation for most officers, but after his time in the service, Sean had gone into counseling, and it had made a world of difference. He didn't think he had anything wrong with him, but he understood the need to have a shrink talk to him. If Sean was being honest having the 'all clear' from the station shrink would give him more confidence.

"I understand. It's standard procedure," Sean said.

"In the meantime, you can work in the office, but no going out in the field," Montoya added. With that, Sean was told to go about his day, and to expect an email from the therapist he was to talk to.

ALISON KAUR sat in the conference room with the Mages, waiting for Sean to be done meeting with the Sergeant.

"Hey, what's up with Montoya?" he asked, walking in the room. "He seems off".

Heidi Decor was in the room looking at some notes, "What do you mean, 'off'?" she asked, perking up.

Sean paused, "Oh nothing really, he just seems a little off. It's nothing."

Heidi raised an eyebrow, but didn't comment further.

"So what have I missed?" Sean asked, changing the subject.

"Not much, to be honest," Alison said. "There has been shockingly little in the way of media exposure on the case as of late, so that's nice. I would have thought the media would be having a field day with the incident in the Highlands."

"Umm...," Amy said timidly, interrupting the conversation, "that's because I thought they would be a nuisance. I hope you don't mind."

"Are you blocking them?" Sean asked, incredulous.

Amy shrugged, "During the attack, I tried to sever phone and Internet connections, but Faith was already doing that. So after the fight, I just made sure people had a hard time dwelling on the evening."

Sean looked as shocked as Alison felt, "You can do that?" she asked the two Seekers, and then to Faith added, "Why haven't you been able to keep videos of raids on the train yard, and safe houses under wraps?"

"It's standard to interrupt communications during a battle. As for the videos, people aren't streaming them directly to the Internet. People are just recording them on their phones, and then uploading them later. I'm not disrupting all electronics. If I do that, your electronics won't work, and if someone in the area has a pacemaker, that would be a problem," Faith explained.

"And making people forget about what they've seen?" Sean asked Amy, sounding a little concerned.

"I don't make them forget. I just make it so they think about other things. If you don't dwell on something, you forget about it or don't give it significance," Amy said, matter of fact.

Alison decided that she didn't need to be surprised about what Faith and Amy could do. They were Mages, and from her experience there wasn't anything Mages couldn't do. Alison brought Sean up to speed with what he'd missed in the last few days, which as she had said; wasn't much.

GABRIEL DECOR'S mind wandered as Alison brought Sean up to speed. He caught Maddison's eye and she smirked at him as they shared a look of 'can we move on yet?' Eventually, Alison had Sean caught up, and they were talking about next steps in the investigation. Gabriel, on the other hand, found himself looking at Maddison out of the corner of his eye. His gazed traced her tight clothes and lingered on her silver hair and red eyes. While most men would find the Beldame mix of beauty and danger to be a little overwhelming, Gabriel liked it. He'd been intrigued with Stella during the war, and found himself feeling the same about Maddison. He thought their mixed appearance was a fitting picture of the world of the Paladin.

"Gabriel," Alison said, causing him to jump, "are you with us?"

"Sorry; I was staring off into space."

"Happens to the best of us," she said, "come on, Montoya needs to see us."

Gabriel followed the others from the room, feeling embarrassed.

"Glad to see you're always on guard," Faith whispered to him jokingly.

There was another man in the Sergeant's office. He stood and turned to greet everyone as they entered the room. He was in his late forties with brown hair, a square face, and a firm jaw. He held himself with pride. Gabriel hadn't a clue who he was or why he was here, but he respected him right off the bat, just for the presence he had.

"This is Agent Hatcher with Internal Affairs," Montoya said, and then to Amy and Maddison, "He doesn't have any jurisdiction over you two, but I wanted you to meet him. Agent Hatcher is here to look into our recent activities."

"But we are under the supervision of the FBI," Sean said, bristling.

Gabriel had heard that most law enforcement had issues with Internal Affairs, something he found odd. *I guess cops don't like having cops … funny.*

"You are, but you are still part of the Denver Police Department," Hatcher said. "I am not here to get in the way; I promise. Or here on a witch hunt," he said, and then to Faith, "nothing against witches."

"She's not a witch, she's a Mage," Sean said acidly.

"Right," Hatcher said without emotion, "as part of my investigation, I will need full access to anything I deem necessary, and will be meeting with each of you. That includes the Mages. I will need addresses and contact info."

"The contact info will be easy, but I cannot give you my address," Gabriel said.

Hatcher made a face, "I'm sorry, but that isn't up for negotiation."

"Correct, it is not up for negotiation," Faith said, "there are five people on the planet who know the exact location of our team's house. The team members don't even know where they live; they just know how to find the jump anchor associated with the house. I am sorry Agent, but we will not give you a secret protected by the Decor family for hundreds of years; no matter your needs. Also, it is against our Pactum."

Hatcher 's face reddened, "I'm sorry; Mrs. Penn, is it? But state and federal law supersede your contract."

"We haven't recognized your government as our own," Maddison said. "Agent Hatcher , I know you are here trying to do your job, as are we. If you don't want us to continue our Pactum, we can leave … but you will find that your supervisors will not support you on this," Maddison said, not unkindly.

SEAN HUGHES was doing his best not to look angry. As for the Mages, they hadn't shown any hostility at all. Even when Faith, Gabriel, and Maddison were telling Hatcher he couldn't know where they lived, the Mages didn't look irritated in the least bit. Inwardly Sean laughed; *I seem to remember that being you not too long ago. Thinking you could boss around people who could wipe out every cop in the station without effort.* The IA agent, on the other hand, looked pissed, but he wasn't losing control.

"Well, we will see," Hatcher said, dropping the subject for the time being, "may I at least interview you?"

"Of course," Faith said.

"Very well, I have things I need to do, but I will be talking with each of you over the next few days. Then addressing Alison and Sean, "Detectives, I will need to see everything you've done during the case." Sean could see indecision in the Agent's eyes, "In light of the danger that Trinity is posing, and that this is a case for the FBI, I think it best if I only see the evidence the two of you have collected. I don't want to slow down your investigation." He turned to Sean, "As you have not been cleared for field duty yet, I will work with you."

Sean figured that was coming. *You better impress the shrink today Hughes, so you aren't stuck with this guy.*

"Agent Alesbury with the FBI will likely want to be present," Maddison said.

Hatcher nodded, "Yes, I need to talk to him. Thank you all for your time; I will be talking with you soon." He left the office.

Sean stood, irritated, "I hate IA!"

"Hughes, we've done everything right, IA won't be in our hair long, and besides it was going to happen sooner or later. The city has a lot riding on this case," Alison sounded like she was also trying to convince herself.

Gabriel made to leave the room, "All will be well."

Sean followed him and muttered, "Yeah, that's because you can vanish whenever you want."

Gabriel turned and gave him a smirk.

Sean laughed, "Prick."

TEN

SEAN HUGHES sat in a small waiting room with cream carpet and off-white walls, flipping through a magazine. The shrink he was sent to didn't work in the police station, and Sean was happy to be having a break from Clint Hatcher of Internal Affairs. To Sean's right, a door opened, and a man came out.

"Hello, Sean Hughes?" he asked.

He was tall, balding, and dressed casually. He had a gray beard with a few small patches of brown. In many ways, he looked the perfect therapist. His very appearance gave an air of being non-threatening, which was aided by a smooth low voice and warm smile.

"That's me," Sean said, standing. He took the man's hand.

"Dr. Glenn Bryant," he said, "please come on in."

Sean allowed himself to be led inside Dr. Bryant's tiny office and took a seat on a couch. Dr. Bryant handed Sean a bottle of water that Sean placed on a coffee table in front of him. Sean looked around the room which was small for an office, but somehow comforting.

Dr. Bryant sat down across from Sean, looking at a folder.

"So it looks like you were in a bit of a scrape. As you know, I have to clear you for duty," Bryant said, inspecting Sean, "my file must be off; it says that you were hospitalized a few days ago, and that you nearly died, but you look fine."

Sean chuckled, "No, that's right, doc. A Mage healer patched me up. Had she not helped me though; I'd be dead. I was just in the hospital for observation, and to regrow blood," Sean explained.

Bryant raised an eyebrow. "You know, five years ago if you'd told me that, I would have sent you to a mental hospital," he said with a smile.

Sean laughed in earnest, surprised at how easy it was to feel comfortable around Bryant, "Yeah … five years ago I would have checked myself in for thinking that."

Bryant closed his folder, "So tell me about the incident that got you in the hospital."

"I don't remember a whole lot, to be honest with you," Sean said, trying to think of details. "I was in the army for a while, and saw a lot of action. I never had a hard time remembering any of that, but I lost a lot of blood in the attack a few days ago, and I was passed out for most of the fight. The doctors and Erin the Mage Healer told me I might not remember everything."

Bryant nodded, "That's common. I thought that might be the case. It's common for people to have a hard time remembering traumatic events, though most times it's the mind blocking the memories. In your case, it's likely the fact that you lost so much blood." Bryant thought for a bit, "When you came back from the army did you see anyone for PTSD?"

"Yeah, I did. I had a few problems with some of the things I saw," Sean said.

Bryant looked pleased with that, "That's good; I wanted to make sure you knew the signs of having problems from events, and wanted to make sure you'd come in to get help."

Bryant talked to Sean for about a half hour, making sure that he was ok. Sean told Bryant what Alison, Gabriel, and Faith had told him about the attack, and if he was being honest, he was happy he didn't remember most of it.

"I'm going to clear you for duty, Detective, on the basis that you come and see me once a week for a little while," Bryant said. "I think you're fine, but I want to make sure. If you remember anything we can talk about it; if you don't remember anything, that's fine too."

Sean wasn't thrilled about having to go in once a week, but it could have been a lot worse. He knew guys on the force who had to come in for months before being put back on active duty.

Bryant changed the subject, "What do you think of the Mages and working with them?"

"Why do you want to know?" Sean asked defensively.

Bryant sighed, "Honestly, it's mostly curiosity. Also, I don't think you will be the only person in here who has been healed by or had dealings with Vis users." He looked a little put out, "We really don't have any training on helping people with magic. It's made for a bit of trouble in my field. We are having to re-examine many of the people we have institutionalized, and also having magic out in the open has caused a whole new set of issues people are having. It's shaken everything we know: politics, religion, you name it," he said.

"And law enforcement," Sean added. "I know how you feel." He shook his head, sitting back further in his seat. "The things I've seen in the last few months I don't even believe half the time."

"That's what I want to know about," Bryant said, "I can help people who are delusional or are overcoming a loss, but how do you help someone cope with seeing …" he looked at Sean's file, "a car getting thrown at them, and seeing a wizard cut said car in half?"

Sean laughed, "Well, first I think you need to remember it's not magic; it's Vis. I know that doesn't sound like much, but for some reason when I think of Vis and not magic, it doesn't make things seem so crazy. I think I have always associated the word 'magic' with fairytales, but Vis was a completely new word to me when Vis users came out in the open. I don't have any association with the word."

"I can see that; words have power with us," Bryant said.

"At first I didn't like the Mages, but it was nothing they'd done, it was all me. I didn't want anyone in my case, and also I was a little prejudiced about Vis. But after Gabriel saved my life, and I gave them a chance, I found that I really like most Vis users. They come from a completely different world than we do, even though they live among us. But they are like we are; some are good, some are bad … and that can be said of Humans too."

"So your views on Vis have changed during your investigation?" Bryant asked, sounding a little skeptical.

"Yeah they have; I really mean that. The group we are going after is scum; sure, but that exists with Humans too, like I said. Most of the Vis users I've worked with have been great, and I trust them completely. And as far as Gabriel and Faith? Well, they are my partners through and through, and I know they feel the same way."

Bryant smiled, "That's good to know."

Sean chuckled, "That was your real evaluation, wasn't it?"

Bryant shrugged, "Yes and no. I was pretty sure you didn't need help on the grounds that it would be near physically impossible for you to remember your trauma, and since the Mages healed your wounds without leaving a scar on you, it's unlikely you'd have any issues. I figured talking to you about your relationship with the Vis users you work with, and the Vis community, would be a good way to see how you are really doing."

"How'd you know I didn't have any scars?" Sean asked.

Bryant tapped the folder on his lap, "I still want you to come in for a few weeks, but you are good to go out and catch bad guys, Detective."

Sean told Dr. Bryant that he was impressed the man was able to pull one over on him, and then went on his way, looking forward to not having any more downtime.

MADDISON BELDAME hung up the phone with Agent Alesbury. He had been out of town tracking Trinity in Oklahoma.

"What's up?" Gabriel asked, sitting across from her in the team's conference room.

"That was Alesbury. One of the Wolves we arrested and let go in Utah has led Alesbury to the rest of his pack," she said.

"Oh yeah?"

"Yeah, we brought him in just a bit before we came to Denver. The bureau cut him loose, saying they didn't have enough evidence to hold him," Maddison said.

"But you did," Gabriel noted.

Maddison nodded, "We had more than enough to put him away for a long time, but I knew that at some point, he'd hook back up with his pack and we could bring them all in."

Gabriel looked thoughtful, "It's taken him a few months to go back to his pack. Did you know he was from Oklahoma? Or was the pack based in Utah?" Gabriel asked.

"Neither, actually. From what we could find, he was from somewhere in the old Soviet Union. The FBI wasn't able to track down his real name, but in the States, he goes by Alex Smith."

Gabriel chuckled, "Not very original, is it?"

"No, it's not. Anyway, since the FBI has found the rest of his pack, I need to go and bring them in if I can," she said.

She wasn't looking forward to trying to bring in a whole Wolf pack.

"Do you want a hand?" Gabriel offered.

Maddison thought about saying no; that she could handle it on her own, but after a moment she decided otherwise. She would be able to handle the Wolves on her own, but with another Paladin and Seeker, there was less of a chance of the Wolves getting killed, and less chance of any Humans the FBI had with her getting hurt.

"That would be great. We'd be leaving this afternoon," she said.

"That's fine; do you have a jump anchor?" he asked.

"Yes. Alesbury keeps one on him; I can lead you to him," she said.

ALISON KAUR looked at her email and saw that she had a meeting with the IA officer later in the day. She sighed, not particularly looking forward to the meeting. Alison understood why IA was in the office, but she didn't have to look forward to the inconvenience in her day. Next to her, Faith was plopped down reading some papers.

"What are those?" Alison asked.

"Nothing much. Do you remember Makina Yamaoto?" Faith asked.

"Sure do," Alison said, thinking about the Air Elemental.

"I have her working on some things for me, and these are just her reports," Faith explained, "she hasn't found anything of use yet, but I have her following a few of the Mutari that were at the train yard."

Before Alison could ask Faith anything else, Gabriel came up to her with Maddison, "Hey Alison, do you need to leave the office this afternoon?"

"No; why?"

Maddison spoke, "He is going to help me with a raid in Oklahoma. Faith, we would also need you," she said.

"What kind of a raid?" Alison asked, not liking the sound of what they were doing.

"It's a Werewolf Pack we've been tracking," Maddison sighed, obviously not looking forward to the assignment.

Alison paused for a moment. She had no jurisdiction outside of Colorado, nor would she be of any help to the Mages if they were going after Mutari.

"Don't worry Alison, we'll be back in a flash," Gabriel said with a carefree smile.

"And what if this is another trap?" Alison questioned.

"Then it's best we spring it without you and Sean in harm's way again," Faith said, moving to stand next to her brother. "If you need us, you know how to get hold of us."

"Fine," Alison said. She knew she didn't have a choice; she didn't have any control over the Mages contractually or in any other sense of the word, "But if you guys get hurt …"

"Erin will patch us up before you even know," Faith said, sticking her tongue out.

Amy came trotting up to them and took Maddison's hand. Gabriel and Faith joined Amy, and before Alison could come up with an excuse for why she should join them, there was a flash of Vis, and the four Mages vanished.

"What was that?" Agent Hatcher said, spinning in a chair a few desks over.

Alison tried not to sound happy about his alarm when she answered, "The Mages are going on assignment for the FBI." But despite her efforts, Hatcher looked irritated with her, and she sighed, resigning herself to an unpleasant afternoon.

"And why isn't anyone from the DPD going with them?" he demanded, "this is our jurisdiction after all."

"If they were in Colorado that would be true, but Oklahoma is out of our jurisdiction," Alison said, reading the look of shock on his face.

"They are in another state?" he asked, incredulous.

Alison turned back to her work smiling, "For all we know, they are on the other side of the world; I don't think Mages have any limits to how far away they can jump."

SEAN HUGHES' computer chirped at him, letting him know it was time to meet with Agent Hatcher . Sean sighed and got up, heading over to where Hatcher was seated.

Sean paused and said, "We need to meet in the conference room."

Hatcher looked up at him, "Why do we need to do that?" he asked, not sounding happy about Sean telling him what to do.

"This office might be bugged. Sorry, but we had a witness die because of this," Sean explained, not liking to start an interview with IA by telling them that a witness was killed during an investigation.

Hatcher stood, following Sean to the conference room without any further questions. Sean didn't shut the door as he walked in, which Hatcher commented on.

"Don't you want to close the door?" he asked.

Sean smiled, "Nah, sound can't leave this room, and our lips can't be read.

Hatcher sat in one of the chairs in the room, pulling out a folder and eyeing the open door with distrust. "That must be nice," he noted, as Sean sat opposite him, "can you tell me about the office being bugged?"

Sean explained how Angelica Vies had been able to plant bugs inside the station, and that there were several other Mages who had done the same. Hatcher looked like he'd swallowed a lemon.

"Makes you feel real comfortable knowing that, doesn't it?" Sean asked.

Hatcher shifted in his chair, "It's not the best news I've received."

Sean laughed slightly, enjoying Hatcher's discomfort, "Yeah, Vis seems to have that effect on us Humans."

"What's it like working with the Mages?" he asked.

Sean knew that Hatcher was trying to make him comfortable so Sean would spill his guts. It wasn't going to work. Still, Sean wanted to be as honest as possible, "At first I didn't like it, and if I'm being honest with you; I miss the days when we didn't have to worry about Vis. That being said, Vis has been dead handy a few times."

"How has it affected your case?" Hatcher asked, "Are you still able to work?"

"Yes I am; I just had to learn a few new sets of skills … and keep Vis users and their abilities in mind." Sean explained.

Agent Hatcher launched into a set of questions about the case, asking Sean about their investigation. This was what made Sean uncomfortable. Hatcher was in essence interrogating Sean, which was a feeling he didn't care for. Agent Hatcher was particularly interested in the death of Hannah Davis, asking Sean why he hadn't been able to protect a potential witness and suspect.

"This is your job, correct?" Hatcher asked.

Sean's anger flared up, "Yes, it is. We didn't know the office was bugged."

"And neither did your Mage experts?" Hatcher asked, referring to Gabriel and Faith.

Hatcher changed the subject before Sean could answer, looking at his folder, "Tell me about this Gabriel Decor and Faith Penn? They are supposed to be at the top of their games, aren't they? Why didn't they think to sweep the station for bugs?"

"They weren't brought in for that reason," Sean said, trying not to sound angry. "They were originally here to protect Alison and me from Vis users. It wasn't until after we found Ramon Tabor dead and were attacked that Faith and Gabriel were brought on to help with the investigation. The bugs were planted long before Faith and Gabriel came on. We wanted to move on Ramon's killer as fast as we could, and Trinity overheard us." Sean gestured to the room around them, "Hence this room." He looked at Hatcher 's face for a moment, reading the distrust and slight disdain on it. "Do you really have any idea of what we are up against?" Sean asked.

"What's that supposed to mean?" Hatcher asked defensively, "Your actions are under question; not mine."

Sean sat back. Hatcher was upset, and therefore off his game. Sean seized the opportunity to gain control of the interview, "Right now they are, yes; but it won't stay that way forever." He leaned into Hatcher , "Do you have a clean room up in Internal Affairs? How are you going to discuss this case with your commanding officer? If you talk about it in his or your office, you'll be leaking information to Trinity. You may not think so, but let me assure you … your offices are bugged."

Hatcher sat uneasily in his seat for a moment. Sean could see that the wheels in the man's head were turning. He wanted to tell Sean that he was wrong, but deep down inside Agent Hatcher knew that Sean was right.

When Hatcher spoke again, his voice was subdued, "Can you tell me about the first raid you went on with Gabriel and Faith? You were targeting a Mr. Javier Davison, correct?"

Sean breathed out in a whoosh. "That was something else," he said, not thinking about what Hatcher would think of him saying that.

"How so?" Hatcher asked.

"I wasn't inside the house with Gabriel, but if what happened outside is anything like what it was like inside, then it was wild."

Sean started telling Hatcher about the Troll that came out of the house, that the officers on-scene started shooting at him. Sean watched disbelief cross Hatcher 's face when Sean said that the Troll got shot over forty times before dropping. Then

Sean talked about the Guardian who came out of the house, and that it was only because of Faith and Gabriel that any of the officers survived.

"The thing is; had Faith and Gabriel not been on the case, we'd have caught up with Davison at some point in time. The only difference is, had it been a bunch of cops rushing into that house and not a Paladin, then you and I wouldn't be talking today."

"Is there anything that you could have done to lower the loss of life during that bust? If I'm not mistaken, several Trolls and Wolves were killed; were they not?" Hatcher asked.

Sean looked down, "All of them were," he said darkly, "they put up one heck of a fight, though."

"And that justifies them dying?" Hatcher asked.

"No. No, it doesn't. I'm just saying Decor didn't have a choice. That being said, had the city contracted with a few more Mages, Gabriel wouldn't have needed to use so much force. Or if we had Pactums with several of the Troll Clubs in the area ..." Sean said.

"So the fault lies with the city?" Hatcher prodded.

Sean shook his head, "Nope, not gonna happen. The situation was what it was. We did the best we could with what we had. History is riddled with 'woulda, coulda, shouldas', and this isn't one of them. Believe it or not, this was a good case scenario," Sean said.

"Not," was all Hatcher said.

Sean tried to shrug off Hatcher 's comment. The man didn't have a clue as to what was going on. He was here on a witch hunt in some ill-conceived attempt to make the city look good on the "if things hit the fan" front.

Hatcher talked to Sean for a few hours about how he'd handled Mandy, and about the train yard. That was when things started to move in Sean's favor.

"You haven't seen the video yet, have you?" Sean asked.

Hatcher looked put out, "No, I haven't; your friends with the FBI said that I could not view them unless it was under the 'right circumstances' as they put it."

Sean got up, picking up a laptop from the corner of the conference room table, "Yeah, they were talking about being in this room with someone working the case."

Sean opened up the laptop. One of the SWAT guys had been wearing a helmet cam during the raid on the train yard for the FBI. Sean put on the vid, turning the laptop to Hatcher . The man quickly took out a pad of paper to write on.

"That can't leave here," Sean said, and then added, "not my rule; it's the FBI's."

Hatcher put down his pen, obviously irritated, and watched the footage. Sean watched Hatcher 's expressions as he viewed the raid, his mouth coming open a few times, sweat dotting his brow. "How is this possible?" he mouthed. Sean let him watch the whole video before speaking.

"That is some of what we are up against. Alison said the fight between the Mages was something to behold. We don't have any video of that, though." Sean turned the laptop back around, and pulled up a picture of the warehouse floor where Gabriel had fought, "But we got this." Sean spun the laptop back around.

"I've seen this," Hatcher said, looking at the picture.

"You see how the floor is all broken up?" Sean said.

"Yes," Hatcher responded.

"It was in perfect condition at the beginning of the fight," Sean said.

Hatcher 's eyes snapped up to Sean's, "But this floor looks like a jackhammer was taken to it!"

"From my understanding, it was caused by rapid heating and cooling, but I'm not a hundred percent sure on what went down in there. Alison said with Seekers in the mix, being in the room was pretty disorienting."

Hatcher sat back in his seat again looking uneasy. After a long while, he regained his composure. "Thank you, Detective Hughes, that will be all for now. I have an appointment with your partner … am I alright to stay in this room?" he asked.

"Someone just has to be in here with you. Sorry agent, that's the FBI's doing. It was the only way we could keep working out of this office. I'll send Alison a text saying you're ready for her."

ALISON KAUR outlined for Agent Hatcher how Sean had been hurt. From what she could gather, he was distrusting of the Mages. She suspected that due to the fact that she and Sean were close to the Mages, Agent Hatcher distrusted her and Sean as well. When Agent Hatcher had come in to the office, she'd hoped that he was there just to cover the city's butts, and that may have been the intent of his superiors, but it was obvious to Alison that Hatcher was on a witch hunt.

"You'll understand when I tell you that everything that you and Detective Hughes have told me about the Mages is a little hard to believe," Hatcher said.

"Didn't you say that Sean showed you footage of the train yard raid?" Alison asked.

Hatcher nodded, "He did."

"Then I'm sorry; but I'm not sure what you are having a hard time believing as you've seen evidence for yourself."

"I'll give you that. I suppose what I don't believe is that you and your partner trust Mages, and the Mutari they have helping them. Don't you think that individuals like this are dangerous?" he asked.

"And should be under more control?" Alison asked.

"Well, not so much as control, but maybe supervision," Hatcher said.

The back of Alison's neck flushed, "Agent Hatcher , are you here to investigate how our case with Trinity is going, or are you here for some other reason?" Instantly Alison regretted what she'd said.

Hatcher was defensive, "I am here on the interests of the people of Denver, Detective."

"So you are here for a reason other than our investigation," Alison said coolly.

Hatcher waved his hand, "That's not what I said. I am here specifically for the case with Trinity, but my job ..."

"Is the case with Trinity," Alison said, fed up with him. "I am sorry Agent Hatcher , but with all due respect you have your orders, and I have mine. Right now we have a mole or several moles in this office. People have, and will continue to get, hurt or killed if those moles are not found. Furthermore, we are trying to suppress a national, and possibly international crime organization. If you are here to serve the people, I suggest you do your job and help up find our department's leaks."

Alison sat in her seat, fuming. Hatcher was silent across from her, his face red. She shouldn't have said what she had, but she didn't regret it. Now was not the time for red tape. Alison stood "if you don't have any further questions about how we are running this case, I have work I need to do." Hatcher didn't say anything, so Alison walked out of the conference room, leaving him to his thoughts. It may not have been wise to leave him alone in the room; but she hoped that showing him trust would make him trust her in turn. However, she wasn't overly hopeful about that.

ELEVEN

GABRIEL DECOR flashed into existence on a hilltop outside a small town in Oklahoma. Faith, Maddison, and Amy next to him. Looking down on the town, Gabriel could see what looked to have once been a booming little factory town. Now most of the buildings looked rundown or condemned; in a few years it would become a ghost town for sure.

"So what are we looking for?" Gabriel asked.

"The FBI got a lead on our Wolf. It looks like he and a few others are taking shelter in a small abandoned factory," Amy said. "Because of the danger that Wolves pose, the FBI has kept their distance, so we don't know numbers inside the factory."

Gabriel glanced over at Maddison, "All right, this is your show," he said to her.

"Amy," Maddison said.

"Faith, let's recon the area," Amy said.

The two Seekers vanished in cloaks of Vis; Gabriel could hear their voices buzzing in his ear.

"I'm over the factory," Faith said, "There are minor concealment wards in place. Do you want me to breach them?" she asked.

"Not yet," Amy answered, "I am checking the perimeter." A few moments later she said, "Everything looks clear, there's nothing outside waiting for us. Break the concealment spells, Faith. Maddison, Gabriel, you are clear to move up to the building."

"Thank you Amy and Faith," Maddison said, "Gabriel you take the rear. I'll go to the front; don't attack until I give you the order."

"Ascendit," Gabriel said, rising in the air, floating down to the back of the factory. The building was one story of dingy brick, windows were broken along its walls, and the ground around it was littered with debris. He landed without a sound, waiting for Maddison's command.

"I've broken the concealment wards," Faith said, and then, "There are six Wolves, some Humans and … dammit, Gabriel, there's a Wraith!"

"Move out!" Maddison ordered as soon as she heard there was a Wraith.

Gabriel drew Iram and thrust his hand forward. "Movere!" he barked. A heavy door in front of him flew from its hinges. Gabriel dashed into the factory, hearing a howl as a Wolf raised an alarm.

MADDISON BELDAME ran inside the factory, entering a large room with old rusty equipment strewn about. She heard the howl of a Wolf and ducked down behind some wooden crates. There was a scuffling sound of paws and claws on concrete. *You need to take one of them in alive,* she told herself. Maddison moved silently, pushing Vis out around her to find the Wolves. She found them. There were three near her, and another presence. It was the Wraith. *Dangit! I was hoping not to have to deal with that.* Maddison hated dispatching Wraiths. The three she'd killed were not pleasant memories.

She decided to take care of the Wolves first if she could, so she could deal with the Wraith without distraction. Maddison made her way around the crate she was hiding behind, making sure to expose part of herself for the Wolves to find. The growling of the Wolves got softer. *Good, they saw me.* She made it look like she was looking in the wrong direction as the Wolves came up behind her.

She spun, ducking as a Wolf took a swing at her with a clawed paw. She slashed her blade, cutting the Wolf's side. It howled in pain, but swiped at her again. Maddison feinted back, "Lubrica," she said. The floor next to her flashed with Vis, and a Wolf stepped on the concrete slipping, its claws scraping the now slick floor, falling to the ground. It slid around on the ground like the concrete was covered in oil. Maddison struck out with her sword Vindictam, catching the first Wolf in the shoulder, the tip of the blade grinding in its shoulder joint and making it howl.

It fell back and Maddison spun, avoiding a lunge from a third Wolf. The one on the slick floor was back up and jumped at her. "RETRO!" she yelled. The Wolf's head wrenched back with a snap. It fell to the floor unmoving. Maddison turned to protect herself from one of the other Wolves. She slashed Vindictam and took off the Wolf's head.

She looked down and followed a trail of blood on the ground. In the distance, she could hear Gabriel taking care of the other Wolves. That's when she saw him. Ten feet before her was a man in his late thirties, wearing a pair of wire frame glasses and a button-up shirt. He was thin and looked like someone who worked at a desk all day. Behind him, the Wolf Maddison had stabbed was leaned against a cage, blood soaking his sides. In the cage were three people: a woman and two children.

"I'm sorry," the man said, "if I don't they'll kill my family."

Maddison looked at him. It was obvious that he hadn't fully turned into a Wraith yet; he wasn't a mindless killer. He yelled, his clothes fluttering. The children in the cage cried, hiding their eyes. The man became slightly transparent. His eyes turned a dark red and his teeth came to points. He was everything from a scary story come to life. He floated off the ground, taking his full Wraith form.

He rushed at Maddison.

"Scutum," she said, holding her palm out; the air before her shimmering with blue.

The Wraith hit her spell, pushing on it. *I don't have a choice,* she thought, letting Vis pour into Vindictam. She moved her shield and attacked. Her blade swished through thin air as the Wraith avoided her attack. It tried to grab her, and Maddison flicked Vindictam up in the air, removing the Wraith's arm. It didn't make a sound of pain, but rather tried to bite her arm. In the background, Maddison heard the pained cry of the woman, "Henry, NO!" Maddison tried not to let the pain in the woman's voice affect her. *That must be his family.* The Wolves must have been trying to force the Wraith to work for them. She couldn't kill a man in front of his wife and kids. *Alright Henry, follow me.*

Maddison pushed Vis into her legs, jumping high in the air and landing atop some equipment. The Wraith flew after her. Maddison dropped behind some boxes out of the view of those in the cage. The Wraith came down in front of her.

"I'm not going to kill you in front of your family," Maddison said.

The Wraith stopped moving toward her; instead, it jerked and twitched. Its face was a mask of pain and rage. It took on more of the appearance of the man she'd first seen. "Will you keep them safe?" he asked, through gritted teeth.

Maddison found her voice catch, "Yes."

His face became one of determination, "I-I can't control myself much longer, do it now while I'm still me."

Maddison felt a twinge in her gut for the man as she always did when she dealt with a Wraith. She poured Vis into Vindictam, and sliced Henry in half. The lower half of his body lost its transparency and fell to the floor. The upper half of his body gushed blood, but a look of peace crossed Henry's face before he died, the rest of his body falling to the ground. Maddison jumped back over the wall of boxes, landing before the cage. Before her was the Wolf she'd injured. Maddison sheathed Vindictam, not wanting to kill the Wolf, but take it in. It grabbed a gun on a table next to the cage. Maddison chuckled. A gun would do nothing to her, but then she saw something she never thought she'd see. The Wolf took on its Human form and smiled at her. Then it held the gun to its head, and pulled the trigger.

The people in the cage screamed, Maddison rushed forward too late to stop the Wolf from killing itself.

Gabriel came into view.

"What happened?" he asked.

Maddison looked at him, shocked, "He shot himself?" it was a question.

Gabriel didn't look pleased, "I killed all of mine; this one must not have wanted us to get any information out of him." He looked at the people in the cage, confused, "Who are you?"

The woman introduced herself and her two kids. Maddison had been right to assume they were the Wraith's family. Gabriel let them out of the cage, and the lady explained that they had all been kidnapped, and kept in the factory. She said that her husband was told if he didn't do what he was supposed to, the Wolves would kill her and her children.

Faith and Amy were back in the factory, along with a few agents from the FBI.

"So they were trying to control a Wraith?" Faith asked, concerned.

"It's not the first time someone's tried." Gabriel said.

"When was the last time?" Maddison asked.

Gabriel's expression turned dark, "During the war, the Nobilis tried it on a handful of occasions. It didn't work then, and I don't think it will work now," he said, breathing out heavily.

Maddison shuddered to think of what it would be like if Trinity was using Wraiths as weapons. They stayed around for a while, making sure the area was secure, and that Henry's family was taken care of. Maddison felt for them. They would never be the same again, and as for the kids ...they would live the rest of their lives wondering if they would share the same fate as their father. *Will you be called on someday to kill one of them?* Maddison wondered.

ALISON KAUR looked up from her computer to see Gabriel, Maddison, Faith, and Amy entering the station. None of them looked like they were in a good mood as they walked over to her.

"What happened?" Alison asked, worried.

"We can talk about it in the conference room," Gabriel said.

Alison followed them into the room where Hatcher was still sitting. Alison called Sean in. Hatcher gave the Mages a distrusting look that they ignored.

"Is it all right to talk with him in here?" Gabriel asked Maddison.

"That's not her decision," Hatcher said.

"Yes it is," the voice of Agent Alesbury said as he walked in, joining them, "and it's fine if he stays in here. I don't want to spend an hour on the phone while his boss whines about not being included."

Alison was shocked by how Alesbury spoke to Agent Hatcher ; he was normally a fairly polite man.

"What happened in Oklahoma?" he asked Maddison, "you said something came up."

"It did," Maddison said, "we encountered a Wraith while we were there."

Alison ran through a list of Mutari that she had in her head. "Those are supposed to be the most dangerous, aren't they?" she asked.

Faith nodded, "Extremely, they can even take out lower level Paladins sometimes."

"We lucked out though," Maddison said, "he was still partly in control of himself. The thing that is so disturbing is that Trinity had his family there, and they were trying to force him to work for them."

"Is that even possible?" Alesbury asked.

"For a time, yes," Gabriel said, "Wraiths lose their minds eventually, and become killing machines, but for a time they still have some control. During the war, Nobilis forces tried on several occasions to control Wraiths."

"Why would one of these Wraiths be useful?" Hatcher asked.

The Mages were silent for a time before Amy spoke, "Fear," she said.

"What was that?" Hatcher asked, "and who are you?"

Amy looked uncomfortable as everyone looked at her, "My name is Amy, and I said 'fear'. We have used both Humans and Mutari to go after Trinity. We have more manpower than they do, but Wraiths instill fear in most Mutari as they know what they are. I think they were hoping to use the Wraith as a way of making Mutari scared to work with us, or maybe to use fear to make Mutari work with Trinity," Amy said.

"That's a possibility," Alesbury said, "Did you manage to take any of the Wolves into custody?"

Maddison frowned, "No, I had one injured and was going to bring him in, but he shot himself in the head."

"I thought guns didn't have a whole lot of effect on Wolves?" Sean asked.

"He took his Human form first. I've never heard of a Wolf doing that. Have you, Gabriel?" Maddison asked.

Gabriel shook his head.

"Perps do it sometimes," Sean said, "Sometimes if the perp is scared enough of their employer, they will off themselves to keep from having to face the music with their boss."

"Is there a bright side to this raid at all?" Alesbury asked.

"Yes." Faith said, "We caught Trinity off guard."

"So the mole isn't in the FBI," Alesbury noted.

"It doesn't appear that way," Alison said.

She didn't know what to think of what Maddison was describing. She wasn't part of the Vis world, and thankfully had yet to encounter a Wraith; so she didn't understand their theory of making Mutari scared. She could, however, understand why the Wolf killed itself. While in many ways the raid in Oklahoma had been a bust, Alison realized that they had narrowed down where the mole might be.

"I'm still not convinced that the leak isn't with the Mages," Hatcher said boldly.

Alesbury rolled his eyes, "I changed my mind; you aren't allowed in here."

"This is a Denver Police Department building. I have more jurisdiction in here than you do," Hatcher said, firing up.

Gabriel sighed, "Why do you think we are the leak, Mr. Hatcher ?"

Hatcher looked at Gabriel, "You are the ones not submitting to any sort of inquiry, you aren't giving me access to your homes, or allowing me to talk to you ..."

"You can question us all you like," Faith said, "Go on, ask away, get it out of your system."

Alesbury huffed, "Fine. Talk to Faith and Gabriel, but as far as Maddison and Amy, they have a Pactum with the FBI. Come on," he said to Maddison and Amy, who followed him from the room.

"Would you like to speak with us one-on-one?" Gabriel asked.

Hatcher looked like he didn't know what to say, "Yes."

"May I start?" Faith asked.

FAITH PENN ushered the others out of the room, leaving her alone with Hatcher . She increased her Vis output to enhance her senses, activating spells to read emotion. These were like the kind Heidi used, though Faith was nowhere near as proficient as a Contractor.

Faith flashed Hatcher her most charming smile, watching his face flush and his emotions twitch. He found her attractive. She leaned over in her chair, resting her elbows on the table and allowing just a hint more cleavage to show. He was very attracted to her, she was happy to see.

"So what do you want to know?" she asked sweetly.

Heidi had learned to use Vis to mess with people's emotions, but Faith had learned a skill of her own. When she wanted to, she could make just about any man melt. It wasn't something she did often, but in this case, she figured it would save her some time with Hatcher .

"I take it I'm still not going to have access to your home?" Hatcher asked.

"Nope," she said warmly, "but you can ask me whatever question you want."

"How do we know you aren't leaking information to Trinity?" he asked.

That was straightforward enough. "You don't," Faith said, and then added, "but if I were a mole would I almost have Angelica Vies kill me, and would I endanger my brother's life? No offense Agent, but the Denver Police Department isn't really a hard target for Mages. Without Gabriel and I here, Trinity could have wiped you all out by now."

Hatcher didn't look pleased with that answer, "Are you convinced they are that strong?"

"You saw the video, right?" she asked.

Hatcher nodded.

"Then you tell me," Faith said.

Faith resisted the urge to mess with Hatcher during the rest of the interview, but she could tell he no longer suspected her or Gabriel anymore.

"Why do you dislike us so much?" Faith finally asked.

"I don't dislike you," Hatcher said.

"Really?" Faith asked, unconvinced, "could have fooled me."

"Do you care?" Hatcher asked.

"Not really, but I'm curious. Sean and Alison didn't like us when they met us either," Faith said.

Hatcher sighed, "I don't trust you." He looked at her, "Don't take it personally, I don't trust anyone, and that goes doubly so for people I don't understand. That's why Sean and Alison didn't like you, and don't like me. They didn't trust you, and saw you as meddling in their business."

"What will it take for you to trust us?" Faith asked out of a sense of curiosity.

Hatcher smiled, "Don't take this the wrong way, but it will never happen. Not trusting people is my job, and I'm very good at it. Thank you for your time, Mrs. Penn, you can send in your brother now."

SEAN HUGHES waited at his desk as Hatcher finished up talking to Gabriel. It was getting close to dinnertime, and he texted Mandy to see if she wanted to grab something to eat. She texted back saying that sounded good.

"Hey Kaur, Mandy and I are going to get some grub. Do you want to come? You and Decor can come too, Penn." Sean said.

"I'm game," Alison said.

"Yeah, we'll come." Faith said.

Once Gabriel came out, they all left the station.

"How was talking to IA?" Sean asked everyone.

"He got on my nerves a bit," Alison admitted.

Gabriel and Faith said they didn't find him to be that bad,

but Sean figured when your day consisted of getting attacked by Werewolves, an IA officer would be a nice break. They met up with Mandy at a trendy pizza place and wine bar called La La's. The interior had cork walls and the open kitchen filled the restaurant with the scent of pizza. They all sat around the table not talking as they looked over the menu.

The server came by to take drink orders. Sean asked about pairing a wine with the pizza he was planning on getting, and waited for the others to order their drinks. For a while, everyone just chatted about unimportant things, but as soon as dinner made it to the table, Mandy said what the Mages and cops were thinking.

"You need to find that mole," she said.

"We know for sure it's a cop," Alison said, "but there are only a handful of us who know enough about the case to be a real threat."

Sean wanted to give Alison a dirty look, but he couldn't. She was right. He didn't want to think about it, but someone in their inner circle was the mole.

"Heidi didn't find anything out." Faith said, "Everyone in a police station is already so distrusting; I don't know if she ever had a chance."

"Amen to that," Sean said, "let's list who would have enough information to be the leak."

"Hmmmm, there's the four of us, and Maddison and Amy," Gabriel said.

"There is Jesse Sanderson in IT, and Montoya," Alison said.

Sean twitched a bit.

"What is it?" Mandy said.

Sean looked down at his food, "I don't know … nah, never mind."

"Hughes," Alison said reprovingly.

"Fine," Sean gave in, "The Sarge didn't seem to care that I got torn up. He comes off as a hard-ass, but have you ever known him not to care about one of his people?"

Alison looked thoughtful, "You're right; he didn't even visit you in the hospital more than the one time."

"But I've known him since I was a rookie. There is no way he could be the leak." Sean said, "I feel bad just thinking it."

"So that's something small that is out of character for him?" Faith asked, serious.

"Yeah, it is. He makes a show of being a dick, but he isn't one deep down. He's probably just stressed out," Sean was defensive.

He noticed Gabriel and Faith exchange a glance. Sean felt guilty for saying something, but another part of him couldn't help but wonder what was up with the Sergeant.

TWELVE

SEAN HUGHES finished up the report he was working on when Gabriel, Faith, and Erin came into the office. Gabriel and Faith were in their signature black overcoats, and Erin looked like something from a fifties sitcom. She had a plastic container in her hand that she set on Alison's desk.

"Hey Erin, how have you been?" Sean asked.

He couldn't help but want to be friendly with Erin. There was nothing that endeared a person more to you than when they kept you from bleeding to death.

"I should be asking you that, Detective. How have you been feeling?" she asked.

"Perfect, I haven't had any problems at all," he said, adding, "What did you bring?"

Erin looked down at the container, "Oh yeah, I have brownies. I thought you guys might like them."

Erin opened the top of the brownies, the scent of them reaching Sean in a moment. They smelled good, but something didn't seem right with them. Sean reached out, taking one and enjoying a bite. It tasted fine, so he didn't think anything of it. Alison also started in on them. Faith and Gabriel said they'd had some at home.

Sergeant Montoya came walking by.

"Is that brownies I smell?" he asked.

Sean held the container up to him, "Sure is; want one?"

"Thanks," he said taking a brownie and biting into it. "What's your plan for the day?" he asked.

"We have a few leads to chase down, sir. Any word on how long we get to play host to IA?" Sean asked.

Montoya frowned, "Longer than they should be here; that Agent Hatcher has been a real pain, if you know what I mean. I didn't know you could cook, Hughes, these things are good!"

Sean laughed, "I didn't make them, Erin did."

Montoya stopped chewing and looked over to Erin, who Sean was surprised to see wasn't smiling at all. In-fact, she looked apprehensive; even shying away from Montoya. Sean glanced to Gabriel, whose hand was on the grip of Iram.

"What's going on?" Alison demanded.

"Erin," Gabriel said softly.

Erin moved behind Faith like a frightened kid hiding behind their mother.

Gabriel stepped forward, moving closer to Montoya.

"Decor?" Sean said, tense.

Montoya, on the other hand, looked worried. He grabbed at his gut, and leaned over.

"Sergeant!" Sean yelled, getting up, moving to Montoya's side.

"Sean, don't!" Gabriel barked.

Sean moved between Montoya and Gabriel, "What did you do!?"

"It's not Montoya," Faith said, "Sean, move!"

Sean looked back at the Sergeant. The flesh on his face was turning a sickly color, his features twisted.

"Damn Mages!" he growled, pushing Sean out of his way.

Sean fell back as Gabriel moved forward. Montoya pulled his gun from his hip and fired at Gabriel, hitting him in the gut.

Montoya turned to run toward the fire exit. Gabriel shrugged off the bullet and ran after Montoya as the station exploded with activity. Officers were drawing weapons all over, trying to figure out what was going on. Sean stood up to run after Alison, who was chasing Gabriel and Montoya.

Sean spilled into a stairwell to find Sergeant Montoya in a glowing net of lavender Vis. Gabriel stood next to him, Iram pointed at the man. Reflexively, Sean drew his weapon and pointed it at Gabriel.

"What are you doing, Decor!?" Sean demanded.

"This isn't Sergeant Montoya," Gabriel said in an icy voice, "this is a Shape Shifter."

"What?" Alison asked.

Gabriel looked over at them, "Sean, last night you said that Montoya had been acting slightly off, correct?"

"Well yeah, but I didn't think he was the mole," Sean said.

"He was acting off because this isn't the real Sergeant Montoya; this is a Mutari who has taken on his appearance, and is a spy," Gabriel said.

Sean lowered his weapon and looked up at the man in the Vis web. His face's features were that of the Sergeant, but his expression wasn't.

"Can he communicate with the outside world? He's managed to get past every one of our other wards," Gabriel asked Faith.

"No, he can't," she said calmly, "I have the office blocked too tightly, I'm confident of this; but sooner or later Angelica is going to figure out her asset has been burned," Faith said.

Before Sean could say anything, the man in the net spoke, "And when she does, the real Montoya will be killed, Mage!"

Sean's blood ran cold. The thing in the web just admitted to not being Montoya.

Sean set his teeth and approached the Shape Shifter, removing cuffs from his belt.

"Decor can this thing break out of cuffs?" he asked.

"Yes," Gabriel said, "He can make his hands small enough to slip out, but he can't break out of a room, and I can restrain his hands with Vis."

"Do it," Sean said coolly. Then to the Shape Shifter, "You're under arrest for impersonating an officer." He began to read the Shape Shifter its rights as it thrashed against the Vis holding it.

ALISON KAUR watched the man sitting in the interrogation room with hateful eyes. It had told Gabriel that its real name was Bryan Harley, but Alison wasn't sure she believed him. After all, how could you ever take the word of something that impersonated others for a living?

"How did you know?" Alison asked Faith, who stood next to her.

"It was a factor in a list of things. The biggest was that Sean said Montoya wasn't acting like himself. Add to that there were no issues in Oklahoma. Montoya was one of only a few people who didn't know we were going." Faith looked away from Bryan and back to Alison, "Sorry, we were going to tell you and Sean that Erin spiked the brownies, but Montoya had one before we could say anything."

Alison breathed out, "It's fine; in truth we wouldn't have been able to let you try that, so it's a good thing we didn't know, I suppose. What do we do from here?"

Faith looked back to Bryan, "We have to get him to tell us where the real Montoya is, and how long he has been planted in the department. From there, we can get what information we can about Trinity out of him, but he won't know much."

"Do you think the Sergeant is still alive?" Alison asked, not hopeful.

"Yes; not only did Bryan say he was, but also they would need to keep Montoya alive for questioning. It's not easy doing what Bryan does," Faith explained.

Alison tried not to think of what the real Montoya had been through, and she hoped they would be able to free him. Inside the interrogation room, the Shape Shifter sat quietly looking at the one-way glass. His appearance was a mixture of faces, Erin having given him something that would make it impossible to completely control how he looked. She said it would stay in his system for a few days. Every now and then a new feature would form on his face or body. At one point in time, he'd grown one breast, and the left side of his face took on the appearance of an old man.

"Do you think he even knows who he really is?" Alison asked more to herself than anyone.

"I doubt it," Faith said. "He's also very skilled at what he does. Remember we know about any Vis object that comes in this office, and he had none on him. When Heidi spoke with him, he did a very good job of controlling his emotions. He was also taking something outside of the office that was suppressing his Vis flow so that Gabriel and I could not tell he wasn't Human."

"Does that mean Trinity has a healer on hand?" Alison asked.

"I'm sure they do, but the concealment potion would have been made by Angelica."

Outside, they heard a commotion. Alison went to the door, and walked out to see Sean and Hatcher nose to nose, their faces red.

"You better watch it, Detective; you're already under suspicion! Bryan Harley is coming with me, not the DPD!" Hatcher roared.

Alison's face flushed with anger.

"He's what?!" she exclaimed.

Hatcher looked at her. "He's coming with me; the DPD has done enough damage in this case," Hatcher said, brandishing a piece of paper. "This is a warrant!"

"Agent Hatcher , this is not a very good idea," Gabriel started to say, but was cut off by Hatcher .

"I've had enough of you and your sister taking the taxpayers for a ride. By the time I'm done, you two will be lucky if you aren't locked up!" Hatcher said, pushing past Sean into the interrogation room. As soon as the door closed, Gabriel came in next to Faith, not looking upset at all.

"Faith, we need to keep eyes on Bryan; if we are lucky, he will escape from IA, and when he does, we need to know so we can move," he said urgently.

Faith nodded, walking away.

"What is this?" Agent Alesbury said, walking down the hall they were in.

"And the whole family is together," Alison said, frustrated.

"Hatcher is taking Bryan," Sean said.

"The hell he is! That man is a suspect in an ongoing FBI investigation," Alesbury said.

"He's going to say kidnapping an officer takes precedence over that," Sean said flatly.

Hatcher came out of the interrogation room with a smirking Bryan in cuffs.

"What's the meaning of this?" Alesbury demanded.

"I am taking this man into custody, if you have a problem with it, talk to a judge!"

"Oh don't worry; I will," Alesbury said.

Bryan started to laugh, "Humans are the kings of this world, huh?"

Hatcher jostled Bryan down the hall toward the elevator. *I wonder what he meant by that?* Alison thought.

The team waited around impatiently while Alesbury tried to work with IA. Finally, after a few hours he came back into the office, and brought everyone into the conference room.

"I'm not getting anywhere with IA," Alesbury said, "but I have a call in to a judge, so hopefully by tomorrow afternoon we will have access to Mr. Harley. In the meantime, we have access to Montoya's home and we can talk to his wife, so let's track down those leads."

THIRTEEN

ALISON KAUR made her way back to her desk, grabbing her keys. Sean and the Mages followed her as she left the station. As Alison drove to the Sergeant's house, her mind was twisting with possibilities and emotions. How had she not noticed the Shape Shifter? She'd known Montoya for years; she'd even spent a few Thanksgivings and Christmases with him and his wife. *How did you miss that, Alison?*

Faith rode next to her in the passenger seat, looking at her, "You're wondering how you missed the Shifter, aren't you?"

Alison glanced at her, "How'd you know?"

"I wouldn't be too hard on yourself, Alison. Shape Shifters can be exceptionally good at what they do; and with Angelica's help …" Faith said, without answering Alison's question.

"We've known the man for years Faith; we should have known that something was up," Sean said from the backseat.

Alison watched Faith from the corner of her eye. It looked like she was going to disagree with Sean, but decided not to. Instead she said, "We will have to see if his wife has noticed anything odd about him, and for how long. It could give us an idea of how long Bryan has been playing the part of Philip Montoya," Faith said.

"Should you two check to see if there are any spells on his house before we talk to his wife?" Sean asked.

Alison hadn't even thought of that. What if Trinity was watching the Montoyas on the off chance that their spy was captured.

"We will check to be on the safe side," Gabriel said, then added, "But I don't think we will find anything. It would do no good to plant a spy, then have that spy found out when we try to make sure everyone on the case's house is safe."

They were entering an old neighborhood in Lakewood west of Denver. The houses they passed were on nice-sized lots with big front yards, and trees that grew well above the houses. Alison pulled into the drive of a two-story brick house with a large sloping front yard. A flower garden grew between the house and walkway to the door. Alison had been to this house a thousand times, but never to deliver bad news.

Once they were out of the car, Alison waited for Faith and Gabriel to confirm that there was no one watching them before she walked the path to the doorway.

Alison rang the doorbell, and a woman in her mid-forties answered the door. It was Nancy Montoya, the Sergeant's wife. She was a short woman with long brown hair and matching skin. Her eyes were kind, her face etched with laugh lines.

"Hello Alison," she said, obviously not expecting to see her. She looked at Sean and the Mages, her face sinking, "Is Phil ok?"

"Nancy, can we talk inside?" Alison asked.

The woman's face fell and she let everyone inside. She led them to a sitting room with a fireplace above which was a big picture of the Montoyas. It made Alison's insides squirm.

"What happened?" She asked. "Come on, Alison, talk to me," her voice was worried.

Sean spoke, "I'm sorry Nancy, but the man you've been living with hasn't been your husband." He raised a hand to stop her from talking, "Today we have learned that he is in-fact a

Mutari, in particular a Shape Shifter. You know what Mutari are, don't you?" he asked kindly.

She nodded her head.

"One has been playing the part of your husband in order to spy on an investigation the office is working on," Sean said.

She didn't look like she believed him.

"What are you saying, Sean? This isn't funny if you're joking around," she said firmly.

"Has there been anything off about your husband for the last month or so?" Faith asked, "Think about it. Think about little things. Does he act the same all of the time?" After watching Nancy for a moment, Faith asked, "How about when he kisses you? Does it feel like he's just going through the motions? Or have you wondered if he is having an affair?"

Nancy looked dumbfounded, "How did you know that?"

"It was because the man you were kissing wasn't your husband," Faith said.

Nancy sat back in her seat, looking down at the floor like she'd been hit in the gut, "How did I not know ..."

Alison was surprised that she believed Faith so easily.

"Where is my husband?" Nancy asked urgently.

Alison frowned, "We don't know. Up until this morning we didn't know that your husband was missing."

"Have you left town recently?" Gabriel asked.

Nancy looked at him, "About a month, month and a half ago; why?"

Gabriel nodded, "I would guess that's when it happened."

"You are that really powerful Mage, aren't you?" Nancy asked.

Gabriel looked uncomfortable, "Yes."

Nancy looked at him differently, and Faith too, "Phil likes you two; he said you could do things that he couldn't even imagine. Is he still alive?" she asked him.

Alison was about to say she wasn't sure when Gabriel and Faith both said, "Yes."

"Gabriel … Faith," Alison said, disapproving.

"He is alive, Alison," Gabriel said, confident. "I promise you." He looked at Nancy apologetically, "They need information out of him. Bryan, the Shape Shifter, may have been able to learn many of the Sergeant's mannerisms from watching him, but the little details of his life, he doesn't know. Those are the things that keep people from thinking there is something wrong with you. They have to keep him alive for information." Gabriel looked at Nancy, "We need to know everything you can tell us about the last month with Phil. He is alive now, but as soon as Trinity finds out that their spy has been caught, they may kill your husband. It is also highly possible that they will keep him alive for more information, but I'd rather not wait and find out."

Nancy looked serious, "Right. We have been having a bit of a rough patch in our relationship, to be honest with you. Nothing major really; marriages have good years, and bad ones. This has been a bad one for us. I lost my job earlier this year, and things have been stressful. To be honest, we don't talk a whole lot. But in the last month, Phil … Bryan," she corrected, "and I haven't been talking much at all. We only made love a handful of times." Nancy all of a sudden looked disgusted, "I can't believe I slept with that thing … do you think I need to be checked out for any disease?" she asked, all of a sudden with a new concern.

"My sister-in-law, Erin, will come by later. She is a healer. If you have anything, she will clear it out," Faith said. "And I'm sorry; I know you must feel violated right now."

Nancy looked down, "I didn't know, and it hasn't hit me yet … hopefully it doesn't." Then she said, "But we haven't talked all that much; we live in the same house, but we are never together."

That made them the perfect target, Alison thought. A part of her started to wonder if anyone would notice if she were replaced.

Sean leaned in to her, and spoke softly as Faith questioned Nancy more. "IA is going to block us on just about everything on this. We can't go after any of Montoya's work files or phone records, but we can go after his personal effects," he said.

Alison nodded, "Nancy do you know your husband's personal email address password?"

"Yes, I do; why?" she asked.

"We would like to look at it to see if the Shape Shifter was using Phillip's personal address to contact Trinity. If it's possible, can you give us any cell phone records you might have?" Alison asked.

"Yes, I can give you his username and password for the email, and let me log in to our cell phone company and download statements for you. If you want, I can give you our address book so you can find numbers we normally don't call," Nancy said, getting up.

"Are all of your husband's numbers in the address book?" Sean asked.

"Sure are, honey; we aren't twenty somethings, we write stuff on paper. Everything should be in my handwriting too, Phil's handwriting looks like a doctor's, so I put everything in the address book. If you find something in his cell phone, he didn't put it in there either; I don't think my husband even knows how to get into his phone's address book," she said.

Alison smiled as she listened to Nancy talk. Sometimes when you told a victim's family their loved one was missing; they lost their heads and were of no help to you. That wasn't going to be the case for Nancy Montoya.

SEAN HUGHES sat at the Montoya's kitchen table looking at their address book and referencing phone numbers on their statement. Sean had always been good at remembering numbers. Soon, he was recognizing some of the common numbers that Montoya called. It looked like the Shape Shifter was keeping up on talking to Montoya's friends, which was saying something.

"I'm not seeing anything," he told Alison.

"Do you think he had a burner phone?" she asked.

Sean leaned back in the chair, cracking his neck, "Every time Trinity knew about a bust we were about to make, it was when Bryan was in the office. I don't think he was dumb enough to use his office phone, but there are lots of pay phones in our building. He could have used any of those. Are you seeing anything in their email?"

Alison huffed, "No, I'm not. He doesn't send a lot of emails to begin with, and this month has been the same. He only checks his personal email a few times a week, it looks like. Maybe Gabriel and Faith have found something in the bedroom."

Sean and Alison made their way upstairs and into the bedroom. The two Mages were looking around while Nancy stood in the doorway looking worried. Faith was bent over, looking at some items she had strewn on the bed. Sean could see down her shirt, and moved his head to get a slightly better view.

"Are you looking down that girl's shirt?" Nancy asked sternly.

Faith looked up at Sean, giving him an icy stare, "Prick," she muttered before turning slightly, going back to work.

Sean thought about making a comment on what a nice rack she had, but decided against it with Nancy in the room. Instead, he just smiled at Nancy sheepishly.

Nancy shook her head, "Well, I guess I can't blame you. You are a man, after all. Phil said you are a bit of a perv … that's probably why he likes you."

Sean raised his eyebrows, "Is the Sarge a bit of a perv too?"

Nancy laughed, "Yeah, he's not as dumb about it as you are, though."

Faith stood up. "Detective Hughes isn't all that bright about many things," she commented, "I'm not finding any Vis objects here. I think it more likely that he was communicating with someone at the office or maybe in person on lunch breaks or things like that. Since we didn't suspect him, he wouldn't have had to work extremely hard to not be found out."

Gabriel came out of the bathroom. "There's nothing in here either," he looked at Sean, disappointed. "I don't think we are going to find anything here, and unless you can find a way to figure out where Bryan was going outside of the office, I don't think we are going to find anything."

Sean looked down, frustrated, "We won't be able to pull credit card records with IA being dicks about everything. We will have to wait for the FBI to get things moving."

"IA?" Nancy asked, "What are they doing in all this?"

"They were looking into the investigation already. When we found out there was a Shape Shifter, they took him into custody, and are trying to stonewall us," Alison said.

Nancy shook her head, "Phil used to complain about IA all the time."

"Yeah they can be a pain," Sean added. "All right, let's get back to the office."

AGENT CEDRIC Alesbury waited outside of a judge's offices with the case's DA, Drew Brent; and a stony Clint Hatcher . They were waiting outside the office of Judge Cathy Climate.

"What do you know about her?" Cedric asked Brent in a low voice.

"Cathy's a good judge, but I don't know her feelings on Vis users. I dare say that will have an impact on this," Brent said softly. "I did some asking around about Agent Hatcher , and he has a decent reputation. Most people think he is by the book, but a little hard to work with," Brent glanced at Hatcher , "He was a cop once. I guess he caught an officer assaulting a woman, and turned him in. From my understanding, Hatcher wasn't very popular after that. It was when he lived out in

Chicago. The officer was never punished, and when Hatcher and his family moved out here, he started working for Internal Affairs."

Cedric thought about that for a bit, "I can't fault him for that, but I'd bet a week's pay he's biased against people who don't work by the book."

Brent smiled, "And our Mage friends don't seem to care at all about the book."

"Would you if you didn't have to?" Cedric asked.

Brent held up his hands, "I wasn't passing judgment; just making an observation."

It was a fair one at that. Since he'd been working with Amy and Maddison, Cedric had learned that firsthand. At the same time, Maddison seemed to have her own code of conduct; a code she never broke. Since Gabriel was Maddison's teacher, Cedric figured Gabriel and Faith also had a code they wouldn't break.

The door to the office opened, and a secretary led the three men into another office with big windows and a big wood desk in the middle. Climate's office was the stereotypical judge's office. Behind the desk was a vast bookcase taking up the whole wall.

The door to the office opened, Justice Cathy Climate coming in the office.

"I hope I didn't keep you all waiting," she said, gliding behind her desk.

Her eyes were blue and kind, her hair in light brown waves. She sat with the air of someone used to being the final word on matters.

"So we are here about a dispute in custody of a …" she looked at some papers on her desk, "Bryan Harley. Who is a Shape Shifter, and impersonated a Sergeant Philip Montoya." She looked up, "Is that right?"

"Yes, your honor," Hatcher said, "the kidnapping of a Denver police officer is the jurisdiction of the Denver Police Department, and in this case the Denver Internal Affairs office."

Brent spoke, "Which affects a current case of the FBI. Internal Affairs is out of line on this one, your honor."

Climate held up her hand, "Save it, both of you. I want to hear from each of you why you should have control of this suspect, and what your end goal is. Mr. Hatcher you may go first."

Hatcher puffed up. "I am looking into the Denver Police Department because they have seriously dropped the ball on the Trinity case."

"They broke the case," Cedric interrupted.

"By killing suspects, Agent Alesbury!?" Hatcher said.

"Enough!" Climate said, "Agent, the FBI will have its turn. Right now it's Mr. Hatcher 's."

Cedric bit his tongue.

Hatcher went on, "Like I said, I am here doing an investigation. One that I must report is not going as well as I'd hoped. The Mages that the department has hired are refusing to let me inspect their homes."

"Which is in line with the State's Pactum with the North American Pactum Guild. Agent Hatcher , please tell me the basis for your investigation isn't because you do not trust the Mages in this case? If so, you need to get over it; you don't have the right to go into their home. For that matter, you don't have the right to investigate anything about them. If you think they are not doing their job, then talk to the Mayor's office about having their Pactum canceled." Climate said firmly.

Cedric liked her. At first he was worried that she wasn't going to be levelheaded about the case, but he could tell she was a no BS kind of gal, and didn't take sides.

Hatcher 's face reddened, "Yes, your honor. My issue with the FBI having control of this witness is that we have an officer who has been taken and replaced with a non-Human."

At this, Cedric noticed Brent relax in his seat.

Hatcher continued to speak, "We need to find the real Philip Montoya, and that shouldn't be the job of the FBI as they are more concerned about their case than about one of Denver's finest officers."

Judge Climate turned to Brent, "What do you have to say?"

Brent looked over at Cedric, and then said, "Maybe I should speak last; I don't want my friend here to explode."

"Very well; Agent Alesbury, why do you deserve the suspect?" she asked calmly.

"Your honor, unlike an Internal Affairs Office, the Federal Bureau of Investigations is trained -- and regularly finds -- kidnapped people. We have resources that Internal Affairs does not, and this is what we do. Furthermore, we are working closely with the Denver Police Department. They have been a critical key in going after Trinity, which is possibly the most dangerous criminal organization in the United States right now. Sergeant Montoya has been a key player in that. To say that we don't care about finding him is frankly insulting. The best chance Philip Montoya has of not being killed is for the FBI to take point on this."

"Drew, what do you think about this?" she asked the DA.

"Cathy, my job is to take care of the people of Denver, which to me means finding Sergeant Montoya, and finding the people who took him. Agent Hatcher has shown his prejudice against Vis users," Brent said.

"How have I done that!?" Hatcher demanded.

"'Non-Humans', Mr. Hatcher ? Honestly. Our Mages have saved the lives of our people, and I just don't think Agent Hatcher has either the resources or ability to find Philip Montoya, and honestly I think he is only hindering our current investigation. Which I might add he has no jurisdiction over."

"The hell I don't!" Hatcher spat.

"Mr. Hatcher , you will keep a civil tone in my office," the judge said.

"Detectives Kaur and Hughes are on loan to the FBI and you have no jurisdiction on this case. If you suspect their conduct on any other cases is in question, then by all means go to town," Cedric said harshly.

"Boys!" Climate said loudly. She turned to Hatcher , "I have to agree with Agent Alesbury and Assistant District Attorney Brent. You have no place doing what you've done. I'm ordering you to transfer Bryan Harley to the FBI at once. As far as your involvement with the Trinity case; this is not your jurisdiction, and I will be recommending to your superiors that you be re-assigned." She addressed the rest of the room, "Thank you, gentlemen. That is my decision; you may leave now."

Cedric left the office happily.

"You'll regret trusting them someday," Hatcher said as he stalked past Cedric and Brent.

"Are you good to go?" Brent asked, ignoring Hatcher .

"We'll get Bryan right away. How'd you pull that off?" Cedric asked.

Brent smiled, "I spend more time in a courtroom convincing people of things than Hatcher does. I know how to work a room and he doesn't," Brent started to walk away, "Get our man back, Agent."

FAITH PENN watched the elevator door open, revealing Maddison escorting Bryan Harley, accompanied by Agent Alesbury. As they walked into the office, people stopped work and clapped, hooting, and hollering. Maddison looked like she was suppressing a smile as she approached Faith and the others.

"Good work, Alesbury," Sean said, earning an eyeroll from Bryan.

"Thank your DA; he worked some magic. Also, Hatcher shouldn't be bothering you as much," Alesbury said.

Sean laughed, "Now that's worth a beer."

At that moment, Heidi stepped into the office from the stairwell; her glasses perched on her nose.

"What's Heidi doing here?" Alison asked.

"If it's alright with you, we'd like to have her interrogate the Shape Shifter," Gabriel said, "she will be more effective."

Alison and Sean said they didn't care.

"I know she's a Contractor, assholes; remember I've been in this office under her nose for a month now," Bryan said sardonically.

Faith smiled, "True, but you don't have Angelica helping you anymore. Have you ever been interrogated by a Contractor?" she asked warmly.

Bryan's cocky smile faded a bit. His face no longer looked like Montoya or an old man. It was now gray without any distinct features; one eye brown, the other hazel.

"Most Shape Shifters take on their natural appearance when they've been drugged. Unless you look like a lump of clay, you haven't; that tells me your own body doesn't even know who you are," Faith noted.

Heidi looked the Shape Shifter up and down. "I'm ready when you are," she said to the detectives.

Everyone piled into the viewing room to watch Heidi talk to the Shape Shifter in interrogation.

"Is she going to be able to break him if he knows she's going to mess with his emotions?" Alison asked.

Faith smiled wide, "Just watch, and see."

HEIDI DECOR focused Vis into her glasses. Without them, she could both see and affect the emotions of others; but with them she felt like a master violinist. Bryan wasn't intimidated by her. He knew they couldn't hurt him as long as he was in Human custody.

"You aren't afraid of me," she pointed out.

He coughed a laugh, "You're right; I'm not. Good luck getting me to talk, Mage. If you're real nice, though, in a few days, I can make a call for you, and Trinity will send what's left of Montoya back to you."

He was bluffing.

"I don't think Angelica is going to answer your call. Do you?" she said. "In fact, I don't think she's going to be very happy with you for getting nabbed. But when you think about it, she had to know it would happen sometime," Heidi mused. As she did she made an obvious change to his emotions, making him uneasy. Most people wouldn't have noticed her touch, but she suspected Bryan would. He was waiting for her to do this.

She could go after him in a few different ways. She could be subtle with affecting his feelings, but he would see past that. She could also be extreme. Even if someone knew they were being manipulated, if you put them in enough fear, they would be unable to keep control. Heidi wasn't going to do these things. She was going to try a mixed approach.

"You're making me uneasy Mage, you came on too strong," Bryan said.

Heidi raised an eyebrow. She spiked his emotions, making him feel scared, "Do you prefer that?" she asked.

His eyes bugged out, and he looked around frantically, starting to shake uncontrollably. Heidi crinkled her nose and turned to the one way glass. "Sorry about that," she said, and then to Bryan, "did you soil yourself?"

"I I I it was'n- wasn't I in my my control," he sputtered.

She dropped the fear. As she did, his natural anger surfaced. This would be one of her greatest tools. Anger blinds all. As his anger at her rose, she helped it along.

"Did you think that was funny?" he asked with gritted teeth.

Heidi shrugged, “You asked for it.”

“How!?”

“You said I was coming on too strong; I was merely showing you that I wasn’t,” she said sweetly.

Bryan’s gray skin turned a deep red, his face taking on sharp features, the skin on his arms turning red as well.

“That’s interesting,” Heidi said, “I’ve never seen a Shape Shifter who can’t control how they look.”

She spurred his anger a bit. He swore at her.

“Where is Philip Montoya?” she asked flatly.

“Screw you, Mage.”

His anger flared on its own. Heidi tried not to smile.

A half hour of Heidi messing with his emotions, keeping him angry and asking the same questions over and over again, was starting to make Bryan tired. His ability to tell when he was being manipulated was getting weaker by the moment.

“You really aren’t going to talk to me, are you?” she said.

His anger was fading on its own now, and as it did, he didn’t notice that emotions he was feeling were not his own. She made him a little confident.

“Nope,” he said.

“Then maybe we should let you go,” she offered.

He laughed, “What will that do you?”

Heidi shrugged, “Well, we won’t be able to save the Sergeant, so we may as well follow you around. Besides, if we let you out; Angelica will think you helped us. All we have to do is make it look like Faith is protecting you. If you go to Angelica to tell her we aren’t helping you, then you lead us to her, and if she thinks you turned; then … well …”

“I’m bait?” he asked.

Heidi pushed some fear into him. She didn’t have to use a lot.

“What?” she said, “we won’t let her kill you; don’t worry. I mean, you did some serious things, but after what she did to that Seeker in the war? We couldn't let that happen even to you."

He licked his lips, and Heidi didn't need to mess with his fear. It was surging all on its own. Part of her worried she might need to keep it in check.

"What if you gave me real protection …" he said.

"We need something for that. Information, but you aren't going to give that to us," she said.

Bryan looked thoughtful, and Heidi started to stand, "Alright, Bryan; I'll go get the DA to cut you loose. It would be a lot simpler for us if you just go to Angelica, ok?"

"I don't know where she is," he sputtered, "I don't know where Montoya is anymore, either."

Heidi sat back down. He wasn't lying; he was too scared to lie.

"I'm listening," she said.

He nodded frantically, "I worked with her in the war. I know what she did to that Seeker." He shuddered, "I can tell you where Montoya was. He might be there, but he might not be. If you hit it tonight, they won't know what's coming. I report in at night when I go out for a walk, unless I have something urgent."

"Where," Heidi said.

Bryan gave her the name of a small warehouse on Santa Fe.

"One moment," she said, getting up and walking out of the room.

SEAN HUGHES gave Heidi a high five as she walked into the viewing room, "Nicely done, Decor, I've never seen anyone fold like that before."

"Thanks," she said, "I don't think he is lying about the location. Can you move on it fast enough?"

Maddison looked at Gabriel who smiled, "We can handle it."

"Then good luck. There is a chance that Montoya has been moved. Make sure you don't kill everyone in case we need to track down his current location." Heidi said, and then added to Sean, "and Bryan shit himself … sorry."

Sean smiled, "Don't worry about it; that's the janitor's problem."

"I'll get a warrant," Alesbury said, walking from the room.

Sean and the others left the viewing room to prepare to move out once Alesbury had his warrant.

FOURTEEN

ALISON KAUR huddled with the others around a laptop in the conference room as Sean pulled up aerial pictures of the warehouse where Bryan Harley said the Sergeant was being kept. The building was just off Santa Fe, putting it in the perfect place for shipping. Santa Fe was lined with warehouses and trucks as they made shipments. Trinity would be able to go relatively unnoticed in an area like that, provided they were using it as a hub for shipping.

Sean and the others looked keyed up. Alison was too. *He may not even be there, Alison, this could be a setup,* she told herself. But another part of her knew it wasn't. She knew they were going to find Sergeant Montoya during the bust. What she wasn't sure about was whether he'd be alive when they found him, and if he was alive, what condition he'd be in. She tried to push those thoughts from her mind as Sean, Gabriel, and Maddison discussed how they wanted to hit the warehouse.

"Do you want people from the FBI?" Maddison asked.

"No," Sean said, "Montoya is one of our own. It will be good for office morale if it's Denver cops who bring him home."

Alison agreed with Sean.

"How do you want to do this?" she asked.

Sean pointed at the picture of the building, "There's a main entrance, a side entrance on the north, and loading docks in back. I'm trying to find a way to keep Trinity pinned down without spreading ourselves too thin."

"Gabriel and I can easily make it so a door can't open," Maddison offered, "that could play to our advantage. We could push them into a corner."

Sean looked at her approvingly, "That might work. If we hit them hard and fast, they also won't have time to react."

He pulled up a blueprint of the warehouse, "This place is pretty standard; it's one big room with a few smaller ones for an office or two. The main room is separated from the front by two small office-type rooms. Would it be possible to make those rooms inaccessible?" Sean asked.

"Yes," Faith said, "Amy or I can enter the front unseen and seal them up; are you planning on entering from the loading area with your full force?"

Sean nodded, "Yeah, that's the plan, a 'shock and awe' so to speak. What do you and Amy need to get this done?"

Faith and Amy looked at each other, seeming to have an unspoken conversation. Faith smiled, "I have an idea." She looked at the others, "We want to take people alive, which I will admit really isn't my or Gabriel's style … or Maddison and Amy's; for that matter," Faith pointed out. Both Paladins nodded their heads in agreement before she went on, "Amy and I need to secure the building from other Seekers prior to your assault. In either case, you will need to wait on us for however long we need." She turned to her brother, "You and I can slip in the front while I cloak us. Once inside we can deal with anyone in there quietly. Then Amy can secure the doors while you put a Vis web inside of the office areas. When you're done, go and help the team in back breach the loading dock."

Gabriel smiled widely. "When they try to leave, they will get caught in the web, and you will make sure they don't see it coming," he said brightly. "It won't be easy … hmm … maybe if the team in back can make a little sound or something, so everyone clears out of the offices, if there is anyone there …"

"I can do that," Amy said, "I can make it sound like someone got hurt or something. Still, you are going to have to move fast; most Mutari will know something's up pretty quickly."

Maddison smirked, "Not wiping everyone out … that will be interesting. How do you want to detain the Mutari if we aren't going to kill them?"

Alison hadn't thought of that, and judging from the looks of the others; they hadn't either.

"Let's cross that bridge when we come to it," Alison said.

No one else had any other ideas, so Alison's *let's just hope it all works out* plan was adopted.

Alison's phone rang.

"This is Alison," she answered.

"This is Alesbury; we have our warrant. Go take the bastards down."

"With pleasure, sir," she hung up the phone "we have our warrant; let's go!"

Everyone left the conference room, entering the main office where detectives and uniformed officers worked. Sean whistled to get everyone's attention.

"We think we have a line on where the Sergeant is. We have the location of where he was taken when he was kidnapped. If Montoya isn't there, then at least the people who took him are. We don't have time to do this right; we don't have time to get SWAT gathered, and we are going in half-cocked … who wants in?"

Everyone in the room got up from their desks or hung up phone calls they were on, and gathered up their weapons. A few people dashed out of the room to get Kevlar vests and rifles.

Sean turned to the others, "Let's load up!"

AMY CALAMUS settled herself on the roof of Sean Hughes' car as officers piled into it. She used Vis to stick herself to the car, and more Vis to keep her from getting cold. She cloaked herself from sight, along with other cloaking spells to hide the team's approach. She looked at Alison's car with Faith atop it. Faith smiled, looking at the top of Sean's car, and then vanished from sight.

Amy looked ahead. She was looking forward to the mission. For the first time in the case the Seekers, and not the Paladins, were going to be taking point. It was an odd feeling. Part of her was looking forward to the change, but another part of her was more comfortable with the Paladins being the main part of a plan.

The car started, moving forward. The sun had set long before; the night was cold and crisp. Her spells warmed her body as Sean drove to the warehouse. Late rush-hour traffic masked the caravan of cars that carried the detectives and other officers. A few squad cars lingered back from the rest of the group.

Faith's voice came over Amy's com, "Are you ready for this?" she asked.

"Yes, actually, I think I am," Amy said surprising herself with her confidence.

"I will have to focus on the inside of the warehouse once this starts; I can cut off communications once we get going, but I will need you to do the bulk of the attack on the building's concealment spells," Faith said.

"I kind of figured it would go that way. Don't worry; I'll take care of everything. Do you need me to mask your entering?" Amy asked.

"No, I'll take care of it. I'll let you know if we need a diversion; we may not. When we get on-scene, I'll make sure to disperse any people who might be outside the warehouse," Faith said.

"Right."

Sean's voice came over next, talking to everyone, "We're just about there. We'll hang back, and let the Seekers secure the area. Amy, Faith, you're up."

Amy focused her Vis. She jumped from the roof of the car, soaring in the air high above the building. She floated there as she released her crystal ball. It hovered before her, pulsing with peach light. She closed her eyes, seeing with the crystal. Faith had been teaching her to use more Vis, and how to build more power. Amy filled her body with Vis, pushing herself hard as Faith had taught her. When she felt like she was about to burst, she lowered her Vis output. At once, she felt energized, buzzing with power. Before learning this technique, using that much Vis would have been uncomfortable, but not anymore. The power rushing in her made her feel like a goddess. She began weaving spells together and then releasing them. She could see the building before her in shades of peach.

Amy extended her first spell, ensuring Angelica would not know the building was under attack. Then she assaulted the building's wards with spells. Waves of Vis crashed into the building, breaking like great waves on a coastline. There were flashes of ruby, citrine, and emerald, as wards buckled under the onslaught. Amy reveled in the power as the building gave itself to her. After a few minutes, she spoke.

"Faith, you're clear," Amy said.

"Good work; thanks," Faith replied.

FAITH PENN looked over at her brother who shared her cloaking spell, "We're up."

Faith released a spell to make the bystanders in the area remember they had something they needed to do elsewhere. As they left, Faith and Gabriel walked to the front door, unseen by others. Faith dampened the sound in the area and disabled the lock on the door. They entered without anyone being aware. Before them was a door to an office area, separating the main room of the building from the front entryway. *Some luck,* Faith noted as they walked in the room. There was no one there. A window looked out into the warehouse floor where Humans and Mutari moved about. Faith noticed another room off to the side that wasn't in the original building plans.

"There's a room to the south that wasn't in the plans. It's small. If I was going to keep anyone in here, that's where I'd do it," Faith said.

"Thanks for the heads up, Faith. We are in place at the back of the building, waiting your go ahead," Sean said.

Faith worked quickly to keep people from coming in the room until it was time.

"Gabriel," she said to him.

"Ok," he said, walking in the center of the room. "Textus," he said, holding out his hands. Bright strands of amethyst Vis flew from them, clinging to the walls, ceiling, and floor. They expanded into ever smaller and finer strands, filling the room with glowing gossamer threads. Gabriel continued to work quickly. Then all save a few of the threads vanished from sight. The last few dissipated after Gabriel altered them.

Faith walked forward, unaffected by the web. She knew she and maybe Maddison would be the only ones who wouldn't activate it.

"It's done," Gabriel said, "good luck. Maddison, can you give me an anchor."

With that, Gabriel vanished in a flash of Lavender as he jumped to where Maddison and the others were.

GABRIEL DECOR unsheathed Iram, pumping power into it. Amy gave them word that the doors around the building were sealed, along with most of the loading dock doors.

"Now!" Gabriel said, pushing against a door in front of him. He used augmented Vis to give his body strength as he pushed. At the same time, he sent cutting spells to free the door from its hinges. The door flew into the room, crashing to the floor and sliding a few feet, making a grinding, screeching sound. Men started to yell as cops poured into the building behind Gabriel and Maddison. The room was filled with mostly Humans and Goblins. Only a few Trolls and Wolves used Vis to defend the warehouse. Gabriel had to give them credit. The Trolls and Wolves had to know they were going to die if they attacked a Paladin, but they did it anyway.

Gabriel didn't even use Iram to take out the first Wolf; rather he sent a ball of Vis at the beast, splitting its head open. Maddison dropped a Troll as a few of the Humans opened fire. There was the TAT TAT TAT of guns as the officers returned fire.

Goblins and Humans ran from the room, trying to leave through the front. One of them moved over to the little office on the side of the warehouse, tossing in something that was on fire. *Dangit!* Gabriel thought, as he realized what the object was. The little room burst into flames. The man had tossed in an enchanted object. Gabriel pushed Vis into his body and moved forward in a flash of speed. If Montoya was here, he was going to be in the little room that was now engulfed in flames.

Gabriel burst through the door, pushing energy into protective wards as he went. "STINGU!" he yelled, putting out the fire. The room was empty save some burned boxes. *Dammit, he's not here.*

The shouts from the other room subsided. Gabriel looked back out over the room, noting stacks of boxes. He walked into the office he'd placed the web in, and found six Humans and four Goblins suspended in the air, wrapped in lavender Vis. The Humans fought the restraints, but the Goblins didn't move, knowing it was over. Faith flashed into existence in the center of the room.

"Sorry boys, I don't think you're going anywhere," she said to the Humans. Then to her brother, "Is he here?"

Gabriel looked down, "No; he's not."

Sean came up to his side, "Any sign of the Sergeant?"

"No. Sorry Sean," Gabriel said, "But maybe one of these guys can give us a lead," he said, pointing to the men hanging in the room.

Sean looked crestfallen for a moment, but pushed the expression from his face and looked at the hanging men, "We'll get information out of some of them."

MADDISON BELDAME felt like the attack was a little anti-climactic, which she told Amy as she came in the room.

"There wasn't much fighting for you to do, was there?" Amy said apologetically.

"Nah there wasn't, and we didn't even get Montoya," Maddison huffed. "You and Faith did great," she added warmly.

Amy beamed, "It may have been boring for you, but let me tell you; it wasn't for us. It's amazing what Faith has taught me, and it was a nice change with the Seekers being point."

"But?" Maddison asked.

Amy made a face, "But I'd prefer it if the Seekers being point was more of the exception than the rule."

Maddison laughed. Amy hated to be the center of attention. "You know during the war the Seekers did a lot of things like this," Maddison pointed out.

Amy smiled playfully. "Good thing the war is over, isn't it," she winked.

A detective came trotting up to them with a box of lighters, "What are these?" he asked.

Maddison looked in the box, "Concealers, it looks like." She sighed, "I bet this place is full of enchanted crap. We better call James. Detective, can you do me a favor and tell everyone to hold off touching items in here; we don't know if Trinity doesn't have any traps in place."

The man blanched a little, "Sorry, I didn't think about that. I'll tell everyone."

He ran off yelling, "Hey you morons! Don't touch anything! What if the wizards have booby traps!"

Maddison shook her head, "Mages …" she said under her breath.

ALISON KAUR was trying not to be upset about not finding Montoya. Instead, she contented herself with walking around with James and Erin as they inspected the boxes in the warehouse. James was finding a fair amount of enchanted objects, but what was more disturbing was what Erin was finding.

Erin held up a tin. "This is bath salts." She said.

Alison knew of them. They were one of the newest drugs to hit the street, making a splash over the last few years. The problem with bath salts was they could make people crazy, and gave them extreme strength. There was a man in Florida who had tried to eat the face of a homeless man, starting Internet rumors of the start of the zombie apocalypse.

"I hate that stuff." Alison said, "It makes people do freaky crap. A guy I know in Vice told me it took four officers to get some fat dude off a couch he was holding onto with his teeth. Once they got him off, he was talking in made-up languages, and bit one of the officer's arm. They beat the tar out of him trying to get him off the officer. On bath salts, you don't feel pain, and are crazy."

"I bet he was naked too, wasn't he?" Erin asked.

"Yeah, the officer told me the whole time they were trying to cuff the guy, he was humping the floor shouting the most perverse things. How'd you know he was naked?" Alison asked.

Erin shrugged, "It makes them hot, so they take off their clothes, and it also makes them hyper-sexual."

"And hard to take down. An officer in another state had a guy on bath salts rush her; she emptied an entire magazine in him before he dropped," Alison said, trying not to think of what that would be like.

Erin frowned, "Yep, they are nasty." She held the tin up, "This one is filled with bath salts that have been altered by Vis; God only knows what it does."

Alison shuddered, "Can you find out?"

Erin didn't look hopeful, "It will take me a while, but my guess is they are trying to remove some of the nasty side effects, and make the bath salts more addictive."

"Why do you think that?"

"They'd sell better that way, wouldn't they?"

Alison agreed with her, going over to Sean, "What do you have?"

"Ten perps going to processing. In an hour or so, we should be able to start questioning them." He looked optimistic, "One of them will talk. Are you ok?" he asked, looking at her.

Was she ok? No, she wasn't. "I just had a feeling that we were going to find him here … I'd have bet my life on it … but we didn't."

Sean put his hand on her shoulder, "We'll get him back Kaur, I promise."

Sean walked off, and Alison tried not to kick herself for having to lean on Sean over something like getting her hopes up. She found Faith standing with Maddison and Gabriel.

"Good job tonight," Alison told Faith.

Faith smiled, "It was kind of fun."

Alison shook her head, "Only Mages find this fun."

Gabriel looked like he wanted to argue, but couldn't find anything to say, and Maddison just smiled.

"It would have been nice not to have to kill the Trolls and Wolves, but I won't lie that sneaking in and setting up that web was pretty fun," Gabriel admitted. Then more seriously, "We'll crack one of these guys. One of the Goblins will know where he is. Trust me; things don't get past them."

Alison nodded, trying not to think about what was happening to Sergeant Montoya.

FIFTEEN

ALISON KAUR woke with a start. She rolled over and looked at her alarm clock. She had a bit longer until it would go off, but got out of bed anyway. Instead of shutting down to sleep, her mind had spent the night listing what could have been happening to Montoya, like some horror film she couldn't stop. In so many ways, she now knew what it was like to be a victim, or the family of a victim. She knew that every moment that went by, the lower his chances were of surviving.

The shower was cold when she stepped into it, shocking her body; giving her a jolt of energy. As the water warmed, her body relaxed as lists of things she needed to do ran in her mind's eye like the end credits on a movie. *How are you going to do this?* she asked herself. She had been at work late the night before, talking to some of the people they'd arrested from the Trinity warehouse, but none so far had talked. This left her with only a few people left to interview. Sean and Alison were taking the Humans; Heidi the Mutari. It was unclear if Heidi using Vis to influence suspects was considered illegal. To be on the safe side, Heidi stuck to the Mutari as Drew Brent, the DA on the case found it unlikely a jury would care about Vis being used on Vis users. In a way, Alison felt guilty knowing that the legal system would be fine exploiting Mutari on the grounds that they weren't Human.

Alison left her house, planning on being at work early. She drove downtown, stopping at her favorite coffee shop. The lady at the counter looked surprised to see her.

"Getting an early start today, are we?" she asked.

Alison acted like nothing was bothering her as she smiled at the woman, "Sadly, there's no rest for the wicked, and therefore no rest for those responsible for catching them," Alison said.

"Isn't that the truth?" A slightly familiar voice said from behind her.

Alison turned to look into the dark eyes of Alexander Fop, Gabriel's Vampire informant. Actually, Alison wasn't looking into his eyes; but his forehead, as he was rather short.

"You look surprised to see me," he said warmly, stepping up to the counter, "these will be together. I would like a tall coffee, please; black."

"Would you like our breakfast blend?" the lady at the counter asked.

Alexander shrugged non-committedly, "Sure." He paid her and turned his attention back to Alison, who was still stunned to see him. "Breathe, Detective; I've already eaten today," he said with a wicked wink.

Alison regained her composure, "Thank you for the coffee Alexander, how have you been?" Alison asked, unsure of how to act around the Vampire.

He led her to a seat with their coffees in hand. Alison needed to find a way to get away from Alexander. She had work she needed to do.

"I was actually planning on visiting your office this morning to talk to our Paladin friend. It worked out nicely you were getting coffee here. I prefer to not go into a police station if I can avoid it," he said.

Alison was taken aback, "Oh ... do you have information for us? Or would you rather I call Gabriel?"

Alexander waved a hand at her, "You will work fine. I'm sorry to hear about the loss of your Sergeant, by the way. I'm sure you will find him, but that is not why I am here."

"How did you know about that?" Alison asked, amazed.

Alexander simply smiled, but didn't answer her question. "We have bigger problems, my dear," he said taking a sip of coffee, wincing, "Does your coffee taste as bad as this?" he asked.

"No, mine is fine; thank you. What problems do we have?" Alison asked.

Alexander became serious, "Please be sure to tell Gabriel everything I tell you, leaving nothing out. The tides are changing, Miss Kaur."

"Excuse me?" she asked.

"I'm telling you that the Decors and Beldames need to keep their eyes on the prize. I don't know what the prize is, personally; but there is more going on here than you are seeing," he said, cryptically as ever.

Alison felt goose bumps on the back of her neck. She didn't know this man, but Gabriel did, and seemed to trust him. From what she had gathered, Vampires were some of the most influential people in the world, and Alexander was a particularly well-connected one.

"What is going on?" she asked.

"Well, it may not seem big to you, but I've had some associates of mine start backing out of deals. These same people are also not looking for any new business. Vampires are like the investment bankers of the Vis world, you see. In fact we, not the Mages, are the cornerstone of the Vis economy. There are a lot of influential Vampires and large Covens that are not investing anywhere … not even with each other. Furthermore, people are going to cash everywhere; myself included. We Vampires have a sixth sense about the world around us, and mine is telling me to batten down the hatches and prepare for the storm."

Alison took a sip of coffee, though the liquid didn't seem to wet her mouth, "What do you think is coming?"

Alexander looked at her with sorrow as he shook his head, "I honestly don't know, but I haven't seen anything like this in years. Not since before the war."

Alison's blood ran with ice, "Thank you … is there anything else you'd like me to pass on?" she said, trying not to show her disquiet.

Alexander shook his head, "No. Just tell him to watch the tide, and to keep his eye on the prize. That goes for his whole family. Thank you for your time, Detective. I hope I didn't disturb you too much."

Alexander rose from his chair, walking calmly from the coffee shop. For her part, Alison took a big gulp of coffee, though it did nothing to warm her. She didn't know much about the war in the Vis world, but something about Alexander Fop's voice told her she didn't want to know. She took out a notepad and jotted down a few quick notes so she wouldn't forget to tell Gabriel anything.

When she got into the office she found Sean and the others in the conference room.

"Is everything ok?" Faith asked her, concerned.

"Can I talk to you, Maddison, and Gabriel?" Alison asked.

Faith looked concerned, but flagged over her brother and Maddison. Alison told them what Alexander had told her. The others looked concerned, but not as concerned as Alison felt.

"You don't seem as worried about this as I do," she pointed out.

Gabriel looked at Alison intently, and then after a moment said, "He wanted you to deliver his message. Vampires can influence your emotions similar to the way Heidi does, though not to the same level. He made sure his words impacted you," Gabriel said.

Alison was miffed, "He used Vis on me?"

Faith smiled wanly, "Don't take it personally. Most Vampires do that to people without thinking about it. Also if what he is saying is true, then we have every reason to take his warning to heart."

"So why aren't you bothered by it?" Alison asked, dumbfounded.

Maddison frowned, "Because we are already aware of the situation. Marcus and Angelica Vies being out in the open has affected the Vis world. We are making sure to keep a pulse of what is going on," Maddison said.

Alison shook her head, deciding that she didn't have time to worry about Vis politics.

She addressed the whole team, "All right, how many people do we have left to talk to this morning?"

Sean answered her, "We have two Humans and one Goblin. Thus far, even with her abilities, Heidi hasn't gotten anything useful out of the Goblins."

"That's not surprising," Maddison said, "Goblins don't fold easily. Years of being good with business deals have trained them to not let their emotions rule them. Plus, they might not know the inner workings of Trinity."

"Hopefully they can give us some information on the group," Sean said, "I think a few days in jail might help with that. I wouldn't want to be a Vis user in prison who can't make themselves strong."

* * *

Sean Hughes looked over the records he had for the next man he had to interrogate, trying to think of a strategy for getting him to talk. He went into the interrogation room where Allen Farrell was sitting at the table.

"Can I get you anything?" Sean asked, walking in, "Maybe some cigarettes to trade when you're in prison?"

Allen shook his head and gave a small laugh.

"You sure you don't want an attorney?" Sean asked.

"Nah," Allen said, "I don't figure one would do much for me."

Sean sat on the other side of the table from the man, "You know you're not getting out of this, huh?"

"Not getting out of what?" Allen said.

"Kidnapping a Denver police officer," Sean said, expressionless.

Allen laughed. "I didn't snag that cop, and you don't have any evidence saying I did. You've got me on a handful of charges, max," Allen said.

Sean nodded, "You do seem to know the system well, don't you?" He looked at Allen's record, "Looks like you've spent almost as much time in jail as you have out of it. Not very good at not getting caught, are you?"

Allen shrugged, "We all have our weaknesses."

Sean was trying to figure out how he wanted to go after this guy. He didn't seem to care about going to jail. Did he just enjoy spending time in jail? Sean needed to figure out what to do with him. There were some people who spent so much time in the system that the threat of jail time didn't affect them. Jail was a place they were not only used to being, but also comfortable. Sean was worried Allen wasn't going to talk.

"Has anyone talked yet?" Allen asked, conversationally.

Sean decided to be honest, "Not yet. You all seem to be pretty loyal to Trinity."

Allen made a face, "Yeah, that's it. Well I ain't gonna talk either, so why don't you just book me so I can get comfy in my cell."

Sean thought for a moment. Allen had made a slip. He was more worried about getting on the bad side of Trinity than going to jail.

"What if I could get you into witness protection?" Sean said.

It would be a bit of a long shot to play this card, but if he had to, he could get Allen into witness protection.

"For what?" Allen asked.

"The location of Sergeant Montoya, and you agreeing to testify against Trinity. Unless you don't know any of the heads of the organization. In which case, I might be able to get you something for giving us the location of the Sergeant," Sean said.

This was the long shot. If Allen could offer up information about Trinity that would lead to arrests or to convictions, it would be one thing. If he only had the location of Montoya, Sean might not be able to get Allen into the protection program.

Allen thought for a moment before saying, "I don't know any of the big people in Trinity. But I can get you the location of your man."

Sean was skeptical, "I can't get you into the program for that. I can offer you a reduced sentence or even get you off on your current charges."

Allen laughed in earnest, "That's a death sentence, man. No; that's not what I want. Here's how this goes. I tell you where he is, and your records show I never talked. I get the same jail time as everyone else, and you interrogate everyone else."

"So what's in it for you?" Sean asked, confused.

Allen looked him in the eye, "There's this kid, see, who takes care of my old man. He wants to be a doctor or something like that. Anyway, for his twenty-first birthday, he got drunk and tried to drive home. You can guess what happened."

"Did he kill anyone?" Sean asked.

"Nah, hit a tree in his own front yard. But the state is going after him for a DUI; I guess that puts a crimp in med school," Allen said.

"You want me to get him off the hook?" Sean asked, "And you'll give up where my man is for that?" Sean asked, unconvinced.

"My pop is pretty sick. This kid isn't a doctor or a nurse or anything, but he lives next door. He goes over every day to take care of my old man. He's been there when I haven't been. Heck, he even called an ambulance once when my dad passed out. He saved my old man's life," Allen said.

"And so you owe him," Sean said.

He thought about it for a moment, and asked Allen for the kid's name. Sean left the room, and called Drew Brent to explain the situation. Brent told Sean he'd get back to him. Sean went back into the interrogation room.

"I'm seeing what I can do," Sean said.

"If he gets cleared, I give you what you want to know," Allen said.

Sean wanted to lay into Allen, forcing him to fold, but this was the easiest deal Sean had ever had to make. Maybe not the easiest to get done, but the best one he'd made. A minute later, his phone buzzed with a text from Brent reading, "Done."

Sean looked at Allen, "It's done; where is Montoya?"

ALISON KAUR looked up a map of the location Allen had given them. It was a house on the outskirts of the city in one of the more rural areas. It was on a large lot that would be ideal for keeping horses, and making sure the people next to you couldn't hear anything.

"It's about forty minutes away from here," Alison said, not happy.

They would need to tell the police department in the area that they were coming, and then make it all the way out there without Trinity catching wind of the raid and locking down or moving.

"This is going to be tricky to do on such a tight time frame," Alison said.

"And for Brent to get us a warrant again so soon," Sean pointed out.

"Our last raid was productive, but you're right. We can't go into this one half-cocked like before," Alison said.

"Maybe we can," Gabriel said. "Alison, Sean, that house is pretty far away for the two of you to drive to, but with Vis;

Maddison, Faith, Amy, and I could be there in a matter of moments …"

"No way Decor, you aren't going on your own," Sean said.

"It's a good idea, Sean," Maddison added, "I understand if you want to be the ones that bring your Sergeant back …"

"It's not that at all," Sean argued, "you guys can't put yourselves at risk like that."

"Sean," Faith said, sympathetically, "we understand what you are trying to say, but the reality of it is, Gabriel and Maddison are already the primary assault in any raid, and without having to worry about you and Alison, they will be able to focus more on offense."

"It's true," Gabriel said, "think about the first raid we did. I went in alone. Had anyone else been there, the raid would have taken longer, and people could have gotten hurt. In fact, the only reason people did get hurt during that raid was because people didn't listen to Faith when the Guardian came out."

Alison listened quietly. She remembered that first raid. She could still see the Guardian throwing blocks of concrete at her and the other cops. She could hear the sound of hundreds of bullets ricocheting off its body, sparkling with the sparks from them. The screams of men getting hit by the concrete still rung in her ears.

"They are right, Sean," Alison found herself saying. She looked at her partner, "This isn't some warehouse where people are coming and going. This is a safe house, Sean. It's going to be a hardened building."

Sean sat for moment, "What about the other day? I was able to help then … and at the train yard."

Gabriel put his hand on Sean's shoulder, "Sean, you are an incredible asset, and one of the bravest men I know. If we had time to bring the Guardians on this assault, then I would insist on your being there, but we cannot do that. And unlike when you had to save my sister's life, this is not a trap. If it is one; Faith and I are springing it willingly."

Sean looked defeated, "We'll be on our way. I swear to God, if you or your hot ass sister gets hurt …"

"We won't," Faith said, and then in a jovial tone added, "And what about Maddison and Amy?" she linked arms with the prior, "These two are smokin! If I wasn't into boys and happily married, I'd be all about these two," she said, lightening the mood in the room.

Maddison blushed deeply as did Amy. Gabriel laughed loudly, patting his sister on the back. "Faith, that's the first time I've ever seen a Beldame blush; I wasn't sure it was possible." He smirked at Maddison, "How does it feel?" he mocked her.

Maddison rolled her eyes, "Can someone get a warrant?"

MADDISON BELDAME waited impatiently for a warrant to come in. Waiting to get the ok to do anything was something new for Maddison, and she still had a hard time with it. In the Vis world, there was no waiting on a judge to tell you that you could do your job. When you found the enemy, you took care of them; end of story. Amy was next to her looking bored.

"There's so much, 'hurry up, and wait', with Humans, isn't there?" Maddison said.

Amy nodded, "You said it. I swear it's a miracle they got out of the Stone Age," she mused.

"They didn't have any paper to make for paperwork back then," Maddison pointed out.

Amy giggled, "So that's how they got so much done. Still, you have to give Humans credit for one thing. They play the part of being organized rather well."

Maddison smirked, "Yeah, they are good at looking the part, but not so good at being organized."

Sean broke into their conversation, "I'm organized."

"You are," Maddison said, "but your society?"

"Nah, you got it all wrong. Everything is organized; we are just inefficient, and no one knows what to do. If anything, we are too organized," Sean said sarcastically.

Maddison chuckled, "I can give you that. Oh my god the paperwork, and forms, and systems Cedric has to use; it boggles the mind. I think he has to write an essay every time he wants to eat lunch."

Sean gave her a quizzical look, "Gabriel and Faith never help Alison and me with paperwork. Do you help Alesbury?"

Maddison shook her head, "No, I don't." She said emphatically, "It's not in my Pactum, and if anyone ever wanted it in a Pactum; I'd triple my rate."

Sean laughed, going back to work. Maddison glanced at his screen, and wasn't surprised to find him working on a report. *Poor bastard,* she thought.

Alison's phone rang and she answered it. After a quick conversation, she hung up, "We've got our warrant. Gabriel, Maddison, you're up. We'll catch up to you."

GABRIEL DECOR had been sitting listening to Maddison and Sean talk with his eyes closed, focusing on controlling his Vis. When Alison spoke, his eyes snapped open and he stood. The other Mages followed suit. Gabriel followed Faith to the roof of the station. He looked in the direction they would be heading.

"Seekers," he said in a commanding voice.

Faith and Amy stood next to their Paladins and cloaked them. Gabriel stood in a bubble of yellow Vis. He could see Amy and Maddison, but he knew that no one in the area would be able to see them. Faith took his hand as Amy took Maddison's. "I'll take gravity." Faith said.

"Ascendit," Faith said.

Gabriel became weightless, lifting into the air; his clothing floating as if he were in water. Next to them, Maddison and Amy were doing the same; Maddison's silver hair twisting in the air.

He looked to where they were going, focusing on his Vis and enhancing his vision to see far ahead of where they were. "Movere," he breathed. He and Faith shot forward, picking up speed. They flew over the crowded city streets, streaking along. Wind buffeted them as they moved, and Gabriel pushed spells out, away from their bodies, blocking the wind. Gabriel loved to fly, though he rarely found a need to do it. It didn't take a Seeker to block one from being seen by Humans, but Gabriel and Maddison needed to not waste their Vis, which was also the reason why Faith and he both shared the energy needed to fly. They moved faster with buildings passing between the two teams as they went.

The tall buildings of the city gave way to suburbs, and soon wide open fields. Gabriel slowed his approach as they closed in on their destination. About a half mile away from the safe house, they slowed to a stop.

"I need to mask us more," Faith said.

Gabriel waited as Faith and Amy worked, making sure no one would know they were coming. This wasn't anything that bothered Gabriel; in fact, he was fascinated by it. He knew many of the spells that Faith used, but unlike her; he was either unable to use the spells or was so abysmal at them, it was like he didn't know how to use them. There were many he could use that were basic, but for the most part Seeking took a great deal of mastery. The same could be said for what he could do. Faith knew a great deal of the spells he used, and knew the theory behind them, but mastering them? That she hadn't done. Seeking was far more subtle than being a Paladin, and that's what he found interesting about it. In many ways, the two disciplines were polar opposites, but in that they were also companions. They were also the hardest of the disciplines to learn, and master. Gabriel thought this was the reason that Paladins and Seekers controlled the Vis world. It wasn't that they were more powerful by nature as many thought they were; but rather they were more disciplined than others, which made them stronger.

"Ready," Faith said, looking at him, her eyes glowing brightly with Vis.

"Ascendit," Gabriel said, taking control of his own gravity. He signaled to Maddison to get ready. He moved over the house, taking the front; Maddison moving to the rear. He looked at her in an orb of peach Vis from Amy.

"Get ready," he said.

Gabriel closed his eyes and felt for the Vis inside of him. Inside, it was like a dam burst; flooding his body with the power it held back. He augmented his body, and activated wards of protection. He opened his eyes, looking at Maddison. Her eyes burned a bright blue with Vis, her body wrapped in a nimbus of sapphire, its deep, rich color highlighted with bright blues. She unsheathed Vindictam as he unsheathed Iram.

"Now," he ordered.

"Descendit," Gabriel said, releasing his flying spell at the same time Maddison stopped hers.

He dropped about fifty feet to the ground, landing in a crouch; his Vis-filled legs easily absorbing the impact. Around him, red Vis flashed as Amy and Faith assaulted the house's concealment wards. The house was two stories tall, and large. In front, there was a garden with a few small statues that looked like planters. Gabriel was sure if a Human approached the house, they would think the owners were eccentric, but wouldn't think anything of the statues. Gabriel, on the other hand, knew better.

"Textus," a whip of lavender Vis lashed out, cutting one of the statues in half. The other one dropped its flower pots and made to attack. Gabriel cut it in half before it could do anything. He ran forward to the house, hearing a bang from the back. *Maddison is in.* He didn't go for the door, but the wall right next to it in case the door had traps. *Abire!* A section of wall glowed purple, and exploded into the house. Gabriel entered the home to see three men with machine guns running to the back of the house. They spun, raising their weapons.

Gabriel could deflect normal bullets with ease, but he didn't like to waste the Vis; and there was always the chance that the bullets were enchanted. He lunged to the left as the men opened fire, shredding wood and shattering windows. Gabriel rolled, using Vis to move faster, and he continued rolling around the room. When he was next to the first man, he stood and slashing upward and to his left with Iram. It shone bright with Vis and sliced the man in two. He stepped forward and slashed slightly down and to his right, removing a head. Then he placed his hand on the top of Iram's blade and thrust forward, stabbing the last man in the chest.

As the men dropped, he saw into another room where Maddison was finishing off a few others. Gabriel looked up at the ceiling, hearing footsteps. Maddison was in the room with him now. "I'll take the high road if you take the low road," she sang.

Gabriel sent a breaking spell into his fist, driving it into the hardwood floor. Wood splintered, breaking around him, and he dropped into the lower level. He landed in a crouch amidst several Trolls. *Lubrica occulta.* The Trolls fell on the slippery floor, and Gabriel slid forward like an ice skater, removing the legs and limbs of those he passed. In the center of the room was a man tied to a chair covered in dirty clothes and blood. A man on the ground raised a gun to shoot.

"Not gonna happen," Gabriel said.

The man fired, his bullet hitting a wall of lavender. The gunman stood, pointing his gun at Gabriel, but too late he jerked dead as Gabriel drove his hand through the man's chest. He fell to the floor gushing blood, as Gabriel looked into the face of the man in the chair.

"Took you long enough," Sergeant Montoya said through a bloody lip, only one eye not swollen shut.

Gabriel smiled down on him, "Finding you in a timely manner wasn't in the Pactum," he said with a wink.

Montoya coughed a laugh.

SIXTEEN

ALISON KAUR was out of Sean's car before it had come to a full stop next to an ambulance. Before her was a two-story house, with two garden statues cut in half in the yard. In a time before Mages, she'd have found that odd, but now she pictured the three foot high statues jumping and leaping about like crazed demon midgets from Hell. What was odd was that the door of the house was closed, and next to it was a hole in the wall. She looked at the hole.

"The door could have been a trap." Sean said from behind her, "We did that in the army, too. People would rig bombs to the door, so we used the walls."

Alison didn't question Sean as she entered the house through the hole in the wall. Bits of wood and furniture littered the main room. The wooden floor and walls were riddled with bullet holes; on the ground were the bodies of three men.

"Humans," Maddison's voice said to Alison's right.

She saw the woman coming down the stairs with Amy trailing behind her. "Sorry we didn't meet you at the door; we have been making sure the house is free of traps," Maddison explained. "We found the Sergeant. He's downstairs with some EMTs," she said.

"Thanks Maddison," Alison said.

Alison sidestepped a hole in the floor that opened into the basement. Alison pointed at the hole, "… and that?" she asked Sean.

He looked at it as they walked by, "I don't have anything for you on that one."

A group of EMTs were tending to a man on a gurney as they came downstairs. The basement of the house smelled of filth and blood. Bodies lay on the floor where Alison presumed Gabriel had killed them.

She moved quickly to the gurney, seeing a familiar form.

Sergeant Montoya had looked better. His face was black and blue, his skin cut in many places. Blood and grime covered his shirt, his wrists raw from restraints. Alison's heart fell to see him. His eyes were swollen closed, but he looked oddly at peace. Standing next to the gurney was Gabriel. His black overcoat, white dress shirt, and black slacks with the hilt of Iram protruding out of the coat gave him the appearance of something from a Manga or comic book. Little droplets of blood speckled his face. Next to him was his sister. She too looked like some dark action hero, beautiful and deadly.

Alison had never seen the Mages in this light before. She'd seen them fight and kill. She'd worked with them every day, but now she saw them the way others must have.

"He's asleep," Gabriel said, "He was up when I got here, and when the paramedics spoke with him, but then I made him sleep."

"He probably needs the rest," Sean said softly, and then looking at Gabriel, "Were there any survivors?" he asked.

"No," Gabriel said.

"Good," was Sean's response, earning a surprised look from a female paramedic.

Alison wondered if Gabriel would have spared any of Trinity's people had they surrendered. After thinking about it for a moment, she decided it didn't matter. Part of her would have held it against Gabriel for showing mercy; and yet another part of her would have held it against him had he not.

"Can you get him up the stairs alright?" Gabriel asked the paramedics as they started to roll Montoya away.

"Yeah, we got him. Are you sure you want us to take him all the way to Denver General? No offense; but it's out of the way, and there are better hospitals," one of the paramedics said.

Gabriel nodded kindly, "Yes, please. My sister-in-law is a Healer. She will be waiting for you there. If it is not too much to ask, my sister Faith will be accompanying you. She will ensure you do not get any unwanted visitors on your way to the hospital."

The paramedic looked over at Faith. A small smile crossed his face, "I'll be driving; she can sit shotgun with me."

The other paramedic, a woman rolled her eyes.

Only emergency response people could be in a scene of death and horror and not be bothered by it in the least bit. Alison felt a twinge of guilt. How many times had she been around victim's families and made flippant comments to another officer? Now she felt like the victim's family, and the thought of a paramedic checking out Faith at a time like this bothered her. *He doesn't even know he should be as shaken up as I am,* she thought. *Maybe you could remember today when you are around victim's families in the future.*

As soon as Montoya was out of the house and the ambulance on its way to the hospital, Alison's mind cleared. She had a job to do. People from the FBI were showing up at the house with Agent Alesbury.

"This is your crime scene, detectives," he said, "Do what you will."

"I want to walk around for a bit," Sean said, putting on a pair of gloves and taking out a digital camera.

She followed her partner inside the house where they found Gabriel and Maddison.

"So, how'd it go down?" Sean asked them.

"I came in through the front. I took out two small Guardians and three Humans with machine guns. I then punched through the floor and entered the basement where I killed several Mutari and a Human who tried to kill Montoya," Gabriel said calmly. Again Alison pictured him on a comic book cover.

"I came in the back. Neutralized two Mutari, then went upstairs where I dealt with a Human and Goblin. They were both armed. I didn't have any Guardians to deal with," Maddison said.

"Did either of you get hurt?" Alison asked.

Both Mages shook their heads, stating they hadn't sustained a scratch.

Sean laughed in awe, "You two are like an army, you know that?"

SEAN HUGHES thoughtfully walked around the house, taking pictures and jotting down the occasional note as he went. There was a heaviness to the air; it was moist and thick with the violence of the day. He looked out of the window of a bedroom. In the distance, he could see another house where a small family was standing on a wraparound porch. They were watching the gathering of cop cars and FBI as they waited for Sean and Alison to give the go ahead to enter the house. In the back of the house, Sean saw a large shed the size of a small horse barn.

"Hey Decor," Sean called for Gabriel.

Gabriel trotted up the stairs and into the bedroom.

"Have you and Maddison checked that out?" he asked, pointing at the shed.

"Not yet. Do you want to go into it?" he asked.

"Yeah I do," Sean said.

Gabriel followed him down the stairs and out of the house. As he passed a group of CSIs, he gave them the go ahead to enter the house. A news van pulled up.

"How'd they get wind of this?" Sean asked himself.

"Do you need to do something about it?" Gabriel asked.

Sean could see Alesbury walking up to the van.

"Nah, looks like Alesbury is dealing with it," Sean said.

The shed was made of weathered wood, rusty hinges holding the door in place. Gabriel went before Sean, placing his hand on the dark wood. He muttered a few things in Latin before opening the shed. They were greeted with boxes stacked to the ceiling. Sean looked at the boxes.

"These are medical supplies," he said, "x-ray equipment I think … that's odd."

Gabriel had opened another box, and was looking at a collection of objects. "Enchanted," he noted. Then looking at a few other things, said, "Here are more of those altered Bath Salts."

Sean didn't know what to make of the contents of the shed. It was a hodgepodge of unrelated items.

"Alright, I'll have some people come over and catalog all of this junk. Is it safe for people to go through?" Sean asked.

"Yes, there were only a few minor spells on the outside," Gabriel said.

"Is that odd?" Sean asked.

Gabriel shook his head, "No; Trinity wasn't planning on us finding this location, I don't think."

Sean looked back to the family from the house next door. He walked over to a wire fence, calling them over. The man and woman walked up to the fence with their young daughter.

"Hello, I'm Detective Sean Hughes," Sean said, reaching out to shake the man's hand. "This is my associate, Gabriel Decor. As you can tell, something wasn't right with your neighbors. How long have they been here?"

"A few years, but they weren't around much; maybe a few weeks out of the year,." the woman said, "real quiet and all. It was a man and woman."

"What did they look like?" Gabriel asked.

The woman thought for a moment, "He had sandy hair and blue eyes, mid-forties maybe … pretty good looking." She said, "And the woman had long blonde hair."

Sean looked over at Gabriel, his face stone. He rummaged around in his coat pocket, holding up two pictures to the family.

"Yeah, that's them," the little girl said.

Gabriel turned to Sean, "Get everyone out of the house."

AMY CALAMUS walked the house with Faith. Everyone had cleared out, and Faith had jumped back to assist Amy. They had been unable to find any traps, but Amy was on edge. This had once housed the Vieses.

"How were we able to breach the house's defenses?" Amy asked Faith as she inspected the walls.

"They lowered the defenses once they started using this place as a safe house," Faith said.

"What do you mean?" Sean voice buzzed in their ears over the com.

"Mage homes, unless they are in a Vis city are very well cloaked," Faith said, "The Vieses have been in hiding for ten years, and we've never detected this house. I suspect it is one of many they used to occupy. With the security they'd have needed on this place to keep them safe from the many Arks looking for them, they would have had to lower the protection when Trinity staff took up residence."

"Do you think you will find anything of use?" Alison asked.

"No," Faith said, "but it's worth a shot. Moreover, we need to make sure Marcus and Angelica didn't leave us any surprises."

Amy pushed the conversation out of her head. She was looking for anything that would be a clue for the case, or more important; danger. Amy didn't feel comfortable being in the house. She and Maddison lived on a small plot of land with two houses on it. It was owned by the Beldame family, and Amy wasn't sure all of the defenses it had. What she did know of them was that it was near impossible to detect the property, and even harder to get in. Should someone make it that far, there were traps and enchantments waiting for them. Amy was no moron. At some point in time, the house she was searching now had also had those types of defenses.

She closed her eyes, searching.

"Found something," Faith whispered.

Amy turned to see Faith looking at the wall. She placed her hands on it and spoke softly.

"Amy, come and see if you can find what's in here."

Amy tentatively approached the wall, placing a nervous hand on it. She closed her eyes and felt. There was nothing there. "I can't find anything," she said. Faith told her how to alter her Seeking spells, and then Amy tried again. She got the faint hint of something.

"What is it?" she asked.

"Gabriel, Maddison, we need you," Faith said, calmly.

Gabriel came into the room with a concerned Maddison. Faith pointed at the wall and spoke one of the most complex spells Amy had ever heard. The wall melted. Inside of it was an object the size of a tennis ball, pulsing with red and gold Vis. Gabriel looked at it.

"Can you disarm it?" Maddison asked.

He looked hard at the device, "No, I can't. It doesn't know we are here yet," Gabriel said.

"What did you find?" Alison asked over the com.

"It's called a detector," Gabriel breathed. "Faith's and Amy's spells are keeping it from knowing something is wrong. but as soon as they release those spells, it's going to activate."

"And then what?" Sean asked.

Gabriel shrugged, "It will let the Vieses know the house has been breached. I would also bet it would kill any Humans or Mutari in here."

"Well, no harm there. If the vultures from the media were able to find out about this raid, then so did anyone with a radio scanner," Sean said.

Gabriel unsheathed Iram, and pointed the tip at the center of the detector. Amy raised every ward she had as he stabbed it … nothing happened. The detector flashed dully before going dark. Then Amy felt it. Her wards were being tested, but it wasn't the ones protecting her. She felt the wards keeping Vis communication from leaving the house being tested.

"Let it go Amy," Faith said, "they know the house is lost; I'm sure."

Amy let her wards fail.

ALISON KAUR looked at her menu, not really seeing it. She was tired from a long day, and wanted to see Montoya. She couldn't go see him until morning; however. Nancy Montoya wanted her husband to be able to rest as did his doctors and Erin. So instead, the team was getting dinner together. Everyone looked tired from the day.

"How do you think Angelica took us finding that house?" Alison asked the table as a whole.

"She's mad," Faith said, "She's been trying to find us for a while now."

Alison lowered her menu to look at Faith, who didn't seem bothered at all. *She really has changed.* For her part, Alison wasn't thrilled to hear that Angelica was looking for them.

A waitress came up to get their orders, which effectively changed the conversation. As soon as Alison had a soda to sip on, she started to feel more alive again, and her mind started filling up with things to follow up on.

"So how was everyone's day?" Sean asked sarcastically.

Alison laughed, to her surprise, and then asked, "Did we learn anything from today?"

"That the Vieses have been in Colorado for some time now. Even if they weren't using that house often, they kept it for a reason. We also know that we struck a nerve with them today, too," Gabriel said.

"How do we use this?" Sean asked. "We don't have any witnesses, and the people we arrested the other day aren't talking," he said, frustrated, "I hate to sound cliché, but every time we cut off a head, two more take its place."

"I'm not sure what else we can do," Amy said.

"I know," Sean said, "I'm just saying this case has a way of getting under the skin, ya know?"

Everyone agreed with him.

"If there's a silver lining of what happened to the Sergeant, it's that he may be able to shed some light for us," Gabriel pointed out.

"What, like locations?" Sean said, not sounding convinced.

"No," Gabriel said, "he could have gained more insight into Trinity itself. We have been reactive up to this point. We don't truly know what they are doing or how they think. I may know how the Vieses used to operate, but from what we've seen, they have changed how they work. Furthermore, they have to be hooking up with Human and Mutari factions. Until we predict their moves, we can't be anything more than reactive."

"What makes you think they are anything more than thugs?" Alison asked.

Gabriel frowned, "I just can't buy that. Ten years ago, they betrayed everyone they'd sworn to protect, and fell off the face of the earth. Why come out now? Just creating Trinity for the money is too much of a risk. They had to know that at some point in time, one of the former Arks would be onto them."

As Alison listened to Gabriel talk, she couldn't help but think of Alexander Fop's warning to her. *Keep your eye on the prize,* he'd said.

"What's the prize?" Alison asked without thinking.

"That's what I can't figure out," Gabriel said.

Alison was surprised he'd known what she was talking about. It must have been weighing on him. Alison knew that for Gabriel, this was so much more than a case or a Pactum. This was his world, the Vieses were people who were wanted throughout the Vis world, and Gabriel had a personal stake in finding them.

The door to the restaurant opened, and Erin Penn came in. She sat at the table with the others. "Good evening," she said when she sat. At about that time, the food they'd ordered came out.

"So, what's Montoya's condition?" Sean asked, as he started to put ketchup on his fries.

"He could be doing a lot worse," Erin said, and then added, "But he could be doing better, too. He will make a full recovery, but it isn't going to be overnight. I was able to heal many of his injuries, but some of them were caused by Vis, and will have to heal on their own."

Alison was starting to lose her appetite. She forced herself to eat, knowing her body needed the nutrients.

Erin went on, "He is weak, and will need to stay in the hospital for a day or two, but then he can go home. That said, he will need to rest, and with how extensive his injuries were, I dare say he will be looking forward to a little downtime."

"Are there any residual spells on him?" Maddison asked.

"Yes; a few," Erin said, "Most of them are gone or will run out of power soon. I think there is something to having both a Paladin and Seeker give him a once over."

"What's a residual spell?" Alison asked.

"Something passive in his system waiting to do harm or to keep him from healing," Erin said, "Thankfully most of the damage done to him was fairly superficial." She paused, "There are signs that Vis was used on him frequently to inflict pain, however."

Alison felt sick, and put down her burger, as did Sean. The Mages on the other hand; did not.

"Eat," Gabriel said softly, but with authority.

Erin muttered something, and Alison found herself ravenously hungry.

"You need the food," Gabriel said, "You are no good to him if you are weak."

Alison thought about not eating just to prove a point, but she was getting terribly hungry. As she ate, she started to feel better. Erin continued to talk for a while, but didn't have much else to say. Alison tried to tell herself that Montoya was lucky to be alive, but it was hard to do. All she could do was think of how she hadn't known something was off with the Shape Shifter, and that had she worked harder, maybe they would have found the Sergeant before anything too bad happened to him.

"You can go and visit him in the morning if you like," Erin said, "but not until then; he needs sleep," she added sternly.

"Kaur, pick you up in the morning?" Sean asked.

"Yeah, that works," she answered.

SEAN HUGHES parked outside of Alison's condo, waiting for her to come down. She came outside and got in the car.

"Thanks for the ride, Hughes," she said.

"Yeah, no problem," he said.

He knew Alison was shook up about the Sergeant being torn up. Sean understood that feeling. The difference was; this wasn't Sean's first time knowing someone who'd spent time in hostile hands.

When they got to the hospital, they found the Mages waiting for them in the lobby.

"Where's Erin?" Alison asked.

"She already saw him this morning to make sure he was doing ok," Faith said, "do you want us to go with you, or should we wait?"

"You're just as much a part of the team as anyone, Penn," Sean said, "though seeing you might give the poor guy a heart attack," he said with a wink.

Faith gave him the bird and went to the elevator.

"That's cold Penn, I was giving you a compliment," Sean called after her.

Outside the Sergeant's room, they found two uniformed officers and Nancy Montoya. She came up to him, giving him a hug, "Thanks for finding him," she said with a tight voice.

"It wasn't just me," Sean said, serious. He nodded to the Mages, "These four were the ones to save him."

Nancy looked at the Mages, "Thank you all so much for bringing my Phil home to me." Her voice turned to ice, "Did you get the bastards?" she asked.

"Every last one," Gabriel said.

"Good," Nancy said, "now you all can go in and talk to him. He's awake, but I don't want you talking about the case, alright?"

They all agreed not to talk about the case.

Sean walked into the hospital room and to the bed where the Sergeant was. Sean stood over him, looking down at his bruised face.

"You look like Hell," Sean said.

"You are such a prick, you know that, Hughes?" Montoya said with a weak voice.

Sean smiled widely, "Glad to have you back."

"It's good to be back," he said.

Alison came up to him, "How are you feeling, sir?"

"Kaur, I spent the last month being tortured by a bunch of criminals. But Erin patched me up pretty good, and the painkillers Mages have are way better than ours." He said, and tried to smile at Alison, "Where is Gabriel?"

"I'm right here," Gabriel said, stepping up to the bed.

"Thank you for coming for me. I think they were going to kill me soon. You saved my life," Montoya said.

"Anytime sir, anytime," Gabriel said.

"How much trouble did you cause?" he asked Faith, "I had to hear about you awhile back. That Angelica lady isn't a big fan of you; you should know that."

Faith grinned, "I know."

"I should be out of here before too long," Montoya started to say.

"And you're gonna stay home and rest," Nancy interjected, "don't make me call that Erin girl."

Sean smiled, "Take it easy for a while. We've got things handled."

"You having things handled is what's got me worried, Hughes," Montoya sighed.

Everyone laughed, including Sean. He was happy to see that the Sergeant's spirits weren't broken. They talked for a few more minutes before a nurse came in to shoo everyone away.

After that, they all decided a day off was needed, so Sean drove Alison home. After dropping her off, he called Mandy to see if she wanted to get together for lunch.

SEVENTEEN

ALISON KAUR stepped out of the elevator to the hustle and bustle of a hospital. She wove her way between nurses, doctors, patients, and their families, headed for Montoya's room. When she got there, she found Nancy sitting by his bed half-asleep. Nancy woke with a start as Alison put down her purse.

"Sorry," Alison whispered, "is he asleep?"

"No," the Sergeant's voice came from the bed.

His voice was harsh. Not angry harsh, but like someone who hadn't had a drink of water in a few days. Alison came to the side of the bed, assessing his condition. His face wasn't as swollen as it had been the day before; his bruises looked as though they'd been healing for days rather than hours.

"You look a lot better," Alison said.

"Erin," was his simple response.

"Are you feeling better?" she asked.

He gave what looked like an attempt at a shrug, "Yes and no. My body is doing better, but my mind …"

"Take your time," she said.

The cop inside Alison sighed in frustration. While it pained her to see her mentor in a hospital bed, she wanted to go out and find the people who'd put him there. To do that, she needed information. Information that Montoya might have. He'd been with Trinity for a little over a month, and in that time Alison suspected he'd learned a great deal about them. But she wouldn't push him.

She took a seat next to his bed, noting as she sat that Nancy was in the same clothes she'd been in the day before. The woman had her eyes closed again, and looked to be asleep.

"Has she been here this whole time?" Alison asked softly as she sat.

"Yes," he said, "she won't leave my side no matter how many times people tell her to." He smiled as he said this. "Funny … things hadn't been all that great before my … capture. Now though, all of those issues don't seem to mean much," He said, looking thoughtful, "I don't even think I can remember what our problems were; they seem so small now." He looked at Alison, "In a way, I'm thankful for this; for that change in perspective."

Alison had a hard time seeing his point of view, "You went through Hell, didn't you?"

His eyes moved back to his wife's sleeping form, "Yes. I think I went through that so I could see that this whole time I could be living in Heaven. I know that sounds crazy."

Alison chuckled, "You're right, it does … sorry sir."

"Phil, Alison; call me Phil. When I'm out of here, then you can call me sir again, but for now I'm not a cop. I'm just a broken man."

Alison felt herself tear up, "Like Hell you're not a cop."

He looked at her, searching, "I'm sorry, Alison."

"Why are you sorry?" she asked.

He looked away, "I feel like I've failed you in so many ways."

"What?" she asked, the breath in her chest catching. "How could you have failed me? I failed you," she said, a tear running down her cheek.

Her hand was on the side of the bed, and Montoya moved his on top of hers, "I have failed you," he said, insistent. "I have watched you for years give everything to your work. I've seen you do amazing things. But life isn't just about catching the filth of the world. I can see that now …" He looked far off, "They didn't even break me, you know? I did it to myself … I had my mortality placed before me, and…" his voice was weak, and full of some unknown pain, "and it was a collection of crimes solved, and criminals put behind bars … but that was it." He looked at her, "My kids … they don't talk to me. They don't know me. How could they? I was never there. I see that now."

Alison couldn't hear this. Montoya was a rock. He was unchanging; nothing ever got him down. He would get mad frequently, but never down. To hear him defeated broke her heart.

"I don't want you to be me, Alison," he said softly.

There was a catch in her throat at his words. She was like the Sergeant in so many ways. Or at least, she told herself she was. She had doubts about her life, sure; but she'd always told herself that her life had meaning. That some day she'd be like the Sergeant. She'd be a rock, she'd be the mentor to someone else.

"But what about all the innocent lives you've saved? And helped," Alison said, in almost a pleading tone.

He shook his head, "No. I can't use that excuse anymore, Alison. I don't regret my career. I've put a lot of filth behind bars in my day. I've made the streets a little safer … but by only doing that, I poisoned myself. I am jaded, and part of me wonders if I hadn't been kidnapped if I would even be able to feel good emotions again. Alison … outside of your job, what do you have to hold on to? What gives you purpose?"

She looked down, not answering. There was no answer. She didn't have anything else.

"The only thing that kept me alive was that woman over there," he said, looking at his wife, "but I'd almost lost her. Still, she was a small dot of hope and life. I clung to that desperately. It kept me from the brink of insanity and despair. What do you have to ground you?"

She dabbed at her eyes with a tissue, staining them with makeup running in her tears, “I don’t have anything.”

The door to the room opened. Alison pushed the tissue into her eyes to soak up the rest of the tears. She pushed back her emotions and turned. Faith was walking into the room alone. She wasn’t in her normal overcoat and white shirt. Instead, she was in a miniskirt and tight shirt, showing a lot of cleavage.

“Are you here for my sponge bath?” Montoya asked from the bed, surprising Alison.

Faith smiled. “I knew Sean got it from somewhere,” she said accusingly, walking to the other side of the bed.

Alison noticed Faith’s gaze linger on her for a moment before she turned to the Sergeant, “So what? All we have to do is give you some painkillers, and you turn into a dirty old man?”

He laughed, and then groaned, “Something like that.” He looked at her seriously, “I heard a lot about your brother over the last few months from the Vieses.”

Faith smiled broadly, “All bad things, I hope.”

He shook his head, “No … quite the opposite, actually. Marcus seems to have a great deal of respect for him.”

Faith smile faded a bit. “I wouldn’t tell Gabriel that,” she said flatly.

“No, I suppose not … Angelica, on the other hand, hates you. Really, my dear; I am worried about you,” he said.

This made Faith’s smile return, “Do tell; how much does she hate me?”

He looked at her, confused, “You seem different,” he noted. “Well, she wants to kill you very slowly, from what I could gather. Honestly, it got a little boring to listen to.”

Faith laughed lightheartedly, “Sorry about that.”

She looked down at him, her eyes out of focus, “Alright Sergeant, Alison and I are going to leave you now.”

“We are?” Alison asked.

“Yes,” Faith said, still looking at him, “His Vis flow is starting to run a little lower than I’d like. Even for Humans, high

Vis flow means you heal faster, and you, my friend need to rest." She said to Alison, "Have any plans for the afternoon?"

"I'm going to the range," Alison said. She didn't really want to be around anyone.

"Take Faith with you," Montoya said, "Have you fired a gun before, Faith?"

"No; actually I haven't. I don't have anything against them, but ... well, I can use Vis," Faith said.

"Try shooting a gun," Montoya said, "Sean will think it's hot, and he'll be pissed he missed it."

Faith looked at Alison, "I'm game. Do you want to teach me how to shoot?"

Alison thought about saying no, but looked down at Montoya, remembering what he'd said about having something to hold onto.

"Works for me," Alison said.

FAITH PENN rode in Alison's car as they went to the shooting range.

"There's a place in Lakewood by me," Alison said, "is that ok?"

Faith shrugged, "Sure."

They didn't talk much in the car; things felt almost awkward. When she'd first seen Alison in the hospital room, Faith had known that Alison was upset. Faith was chocking that up to seeing her commanding officer hurt, which made perfect sense. But she was worried it would shake Alison from her game. *Maybe shooting something will be good for her.*

They got off of 6th onto Wadsworth, passing a shopping complex and Alison's condo. Faith found it relaxing sitting in a car. Strictly speaking, she didn't travel in them often. James had one that he liked to play with, but for Faith's part, she would rather fly or jump wherever she needed to go. They turned down Jewel, and Faith decided that driving around would make it simpler to find places. It was always a pain to try to find someplace new. With street signs at least, you could find your way around.

They parked in a lot behind a small building. Faith reached out with Vis, finding that below them was a large room with people at one side. *That must be the range.*

It was cold outside, making Faith use a little Vis to keep herself warm. She turned some heads upon entering the building. It was a store with people standing at a large glass counter. A few people gave her looks that she thought had to do less with her attractiveness, and more to do with her being in summer clothes. She looked over at Alison, who was huddled in a heavy coat.

"I kind of stick out, don't I?" Faith said.

"It's freezing outside Faith, and you look like it's July." Alison said.

"Amy is better at blending in than I am, isn't she?" Faith asked as they walked down the stairs.

Alison coughed a laugh, "You think?" and then added, "but Maddison …"

Faith could hear the loud bangs of guns being fired. Alison had Faith fill out some paperwork, and there was a small discussion about her not having an ID. Faith solved the argument by making the clerk's gun come off his waist and aim at him.

"See, I can use Magic; I don't have an ID," Faith said, hating to call Vis "Magic."

"I I I thought it was called Vis?" the clerk asked.

Faith rolled her eyes. Of course he knew what it was called. "Yeah, but Humans don't seem to call it that," she said, irritated, and making his gun go back in its holster, "Sorry, that was a bit extreme."

The clerk just looked happy she hadn't shot him with his own weapon, "That's ok, since you're with a member of law enforcement and all; I think we can skip the paperwork."

"Thanks," Faith said brightly.

"But you still have to follow the range rules," he said, handing her a set of headphones and safety glasses.

Faith looked at them in slight disgust before putting them on. She was disappointed that they'd only be shooting at paper targets, and Alison forbade Faith from making more interesting targets with Vis.

"Ok Faith, you hold the gun like this," Alison said. "Are you paying attention?"

"Yeah, yeah, two hands, right; I got it, squeeze the trigger and point it at the piece of paper," Faith said, holding the gun in front of her. Alison seemed to be hovering. Faith rolled her eyes and turned to her, "Alison, I have loads of wards protecting me. I could shoot myself in the head and not get hurt. Do you want to see?" As she turned to speak, the gun came around, and Alison gently pointed it back down-range.

"No; I don't want to see, and I don't have wards on me, nor do any of the other people here," Alison said nervously.

Faith rolled her eyes again, and pointed the gun down-range. The gun had three little dots she had to line up to hit what she wanted. It was a bit of a pain to do, but Faith finally had the paper man in her sights. She squeezed the trigger. BANG! The gun jerked in her hand, surprising Faith. She didn't drop it, but she looked at it.

"That thing has some fight in it!" she exclaimed.

Alison smiled and laughed, "Yeah, it does."

Faith fired several more shots, emptying the magazine.

"This is fun!" she said, making the target come back to her.

She looked at it. "I hit it ten times," she said to Alison, looking at the bullet holes all over the target. "...how many times did I shoot?"

"Fifteen," Alison said.

Ten out of fifteen didn't sound bad to her.

Alison put up her own target and moved it further down the range than Faith's had been. Alison pushed a button, making the target rush at her; she fired her gun quickly at the moving target. Faith thought it looked fun. When the target came back, her mouth fell open. All of Alison's shots were around where the heart of the target would have been if it were a real person.

She looked at Alison, "I SUCKED!"

Alison laughed hard, "Yeah … yeah Faith, you really did."

Faith put her target back up, "Nope, not gonna happen."

"No using Vis to steady your hand," Alison taunted.

Faith stuck out her tongue and turned back to the range, determined to master shooting.

"Why don't you come over for the evening?" Faith said to Alison as they left the range.

"I don't know …" Alison started.

"Oh, come on. Mandy and Sean are coming, and so are Paul Labus, Maddison, and Amy. Gabriel has some things he wants Paul to look at from the last few raids, so really you can count this as work," Faith said.

Alison looked at her for a while, "You won't drop this until I say yes, will you?"

"Nope."

"Fine," Alison relented, "Let me pack a bag."

Faith rode with Alison back to her condo so she could pack a bag for the night.

"I feel like I'm getting ready for a sleepover, like when I was a kid," Alison said.

"What's a sleepover?" Faith asked.

Alison stopped what she was doing, "Ya know, like when you and all your girlfriends stayed the night at each other's houses when you were kids."

Faith thought for a moment "yeah I'm pulling a blank. Alison I came from a Paladin and Seeker family, we didn't do sleepovers."

"That's too bad," Alison said.

Faith waited for Alison to get ready to go. They were in her living room, and Faith took her hand.

"Are your doors locked?" Faith asked.

"Yes," Alison said, closing her eyes.

Faith snickered. She didn't get Sean and Alison's fear of jumping. Vis welled up in her as she locked onto the house, releasing the power in her. With a bright flash of yellow, the team's house appeared before her.

Alison opened her eyes and sighed, "I do have to admit your way of traveling is pretty fast. You really can't tell me where we are?" Alison asked.

"We are in North America," Faith said with a wink.

She took Alison to her room before leading her back down to the house's living room. There they found all the Mages along with Sean, Mandy, and Paul.

James came up to her, giving her a hug and kissing her, "How was shooting a gun?" he asked.

Faith grinned, "So much fun, we are making a range here," she turned to Gabriel, "you'll love it!"

"Have you ever held a gun?" Sean asked Mandy.

She gave him a look. "I have a concealed carry permit," she said dryly.

"You what? Are you armed right now?" Sean asked, disbelieving.

Mandy looked at him for a moment, and then reached up under her shirt. There was a snap of something, and Mandy held out a little black gun, "Beretta Nano," she said, "twenty bucks says I can out-shoot you, too." she added.

Sean and Alison both looked amazed. For her part, Faith walked over to Mandy to look at her gun.

"It's so small … it's cute; do you keep it in your bra?" Faith asked.

"Nope," Mandy said with a smile, "Well kind of nope; I have a holster that attaches to my bra."

"You just got hotter, you know that?" Sean said to Mandy.

Faith noted that Mandy seemed to like the praise. She turned her attention to the others as Mandy and Sean started to talk trash.

GABRIEL DECOR was in pretty high spirits as everyone got settled in, and they made their way to where James was storing some of the enchanted objects the team had taken from Trinity. Normally the police department wouldn't allow evidence to be kept outside of a station, but in the case of enchanted objects they seemed all too happy to let Gabriel and Faith store them.

James was showing Paul around the many boxes of items.

"So what do you think?" Sean asked him.

"I think you guys have a lot of merchandise … hey, do you think when the case is over the department would be willing to sell this stuff? I'll give you a good price," Paul said.

Sean laughed, "You want this stuff back on the street?"

Paul looked confused, "Yeah. There isn't anything in here that is illegal. Besides, what are you guys going to do with it?"

"What can you tell us about it?" Alison asked, changing the conversation.

Gabriel saw Mandy mouth to Sean, "Goblins are always looking to make a deal."

"Well …" Paul said, looking around, "you have a lot of things here. Not all of them are for anything shady though." He picked up a plate, "Like this. It keeps your food hot."

"Why did they have that?" Sean asked.

"Well, for one thing, if they were housing a lot of Mutari, things like this are going to be common. But also, they sell well, even to Humans. There's no way Trinity is only moving things that are for crime. Goblins just don't think that way, and from what Gabriel has told me, you've been picking up a lot of Goblins." Paul said, "But after dinner, I can take a better look, and maybe separate out regular household items."

"That works," Sean said.

Paul picked up a clock. "No way," he said.

"What is it?" Alison asked.

"It's a detector," James said.

"Yeah, and they sell like nobody's business. Hard to get your hands on them right now. With everyone in the Vis world being on the lookout for the Vieses, they have been buying these things left and right," Paul said, half-disappointed.

"What do they do?" Sean asked.

"I destroyed one at the Vieses' old house," Gabriel said, "It would have let them know the house was under attack."

"Yeah, but you can have them do a bunch of other crap too," Paul said, excited, "Hey James, I've been meaning to ask you something."

"What is it?" James asked.

"Can you make something so that, say, a Troll could jump to a location?" Paul asked.

James made a face, "Yeah, why?"

Paul got all happy-looking, and Gabriel was waiting to hear what his latest business idea was.

"Ok, here's the idea. So Humans have security systems that call the cops when there's a break in, but they aren't that fast." He turned to Alison and Sean, "No offense."

"None taken; we can only get to a house so fast," Sean said.

"See, here's what I'm thinking. Could you make detectors that could tell when someone was around who was going to hurt homeowners?" Paul asked James.

James nodded, "Without a problem."

"Great," Paul said, "Could that same detector then prompt an enchanted object that would then jump a Troll or Trolls to that location?"

"That's pretty smart," Sean said.

Paul pointed at him, "Right! When the bad guy comes in your house, help literally appears out of nowhere."

"Who would you sell this to?" Sean asked, interested.

"Humans," Paul said.

Sean looked down, "There's a problem."

"What? It's not that your kind won't buy Vis stuff. I have a vendor who sells loads of it," Paul said.

"No; not that. The Trolls would probably kill a perp, and that could be a legal nightmare," Sean said.

"Why Trolls?" James asked, coming back to the conversation.

"Who else? No one can afford Mages on call," Paul said.

James shook his head, "I just didn't know if there was a reason. What if it were Guardians that were designed not to kill, but to restrain the intruder until Human law enforcement got there …"

Paul looked like he was going to explode, "YES! James you are a genius … so, could you do it?"

James made a mock look of offense, "Yeah, I could do it."

As the others started asking questions, Gabriel started thinking about Paul's idea. He knew James and Paul were talking about basic Guardians for what Paul would need, but Gabriel was thinking about the possibilities of using more advanced ones. It could mean having everybody on the case protected. What had happened to the Sergeant could have been avoided by simply having a detector at his house. In a way, the team was already using this for Alison and Sean. If they ever got in a tight situation or were feeling an extreme emotion, Alison's necklace and Sean's watch would notify Gabriel and Faith. They would then use those same objects as anchors to jump to them. It had saved Sean and Mandy's lives not long ago.

"You see this is the future of Vis," Paul was saying.

Gabriel perked back up.

"How so?" Sean asked.

"Vis products man," Paul said, "Think about it. Humans would buy stuff like this instead of security systems. Mages make it, and Goblins sell it for a cut of the sticker price, just like we do now. But instead of selling only to Mutari we sell to your race," He said.

"Are there enough Enchanters out there to handle that?" Alison asked curiously.

"Yes," Gabriel said, "there are many more Enchanters and builders than any other type of Mage."

"Really?" Sean asked.

"Yes. Our team may make it look like there are an equal number of Paladins, Seekers, Builders, Enchanters, Healers, and Contractors; but that's not the case. Seekers and Paladins combined make up only ten or fifteen percent of the Mage world. There are even fewer Healers, and Contractors are only slightly more prevalent than Paladins and Seekers," Gabriel explained.

"But I thought it was your families that controlled things," Sean asked.

"There are many prominent families that are Seeker and Paladin families. And in the time of war; yes, we control the Vis world. When there is no threat, no one is in charge. If anyone were, it would probably be the Enchanters and Builders; they are your normal Mages," Gabriel said.

Sean looked like he wanted to ask more questions, but held off. There was a lot of truth to what Gabriel had said. There was no real leader of the Mages, and therefore the Vis world, but he wondered if that would change. The need for Pactum teams was starting to go away, and while for centuries, Seekers were needed to keep Vis from the open; they were not as needed as before. Gabriel wasn't dumb. He knew that despite what he'd said, the big Seeker and Paladin families held more sway than those that weren't. *Will it always be that way?* Yes, he decided. There had always been more Enchanters than Paladins, but on average, Paladins and Seekers were far stronger than any Enchanter. James was in many ways a rarity. Being around Faith made him push himself in ways that most Enchanters didn't. No; Seekers and Paladins would stay at the top of the social ladder, and in a way that saddened Gabriel.

EIGHTEEN

ALISON KAUR woke to the sound of gunshots outside. Her mind snapped into awareness as she rolled out of bed and groped for her gun on the nightstand. After about a month of being a cop, Alison started sleeping with a gun next to her. She crept to the window, trying to peer outside and keep herself from view. It took her mind a moment to realize that she was in the large compound- style house the Mages lived in. Outside were several people facing away from the house.

Alison squinted to look at the figures. Further away from them was a gray statue walking back and forth in a line. There was another bang from a gun. Alison flinched, and then took a harder look at the people as she heard a familiar voice shout, "Take that!"

Holding a pistol Faith was with her brother, her husband, Mandy, and Sean. The figure that was standing away from them was a Guardian. Alison watched Faith fire at the statue again. She wasn't hitting it, but Alison could see she was having a fantastic time trying to. Alison laughed, watching Faith. She got dressed quickly and made her way out to everyone. By the time she reached the group, they had been joined by Erin and her husband Guy. Mandy was shooting now. No one knew Alison was there yet. She stood still, not wanting to distract Mandy. Alison held her hands to her ears as the woman fired. To her surprise, she couldn't hear the shot.

Gabriel turned to her with a smile, "If you're within fifteen feet of the gun, you can't hear it go off," he said to her.

"That's handy," Alison said, approaching the group.

She watched Mandy shoot. No matter how fast the Guardian moved, Mandy always hit it. Alison was impressed. Mandy fired her last round and turned to Sean, "Pay up." Sean looked part annoyed, part in awe as he handed Mandy a $20.

Alison chuckled, "Hughes, did she out-shoot you?"

Sean rounded on Alison, "She'd out-shoot you too." He looked at Mandy, shaking his head, "You sure you aren't using Vis to steady your hand or anything?"

"It's called focus, Sean," Mandy taunted, "I can teach it to you sometime if you want."

Everyone laughed.

"So where are you guys getting the ammo for this?" Alison asked.

Sean looked down guiltily, but Faith grinned and pointed to a pile of ammo that looked like it would have a hard time fitting on a shipping pallet.

"Ho-how how …" Alison sputtered.

Guy piped up, "Ammo is easy to make. Sean and Mandy each gave me a round, and boom! Within about twenty minutes or so, I figured out how to replicate it."

"Look Kaur, I know this is technically illegal or should be if it's not …" Sean started.

"It's against the law to make ammo?" Faith asked, confused.

"No," Sean said, "But most of this stuff here is patented, so making copies of it would be illegal."

"I'm not even mad," Alison said, "Frankly, I'm in awe yet again of what Vis can do. Just don't take it to the range or sell it, all right, guys?"

"We won't; don't worry," Faith said. Then to her husband, "Can you make the Guardian scream when it gets hit?"

"Faith, that's sick," Sean said, choking a laugh.

Faith looked confused, "What? You guys play those video games all the time where people get blown up."

Alison couldn't help but find the Mage entertaining.

She took part in the shooting free-for-all, and then Guy said he'd go to the store and get a box of every different type of ammo he could, so they could practice with whatever they wanted. As they walked back up to the house, Sean said to Alison in a soft voice, "Way to turn them into a bunch of rednecks. As if they weren't dangerous enough with Vis."

Alison laughed, "I know, right? Who would have known they'd have so much fun with it."

SEAN HUGHES sat down, taking out a pad of paper and a pen next to Sergeant Montoya's bed. He clicked the pen and jotted down a few notes and questions he wanted to ask. Even though he was talking to someone he knew; Sean wanted to make sure he did a good job with the interview. They couldn't afford to make any mistakes with Trinity. Sean also placed a recorder down next to Montoya.

The Sergeant looked like he was fully healed, thanks to Erin; but he was still tired, and would need to stay in the hospital at least one more day before he could go home. From there, Sean wasn't sure what would happen. It would take a while before Montoya was cleared for duty, and the department was insisting that he take at least a month off.

"Are you ready?" Sean asked Montoya, and Alison, who was seated next to him. On the other side of the bed were Faith and Gabriel. In the back of the hospital room, Maddison and Amy stood leaning against the wall.

"Yeah, I think I'm ready," Montoya said.

Sean turned on the recorder, "Can you state your name for the record?" Sean asked.

"Philip Roger Montoya," he said.

Sean looked at Gabriel and Faith, "Can you confirm that the man before us is indeed Philip Montoya, and not the Shape Shifter Bryan Harley?"

Both Mages confirmed that it was indeed Montoya before them.

"Can you state your job, and your relationship with Detective Kaur and me, for the record?" Sean asked the Sergeant.

"I am a Sergeant in the Denver Police Department over homicide. Detectives Hughes and Kaur are my subordinates," he said.

Sean was impressed at how steady and clear the Sergeant was being. Perhaps it would be easier to interview a witness who was in law enforcement.

"Do you know why we are talking to you?" Sean asked.

"Yes. I was kidnapped by an organization called Trinity. You are interviewing me for the sake of the case you are working," he said.

"Can you tell me what happened? From the beginning," Sean asked.

Montoya took a deep breath, "Sure. I was attacked in my home by a man named Bryan Harley. He is a Shape Shifter, and was in my house for the purpose of capturing me to then take my place at my job so he could spy on the investigation of Trinity.

"I was drugged in my home; when I woke up, I was in a warehouse. I was tied to a chair, and was introduced to Angelica Vies, Marcus Vies, and Keith Spencer. Later I would speak with several Humans and Mutari along with another Mage named Tracey Hope."

Montoya started to outline how he was kept in a room by himself, where he had limited interaction with people. He said that from time to time, Angelica would ask him questions about his life and events that had taken place. He said that on a few occasions, he gave her false information.

"What happened when you did that?" Alison asked.

Montoya looked down, "Angelica used Vis on me then … I didn't know you could feel pain like that … she did that a lot when I wasn't talking to them, or I tried to resist. A few times they threatened to kill or harm my wife, but it didn't work."

"Why was that?" Sean asked.

"Had they attacked Nancy, it would have gotten the attention of the department, along with Gabriel and Faith. They didn't want that, and I knew it."

"So what happened then?" Sean asked.

Montoya shrugged in his bed, "They used more Vis on me, and beat on me a bit, but for the most part they used Vis."

"Was it always inflicting pain?" Gabriel asked.

Montoya looked at him questioningly. "No … how did you know that?"

"Mages will often affect the emotions of those they are trying to get information from," Gabriel said simply.

Montoya nodded, "They did that. Honestly I think had they stuck to torture, I could have held out. Getting beat up isn't fun, but it's not going to make someone like me fold. It wasn't until after they broke me that I realized they were just hurting me to keep me from thinking about how I felt …" He looked at Sean, "For the first week or so I was with them, they made me feel like I'd never get out. Like I was theirs, and I was going to die in that warehouse, but then I started to feel a little hope, and tha-that's when I lost it." He looked at Sean and Alison, his face strained. "I'm so sorry."

"You have nothing to be sorry for," Alison assured him.

"But I do," Montoya said, "I told them whatever they wanted to know. Eventually, they beat me down far enough physically and emotionally that I was completely theirs." He looked away from them, his eyes dark and in a far-off place, "I told them about the case, the department, and even personal information about anyone working the case. The names of family members, friends … where people lived; you name it."

Sean felt a twinge knowing that Trinity now knew everything about him, including those they could hurt to get to him. He glanced up to Gabriel who mouthed, "We'll talk after." Sean tried to re-focus on the interview. The Sergeant described how he was eventually moved to the location where Gabriel and Maddison found him.

"How long were you there?" Sean asked.

"I don't know; maybe two weeks or so," he said.

"What was Marcus like?" Gabriel asked.

Montoya frowned, "Calm, relaxed. He was extremely collected. Angelica was too, most of the time, but on a few occasions she would lose her cool." Montoya shuddered, "She would take her anger out on me …"

Sean looked down at his notepad, trying not to think about Angelica Vies' anger.

"But Marcus would stop her," Montoya said, looking up at Gabriel, "He doesn't lose his cool, does he?"

Normally no matter how bad the situation was, Gabriel seemed lighthearted and carefree. Not at the moment; his face was a mask of carefully controlled rage.

"No; Marcus Vies is the most controlled man I have ever met," Gabriel said, "What did he say to you?"

Sean was curious to find out more about the Vieses, and how they thought.

"He asked questions mostly," Montoya said. "He talked to me a lot. He would ask me about how the Human world worked, and what I thought of it." He looked at Gabriel quizzically, "He kept asking me what gave Humanity the right to be the dominant race of the world."

Gabriel nodded slightly.

"Does that mean anything to you?" Montoya asked Gabriel.

"Yes actually, it does." He sighed, "Well, now we know why he betrayed the Arks. The Nobilis wanted to rule over the whole world, Human and Mutari alike. They thought it was the role of the powerful to rule over the weak."

Montoya nodded, "You agree."

Gabriel stiffened and then relaxed. "That is how the world is, with the exception of Humans not being part of the rest of the world," Gabriel said, and then asked another question, "What is he planning?"

Montoya's face darkened, "I don't know. But I can tell you this; they are not what we thought they once were. They aren't a group of criminals that created Trinity for money."

Gabriel looked down and started tapping his knee, "Watch the tide," he said to himself.

"Did anything seem off about the place you were held?" Gabriel asked.

Months ago, Sean wouldn't have let Gabriel highjack an interview with a victim, but a voice in him told him to let the Mage work. With the voice, Sean felt goose bumps creep up the back of his neck. Gabriel was onto something.

Montoya started talking about old medical equipment being brought in. He said that Marcus would make Montoya help unload it and put it in the shed, as a reward for talking. He told them that any chance to get out of the house's basement, and a chance to move was worth more to him than anything.

"What type of medical equipment?" Sean asked.

"X-ray and things like that. There was some other equipment; why?" Montoya asked, "Surely when you inspected the property, you saw it. I think they are planning on enchanting it to do something," Montoya said.

Wheels were turning in Sean's head. Lists of items recovered from the last raid scrolled in his mind's eye as little links of events came together in his head. He swore under his breath, and stood up.

"Sean!" Alison said.

"We found fertilizer at that warehouse, Alison, and at the safe house they had a bunch of stuff that's radioactive!" he said.

Alison and Montoya looked confused for a moment before going pale. The room was silent for what seemed like an eternity as the three cops realized what Trinity might be up to.

"What?" Faith asked, frustrated, "Is this what it's like when we don't tell you things?"

"Hughes, why would they want to make a dirty bomb?" Alison asked, "and do you even think they could do it?

"What's a dirty bomb?" Gabriel asked.

"It's a bomb that has a bunch of radioactive stuff in it. The basic idea is that it will make cancer rates go up in an area, and kill a bunch of people. It's not like a nuke; it won't kill millions of people, but as a weapon for terrorists ..." Sean explained.

Sean thought more, then said, "No; it can't be that ... most of the equipment you're talking about was old, and wouldn't have anything radioactive in it anymore," he said, calming down.

"But would Mages know something like that? And what would be their purpose in it?" Alison asked.

ALISON KAUR waited in the silent room, but no one seemed to have an answer for her. Finally, it was Gabriel who spoke.

"Destabilization," he said, almost to himself. His tone was that of someone who has had a grim realization. "Marcus is looking to destabilize the city, or maybe even the country," Gabriel said.

"What purpose would that serve?" Sean asked.

Gabriel stood and started to walk the room. "It makes so much sense ... why Vampires are not investing, why Mutari, and some Mages, are going to ground. They see what is coming," Gabriel said more to himself.

"And what is that?" Faith asked.

Alison felt cold.

"He is trying to shift the relationship between Vis users and Humans. If a criminal organization run by Mages kills a huge amount of people, how would Human society react?"

"They would turn on Vis users," Alison said, having a realization of her own.

Marcus was making a power play. He was looking to turn the world against Vis users; but why?

"How would this help him take control of Humanity?" Maddison asked from the other side of the room.

Gabriel shook his head. "It wouldn't," he said. "At any moment, Vis users could vanish from society. Humans would have no way of finding us." Gabriel said, "All it would take is for Mages to decide that it was time to hide again. We allowed Humans to know about us because we thought we could live together. If Humans turned on us, we would simply hide. Marcus could separate us, and divide us …"

"You think he wants to start another war?" Maddison asked. Alison was slightly bothered that it didn't sound like Maddison found the possibility of another war being so hard to imagine.

Gabriel looked at her, "He might be. But it doesn't fit." Gabriel said urgently, "Marcus could have turned on us at any time during the war if he sympathized with the Nobilis … even now there aren't many who would support them …"

"But if enough Mutari and Mages were killed …" Maddison said.

"That would turn many against Humanity. More than that, leaving society would ruin many in the Vis world. Many of those who opposed the Nobilis have invested heavily into working with Humans," Gabriel said.

Alison was having a hard time keeping up. The conversation had moved from a possible weapon of mass destruction to Vis politics. Add on top of that, she'd just spent an hour hearing about her mentor being tortured. Alison couldn't take any more.

"Enough," she said, "We need to finish interviewing our victim," she said.

Maddison and Gabriel went silent, the latter apologizing.

Alison turned back to Montoya, "Can you remember anything else?"

"Yes," he said, "I could sometimes hear them talking. They are moving drugs. I don't know what drugs they are moving, but they are moving them. They are trying to move more if they can. It also sounds like our raids have been doing a fair amount of damage. They only have a handful of locations left in Denver."

"We found some of those drugs in the warehouse," Sean said, "Is there anything else?"

Montoya thought for a bit, "Not that I can think of right now."

Sean nodded, "Let us know if you do, ok?"

Montoya nodded.

"All right, old man, we will let you get some rest so you can get back to work," Sean said, getting up.

Montoya shook his head, "Sean, I'm not coming back to work."

Sean shrugged off his comment. "We'll see how you feel about that in a month," he said.

FAITH PENN closed the door to Sergeant Montoya's room softly behind her. In the hall, the rest of the team waited.

"We need to make sure your loved ones are protected," Gabriel said in a matter of fact tone.

Faith agreed with him. It was unlikely that Trinity would attack Alison's or Sean's families, but there was a chance.

"How are you going to do that?" Sean asked, "You can't spread yourselves too thin."

"Do you remember what Paul and James were talking about last night?" Gabriel asked.

"Yeah," Sean said.

"I think we should put detectors in your family's houses, and maybe on them. If the detector senses something, a Guardian will go to them. James can make sure the Guardians will do a bit more than just restrain a perp," Gabriel said, "if you don't want to frighten your families, we can plant the detectors on them without them knowing."

No one objected. It was obvious that Sean and Alison both were shaken up about the Sergeant. Faith could understand that. As they left the hospital, Faith sidled up next to Alison, "Are you still planning on staying with us tonight?" she asked.

"Yeah, I think so," Alison said.

It was mid-afternoon, and Faith asked if the detectives were done with work for the rest of the day. Sean said that he was going to type up the notes from their interview with Montoya, but other than that, he didn't have anything to do for the case. This made Faith happy. She knew that very soon, life was going to be changing, and when it did; downtime wasn't going to come around that often. She could tell that Gabriel felt the same way by the way he was carrying himself. Faith wasn't anxious about the future. She was doing the best she could, and that was that. *Hopefully, Gabriel is wrong, and Trinity isn't trying to destroy the years of work that Vis users and Humans had put into building a relationship,* she thought.

NINETEEN

SEAN HUGHES walked into the conference room at a fast clip, the other members of the team behind him. His mind was racing. Trinity was a huge threat, this he'd known for some time. He also knew Trinity had been into arms dealing on a small scale. Possibly making dirty bombs was completely different, however. *They aren't making them,* Sean reminded himself. But they were selling what people needed to make them, which was almost as much a threat as if they had been making them for their own use.

"We need to get our crap together," Sean said, pacing around the room, not wanting to sit down.

Sean didn't like having to wait to get back to the station to talk, but they couldn't afford for Trinity to overhear any of the team's planning.

Agent Alesbury had joined them. "First we need to figure out what their intentions are," he said.

"Why?" Sean asked, "We know that they are planning to sell the parts needed for weapons of mass destruction. Or they are planning on using them. Don't we need Homeland Security for this?" Sean asked, trying not to sound agitated.

"There's a big difference, Sean." Alesbury said calmly, "If we think that Trinity is planning on using them, then yes; we need to get Homeland Security in the loop, but even then the FBI will do the heavy lifting. On the other hand, if they are only planning on selling what could be used, that's different. For all we know, they were planning on modifying that medical equipment for some other purpose. A team from the FBI has been over there, and did not find high amounts of radiation from the equipment. Whoever Trinity got it from had done their job and made sure the equipment was harmless."

That did make Sean feel slightly better. Being run by Mages, Trinity's major weakness was not understanding the Human world. They'd likely heard of what a dirty bomb was, and in essence how to make one, but didn't understand enough to make an effective bomb.

"But what's with the fertilizer?" Sean asked, thinking about containers of fertilizer that had been found in the raid of the warehouse. At the time, Sean hadn't thought anything of it, but now?

"That points to them selling it," Alesbury said, "think about it. If Trinity was going to make a dirty bomb, would they actually need Human explosives?"

Sean looked to Gabriel, who gave a "he has a point," shrug.

Everything Alesbury was saying made sense to Sean, and as he thought about it, he became more convinced that Trinity was planning on selling parts for a bomb. *Parts that for the most part won't work*. He relaxed.

"So dealing, then?" Alison said.

Alesbury nodded, "Yes; they have a lot of guns, we know that from our raids."

"No," Gabriel said, "I think they want to attack."

Everyone looked at him.

"I agree with Alesbury about the fertilizer," Gabriel said, "I don't think they need that for a bomb. Selling that makes sense to me. But as for the equipment … I think they are doing something of their own."

"I don't know, Gabriel …" Alison started.

"Trust me," he said urgently, "Marcus Vies is no thug; he has a bigger plan. The whole of the Vis world sees it."

"Look, in general your input seems to be spot on," Alesbury said, "but in this case, I don't think the evidence points to some master plan of theirs. I think Trinity sees an opportunity with arming people, and possibly even arming terrorists, both foreign and domestic."

"I agree with Gabriel," Maddison said, "I think Marcus is looking to shift public view of Vis."

Sean thought about it for a moment. Conspiracy theories sounded great in books and movies, but not in real life. Furthermore, to do what Gabriel and Maddison were suggesting was a lot harder than it sounded. A single attack on Americans would not galvanize the world into hating Vis users.

"It wouldn't work," Sean said, "Think about it." He urged, "Say you're right, and they are trying to shift the population's views. Let's say they attack some major city with a dirty bomb; what would that do to the world's views on Vis? Nothing. It would make headlines for a few months, and people inside the US would be frightened. Maybe even here in the US, Vis users would need to go into hiding. But around the world? The rest of the planet would forget about the attack in a week, two tops."

Gabriel deflated a bit, "I suppose you're right."

GABRIEL DECOR could tell that he was not winning over the Humans, and could he blame them? Their world was so much different from his. If he wasn't able to get Alison, Sean, and Alesbury on board with thinking that Trinity was a terrorist group, that was fine; he would do his best to get them to hunt them down as arms dealers.

"So we are agreed there is no danger of an attack?" Gabriel said.

He noticed Maddison give him a look. He met her eye and gave an almost imperceptible nod. Her stance relaxed.

"Yes," Maddison said a little stiffly. "What do we do from here?" she asked the room.

The cops looked thoughtful for a bit.

"We need to stop looking for locations," Faith said.

"And how will not looking for the enemy help us, Penn?" Sean asked sarcastically.

Faith gave him a cold look before speaking, "I didn't say we shouldn't look for the enemy; I said we shouldn't look for locations anymore. The Sergeant made it sound like we'd hit most of the locations here in Denver, but the Vieses are still holding to this area. I think this is their center of command. The people we are getting in safe houses and other locations have no clue where the leadership is. Montoya said that Marcus all but talked down to him about Humans, do you truly think that any of the Human staff knows where the real headquarters for Trinity is?"

Everyone was silent. Faith was right. They needed to rethink how they were hunting.

"What about Mutari?" Alesbury asked, "Would any of them know?"

"I don't think so," Amy said, "from what we've been able to gather, there is at least one Goblin Guild that is ignoring all of this. If a guild is ignoring things, that can only mean either a high-ranking guildsman or Vampires."

"Vampires for sure," Maddison said. "If they aren't helping run things directly, they are bankrolling Trinity."

"So this means we can't keep raiding locations because Mutari won't talk?" Sean asked, confused.

"It means that the people we are working with will have had only a little contact with middle management. Anyone who could connect us with the head of Trinity is going to be too shielded for us to ever find. Trinity members see Marcus and Angelica on a regular basis, and know they are the heads. This would keep people in line, but as far as the day-to-day management of Trinity ... we will never find those people, or at least not enough of them to do any damage," Gabriel said.

"What makes you so sure?" Alesbury asked.

Gabriel shrugged, "We used similar techniques in the war. Marcus was a master of making an organization near impossible to infiltrate. During the war, countless groups on our side were breached; but the way Marcus had everything set up, not only did the Nobilis spies not find out anything that helped their side, but we were able to find them quickly and easily." Gabriel explained, "He set things up so well even when we took a significant loss, it didn't drastically affect our forces as a whole."

FAITH DECOR watched Gabriel as he spoke, his eyes like glass as he looked off to a time she had trouble remembering. She was struck by what a team Angelica and Marcus were. What Gabriel spoke of sounded like the perfect brainchild of a Seeker and Paladin working seamlessly together. Faith no longer doubted that she could beat Angelica Vies, but part of her wondered, *will Gabriel and I ever be that effective as a team?* Marcus and Angelica were married, which would make one think that they would be the perfect team. But Gabriel and Faith were brother and sister. They'd known one another their entire lives. *We can and will be a better team than they,* Faith told herself, *now that I am pulling my weight, it will happen.* There was a peace to this realization.

"So how do you want to go about this, then?" Alesbury asked.

"Amy and I will focus on the highest-ranking people we know of," Faith said, "We will directly hunt Tracey Hope, Keith Spencer, Angelica Vies, and Marcus Vies."

"Aren't you already looking for them?" Alison asked.

"We haven't been dedicating one hundred percent of our resources to it. We have been looking for safe houses and various leads." Faith looked over to Amy, "Besides, Amy has come a long way in broad Seeking in a very short time. I'm certain the two of us can come up with a plan to find at least one of the Mages. I don't think it likely that we will be able to find the Vieses as they have been in hiding for so long. But as for Keith and Tracey . . ."

"You think there's a solid chance of getting a line on them?" Sean asked, not sounding convinced. "And what about tracking the weapons they are selling?"

Faith tried not to be put out that the detectives were not on board with her. *Convince them,* she said to herself.

"Now that we have hit so many locations, Keith and Tracey will have to start taking a direct approach to protecting what Trinity has left. I think if we find them, we will be able to find a lot more than weapons. Those two must know the location of every Trinity safe house in the country." Faith said, and then seeing that Alesbury didn't look overly convinced; sighed and said, "Or if you aren't comfortable with that, Amy can search out new locations to hit, and I can focus on the Mages."

This seemed to get a few more nods of approval from the others.

"I like that idea," Alesbury said, "Kaur, Hughes, thoughts?"

Both detectives shrugged. Alison said, "I think this seems like a good plan. I hate to lose Faith on finding locations, but at the same time we have to start looking for those two Paladins. They have been a headache for us from the word go. Getting one of them could turn this case for us. I think it's worth losing Faith for a bit."

"Personally, I'm with Faith," Sean said, surprising her "we've been taking out little bits and pieces of Trinity, and we need to strike its head and set it down for good. We do that, and we won't need to find safe houses."

"Decor?" Alesbury asked.

Gabriel looked passive, "We are under Pactum with you. Whatever you want to do is what we will do. As for my input, I would like to dedicate one hundred percent of our Seekers' efforts to finding the largest threat, which in this case is Trinity's Mages; and the weapon they are developing or selling."

His tone was calm like he always was, but Faith noted the slightest lack of command to it that there should have been. *He's not telling us everything he's thinking,* Faith realized, *he doesn't care about what is going on here … he has other plans.* Her brother was moving independently of what the department was doing. Or was planning on it. Faith also noted that Maddison was not being a dominant force in the conversation either. *She's with Gabriel.* The others in the room didn't seem to notice Gabriel's lackluster attitude about their current plan.

"It's decided, then," Alesbury said. "Faith, you will take looking for the Mages; Amy, you will look for locations, and the rest of us will work as normal." He addressed Alison and Sean, "I want you two to track down everything you can. I want to hinder these bastards."

Faith zoned out, not focusing on the room or conversation. The nice part of being a Seeker was that people expected you to not pay strict attention all of the time. Faith checked a few wards and spells, but for the most part she just relaxed her mind.

"Faith, it's time to go," Gabriel said.

"Ok," Faith replied.

She said her goodbyes to everyone for the night, and told them she might not be in for the next few days or if she was; she might not be around a lot. Once they were out of the station, Maddison spoke to Gabriel.

"What is the real plan?" she asked.

Amy looked a little surprised, but didn't say anything.

"How are your parents?" Gabriel asked.

"Fine," Maddison said.

"I'm glad to hear that. I ask, because my father has been meaning to contact them recently … you know, to catch up," Gabriel said.

Maddison nodded and Amy looked even more confused.

"I'll let them know to be expecting a call," Maddison said.

MADDISON BELDAME stood in front of the Decor's home. On her right side stood Amy; on her left her parents. The front door opened and Edward Decor stepped from the house to greet Maddison's mother Olivia, taking her hand. Her mother was slightly tall for a woman, and had long, curly blonde hair, elegant features; her eyes a deep red.

"Olivia," Edward said in greeting, "it is so wonderful to see you." Greeting her first was the custom.

He turned to Maddison's father, Matthew. He was tall with a square face and kind eyes. Edward greeted him with a handshake, clapping him on the shoulder. Next, Edward greeted Maddison, and then Amy. Melinda came outside, welcoming their guests in the same order, as did Gabriel and Faith.

"Please come into our home," Melinda said, ushering Olivia through the door.

Maddison fell in step beside Gabriel, following his parents to the dining room. There was a table with glasses, and a plate of snacks in the center. Edward uncorked a bottle of wine and poured everyone a glass.

Amy made to motion to decline hers, but Maddison gently stopped her and whispered, "Take the wine."

Amy looked uncomfortable, but took the glass.

On one side of the table was the Decor family, and on the other side, the Beldames. The two families exchanged a few pleasantries for a moment before Maddison's mother spoke.

"So Edward, you contacted me as one head of family to another; you say we have important matters to discuss," she said conversationally.

The Decors and Beldames had a long reputation for being friendly with one another. Maddison knew that her parents and Gabriel's parents were extremely close friends, and had been their whole lives. It sounded odd for them to speak so formally.

"I don't suppose this is about a potential union between our two families, which is long overdue," Matthew said.

Maddison's face flushed with embarrassment.

Melinda smiled, "Sadly no; it's not ..." she looked at her son, "but we could always change that."

"Yes," Maddison's mother said, "Maddison has always had a crush on you, my boy," she said to Gabriel.

Maddison felt her heart stop as her mother went on, "Don't you think she's pretty? You two would make a wonderful couple, you know."

"Yes, Gabriel, that's right," Melinda piped in, "don't you think Maddison is a pretty girl? You always tell me how much you enjoy being around her. What's the hold-up?"

Gabriel spluttered, "We- well, it's not that ... I I just. I mean to say, Maddison is very good looking." His eyes bugged out, and he looked at Maddison, "Not that I've been looking at you in an inappropriate way."

"What a shame," Matthew said in a dry voice.

Maddison wanted to disappear.

Both sets of parents laughed good naturedly, and Maddison's mother spoke, "Oh Melinda, we should move back to the States. I miss tormenting our children together, don't you?"

"That I do," Melinda said with a smile.

There was a pause, and Olivia addressed Edward, "But on a serious note, may I ask what the topic of conversation for the night is?"

Edward took a sip of wine, "While I may be the official head of the Decor family, Gabriel is truly the acting head. This meeting tonight was at his request."

Olivia turned her gaze to Gabriel, and inclined her head in respect, "When an Ark calls a meeting, one would be wise to take it seriously."

"Thank you, Olivia," Gabriel said.

Maddison felt herself squirm on the inside. She still felt embarrassed, but all signs of Gabriel's embarrassment were gone. He was holding himself with dignity and honor. He was in command of the room; there was no denying it. Her heart skipped a beat, and her mind played with unbidden thoughts of how happy she would have been if the meeting tonight really was about joining the two families.

"Marcus Vies is on the move," Gabriel said with authority, "I have it on good word that Vampires have been pulling out of the market and are readying themselves for hard times. We also have discovered that Trinity, the organization the Denver Police Department and the FBI are investigating has been gathering supplies to make what Humans call a dirty bomb."

"I've heard of them," Matthew said, "My spies in the State Department for this country have relayed that the Human government fears these dirty bombs for their ability to instill fear in the populous."

AMY CALAMUS tried not to show her surprise as Matthew Beldame said that he had spies in the US State Department. The Beldames were a large and powerful family; it was natural that they kept a finger on what was going on in the world.

"I think Marcus is going to use these bombs to try to destabilize Human and Vis user relations," Gabriel said.

"But not by only attacking one city," Olivia said.

"No, I agree," Gabriel said, "he might be planning a more extensive attack than that, but I don't think he has the resources to accomplish an attack in enough places around the world to truly destabilize what we have built."

"I have our spies checking to see what they can find out. We have Mage teams that have been working with both the US and British Secret Services," Edward said, "they are Seekers the Services has paid to keep an eye out for assassination attempts, but they are also branch families, and are reporting to me."

Amy again tried not to show her surprise. The Decors and the Beldames had managed to infiltrate the top levels of at least two Human governments, and in the case of the Decors, they were even getting paid for it. *I wonder what the other prominent families are doing?* Not being from a prominent Seeker or Paladin family, Amy wasn't used to the role the families played. She could see now that those families were ever-vigilant, always looking for danger on the horizon. The rest of the Vis world didn't see this. They weren't privy to the secret meetings of the heads of houses. Nor were other families as organized as Seeking and Paladin families. *How many disasters and threats have these families shielded the rest of the Vis world from without us even knowing?* She refocused on the conversation.

"It is possible that Marcus wants to use Denver as a testing ground. Perhaps by slowly attacking cities around the world, he will be able to hold them in fear," Gabriel said.

"Or this dirty bomb could be only one of the weapons he is going to use. Perhaps a combination of attacks around the world could be his plan using a variety of methods," Olivia said. "Why are you talking to us, Gabriel?" she asked abruptly, "Is it because Maddison is on this case, and you feel it wise to keep us in the loop?"

"We need your help," Gabriel said, "My father has the commitment of the Decor branch families, but we need the Beldames. Will you join with us?"

Olivia Beldame looked more serious than Amy had ever seen her as she considered Gabriel's request. She looked at her daughter; Olivia's red eyes focusing on Maddison, and then they shifted to Amy. Amy didn't look away from Olivia's piercing gaze, though she wanted to. She seemed to make a decision.

She turned back to Gabriel, "Yes." Then she said to Maddison, "Edward is right to transfer his authority to the most powerful Paladin in his family. I will follow his example; until the time I say otherwise or until you die, you are the acting head of the Beldame family. Do what you will with me and your father, as well as the branch families."

Amy could almost see Maddison's shoulders sink with the weight of the mantle that Olivia had just placed on her, but she did not break. Maddison didn't even flinch. Amy was in awe of her friend. Never before had she understood what it was to be from a prominent family. She'd never seen the weight they carried. She soon would. As Maddison's Seeker, Amy would now be in charge of all of the Beldame branch family Seekers.

Maddison looked to Gabriel, "What are your orders?"

FAITH PENN tried to calm her mind. The meeting with the families was over, and Amy was with Faith in the study of the Decor house.

"So what do you want me to do?" Amy asked, slightly timid. "Are we planning on violating our Pactums with the police and FBI?"

"No, we aren't. We are just going to be doing more than what's in the Pactums. I want you to start looking for radioactive material," Faith said, "You should be able to find a sample fairly easily. From there, I want you to start looking for it around the city. When you find some, investigate to make sure it's not a threat."

"So you want me to look for a bomb?" Amy asked.

Faith nodded, "Yes, I think this will be the best way to accomplish our goals. By looking this way, if you find a large pocket of radioactive material that shouldn't be there; it's likely you will have found a Trinity location."

Amy said she understood.

"And the Beldames?" Amy asked.

Faith thought for a moment, "Trinity is spread around the world. We need to start looking for them. If you have anyone that is on Pactum, leave them be, but if you have Seekers that aren't, have them try to find Trinity where they can. It will be up to Gabriel to decide whether or not to move on those locations, but for now, tell them to keep an eye out."

Amy looked uncomfortable.

"What's bothering you?" Faith asked.

Amy sighed, "I don't know … I've just never been good at telling people what to do. I also kind of never thought I would be involved in anything more than working Pactums, ya know?"

Faith honestly didn't know. Some of her early memories were during the war. For Faith, the current dealings were an inevitability; she'd always known at some point in time that she was going to be actively hunting the Vieses.

"I'm sorry Amy; I don't," Faith said honestly, "For me, this is what my life was always going to be. I can understand feeling like you are in over your head, though."

"What if I screw up?" Amy asked.

"You will," Gabriel said, coming into the room with Maddison. "We all make mistakes," he continued, "it's not about what you mess up, but how you recover from your mistakes."

Gabriel turned to Faith, "Do you have a plan?"

"It's in the making, but for the most part; yes. I have Amy and the Beldame Seekers looking for Trinity locations around the world, unless you would like them to focus their search to the US," Faith said.

Gabriel thought for a moment, "No, I don't want that. Have them search the whole world. If we can prove that Marcus is working around the globe, we may be able to garner support from other families and former Arks."

"I am planning on looking for Trinity Mages," Faith said.

"And with the Decor Seekers?" Gabriel asked.

"There are still many Mages out there who fought with the Nobilis, and others who had parents and family members who were with the Nobilis. I am going to have our Seekers start to track them down and keep tabs on them," Faith said, "Is there a plan of attack you have that you want me to prepare for?"

Gabriel shook his head, "I want to get a better idea of what Marcus is going to do. I like where you are going though," he said to Faith, "If we are able to find the bulk of their organization, we can take it out in one swoop and cripple them. Also, by looking for former Nobilis supporters, we will have a better idea of who is supporting Trinity."

Faith beamed on the inside at the praise. *You and Gabriel are as effective as Angelica and Marcus.* She thought with pride.

"I am going to have Makina and some of the other Mutari helping me here in town. We will keep heavy pressure here in Denver. My hope is they will not figure out we are looking into their organization around the world," Faith said.

Gabriel nodded, "Good. As for them not knowing about us looking into them, I do not think we will be that lucky. Unless I am mistaken, Marcus would be highly surprised to find out that we haven't been working on a global level already."

TWENTY

SEAN HUGHES fired ten rounds in rapid succession as the paper target flew towards him. His gun clicked empty, and he pulled out a marker. The Target stopped right in front of him. It was a silhouette of a person. Sean circled his latest bullet holes. It had been over a month since they'd rescued Sergeant Montoya, and Sean was getting frustrated with the lack of progress on the case.

He reloaded the magazine, and slid it back into his gun, a Glock 23. He moved the target back down-range, and took aim. This time he didn't have the target come towards him. TAT TAT TAT *what am I missing?* TAT TAT TAT *is it possible that Trinity has gone to ground? That they are keeping a low profile for a while?* TAT TAT TAT TAT. No, he decided. Trinity wasn't keeping a low profile; the team was just out of leads. The Glock was empty, and Sean repeated the process of marking the target. He was starting to feel a little worthless. With the team not having much in the way of leads, they'd been tracking down older leads that hadn't been promising at the time, in hopes of picking up a trail on Trinity. Gabriel had suggested that Sean and Alison take the time to hone their skills and to prepare for when Faith or Amy found something.

That was fine and dandy for Gabriel. Sean admired the man for his patience; it wasn't a quality that Sean possessed. Gabriel had been hunting the Vieses for a decade; he'd bided his time, and knew that the time would come when he would get a line on them. Sean needed to think the same way. Time would end up helping the case. Sooner or later, someone with Trinity would slip up in some way. Sean and Alison had a few people of interest that they had yet to track down. What would happen sooner or later is that one of those people would do something small and dumb, like get pulled over for speeding. When that happened, the case would start to move again.

Sean swapped out the silhouette target with a cheesy zombie one. The picture was of a green man covered in blood and gore. They were popular targets, not because they were better at teaching you how to shoot; but who didn't want to shoot the occasional zombie? Sean sent the target down-range.

"Seriously, Hughes?" Alison said, poking her head into his stall, "a zombie target?"

Sean looked back at her with a smile and shrugged. Alison shook her head, disappearing behind the little wall separating their stalls. Sean unloaded on the target, having more fun than he probably should have. He was out of bullets. He put the Glock back in its case, and went behind Alison to watch her finish off her box of ammo. Alison was an incredible shot. Sean was always impressed watching her shoot.

When she was done, they left the range. "Wanna grab some lunch?" he asked.

"Sure why not; The Oven?" she asked.

Sean said that was fine. It was starting to get nicer outside, and despite Sean's poor mood about the case, it was hard for him to stay upset with the mild day. The sun was out, making it feel warm in the light, and the sky was a pale blue. The air still held a bite of winter to it, but overall it was a wonderful day.

The Oven was Alison's favorite pizza place. Sean and Alison ordered their food, and they started talking.

"Have you talked to Faith this week?" Sean asked.

Alison nodded, "Yes, the other night she came over for a bit to have a drink."

Sean smiled, "Look at you. Someone might think you have a social life."

Alison rolled her eyes, "Yeah, I'm trying. Why did you want to know?"

He finished a bite of pizza, "I haven't seen her in a few days … heck, I hardly see her at all anymore, and when I do, she's like when we first met ya know? She's in the room with you, but not really."

"I guess while we have been bored, the Seekers haven't been," Alison said, "Faith told me that she's been working nearly non-stop, and so has Amy." Alison said.

Sean could understand having a lot of work to do, but the thought of using Vis to find people, and to fight, still gave him a sense of awe. He knew that Amy and Faith were doing things that he couldn't even grasp. It also made him feel a little useless. They gave each other a hard time, but he and Faith respected each other and the other person's skills a great deal. Sean knew that Faith could do in an hour what took him a week. To think of her having to work constantly and still not getting anywhere made him wonder what he could ever do.

"What are you thinking?" Alison asked.

"Nothing," he said, and then, "do you … do you ever feel a bit like a rookie being around Faith and Gabriel? Like you don't honestly have a clue of what's going on around you?"

Alison laughed lightly, "Every day," she shook her head, "The things those two have done, and seen … I just can't get my head around it. Especially Gabriel. Every time I hear more about him and his past, and from what I've seen … the Mages are so different from us."

"All Mutari and Mages seem to be that way," Sean said.

"Even Mandy?" Alison asked.

"Yep," Sean said, "Her views on the world are so much different than anyone I've ever met … well, I shouldn't say that. Her views on Humans, and Human society. She lives in the city around us, goes to the same stores, the same schools, but she's not actually with us, if you know what I mean." He shrugged, "That's what makes her so fascinating to me."

"Have you told her how you feel?" Alison asked smugly.

Sean became defensive, "What are you saying?"

Alison sat back in her chair, rolling her eyes again.

"Fine," Sean relented, "I guess there's no point trying to hide something from your partner, especially when she's a cop. No, I haven't. I don't want her to feel uncomfortable around me. Her wellbeing is way more important to me than her knowing how I feel."

"I can see that," Alison said, going back to her food.

He chuckled, "What, no sisterly advice?"

Alison raised her eyebrows, "I haven't been in a relationship since college, Hughes; do you honestly want advice from me?"

Sean thought about it for a moment. "Yeah, you've got a point," he said lightheartedly.

MADDISON BELDAME raised Vindictam above her head, blocking Gabriel's sword Iram. She pushed Vis into her lower body, pivoting, moving away from him. She tried to move behind him, faking an attack on his back with Vindictam. She was blocked. "Retro," she breathed, flying backwards in a flash of blue Vis.

"Aer ignis!" she barked, slashing Vindictam. The space before her filled with blue flames as the air itself lit on fire. *Movere,* she thought, moving to the side. Gabriel wouldn't be stopped by the fire, but he couldn't see her through it. She was finally going to get the drop on him. Lavender filled her vision, and her wards strained. Maddison raised her blade, sending Vis out of it to block Gabriel's attack. She stumbled back. Her own fire spell was blocking her view now. She extinguished it. As the flames vanished, Gabriel came into view, Iram rushing towards her head. Vindictam caught Iram, Maddison pushed Vis into her arms and shoulders, holding back his attack. Gabriel's hand thrust forward, hitting her in the gut and knocking the wind from her. Maddison tumbled backwards.

She landed on her side and rolled, coming back up on her feet *I had no idea he was this powerful!* Maddison was used to winning. Even in the last few months, she'd beaten him a few times in training, but not today. *He was holding back before,* she realized. Part of her knew that he was still holding back.

She gritted her teeth, letting Vis tear through her. She moved forward, slashing with Vindictam.

An hour later, Maddison sat on the ground covered in sweat, her hair sticking to the back of her neck. Next to her, drinking a bottle of water was Gabriel. She was happy to see that he looked tired as well. Maddison took a long pull on her own bottle of water. She closed her eyes and rested her head on the wall behind her. She breathed deeply, playing back the fight with Gabriel in her mind.

"You've been holding out on me," she accused.

He chuckled, "Yeah … I have."

She looked over at him, "So? How'd I do?"

Gabriel looked at her with a small smile, "You did well."

"Were you testing me?" she asked.

He closed his eyes, resting his head on the wall. "More myself," he admitted, "I haven't fought anyone up to Ark level in years," he said.

Maddison felt a flutter inside of her when he said *Ark level.*

"So are you saying I'm at Ark level?" she asked.

He sighed, "If the Arks were formed today, you would be one of us." He was matter of fact, "I would say … sixth seat, if I'm not mistaken."

"Stella was eighth," Maddison said, referring to her sister.

Gabriel nodded, "You are more powerful than she was, and more skilled. Though she was better at Vis flow than you are currently."

"Thank you," Maddison said, honored.

Maddison didn't know what to think. She'd been dominated by Gabriel, and yet he was saying that she was one of the top Paladins in the world. She wondered, "Have you progressed now that you don't have anyone to pit yourself against?" she asked.

"Yes, I have. I may not have had an equal to train with on a regular basis, but I have not stopped working as hard as I did before, or during the war. I am more powerful than Marcus was during the war," he said, without a hint of boasting, "but Marcus will be stronger now as well."

Gabriel stood up, offering her a hand. Maddison took it, lifting herself. He told her that they were going to work on Vis output exercises.

FAITH PENN felt a bead of sweat roll down her back as she focused on keeping her Vis output high. *I'm stronger than you,* she thought to herself. Angelica was fighting hard. She relished the exertion in a way she never thought she would. She no longer saw Angelica as her superior; but her equal, if not her inferior. The two Seekers were going toe-to-toe, and Faith felt the more experienced Seeker become weak. It would only be a matter of time before Faith would win.

Currently, Angelica was trying to break Faith's defenses. *I will not let you win.* In so many ways, the battle was pointless, and a waste of energy. Unwittingly, Angelica was trying to find the physical specs of a dummy location Faith had setup. She could let the other woman break down her spells just to find that she'd uncovered a tree on the north side of town, but Faith wanted to beat Angelica. She was going to make the woman respect and fear her.

Waves of energy crashed into the tree's concealment spells. Angelica was using a broad Seeking technique that Faith didn't bother trying to deflect. After what seemed like hours, Angelica gave up. Faith waited for Angelica's attack to resume, or for one of her other defenses to be tested, but they weren't. Faith opened her eyes, and looked to Amy who sat next to her.

Amy looked worried, and even a little scared. Faith smiled, "Are you ok?"

"Are you?" Amy asked, concerned, "I could feel your Vis … it was incredible … are we in danger?"

"No; there's no way she could breach the team house's defenses. She was attacking one of my decoy locations … it was a cottonwood," Faith explained.

"You have been sitting here for two hours exerting yourself to defend a tree?" Amy asked, sounding worried about Faith's sanity.

"Yes, and now Angelica not only thinks she found a critical location, but she also knows that I can beat her," Faith said.

Amy didn't question her, but Faith could tell that she still thought Faith was nuts. Faith took a moment to check all of the real locations she was protecting, which was mostly a collection of the homes of the Mutari who were helping the team. None of them were under attack.

"I'm sorry to keep you waiting Amy," Faith said. They had been in a meeting when Angelica had attacked, "What were we talking about?"

"The Beldame progress with Trinity," Amy said.

"Right. What have you found out?" Faith asked.

Amy didn't look happy, "Nothing yet. We think we have found a few possible locations, but for the most part we haven't found anything useful."

Faith wasn't surprised to hear this. It had only been by chance that they'd found out Trinity to begin with.

Amy and Faith met up with Maddison and Gabriel, who both looked tired.

"You two look tired," Faith said, and then added, "Working on a niece or nephew for me to play with?"

Maddison turned red, and Gabriel laughed, "What have you been doing? You look a little beat yourself," he asked her.

"I'll have you know I just overpowered Angelica Vies," Faith said, proud.

Gabriel smiled, "Good, were you protecting something or trying to find something?"

"I protected a tree," Faith said.

Gabriel laughed heartily, "Well done, Faith. Are you going to let her find it the next time she looks?"

"I wasn't planning on it. I figured she would think she'd found something of interest," Faith said.

Gabriel shook his head, "Think of your enemy; when does she make mistakes?"

"When she's angry," Faith said, "The next time she looks, I won't put up much of a fight. I don't think she'll appreciate how much effort she put into something that didn't matter." Discovering that she'd been spending so much energy on a tree would just enrage Angelica.

"That she won't," Gabriel said.

SEAN HUGHES was watching over Paul as he finished cataloging the last of the Vis objects the team had taken.

"You know, if you let me sell some of this stuff, the department wouldn't have to pay me," he said.

"Always trying to make a deal, aren't you?" Sean asked.

Paul shrugged, "I'm a Goblin."

Sean sat on an old chair and took out his phone to play a game. A question came to him.

"Hey Paul, I'm curious … what's Vis society like?" Sean asked.

"What do you want to know?" he asked, "That's like me asking you to explain everything about being a cop."

"How do you live in such a violent society?" Sean asked.

Paul stopped what he was doing and looked at Sean, "What do you mean? Vis society isn't that violent. We don't even have as much crime as you do."

Sean gave him a look, "Come on, I've seen what Mutari and Mages are like."

Paul shook his head with a smile, "No man, you've seen what Gabriel's team is like, and Trinity."

"That isn't par for the course?" Sean asked.

"No man; are you serious? I heard about that train yard raid. Come on man, you have been around some of the best of the best." He pulled up a chair, "Ok how many Mutari did you all kill at the train yard? Or Hell; total in this case."

Sean thought for a moment, "I don't know. Off the top of my head, a lot."

"Ok, and how many Humans have been killed? Not on our side, but theirs."

"Loads," Sean admitted, "It's been excessive to be honest; normally we try to avoid having to kill suspects."

"Ok, and how many casualties has our side taken?" Paul asked.

"I don't know … a couple people at the train yard and … that's it. We've had a few people get hurt," Sean said.

"Don't you find that a little odd? Come on man, you can't be that dense," Paul said.

Sean was about to get defensive when he thought about it. When he thought about it, his side hadn't taken hardly any casualties.

"So Gabriel's team is above average?" Sean asked.

"Average doesn't touch it; even those obnoxious Banshees are top notch. Gabriel doesn't really work with people who aren't good at what they do. Even those with Trinity are above average, and they haven't stood a chance against Gabriel's people. Look, most Vis users aren't that good at using their power. They just don't have the Vis flow or Vis output to hold a candle to Gabriel," Paul said, and then added, "Gabriel Decor is the best Paladin in the world man, and if Faith isn't the top Seeker, she is right up there. Gabriel's a freaking legend in our world."

"So most Mutari aren't that violent?" Sean asked, "And you said you don't have as much crime as we do. How is that? Are there cops?" Sean asked.

"No man, most Mutari are normal people … well, normal for us; but they aren't mean or violent. I thought Gabriel took you guys to Domum? Did that look like a sketch place? As for crime, we are a little different than Humans. We don't have the legal system that you guys have," Paul shook his head. "Honestly man, I don't know how you guys come up with so many laws."

"What, so everyone is just sweet and nice, and they don't rob stores or anything? And yeah, Domum was nice," Sean admitted.

Paul laughed, "No, everyone isn't sweet and nice. I have a Troll in my shop man, would you try to knock off a place with a Troll in it?"

Sean was brought up short, "No, I wouldn't. But there has to be some crime."

"Sure there's some; if someone is a real piece of crap we do have jails, but for the most part, Mages are able to keep the real scum under control," Paul said, "But aside from that, Mutari take a much more practical approach to personal safety."

"What do you mean by 'personal', and what if the Mages get out of line?" Sean countered.

"Well, most Mutari can do a lot of damage if they want. But that aside; most of us are armed, and we really aren't into being victims, man. As for the Mages, if one of them needed to be put down, a Paladin takes care of it," Paul said.

Sean sat back, "You just off them?"

"If they are killing people and stuff, yeah; does that surprise you?" Paul said. He looked at Sean, then nodded, "I get it, you keep comparing everyone to Gabriel and Maddison. I can see why you're confused now. Look man, the strongest Enchanter in the world doesn't have half the Vis output of any Ark. Heck; most of the Decor branch family members have a higher Vis output than eighty percent of the Mages out there."

Sean was confused, "What's Vis flow and output you keep talking about?"

"Ask Mandy. Succubi and Vamps have incredible Vis flow control. Look dude, I want to get this done. Just know that Gabriel and Faith are both prodigies. If you want to have a better idea of how special they are, the next time Erin is in the office talk to her about it," Paul said.

He got up and went back to his work, leaving Sean to stew over what he'd said.

After leaving work, Sean drove to Mandy's apartment with a bag of Thai food.

"How are you?" she asked, letting him in.

"Good; how was your day?"

"Fine, what's for dinner?" she asked.

"Drunken Noodles -- do you like them?"

Mandy looked happy, "You are a mind reader."

They sat down to dinner, and Sean couldn't help but think how much this was starting to feel like a routine. Mandy had become his best friend. Gone, it seemed, were the evenings of trying to pick up women, and late nights. Now he spent most evenings with Mandy, at his apartment or hers. *You aren't even with this girl, and she's changing you,* he thought. He tried not to think about that, but it was hard with Mandy across from him. Sean lost himself for a moment as she looked down at her plate. Her skin looked soft, and she wore a tank top that drove Sean crazy. *God, I wish you were my girlfriend,* he caught himself thinking. *No, you can't think that way, you need to be here for her.*

Sean thought of his conversation with Paul, "Hey, I was talking to Paul today, and he kept talking about Vis flow, and output, and junk like that. What is it? He said being a Succubus, you'd know a lot about it."

She nodded, "Vis flow is how you use Vis in your body," Mandy said. "It's how I keep myself looking young. If you aren't good at regulating your Vis flow, you age, and waste Vis. Well, I should say you age if you're a Succubus."

"Ok, I think I understand that," he said.

"There are instances when Humans can do it too," she said, "everyone has heard of mothers lifting things off their kids, and whatnot. That's augmenting Vis, it's when you change how Vis is flowing in your body, and in the case of the mother; she is augmenting her body's natural abilities. Though Humans can only do this in rare cases, and only a handful of Humans seem to have that ability."

"I always thought it was adrenaline," Sean said.

She nodded again, "Yes that's there too; adrenaline makes your body produce more Vis."

"Ok, and what about Vis output?"

"This I can't do as I can't make my own Vis," Mandy explained, "but it's basically how much Vis you can produce, and how long you can sustain it. Think of it like when you work out; you can only do a handful of reps at the amount you max out at."

"That makes sense, thanks," Sean said.

They went back to eating, and he thought of another question, "Sorry to keep bugging you about this," he said, "but how is Gabriel different?"

"It's ok," Mandy said, "I don't mind answering questions. Gabriel, Faith, Maddison, and Amy are different because they work on mastering both Vis flow and output. When Gabriel moves fast, that's augmenting Vis, and you've seen when he fights. I'm not a Mage expert, but from my understanding, you have to master a spell before you can use your max Vis output. I guess there are a lot of Mages who can make a lot of Vis, but can't do anything with it. For Gabriel, on the other hand …"

"Yeah, he's extremely powerful, and a master," Sean said.

He didn't ask her any more questions during dinner about

Vis. He was thankful to have someone to ask about that kind of stuff. The more contact he had with other Vis users, the more he started to realize that Gabriel and Faith were very private when it came to Vis, and what they talked about.

"Are you sure you want to do this tonight?" Mandy asked him as they sat on the couch.

"Yeah of course," Sean said, "do you mind if I crash here after?"

"Sure," she said.

Sean got comfortable on the couch, leaning back. Mandy leaned over him, her face inches from his. *It would be nice to kiss you for reasons other than Vis* he thought, as their lips touched. The feeling of his life force leaving him didn't bother him anymore, and he never felt sick anymore. He would, however, feel very tired, and fall asleep. Most nights they did this, Sean got ready for bed, and was in bed when Mandy took his Vis. She would lock up on her way out, and Sean would sleep.

It almost felt good sometimes, feeling his Vis leave. The first few times he gave it to her, his body fought the feeling, but now it just relaxed. When Mandy pulled away, his head was buzzing, and he almost felt drunk. He mumbled a few things, and then lay down on the couch.

"Come on," she said, "I feel bad leaving you on the couch after you gave me Vis."

"Did you call me a cab?" he asked, groggy.

"No; come on, you can sleep in bed with me," she said.

Sean was all too eager to take her up on her request as he stumbled from the couch and tottered into the bedroom. If he had any thoughts of his and Mandy's relationship taking a turn, he would have been disappointed. Sean was out as soon as his head hit the pillow.

TWENTY-ONE

Faith Penn concentrated on some of the seeking spells that she had working. Over the last week, she'd managed to break down the defenses of several of Angelica's decoy locations. Faith knew that for most people, it would be disheartening to only uncover decoys, but Faith didn't see it that way. With each fake location she removed, she was closer to finding a real target. Sooner or later, Angelica Vies was going to be backed into a corner.

Faith had also redirected some of the branch family Seekers to assist her in breaking down Angelica's defenses. It wasn't that the branch families were anywhere as close to being as powerful as Faith or Angelica, but Faith knew it would help to overwhelm the other Seeker, and the strategy was working.

One of Faith's broad spells pinged her. The spell was working to find spikes in Vis usage. Faith liked to use it as a catch-all spell. It was set to ignore those using small amounts of Vis, like Mutari, but if a Mage was using large amounts without doing a good job of concealing their usage, Faith would find them. The spell used to be a common one back when Vis wasn't in the open; Seekers would use the spell to find Mutari and even the occasional Mage who was a possible threat to Vis users' secrecy. Now the spell was all but useless, and therefore Mages didn't use it anymore. The spell was telling her that in Aurora, someone was using a lot of Vis.

Faith used other spells to hone in on the area, and found that a Mage was trying to keep their Vis concealed, but not doing an overly good job of it. Faith moved to one of her other broad spells using birds, directing a few that were close to the Vis user. She watched with their eyes as they came in on a backyard. The yard had a lot of trees blocking the view of neighbors, and there was a small pool.

In the yard was a group of people, all sitting around. Faith couldn't tell with the birds if they were Human, Mutari or Mage, but it was a group of women around a man. Faith made a single bird fly overhead, trying to see who the people were. The man held up his hand towards the pool. The water glowed orange, and twisted into two crude forms of the upper halves of people. Faith stopped the bird and watched as the two water people boxed. Faith didn't need to look at the man's face to know who it was, but she still confirmed with the bird. The girls were clapping, oohing, and ahing. *Moron,* Faith thought, watching Keith Spencer take a bow.

MAKINA YAMAMOTO stood on a rooftop next to Faith. Faith had asked her to follow another Mage, which was something Makina would normally not want to do. But Faith had cloaked her thoroughly, and as she watched her target, she felt more comfortable.

"This guy is an idiot," Makina said flatly.

Faith nodded her head slightly, "Yeah, Trinity must have been pretty desperate when they brought him on. He's been nothing but a liability for them, and has no respect."

Makina turned to Faith, "So you just want me to follow him around?"

"Yes, but keep a distance if you can," Faith said, handing Makina some enchanted glasses, "These will work like binoculars, and also night vision should you need it."

Makina put the glasses on. There was an odd feeling in her head and eyes that quickly went away. She focused on Keith, the glasses zoomed in on him. "Handy," she said.

"They are yours," Faith said, "just give me feedback on them; James wants to offer them as a new line of products."

Makina smiled, "If he has anything else he needs tested …"

Faith chuckled, "You'll be the first to know, and yes, actually; he does have a few things, but they aren't ready for a field test like this yet."

Makina was an Air Elemental, which gave her complete control over the air. She was able to feel its vibrations, and her senses were so attuned that she could even hear Keith speaking though he was far away.

"He's boasting to those girls. I think they are Human," Makina said.

"They are," Faith said with a sigh, "He's been doing everything he can to impress them for over an hour."

Makina watched the girls. Keith's attempts seemed to be working. She sighed on the inside, not looking forward to having to watch him.

"How long do you want me to tail him?"

"Until he leads you to a base of operation. At that point, contact me," Faith said.

"Like the train yard, huh?"

"Yep … well kind of, we are targeting Mages this time."

"Why not just move now?" Makina asked.

"We can kill two birds with one stone this way. If we are lucky, he will lead us to Angelica or even Marcus," Faith said.

Makina was surprised at how casually Faith spoke about hunting down the Vieses. For her part, she didn't want to find Marcus. She wanted him to be taken out, but Makina didn't want to cross paths with the Paladin or his wife. *Gabriel will defeat him,* she told herself. She had complete confidence in Gabriel, and even in Faith. Add on top of that that a Beldame was in the mix. *The Arks are coming together,* a voice in her head almost seemed to speak. That thought she pushed from her mind.

"All right, I'm going to take off. I have other things I need to check on. Are you good to go?" Faith asked.

"I'm good; I'll keep you up to date on what's going on," Makina said.

"Oh," Faith said, taking a bracelet out of her pocket, "This is for you. If you get into trouble, it's a jump anchor. Gabriel and I will come to your aid."

Makina put it on, "Thank you," she said, as the Mage left. As Faith vanished, Makina felt slightly more comforted knowing that Gabriel would come to her if she got into a pinch. *Just don't get into a pinch, Makina!*

Makina watched as Keith continued to woo the girls for a few hours. As the sun was setting, he finally sent them on their way and left the house. She was worried about trying to track a Mage who was on the move. Makina could keep up with a flying Mage, but if he cloaked himself, she'd have to wait for him to come back to the house. Thankfully he didn't use Vis to travel. Instead, he had a flashy convertible. *Figures,* she thought. Makina followed Keith as he drove around. He was a jerk, and she felt bad for the people driving around him.

She followed him as he left the city, going into more rural areas. Makina had to work to keep herself from being seen, but she was able to manage. He turned onto a dirt road. Makina didn't go onto the property, instead waiting outside. She focused with her glasses. There was a house surrounded by fields, and several large sheds. It looked like a large farm, but Makina knew better.

"Faith," she said, over the Vis com they were using.

"Have you got something?"

"Yes," Makina said.

"I'm sending Amy; I can't get away from what I'm doing," Faith said.

Makina waited. it only took Amy a few moments to arrive.

"What do we have?" she asked.

"Looks like a farm," Makina said.

Amy looked intently at the farm, "It's protected, but I don't think as much as the train yard was."

"Do you think it was a backup location?" Makina asked.

Amy made a face. "I don't know; it might be. They could also be trying to lock down the locations that they have left."

"What do you want me to do?" Makina asked.

"I dare say Gabriel is going to want to work on this quickly. Get some rest," Amy said.

* * *

Amy Calamus was careful to not be found as she poked around the farm. At first, she'd thought that they'd found a backup location to the train yard, but now Amy could see that wasn't the case. However, Trinity had been learning from its past. *This place is locked down tight,* she said to herself, *we are going to have to hit it with a lot of force.* Even the concealment spells on it were high-end. Amy figured that was a reaction to Faith's constant assault on Angelica.

Maddison joined her, "What do we have?"

"This place is locked down pretty good. It doesn't feel like the safe house or the train yard, but Angelica isn't taking any chances."

Maddison didn't say anything for a while. "Yeah, the defensive wards here feel like they aren't messing around." she said, not sounding pleased.

"Not looking forward to taking this place?" Amy asked.

"Not looking forward to having to risk so many people," Maddison said, "Normally, Gabriel and I are able to take care of most of the real danger, but here … well that won't be the case." Maddison paused again, "We need to have Gabriel and Faith out here."

Amy contacted Faith, telling her that she and Gabriel were needed. While they waited, Amy checked around the area to ensure that there weren't any traps. When Gabriel and Faith arrived, Amy and Maddison brought them up to speed.

ALISON KAUR listened to the Mages go over what they'd found. It felt good to have a lead again. Though it didn't look like they were going to have an easy time of taking this location.

"So are you planning on moving on this place?" Alesbury asked.

"Not sure," Gabriel said, "We want a Mage out of this," he said, "We don't want to hit this location and then not get any real information out of it."

Gabriel looked like he was deep in thought, "We know that Keith Spencer is there now. He's Trinity's least skilled Paladin, but he should still have plenty to tell us."

"Do you think you can take him alive?" Sean asked.

Gabriel didn't look as sure about that, "Well … we will need to make sure that he can't jump out of the farm …"

"And not killing him?" Alison asked pointedly.

"Well, between Maddison and I …" he started.

"And if Tracy or Marcus is there?" Alison asked.

"Well, that could be kind of nice," Maddison said, "I mean, if Tracy is there, then if Spencer dies we have a spare …"

"And Marcus?" Sean asked.

"Then we have the top of the organization; without him Angelica won't be able to defend herself. She'll have to go into hiding if she doesn't try to avenge her husband's death, and without his leadership, and her having to hide Trinity will fall apart." Gabriel said, sounding confident, "So really, we should hope that he's there."

Alison wasn't convinced she wanted Marcus or Angelica Vies to be at the farm.

Gabriel breathed out, "We will watch the farm to ensure that Keith doesn't leave, and if he does, we will track him down. As for you and Sean," he said, "You will need to spend a bit of time brushing up on using the Guardians. I will also have to get some of the Mutari we used at the train yard."

Sean perked up, hearing that he got to use the Guardians again. Alison wasn't terribly excited about having to use them. Alesbury and Sean started asking technical questions about the farm so they could organize an FBI SWAT team. Alison tried not to let her mind wander as they talked. Working the case with Trinity was making Alison feel more like she was in a war instead of a case. They'd made many arrests. Just in Humans alone, they'd taken over twenty into custody in the locations they'd hit. Oddly, she longed for the days of having to solve murders. She didn't think she'd want those days back. It was a time when she was able to focus on justice for a victim. She was good at that job; she'd put a lot of dirtbags behind bars, and taken them off the street. In her whole career up to the Trinity case, Alison hadn't even discharged her weapon on a case. Now … she had a hard time thinking of how many times she'd used her gun. *What have you gotten yourself into, Kaur?* She didn't know anymore.

In her mind, she saw Montoya in his hospital bed talking about his life and its shortcomings. Alison couldn't help but think of her own life. Even now, as she should have been listening to others plan how they were going to go after Trinity, all she could think of was that her life had turned into a constant hunt. A hunt that was now punctuated with violence and death. Outside of the conference room, officers were leaving for the day. They were going home to families and loved ones, but Alison was yet again going to be spending an evening working. There were other divisions she could work in. There was a group of cops that chased down white collar criminals. They didn't deal with murders or Vis users intent on killing. *Maybe it's time to look at transferring,* she thought, *when this case is over.* She added as an affirmation.

"So in the morning, then?" Sean asked, bringing Alison's attention back to the conversation.

"Yes in the morning, we will come in hard and get Spencer. He is the top priority; don't worry about anyone else unless they are a Mage," Alesbury said.

SEAN HUGHES checked over his Guardians one last time. He didn't have as many as he had at the train yard. This time, he only had offensive ones, as did Alison. He looked over at her. She didn't look happy to be in control of the statues, but Sean enjoyed it. His emotions almost seemed to transfer to them as they tensed, ready for the command to move forward. In front of him, Gabriel stood with Iram drawn. The blade shone brightly with Vis licking up its edge. Gabriel was going to be hitting the farmhouse and Maddison was going to take the sheds. Sean looked around at the FBI SWAT members he had in his control. They watched him intently, waiting for a command.

Faith was nowhere to be seen, she'd already cloaked herself; and from Sean's understanding, she and Amy were going to take down any wards placed by Angelica. After that, Gabriel would lock down the property, making sure that Keith would not be able to jump out.

Gabriel turned to look at Sean, his eyes glowing a bright purple. "It's time," he said.

"Get ready," Sean said to the FBI.

Gabriel held Iram before him and yelled something in Latin that Sean couldn't make out. Sean yelped; covering his eyes as a blinding beam of Vis left Gabriel. There was a roar like thunder, and the area around the farmhouse turned gold. *Gabriel said that's the color of Marcus Vies' Vis.* The two colors fought each other before the gold started to flicker. The gold bubble around the property vanished, and Gabriel flew forward.

Sean urged the Guardians forward, as he ordered his men on. The statues moved quickly, going faster than the running SWAT team. Sean breathed hard as he moved forward, his chest constricted by a bullet-proof vest. He held his gun at the ready before him.

Gabriel was at the house. Four Guardians came out at him.

"I got them!" Sean said.

Gabriel slipped by the statues with ease. Sean fired at the Trinity Guardians, making them turn in his direction. Sean's Guardians attacked the others.

Sean looked at two of the SWAT guys with assault rifles. They looked terrified. He pointed at the statues, "Keep your fire on the enemy Guardians," he ordered.

"Sir?" one of them asked.

"Do it!" Sean roared.

The men did as they were told. Sean's ears rung with gunfire. The men's bullets did no damage to the Guardians, but Sean was happy to see that it distracted them, which gave his an advantage.

"Move around the house!" he ordered, and then to Alison, "Have your Guardians circle around back, one on each side."

Alison nodded. She had two Guardians compared to Sean's four. Hers stayed in front of the FBI agents as they moved around the house. Sean was at the house, and ran to a hole in the wall Gabriel had made. Inside was destruction. Gabriel was in a big room dealing with four Trolls that wore what looked like armor. Sean fired a few rounds at them, distracting them. One turned its attention away from Gabriel, who took off its head. Several of the FBI guys started firing on the Trolls. The bullets bounced off their armor, sending the bullets in all directions.

"Hold your fire!" he yelled.

The men seemed to figure out that it wasn't a good idea to shoot the Trolls. Instead, Sean led them up the staircase. From the behind house, he heard an explosion.

MADDISON BELDAME descended from the sky on the shed in the back of the property. She landed on the roof as a team of SWAT came up from the rear. She slashed Vindictam at her feet, slicing the metal roof. She dropped into the shed, landing in the center. The room was filled with boxes. Maddison saw several Mutari and Humans flee. Before her were a surprised Keith Spencer and Tracy Hope. Maddison smiled at them, letting Vis run down Vindictam's length.

The two Mages stood with orange and green Vis swirling around them. Keith looked at her with a cocky smile.

"Thanks for showing us how to get here," Maddison taunted.

Keith's face twisted with rage.

Before he could speak, Tracy said, "Who are you?"

Maddison appreciated that the girl had manners.

"I am Maddison Beldame; my blade is Vindictam. Who are you?" Maddison asked.

She knew who they were and vice versa, but if Tracy was going to follow tradition, Maddison would give her the same respect.

Tracy's chin came up a bit, "I am Tracy Hope; my blade is Dolor."

Maddison looked to Keith.

"I'm the guy who's gonna kick that pretty ass of yours," he said in a biting tone.

Maddison made a mental note to teach him a thing or two. His Vis flow and output were pathetic; Tracy on the other hand, looked like she knew what she was doing.

Keith came at Maddison. The move looked so obvious she thought he had to be feinting or setting her expectations up. Then she remembered Gabriel saying that Keith was exceptionally unskilled. Maddison pushed Vis into her pelvis and legs, using her center of gravity to wind around his thrust. His eyes widened, and she sent an elbow into his chin. He stumbled back.

"That was for leading us here," Maddison said, "Do something dumb like that again, and I'll kill you."

Keith gritted his teeth, but Maddison couldn't pay him any attention as Tracy was attacking. Maddison blocked and parried a few attacks, testing the other Paladin. *She's better than the last time you fought her,* Maddison thought. Tracy managed to get Maddison slightly off balance, but before she could capitalize on it, Keith attacked again. Keith stepped in front of Tracy's attack, making the other Mage back away.

"She's mine!" Keith said.

He struck his hands on the ground to break the floor. Maddison hardened the ground, countering his spell. At the same time, she held her breath and pushed the air in the area away. Keith gasped for air, and dropped his guard. Maddison was about to cut him when she decided that he wasn't worth killing with her blade; and at any rate, she was supposed to try to take him alive.

"Scindam!" Maddison yelled.

Ribbons of blue Vis extended from her hands. To Maddison's amazement, Tracy stepped in front of the spell. Her wards lit a bright green, and then failed. Maddison's Vis sliced into her, cutting her face, neck, arms, chest, and torso. She flew back with a scream. Keith looked terrified as his companion landed on the ground. He looked at Maddison in fear. She moved forward to attack him. Maddison was hit with a burning spell from Tracy. Maddison's wards flared. She ducked away from the spell, and countered with a spell that made the air concuss as a shockwave ripped towards the other Mages. Keith's wards turned orange. As for Tracy, her strength was being diverted to keep herself from bleeding out. She took almost the full force of Maddison's attack, sending her flying back into some of the boxes, knocking her out cold.

Keith turned to Tracy on the ground, then he looked at Maddison without a hint of cockiness. He ran, and ran fast. Maddison made to chase him, but stopped. She looked down at Tracy's form on the ground, blood pooling around her. Maddison kicked Dolor away from the girl's hand, and leaned over her, breathing a spell to stop her bleeding.

Maddison put a finger to her ear, "Gabriel I have Tracy Hope in custody; but I need Erin now!"

ERIN PENN came running into the shed of the farmhouse. She'd been waiting to tend to the wounds of Humans and Mutari, but not one of her own kind. Tracy lay on the cold floor of the shed with Maddison and Gabriel standing over her, keeping her from bleeding to death. Erin did a quick assessment of her wounds. Lacerations covered her body. Without Maddison and Gabriel keeping her alive, she would have bled out quickly.

"Why didn't her healing wards seal this?" Erin asked, confused.

"They would have, but when I attacked Keith she got hit as well. I don't think she had any strength left," Maddison explained.

"I see," Erin said.

So much blood, she thought. Erin pulled out her wand and started to tend to the wounds. She noticed blood coming from Tracy's ears.

"What kind of spell was it?" Erin asked Maddison.

"Shockwave."

Erin waved her wand over the girl, "She's bleeding on the inside, too."

She knew there was no avoiding it, but Erin deplored the violence. Maybe it was because she was a Healer, or maybe because she was just a non-violent person by nature, but she hated having to patch people up after a fight. She didn't hold anything against Maddison or Gabriel; they were doing what needed to be done. She just wished it didn't need to be done.

"How long until she is awake?" Gabriel asked. His voice was cold, a tone that Erin wasn't used to coming from him.

"You won't be able to talk to her for a little while," Erin said.

"Erin, this is not a normal suspect or one of our own. When will she be up?" he said, more commanding.

"Two, maybe three hours. What are you going to do when she's up?" Erin asked, worried to hear what his answer was going to be.

"We need to have a talk."

"And after the talk?" Erin asked, looking into his eyes. Eyes that were like cold dark stones. She fought the urge to shiver. His eyes softened.

"Erin," he said softly, "You know we cannot contain her, and we cannot let her go free."

"So you will kill her?" she asked.

His eyes looked sorrowful, "Not if I can help it."

Erin wasn't a moron. He was saying that to make her feel better. Erin knew that Tracy would die.

"If she leads us to Marcus and vows to not harm anyone, I will let her go free," Gabriel said, surprising her.

"Really?" Erin asked.

Maddison, on the other hand did not look surprised, and was the one who answered, "Tracy seems to be an honest one."

Erin went back to her work, saying a little prayer that Tracy would come around. Erin knew it wouldn't be a fast process, but she had a hope that her patient wouldn't be slaughtered.

TWENTY-TWO

ERIN PENN was about to clean up an unconscious Tracy when Gabriel told her to stop.

"Why?" Erin asked.

"Sean, is there a chance we can get some of the CSIs in here to take pictures of this crime scene, and we can put her in a body bag?" Gabriel asked.

"But Gabriel, she's alive." Erin said, confused.

He smiled, "But she was very badly hurt; Keith saw that. If we play our cards right, Trinity will think that Tracy is dead."

"Do you think they'd try to rescue her?" Alison asked.

"No," Gabriel said, "They will know she will be in a secure location; it would force them to change any plans and they'd might have to leave locations. Tracy knows too much about them." He turned to Erin, "How long is she going to be out?"

Erin shrugged, "A few hours … if you like, I can make sure she stays asleep longer."

Gabriel nodded to her, and told her to do that.

"We need to talk, Gabriel," Alison started, but was cut off.

"Alison, the city does not have any place that can hold Tracy. My family does. I know you want to ensure that your suspect is safe so you can get information from her, but I will tell you, it is extremely difficult to detain a Mage. If Tracy is able to escape, everything that we have worked for over the last month will be for nothing," Gabriel said.

Erin watched everyone talk, not for the first time being thankful she didn't have a more influential part of the team's current Pactum. The detectives and Gabriel spoke for a while longer, and Erin focused on making sure Tracy would not wake for several hours. After that, she tended to a few minor injuries that suspects and FBI agents had sustained. She was packing up when Sean came up to her.

"Need a lift back to the station?" he asked.

"Sure," she said, "Your department makes me write an essay about everything I do for you."

Sean laughed, "Trust me, you've got it easy. I could have written about a hundred novels by this point in my career."

It was just her and Sean in the car as they drove back. Gabriel and Faith were taking care of moving Tracy to a secure location. Sean seemed more quiet than normal.

"What's up?" Erin asked.

"I was just wondering … how many times have you seen Gabriel fight? Or have you even seen him fight?"

Erin sighed. She'd never seen Gabriel in combat, though she'd seen the aftermath of him in combat.

"I have, but it was before the war," Erin said.

Sean perked up, "Really?"

She nodded, "Yep. There was a tournament, and my parents and I went."

"What was it like watching him?" Sean asked.

"I was young, and I remember that Gabriel was supposed to be too young to be in the tournament. My father said that Gabriel being in was the Decors throwing their weight around; he didn't think Gabriel would be able to do anything. How much do you know about Vis flow and output?" Erin asked before she went on.

Sean told her what he knew, and Erin filled in a few gaps, "When you increase your output, people can visibly see your Vis."

"Like when Maddison and Gabriel look like they are in a bonfire of Vis?" Sean said.

"Yes, like that. Anyway, there was a lot of Mages in the tournament who looked really powerful, but they couldn't sustain that power or couldn't use it," Erin said, remembering back to watching Gabriel. She could remember the day like it was yesterday. "The first Paladin Gabriel fought looked very powerful. I remember his Vis was blue like Maddison's. He made a big show of how high his output was."

"I bet Gabriel put that to shame," Sean said.

"No he didn't," Erin said, "You couldn't even see what color his Vis was. He looked totally unaffected by the man before him. I remember my father commenting on how arrogant he thought Gabriel must have been for not even trying to equal what his opponent was doing." Erin shook her head, "Then the man attacked, and Gabriel sidestepped him. He moved so fast," Erin said, having a hard time trusting her memory, "He was like a flash, his control of augmenting Vis was beyond impressive. The other Paladin slashed at Gabriel with his sword, but Gabriel never even drew his. He took the man out with a single hit to the chest. Gabriel sent him flying across the arena."

The car was quiet for a moment before Sean spoke, "What did your father say then?"

Erin laughed, "He was in awe that someone so young could do what he had. My father told me that he had been wrong to think low of Gabriel and the Decors. From there, we watched Gabriel dominate one person after another. He didn't draw Iram until his fifth match up."

Erin could tell Sean wanted to ask more questions, but they were back at the station.

ALISON KAUR walked into the conference room with the rest of the team behind her. Maddison was taking care of moving Tracy.

"What do you think we need to do?" Alison asked Gabriel, "Tracy is still in DPD custody."

"No she isn't," Sean said, "Not until an arrest report is made."

Alison gave him a look.

"It's worth noting, Kaur. As far as the rest of the world is concerned, Tracy Hope is dead." He looked at Gabriel, "There was a reporter for the Post there; I made sure to let him overhear me say she was in a body bag," Sean said, "Which she was," he smiled.

"Do you think Marcus will buy it?" Alison asked.

"He doesn't have any reason not to," Faith said, "Maddison said that not only did Keith run, but he looked terrified at the same time. By now he's told Marcus that Tracy is dead. There's no way a coward like him is going to cop to letting a teammate get captured."

Alison thought about that. She suspected what Faith said was accurate. From what they had gathered about Spencer, he was mostly show; and when it came right down to things, he was a hothead and a coward. In a big way, today had been a huge win for the team. Tracy was far more skilled than Keith, and having her in custody would do more damage to Trinity than had they lost Keith. Part of Alison even wondered if Keith wouldn't be a liability to Trinity.

"Will she talk?" Alison asked the Mages.

"Yes, eventually." Gabriel said, and then added, "I won't torture her, Alison."

"Yeah, I know you won't," she said.

She wasn't lying. There was a time when she believed that Gabriel would have tortured someone, and part of her knew that he still would if he thought it to be best.

"What makes you so sure she'll talk?" Alison asked.

"She's dead, remember," Gabriel said, "and she's being held in a secret location. Sooner or later, she is going to talk."

"How are we going to handle this?" Sean asked Alison, "We have a suspect we are holding without arresting; we are completely ignoring her civil rights."

Alison sighed. How were they going to get around this? Trinity couldn't find out that Tracy was alive, and possibly talking; but Alison couldn't ignore someone's God-given rights.

"There is a provision in the Pactum that the city of Denver has with the North American Pactum guild, giving Paladins permission to handle other Mages as they see fit. It was added to ensure that Mages could still police the Vis world without violating Pactums." Gabriel said, "I'm not sure how public opinion would be on it ..."

"We couldn't ever charge her with any crime," Alison said, "Not after keeping her locked up. Not only would a defense attorney be able to tear us apart, but the public would be enraged."

"Were you going to charge her with a crime anyway?" Faith asked, "Seriously, how were you going to keep her in custody."

Alison didn't have an answer for that. It wasn't her problem, it was the state's issue to figure out; Alison's job was just to find the bad guys, and let the system take care of the rest. *How can the system deal with this?* she wondered.

"There is something else," Gabriel said, "Tracy is not going to talk to a Human."

"I figured as much," Sean said, "but we need to be there."

"Tracy is being kept in a room with stone walls, but we should be able to make sure you can watch and hear our interrogation." Faith said, "But we will not be able to tell you the location."

"Won't it be at the team's house?" Alison asked, surprised.

"No," Gabriel said, "It's at another location. Only four people in the world know where it is."

Alison wasn't going to argue. It wasn't that she was happy with how things were going, but she didn't see any way of getting around their situation, so she resigned herself to doing more things not by the book.

TRACY HOPE'S eyes flickered open. The world was foggy, her back and arms were sore, her mind fuzzy, and she was cold. As the room came into focus, her vision swam, and she felt like she was going to vomit. She closed her eyes and took a few deep calming breaths, then she opened them again.

She was sitting on an uncomfortable chair with her hands behind her back. Before her was a dark metal door. The walls were made of a stone that was dingy and dark. Where was she? How did she get here? Her mind flooded with memories. Maddison Beldame was before her, using a cutting spell. Tracy couldn't remember the pain, but she knew she'd felt it at the time. There was more. Keith had been a moron, and almost gotten himself killed, along with her. *I swear one of these days I'm going to let you fall on your butt, Keith,* she thought. That explained where she had been, but where did Keith take her once she was knocked out? *He didn't take you anywhere,* a voice in her said, *He's a coward, and left you. Think Tracy, if Keith had rescued you, why would your hands be tied?*

She was starting to get a better grip on her senses. She looked around the room, seeing that it had a high ceiling with a single glowing light, and the walls were all stone. They were cast in a lavender light that seemed to be coming from behind Tracy. She flexed her arms a bit, feeling bonds on her wrists tying her to the chair. Her forearms were tied too. She looked down, seeing her ankles were also tied to the legs of the chair in bands of brightly shining purple Vis. The chair was part of the floor. Tracy was in trouble.

You've been captured. She started to feel a sense of panic. How long had she been out? And where exactly was she? *How long will it take Marcus to find you?* she wondered. The heavy-looking metal door opened, swinging in the room towards her. In stepped six people. The first was a man in his mid-fifties with full dark hair. He looked like an older Gabriel Decor. Behind him was a lovely woman with long bronze hair and delicate features. Tracy knew these people. They were followed by their son, Gabriel. A tall man with a square face came in next with a blonde woman who carried herself with confidence; her eyes were a deep red. It was the Beldames, and their daughter was with them. Tracy felt sick to her stomach.

Maddison and Gabriel stood before Tracy with their parents on either side of them.

Edward Decor spoke first, "My name is Edward Decor. I am the head of the Decor family. Who are you?"

"Tracy Hope," Tracy said, trying to make herself sound unafraid, but her voice came out in a squeak.

Olivia Beldame smiled as Tracy spoke.

"You have some very interesting friends," Olivia said.

"Friends who will find me," Tracy said with more confidence.

Angelica would be looking for her as they spoke, and soon Marcus would come to save her.

Gabriel frowned, "I do not think so," he said. He pulled a bit of paper from his pocket, and unfolded it. He held it for Tracy to see. It read, "Denver Police Raid Trinity Location: Suspect and Mage Tracy Hope Killed in Attack." Tracy started to read the article, but it was pulled away by Gabriel.

"They think you're dead, Tracy," he said not unkindly, "We even put you in a body bag and took you out in it."

"We have people in the station. They wi-" she started.

"Have no idea that it was a hoax. There are only fourteen people in the world who know you aren't dead." He said, "The Human papers are going to have a field day with it. What do you think Keith is going to tell Marcus?"

She wanted to tell him he was wrong, but Tracy knew what Keith was going to say. She'd been badly hurt in the fight, and he didn't take the time to save her. Tracy knew that Keith would tell Marcus that she was dead, if for no reason than to keep from getting in trouble for leaving her behind. *No one is coming for you,* the voice in her head said.

A chill ran down her spine. She wasn't trained to be interrogated.

"You know you're going to talk," Gabriel said.

Tracy's eyes snapped up to him. Unconsciously, she flexed what little Vis she had and tried to move. She gasped as a line of fiery pain cut into her wrists where the Vis bonds were. She felt hot liquid run down her fingers. Gabriel looked put out.

"I wish you hadn't done that," he said, "I was just about to tell you that if you try to escape, you'll just hurt yourself. You should have known better."

She was nowhere near as strong as Gabriel, but she could have broken her restraints eventually. However, in her weakened condition, she didn't have much Vis left. She felt her healing wards start to sap energy from her as they tried to repair the damage to her wrists. They would be small cuts, but Vis came from every cell in one's body. Tracy had lost a lot of blood in the fight, she was sure. She was weak, and while she could normally break free from Gabriel's cords, she couldn't now. The cuts in her wrists would continue to open, making her already weak body heal itself. Tracy would never get the strength to break free.

Her heart thumped and she felt sick again. She had no hope of escape.

"So is this the part where you offer me the chance to talk before you torture me?" she asked, her voice weak.

Gabriel gave her a tight smile, "No Tracy; that isn't how this is going to work. Like I said, Trinity thinks you are dead. We have all the time in the world. You will talk; I'm sure of it."

"So what? Are you saying that you aren't going to hurt me?" she asked.

He shook his head.

"What makes you think I'm not just going to let my strength recover and escape? I can keep from cutting into my wrists for a while," she said, a bit more firm this time.

Gabriel almost looked sad for her, "No Tracy; that won't happen. It will take you days to get enough strength up to break those restraints, even if they weren't cutting into you. But even now they are." He said, "They numb the area they are in; if you feel your wards, you'll feel the pull on them."

Tracy took a moment to feel for Vis leaving her. It was there. She felt Vis leaving her body, but it wasn't a lot. Even if they didn't feed her well, she would be able to break the bonds in a week … maybe a week and a half, but what then? She wouldn't have enough energy to break out of the cell. So, maybe two weeks until she could.

"Tracy," Gabriel said, getting her attention, "I take it you're trying to figure out when you will be able to leave here. You are correct in thinking that you can become strong enough in a few weeks if that is what you are thinking. That is your choice, but that won't be what you choose."

"Ha. What makes you think that?" she asked, feeling much more confident just by knowing they weren't planning on torturing her.

Gabriel looked at her like she was missing something, "The chair," he said, "How comfortable is it?"

How comfortable? As he said the words Tracy noticed how her body felt all of a sudden. She wasn't comfortable at all. The seat dug into the back of her legs and her lower back was hurting. She could feel her neck tightening up almost imperceptibly, and the angle her arms were tied to the chair was pulling oddly on her shoulders.

She sighed, "So what; you think a little discomfort will keep me here?"

He shook his head, "You have been in that chair for thirty minutes," he said, "It's made to be particularly uncomfortable. It will make muscles tighten and pinch nerves. To Humans, a day in it would be like torture. They would be moaning from pain, but for a Mage …"

"I can use Vis to make myself not hurt," Tracy said.

Part of her wanted to scoff at him. Tell him that no matter how much discomfort she was in, she could withstand it. That would be a lie. She'd heard of chairs like this one. They were perfect for keeping weak Mages in a jail cell. With Vis, Tracy could make herself feel comfortable for weeks on end in the chair. But using that Vis meant that in her weakened state, she would never gain the power needed to free herself. If she tried to tough it out, however; she wouldn't sleep, and would start to feel extreme pain after just a day or so. It would be her choice. Weeks of pain that she might not be able to bear, which would make her tell Gabriel whatever he wanted to know, or she could stay in relative comfort until she talked.

"You aren't dumb, Tracy Hope," Gabriel said, "Sooner or later being here in the room, you will talk. You know it, and I know it." he started to move away.

"Where are you going?" she asked.

"Unless you are planning on selling out your organization now I am going to leave you alone," he said, and with that, Gabriel Decor and the other people left the room. As the door closed, Tracy realized that she was truly and utterly alone, and for the first time in years, fear started to enter into her mind.

TWENTY-THREE

GABRIEL DECOR relaxed in the conference room, waiting for the meeting to start. Sean was sitting at his laptop clacking away. Maddison was leaning back across from Gabriel with her eyes closed. Faith and Amy were absent as was becoming the norm. Alison came in the room to see an unexpected face.

"Sergeant!" Gabriel said, "I didn't know you were coming back today."

Sergeant Montoya was in a pair of jeans and a sweater. He sat in a chair next to Maddison, sighing.

"I'm not back on full-time yet," he said. "Hughes, are you even gonna say hello?"

Sean looked up from his laptop with a start, "Oh ... good to see you sir. FYI, it's not casual Friday," he said with a wink.

"Prick," Montoya commented.

Alison sat next to Gabriel, clearing her throat, "Ok Sean, why are we here?" she asked.

Sean looked up from his laptop. "Thanks for coming in," he said, plugging the computer into a projector that projected his screen on to the wall. It was a list of Trinity locations and items found. Sean got up, walking to the wall. "I think we have been looking at Trinity the wrong way. Here you can see the different locations we've hit. Next to each location's name is the date we've been able to figure out Trinity started using it. Below each location name are items that were recovered." Sean explained, "We have found guns, ammo, and bomb-making supplies at many of these locations."

"Yeah, we have been working the last month under the assumption that Trinity is an arms dealer, and possibly trying to supply terrorist groups," Alison explained to Montoya.

Sean shook his head, "I don't think so anymore." He pulled up another list of items, "We know that Trinity has been making their own guns. All of the guns we have found have been identical, down to serial numbers and ballistics tests, which shouldn't be possible. After we shot over at the team's house and Guy made all that ammo, it got me thinking. What if Trinity was doing the same thing? What if they were going for easy money?"

"But selling arms isn't easy money," Montoya said.

"It is if you can make your own guns. Gabriel, what would it take for Guy to make a warehouse full of guns?" Sean asked.

Gabriel thought for a moment. He wasn't a Builder, and admittedly it was the discipline he knew the least about.

"You would need the raw materials needed for the project … but Builders can mine with ease. Getting all of the raw materials would take maybe a day, and then if they had a gun to copy … I would have to ask Guy, but I would think they could make a warehouse full -- start to finish -- in two, maybe three days," Gabriel said.

Next to him Alison tightened up, and Montoya pinched the bridge of his nose.

"They wouldn't need a supplier, so they have no risk of being found out on that end of a deal, and they could use Vis to move weapons, and they make a hundred percent profit," Alison said, sounding sick. "How much do you think they could have moved in the last few years?"

Sean looked almost happy, "I don't think they've moved much. Many of the boxes we have found have been covered in dust. They haven't been touched in years. Trinity has loads of guns that you see on movies, but not that your common criminal is going to use. Also, I took a look at the fertilizer we found a month back, and there were three different kinds."

"So?" Maddison asked.

"So that tells me they didn't know how to make explosives; you can only use certain types to make ANFO," Sean said, "and think about the medical equipment we found. It was unusable for a dirty bomb, but they had loads of it sitting around."

"They have been working off of what they've seen on TV and movies …" Gabriel said.

"Yes!" Sean said, "I think that's why they brought on Cory McLoughen; they needed someone with more knowledge and the networks to distribute arms."

"What's with the hookers and altered drugs then?" Alison asked.

Sean shrugged, "Product testing. Plus, drugs *are* easy money, and would be a part of any Human crime syndicate. Trinity was just using the current system."

"So the Human element allows Trinity to expand distribution, and find out what products to make," Montoya said.

"From my understanding, most drugs have an organic base," Gabriel said, "That means a Builder to grow them or having to buy drugs, and then alter them to make them more addictive or powerful." He said, thinking out loud, "Like with arms, they would have complete control over production."

"Bottom line is Trinity could have the corner on the market in black market arms," Sean said, "Think about it. They have been building the connections here in the US, and probably overseas, and they have enforcement to ensure that other Mages aren't doing the same. Add on top of that they can move drugs and enchanted objects."

"They would be the biggest clearinghouse for anything the criminal world needs," Montoya said, "If you work with Trinity, you get whatever arms, drugs, and Vis objects you want without having to worry about law enforcement," he shivered.

"That would give Marcus the power to start working in the Vis world," Maddison said, "It would give him wealth to buy any guild that he wanted or whomever he wanted. In the whole process, he'd be building an army of some of the most dangerous Humans there are."

"We have found foreign currency at Trinity locations, so we know they are working outside the country. If the guns are copies, then we know they have at least one Builder on staff, and the drugs mean a Healer," Gabriel said.

"And Enchanters," Maddison added, "If they are trying to make themselves a clearinghouse, they'd need several of them. Guns are one thing, but enchanted objects take a lot more time."

"We need to find locations where they do production," Alison said.

"That doesn't change what the Seekers are looking for," Gabriel said, "They need to still be looking for Mages and locations. I do not think finding the production center will be easily done, but we have Tracy, and she might know where it is," Gabriel said.

"How goes getting her to talk?" Sean asked.

"I think it will go well. We have let her sit for about a week. By this time, she has to be realizing the only way she is ever going to get out of that room is to talk," Gabriel said.

Sean nodded, "Ok, keep us posted."

TRACY HOPE woke, lifting her head. She turned it from side to side trying to pop her neck, but her muscles were too tight. She fought back a shiver and tried to push her discomfort from her mind. She closed her eyes and checked on her Vis. There wasn't much there. She couldn't say that she hadn't learned a thing or two since being captured. When she'd first seen Gabriel and he explained her situation, part of her thought that she would be able to slowly regain her strength. She knew it could take her months to do, but she thought she could do it. Tracy was no stranger to discomfort or the cold, but she hadn't taken into account the other things she'd need Vis for.

Her bare feet were freezing cold on the stone floor. The room was cold. This left Tracy with a choice. She could be cold, and run the risk of getting sick, or she could use Vis to keep herself warm. Her muscles were in knots that caused pain and stiffness. She could heal them with Vis, but that would exhaust what Vis she had, and as soon as they were healed, the position she was in would start to make them cramp again. So instead, Tracy was just dulling the discomfort with Vis, using as little as possible. There were small blades in her wrists that would cut her if she moved, so she had to make sure to keep herself comfortable enough that she didn't fidget. With all of that, eventually she could have escaped.

What she hadn't counted on was little things like eating, drinking, and going to the bathroom. A tray of food was given to her every few hours. The food was bland, but filling. The catch was, Tracy was tied up; and therefore had to use Vis to eat her food. The food had additives that made her thirsty, so she had to use Vis to drink. There was a slot in the wall where the food came in; next to it was a basin of water that never ran out. Tracy would make her food float over to her and to her mouth so she could eat. Then she'd have to make tendrils of water flow into her mouth. As if that weren't enough, if she wanted to go to the bathroom, she had to use Vis to move her waste to a hole in the floor unless she wanted to soil herself; which was something she refused to do. All of these little tasks, along with keeping herself semi-comfortable, exhausted what little Vis Tracy's body was producing.

She wasn't sure how many days she'd been in the room. The light never turned off, and no one visited her. Her meals were evenly spaced out, and no one came in the room. She thought maybe she'd been in the room two weeks. Gabriel had come in to talk to her once, but Tracy had refused to talk to him. She regretted it now. Vis couldn't help her from not having contact with people. It was something she didn't think she'd miss. Maybe it was because she couldn't go outside either or move around, but being left alone with her thoughts was taking a toll on her.

The door opened and Tracy focused, hoping she would see Marcus Vies come in. It wasn't him. It was Gabriel, carrying a small stool. He placed it before her, but didn't sit on it.

"Are you going to talk with me today?" he asked, calmly.

She looked over at the door, but it had shut behind him.

"I'm not giving up Trinity," she said, her voice croaking.

Was that really her voice? The last time she'd used it, she was screaming insults at the door, but that had been a few days ago.

Gabriel sat on the stool, and Tracy felt a jolt of happiness.

"That's fine; we can talk about something else," he said.

"How long have I been in here?" she asked.

"How long do you think?" he asked.

This made her angry; but she didn't want to make him leave so she answered honestly, "Two weeks."

"No; it's been just over a week," he said.

What? Time was moving that slowly?

Her shock must have shown on her face, "You lose track of time in here. Also, we time your food out over a full twenty-four hours. Don't bother counting meals to figure it out. Some days you get four meals, others you get five. Not that it matters anyway."

"Why doesn't it matter?" she asked.

He shrugged, "You are going to be here as long as you want."

"As long as I want? You mean until I tell you what you want to know," she spat back.

"Yes," Gabriel said, "So since we aren't talking about Trinity, why don't we talk about you. Where are you from?"

"Bite me," she said, "I'm not telling you anything about myself."

"But you already have," he said. He stood walking to the door. He opened it, and for a moment Tracy thought he was going to leave. Instead, he brought in a broad sword. It was Dolor, her blade. Gabriel sat on the bench, hefting the blade. It felt like a violation to her seeing him hold Dolor, but she didn't speak. She was more frightened that he would leave her again for several days.

He inspected the blade, "Hmmm. Did you know that fighting styles and weapons tend to dominate regions of the world?" he asked, "For example, most Paladins who learn to fight in North America and Eastern Asia use Katanas like I do. In western Asia and northern Africa, they prefer Axes. Southern Africans likes war hammers, and the Australians use spears. Central and South Americans prefer rapiers." Gabriel said, "And Paladins in Europe; they use broadswords," he said, looking into her eyes.

Tracy looked down, not wanting to give him the satisfaction of being correct.

He leaned into her, "Tracy Hope is a pretty generic name, so that means you took it on when you came to the States. You have very pale skin, blue eyes, and bright blonde hair, so I'm going to guess you are Scandinavian."

Her heart picked up a bit. How had he figured that out?

He backed away from her, "And you don't go for normal Mage protocol like using a dedicated Seeker, so I'm going to go out on a limb and say that your parents were Human?"

She looked up at him, "How … how did you know that?"

GABRIEL DECOR looked her over. She was obviously uncomfortable, and he had to give her credit for trying to increase her Vis. She looked amazed that he'd been able to figure out what part of the world she was from.

"I have a little experience," Gabriel said, "Marcus Vies used to fight with a Katana. Did you know that?" he asked. Then before she could answer, Gabriel said, "But he switched over to a broadsword shortly after I started training. Most people don't do that. I think he thought it gave him a unique style of fighting, and it did. You show a lot of that style of fighting, but not completely. You got your foundation from someone else, didn't you?"

Her chin turned up just a bit, "Yes I did," she said.

Gabriel nodded sagely, "I thought so. Well, you do Marcus proud," Gabriel told her honestly, "Your partner Keith, on the other hand …"

Her cheeks reddened at his comment, but she didn't argue with him. *She must know what a problem Keith is,* he thought.

"So, how did your parents feel about you being a Mage?" Gabriel asked.

This question was out of curiosity. In so many ways, he felt for those not born in Mage families.

Tracy looked down at the floor, and Gabriel regretted asking.

"Did they kick you out?" he asked softly.

She looked up for a moment, and then back down, "Yes. I wasn't even eight the first time I used Vis around them … they left me on the street."

Gabriel was shocked she'd told him that. *She must be close to breaking,* he realized. The room they were in was very effective at what it did, but he was surprised that it had worked so quickly on Tracy. *She looked relieved to see you. She was abandoned to a hostile world as a child, and now she finds herself in another hostile situation with the knowledge that no one is coming to her aid.* Gabriel had nearly broken her by pure dumb luck. Tracy was from the street; hurting her wouldn't have been effective. She would be used to pain, but Marcus had taken her in, had given her hope. In Gabriel's experience, when someone who never had hope gained it and then lost it again, their whole world shattered around them. *She doesn't even know that she's letting you in. She's just desperate to keep you in the room, to keep you from leaving her alone.* He needed to tread carefully.

"If Marcus wasn't the one to pull you off the street; then who?" Gabriel asked.

"I'm not going to tell you her name," Tracy said.

So you still have some fight left in you.

"Will you tell me anything about her?" Gabriel asked.

Tracy looked up with fire in her eyes, "Yes. She was killed by the Ark Dietrich Collier! That's why I hate the Arks," she said bitterly.

"Why did Dietrich kill her?" Gabriel asked, "Was she Nobilis?"

"She was defending her home," Tracy said, "He murdered her; she was trying to protect us!"

Gabriel didn't say anything for a moment as he thought back to the war. Dietrich hadn't spent a great deal of time in Northern Europe, and the time he'd spent there was very heavy action. *Where would she have been living that Dietrich would have been attacking a place where civilians would have been?*

"The battle of Hiems," Gabriel said.

Tracy looked back to the floor, her face red and her breathing heavy. Hiems was an all-Vis town in Northern Sweden; it was controlled by the Nobilis, and was one of their hometowns. It was a big win for the Arks when Dietrich had taken it.

"You hate the Arks, yet you serve their former captain," Gabriel said, almost as an accusation, "That seems a bit of an insult to your teacher's memory, doesn't it?"

"He killed Dietrich," Tracy said, "He told me he never ordered him to attack that city," she said, looking into Gabriel's eyes again.

Dietrich had been the second in command of the Arks. It was true Marcus had killed him.

"You are right Tracy; Marcus Vies never commanded Dietrich Collier to attack the town of Hiems," he said.

Her expression was one of satisfaction, like Gabriel had just conceded his argument.

"No; Marcus did not command Dietrich Collier to attack and destroy the town of Hiems. He ordered me to do it," he said, "But I was injured prior to being able to leave, so I asked Dietrich to go in my place."

Tracy was silent for a moment. Gabriel remembered that time well. He was loath to destroy a town in the hopes it would shatter Nobilis morale. Dietrich didn't want to do it either, but Gabriel was hurt and therefore could not fulfill his orders. Marcus had known and approved of Dietrich going in Gabriel's place.

Dietrich's forces had met heavy resistance at Hiems, but he fulfilled his orders. And after Hiems' defenses fell, the battle had turned into a slaughter. Dietrich wasn't right after that. Part of Gabriel hated Marcus for ordering the attack, but as Marcus had hoped, the annihilation of Hiems broke the Nobilis' back. Their troops' morale was broken, and it wasn't long until the war came to a close. Gabriel refocused his attention on the silent girl before him, her eyes wet.

"I don't believe you," she said in a small voice.

"You can believe whatever you like," Gabriel said, "but Marcus was in command of the Arks. You know how he leads an organization; do you know him to not have full control over what his leadership is doing?" he asked her.

Tracy was about to speak; then stopped, her retort catching in her throat. Gabriel had won. He could see it in her eyes; the wheels were turning. Not only had Marcus left her for dead, but he'd also ordered the destruction of her home city, killing her only family figure. He'd also lied to her.

"Marcus had to know you were from Hiems, didn't he? He knew what he'd done to you, and he lied to you, and used you. I am sorry Tracy; truly I am. I too, have trusted Marcus Vies, and lived to regret it," he said.

He wasn't sure Tracy was paying attention to him. Her breaths were short pants, her skin was red, and her expression moved back and forth between disbelief, rage, and sorrow.

"Have I been here eight days?" she asked.

"Yes today will be the ninth," Gabriel replied.

She looked up at him, her face fixed on rage, "4:00 p.m., Cheeseman Park, there is going to be a bomb." She said, and then almost at once she looked shocked, "Oh my God, what have I done?" she exclaimed, realizing that she'd just given Gabriel vital information.

Gabriel looked at his watch and swore; it was 3:40 p.m.

TWENTY-FOUR

ALISON KAUR sat with Sean as they ate lunch at a burger place on 16th Street. It was a mild day, and Alison found her mind wandering as she ate. It felt good to not think. Across from her, Sean looked the same; his eyes out of focus as he stared off out the restaurant window. Alison watched street kids panhandling, weaving around people as they walked the mall.

"Got any plans for the weekend?" she asked Sean.

"Nah, it's only Wednesday," he said, "but I'm sure Mandy and I will hang out. She keeps talking about some movie that's out, so we'll probably go to that. You?"

Alison shrugged, "Nope. Faith has been so busy with the case, I don't talk to her very much. I called an old friend this weekend, so maybe I'll get together with her."

Sean looked mildly surprised, "Oh yeah?"

Alison smiled, "Yeah," she chuckled, "She's one of my oldest friends, and I haven't talked to her in a few years. Last time I talked to her she was pregnant with her first kid. She's had another since then."

"Good for her," Sean said.

Alison nodded.

"So now that you're trying to be all normal, are you going to try to find some guy to marry and make babies with?" Sean teased.

Alison made a face, "Nah, nothing like that," she joked. Then added seriously, "I just don't know how well it would work with this job, ya know? Plus I've seen so many things; I don't want to bring a kid into my world."

"Amen to that," Sean said, "I think it's hard on spouses, too."

"Yeah," Alison said, thinking about James Penn, Faith's husband. *I wonder what it's like for you?* she thought. Faith wasn't a Paladin, but her profession was dangerous in the extreme, and she was at the top of her field. James would remember the war and know stories of the Ark and Nobilis squads fighting. He may have been able to forget that world ever existed, but now that Marcus was back in the open? James had to know that his wife would be forced to fight the Vieses.

"What are you thinking about?" Sean asked, "You look all thoughtful and concerned."

"What do you think it's like for James?" Alison asked.

Sean considered the question for a moment, "Are you talking about Angelica?"

Alison nodded.

"I think he has a particularly stressful life at the moment. I can't imagine what it is like for Heidi either; Marcus killed her husband," Sean pointed out.

Alison had forgotten about that. For Heidi, her life had been on hold since Marcus betrayed them. For her, Marcus being in the open must have been a horrid mix of feelings. On the one hand, Alison figured Heidi would be looking forward to the day when Gabriel put Marcus Vies in the grave; but on the other hand, Heidi would have to live in fear that Marcus wouldn't lose. And what if he disappeared again? No, Alison decided. Marcus Vies had no intention of fading into darkness again.

Alison's phone rang, and she looked at it. *Speaking of Gabriel.*

She answered the phone. "We're at lunch if you want to join us," she said conversationally.

"There's a bomb in Cheeseman Park set to go off in twenty minutes," he said urgently.

All at once, Alison's world came to a grinding halt. Her gut turned to stone, her heart felt as though it was no longer beating. She swallowed hard, her throat all of a sudden dry; the saliva in her mouth thick.

"You are sure?" she asked.

"I'm heading there now. I told Faith; she is having Maddison and Amy meet us there. It is your choice what you want to do. Maddison and I will find the bomb and contain it if we can," he said.

Alison stood quickly from her seat, Sean following her lead and reading her body language.

"Sean and I will meet you on scene; do you need backup other than us?" Alison asked.

"If I do, it won't be Human. I don't want Marcus to be tipped off if we can avoid it. Also, your bomb squad would be worthless against a Vis bomb," he noted.

Alison hung up the phone as they walked quickly out the door. She trotted down 16th with Sean on her heels.

"What have we got?" he asked, his voice controlled.

"We have a Bravo Tango in Cheeseman Park." Alison said, using the code for bomb threat so as not to freak out any civilian who might overhear them.

Sean picked up his pace.

"The Mages will meet us on scene." she said.

SEAN HUGHES sat in Alison's car on the phone with dispatch, telling them the situation. They were going to have EMS prepared if needed. *I don't like not being able to evac the park,* he thought, but if they did, there was too high a chance that

Marcus would set off the bomb early. He texted Mandy to see where she was.

"Home. Why?" she asked.

"Just stay there, please," Sean sent back.

It felt like an eternity before she texted back, "Ok".

Alison drove quickly to the park, pulling up in the lot with just minutes to spare. Sean didn't see Gabriel or Maddison when he got out. There was a flash of peach next to him as Amy appeared.

"We are masking our presence and yours; hopefully Angelica won't find us," she said as Maddison flashed into existence next to Amy, followed by Gabriel and Faith.

"Nothing yet," Maddison told Gabriel.

"Sean, Alison," he said, "we don't know what we are looking for. We need your help. Alison, you are with me; Sean you are with Maddison."

Sean didn't argue with him. The command in Gabriel's tone was impossible to ignore.

Amy vanished again, and Sean walked quickly with Maddison.

"What are we looking for? I don't know how to find Human bombs," she said.

"Anything that doesn't look like it belongs … can you see into cars?" he asked, having an idea.

"Yes," she said, "But Amy will be better; she can break a cloak if she finds one."

"Amy, can you hear me?" Sean asked.

"Yes I can," her voice said next to him.

Sean continued looking around with Maddison as Amy searched the insides of cars. They didn't have very long, and a part of Sean worried that not only he, but innocents were going to be killed if Gabriel had reliable information. He couldn't help but notice people in the park. With the mild weather, people were going out for runs and walks, or were enjoying their lunch breaks eating outside. A car caught his eye. Sean couldn't place exactly what was wrong with it. Maybe it was parked too perfectly, or maybe it was just his gut telling him something was up.

"Amy; white sedan," he said, as he and Maddison went over to the car.

Amy couldn't find anything, but Sean looked underneath it. There it was, or rather there it wasn't. The whole gas tank of the car had been replaced with a giant bomb.

MADDISON BELDAME didn't need Sean to tell her they'd found the bomb; his body language said it all. She looked at the time, it was 3:59 p.m. *Dammit,* she thought. In a rush, she pulled on her Vis, letting it flair inside her. She pushed Sean back as she spoke, "Continent," making a blue bubble encapsulate the car. "Gabriel, we found it!" she said, and then the car exploded.

Her ward flashed so bright, it nearly outshone the winter sun. Maddison's heart raced from the drain on her Vis. She dropped to a knee. In the background, she noticed Sean jump away, calling out. The ward was weakening; Maddison needed to control the energy inside. Instead of exploding and being over in a flash, the air inside the ward was superheated, being a bomb itself. "Frigus," she said, freezing the air inside. As the air froze, her containment ward stopped draining her. It was over. Maddison let her Vis go. As the spell disappeared, all that was left of the car was a hunk of blackened metal on charred and melted ground. People around the park had been taken off guard by the flash of light, and were now starting to panic.

Maddison breathed, out feeling exhausted. From behind her there was a bright flash of lavender light.

ALISON KAUR shielded her eyes from bright blue Vis. She looked to where Maddison and Sean had been. Maddison was kneeling on the ground; Sean was standing up. Before them was where a car had once been. Gabriel had left Alison's side; and none too soon. A man with a sword came out of nowhere, sending Vis at Maddison. Gabriel blocked it with a wall of purple.

Alison drew her weapon as she saw other Mages arriving. There were four others. Alison made to fire at one, but stopped as a hand gripped her arm. Her head snapped to the woman who stopped her.

"That will be enough Alison; we will take it from here," Melinda Decor said.

Next to Melinda was her husband Edward, Olivia, and Matthew Beldame.

Alison was wrapped in a cocoon of blue Vis as she and Melinda lifted into the air. On the ground, Matthew Beldame vanished in a burst of maroon Vis. Melinda was muttering to herself, and Alison watched as Edward and Olivia drew Katanas. Anyone left in the park was running away, so Alison didn't feel worried as she watched Edward and Olivia approach the other Mages. Columns of Vis shot into the air from the Mages they approached. Edward stopped, a column of emerald Vis surrounded him and lighting up the park. A bright pink column enveloped Olivia, and Alison felt a chill run down her spine.

GABRIEL DECOR moved behind Maddison, blocking a spell. He stood tall, looking into cold blue eyes. The man before him had sandy hair with a firm square jaw; he wore a white coat with his hand on the hilt of a broadsword.

"You've become quite the fan of attacking people from behind, Marcus," Gabriel said in a voice like ice.

Marcus Vies smiled tightly, "It's about defeating your opponent, Gabriel; you know that," he said, and then added, "so it looks like Tracy wasn't dead after all."

"You sound disappointed," Gabriel noted.

Marcus shrugged, "A little; I honestly thought you'd take in Keith," Marcus said, looking to his right where the other Mages fought; Keith among them.

Gabriel laughed once without humor, "You planned on us taking in one of your people? You lied to that girl so she'd lead us here?"

Marcus looked back to him, "I lied to both of them. Everyone breaks, Gabriel; if you got one of them, it would only be a matter of time … though I would have preferred it wouldn't have been Tracy; she had potential."

"Had" was the key word. Gabriel knew that if Tracy ever tried to return to Trinity, she'd be killed.

"So what was the point then; why continue your attack if you thought she was dead," Gabriel asked. When he'd talked to Tracy, he didn't think about what a bad target a park was. It was wide open with not that many people, compared to something like a mall.

"You, of course," Marcus said, "I can't have you and your sister messing with Trinity anymore. Sorry, Gabriel." Then, "Tell me why do you work with them?" his tone was legitimately curious.

"With whom?" Gabriel asked.

Marcus scoffed, "Humans … honestly; the country we are in is supposed to be the strongest of them; and still the Decors and Beldames could take it down with the help of your branch families. Two families could do that to their most powerful country; so why serve them?"

"You know the answer to that question," Gabriel spat.

"At one time maybe, but while morals may have kept me from fighting to enslave them at one time; I no longer feel that way. Honestly Decor, you work with them; you must see how truly weak they are. I'm not talking about Vis either, but Humans as a group," he accused.

Gabriel bit back a retort.

"You can't disagree with me without lying can you? HA! How can you work with such a pathetic group? They punish the strong and encourage weakness," he said biting, "They help put others into power who promise them the world and then enslave them," Marcus laughed, "Then they don't even have the courage to remove them from power. How many dictators have Humans had? Tell me Gabriel, what dictators has the Vis world had? The closest were the Succubi; but that empire fell hundreds of years ago. How can Humans be left to rule themselves? How long until one of their dictators wipes out everyone in the world? Surely you see it's only a matter of time. Even they see it. They consume stories of the end of the world like a child would candy. They fear their own power, but do nothing to control it; they let the wicked and tyrannical run rampant. They are weak!"

Gabriel didn't have an answer for him. These were all questions he'd asked himself. But that was before Alison and Sean. At one time, he would have agreed with Marcus wholeheartedly, but no longer. He thought of those he was now friends with, *no; the strong have not died out yet.*

"You work with murders, pimps, and drug dealers. It's no wonder you think the way you do. You claim they are weak; but how many of those tyrants have they removed from power? Some have stayed in power, yes; but if you recall we had some of our own who tried to take power. Or do you not remember the Nobilis?" Gabriel said.

Gabriel could see out of the corner of his eye as the Trinity Mages were being taken out by Olivia and Edward. There was a flick of Vis in the air uncloaking a Seeker. Marcus and Gabriel both turned their heads to watch as the Seeker was hit by maroon and blue Vis, his body being torn to shreds as he screamed. At once, the Trinity Paladins started to lose badly. Gabriel turned away as Olivia cut the legs off one.

"Re-growing limbs can take some time," Marcus said, "But reattaching them is a snap, isn't it?" he said.

Gabriel flexed his left hand and forearm, remembering when Marcus had cut them off. The pain was a memory that Gabriel could never forget. With his right hand, he gripped Iram, "Enough talk," he said pulling the blade from its sheath.

Marcus smiled widely, drawing Amare his broadsword. He'd once told Gabriel that he'd chosen to name his blade love because he used it to protect that which he loved, but now Gabriel looked at the blade with hate. Vis pulsed inside of him. Marcus was enveloped in gold Vis, Amare burning brightly. Gabriel pushed Vis into Iram.

He yelled as he ran forward, as did Marcus. The two blades met with a clang, the Vis from them pushing against one another. The massive amounts of energy had nowhere to go except to the sides, up and down. A wave of Vis cut into the earth as cars in a lot by them were sliced apart. Gabriel pushed with all his might on Marcus's sword. He wasn't able to move forward. The two separated.

Marcus swung his sword, making a tendril like a whip lash out at Gabriel. The whip smacked against a purple sphere around Gabriel. He jumped in the air, pushing with Vis and making it appear he was going to attack from above. Marcus did the same. Gabriel zipped to the ground to out-flank Marcus, but it didn't work. *Think, Gabriel! Dumb tricks aren't going to work on him,* he chided. He swung Iram at Marcus's side, but was deflected. Marcus attacked, and Gabriel defended. He pushed more Vis into his body augmenting it, and they both moved in a flash. Their movements were graceful, though deadly. There was a kind of joy in meeting your match. For every inch Gabriel took, he lost one.

Marcus lifted himself in the air while sending a car not at Gabriel, but at one of the apartment buildings around the park. Gabriel stopped it, but as he did, Marcus attacked him and cut Gabriel's arm. In that moment, Gabriel's heart sunk. Gabriel would have to choose. Did he protect the people in the area, and perhaps not defeat Marcus? Or did he let them die, and defeat his enemy of ten years?

Gabriel backed away from Marcus as he threw a tree at him; it glowed with gold Vis that made it strong. Gabriel struck it down, but missed another that Marcus threw. He watched in horror as it careened toward an apartment building. It struck a wall of blue.

Maddison's voice buzzed in his ear, "I'm weak; but I can keep him contained." Olivia's voice came in, "Your father and I will help her Gabriel; and Amy, Melinda, and Matthew are keeping this out of the notice of those in the area no matter how high you go. No Human will see this outside of the park, and Matthew is evacuating the few remaining here. You are good to go full power."

Gabriel gritted his teeth, letting Vis explode inside himself. Below him was a large stone pavilion that could hold dozens of people.

"Effodiunt volare circulus!" he roared.

ALISON KAUR watched as Edward killed the last of the enemy Mages. Like his son, Edward was anything but passive and harmless. Gabriel was desperately trying to ward off attacks from Marcus to keep others safe. She saw the blue Vis that stopped a tree.

"What's happening?" Alison asked Melinda.

Melinda was silent for a moment and then she pushed her finger to her ear, "Matthew, find innocents; get them out of here. Amy, block outside Mages; I will make sure no one can see this fight. We don't need to send the city into panic as two Arks try to kill one another." Melinda turned to Alison, "All we can do is contain; it is up to Faith and Gabriel to deal with the Vieses."

"Are there Mages from outside trying to attack?" Alison asked.

"Perhaps. Seekers started to look into the park as soon as they sensed Marcus and Gabriel fighting. It has been years since two Mages this powerful fought." Melinda smiled tightly, "There was a time that when your kind saw two Paladins this strong fight, they thought it was the gods going to war."

Alison turned away, trying not to think about Melinda's last statement. Alison gasped as the stone pavilion broke into pieces; some the size of cars, lifting to swirl in the air around Gabriel. Her mouth fell open, thinking of the power it would take to lift one chunk of stone the size of a car, let alone dozens of them. They orbited Gabriel, blocking cars and trees that Marcus sent at him. Alison watched as the park was destroyed, and neither Mage was hurt. A tear rolled down her cheek, *the gods are at war.*

FAITH PENN altered the air around Gabriel, trying to shift his appearance. Angelica blocked her. Faith sent little spells out all around her, trying to find the other woman. Try as she might; she was unable. *You can do this Faith, you have beaten her before, and you will now!* Faith dropped in the air, changing her location. Vis was bombarding her; she was having a hard time diverting it. Faith sent out waves of Vis, trying to detect Angelica's location.

There were bursts of red Vis that crashed into Faith's cloak, cracking it. As it weakened, Angelica attacked harder. Faith had to move focus away from finding her, and protecting Gabriel. She strained to keep her defenses up as she bobbed around above the park. Her cloak broke, and Faith moved out of the way of a knife too late. The blade dug into her arm. Faith cried out, but didn't waste any Vis to stop the pain. She had to get her cloak back up. She pushed Vis into wards, keeping any other attacks Angelica had at bay.

She struggled to re-cloak herself, and finally managed to. In the time it had taken her to do that, Gabriel was starting to lose. *He needs you if he is going to beat Marcus!* Faith was livid with herself for failing, even if only for a moment. She doubled her efforts at protecting Gabriel, not worried about her own defense for the moment. Gabriel was able to keep Marcus at bay, and was now starting to get a slight upper hand. Faith decided to take a risk. She weakened her cloak just a bit. She felt Angelica attacking, and acted like she was fighting the other Seeker.

At once, Angelica pushed hard on Faith's cloak. Faith closed her eyes, bringing her crystal ball in front of her. She looked with it, seeing where her Vis flowed, looking for areas that were off. "THERE!" she opened her eyes. Vis rushed from her to where she thought Angelica was. The air turned ruby, forming into a sheer. Faith attacked her with all she had. Faith pushed on the cloak, and soon she could see the face of Angelica Vies contorted in rage and effort. Angelica looked at her.

Faith let her Vis roll into a spell, "Rumpere brachium." The spell met resistance, but Faith pushed harder. Angelica yelped, and Faith watched her arm twist as it broke. Angelica's defensive spells broke for a second, and Faith said, "Dolorem."

Angelica's face twisted in pain, but she continued to keep Faith at bay in the fight with the Paladins.

Sorry Gabriel, you need to be on your own for a moment, Faith thought, removing her protection from him. Focused completely on her pain spell, she lit up every pain receptor in Angelica Vies' body. The woman screamed and fell from the sky. She landed hard, writhing on the ground in pain and screaming at the top of her lungs. Faith looked to the fight with Marcus and Gabriel, the prior pausing at his wife's screams. Faith threw herself into making Marcus Vies' world turn. Still keeping Angelica paralyzed with pain, she made images appear in front of Marcus, keeping him from seeing Gabriel.

Gabriel attacked Marcus, slashing at him with Iram. Marcus barely blocked the attack. Gabriel swung again and again. Marcus was beaten down to the ground, taking injuries left and right. Faith grinned, throwing all she had at Marcus, as she watched him trying to defend himself. He was next to his wife and stood over her. At once, her screams stopped. Pain was the spell of a Paladin, and Faith was no match for Marcus blocking her spell. The two of them vanished in a cloak of ruby, and with that the Vieses were gone.

Faith touched down on the ground, the park around her devastated. There had been a terrible cost to this victory. Cars were strewn about, trees ripped from the ground and the white stone pavilion was in pieces. Her brother landed next to her. Erin rushed into the park to tend to the injured. Faith's mother came up to her with a proud smile on her face. She squeezed her daughter tightly, "You beat her on your own as I knew you would."

Melinda held her at arm's length, looking into her daughter's eyes, "Today you did things that I would have never thought to do, and showed mastery beyond that of my own," Melinda said. Faith felt a catch in her throat. Her mother had never said anything like this to her before. "Before today, Angelica and I were the two best Seekers in the world; but no longer. Today you proved that you are truly better than both of us. I am proud of you."

Faith wanted to cry. She was feeling so happy and overwhelmed at the same time, but she didn't cheapen the moment by doing that. Instead, she thanked her mother, and said that she would do her best to continue to make her proud.

SEAN HUGHES directed uniformed officers and emergency response as they locked down what was left of the park. He'd never seen destruction like what he'd witnessed that day. The worst part was that the park had been built on one of Denver's original cemeteries. The ground was torn up from the Mages' fight, sending bits of wood and bones from the old graves. It made for a truly macabre scene.

"So is Homeland Security going to take over from here?" he asked Agent Alesbury.

"Nope. The bomb didn't hurt anyone, and they told me that it wasn't a terrorist attack. Gabriel and Faith were the targets here." Alesbury said, "So you're still stuck on the job."

Sean smiled, "Good to know."

He walked up to Gabriel and Faith, "Way to save the day, guys."

"How so?" Gabriel asked, "We didn't kill Marcus Vies."

"No, but you beat him. Today is a win. It marks the end of a long string of crap, from the Sergeant to today. Trinity is on the run now," Sean said.

Sean breathed out. For the first time in a long time, the tides had changed. No longer was Trinity calling the shots, and that felt good to Sean.

EPILOGUE

SEAN HUGHES cracked open a can of soda. He would have rather been having a beer, but they were on duty. He, along with the whole team except Erin, was in one of the station's large conference room celebrating their victory. In the corner of the room, a TV played a recording of the news that morning.

"A group of Mages destroyed Cheeseman Park yesterday, as Denver Police Department Mages Gabriel Decor and Faith Penn tried to bring the head of an organized crime ring into custody. The man they fought is named Marcus Vies, and is at large and considered extremely dangerous. The Mages working for the city were able to contain a bomb and stop an attack on several apartment complexes. No humans were hurt in the attack, but several Trinity Mages were killed. The Mayor is calling Gabriel, Faith, and the other Mages, men, and women who have been working the case heroes …" the anchor said.

Sean didn't think it would ever get old hearing that. Trinity was far from dead, but for the most part, they'd been pushed out of Denver. Sean didn't know how long the FBI would keep him and Alison to hunt Trinity in the rest of the country, but he didn't care at the moment.

GABRIEL DECOR did his best to be in a good mood. They had made progress, and he could see why Alison and the other cops and FBI agents were happy; this was a signal to them that the tides had changed. Trinity had taken heavy losses, and both Gabriel and Faith had defeated their opponents. They could beat Trinity. But Gabriel found it hard to celebrate, knowing that Marcus and Angelica were still out there. He knew they weren't beaten yet. Nor would they be until they were dead.

Maddison was next to him. Gabriel was impressed with her. She'd stopped a bomb all on her own, which was saying something. The car that held the bomb was beyond gone, and therefore CSIs were going to be unable to learn more about the bomb the car held, but Sean had told Gabriel that the bomb would have taken out most of the park. Even many Arks wouldn't have been able to contain a blast like that; never mind being able to help in a fight after doing it.

"What?" Maddison asked, noticing him regarding her.

"Just thinking about how impressed I am with you and your performance yesterday," he said honestly.

She blushed, making Gabriel laugh. She was serious, "the fight with Marcus … thank you for saving my life," she said.

"Anytime."

"What was it like?" she blurted, "Fighting someone that strong? I saw the two of you use spells I have never needed in real or fake combat."

Gabriel paused for a bit, "Good in so many ways. He's stronger than before," Gabriel smiled a bit, "But so am I."

Their conversation was cut short by Erin coming into the conference room quickly. She looked frazzled.

"Thanks for coming Er-" Sean started, "What is it?"

The room went silent.

Erin looked at Gabriel, "There is something wrong with the drugs you took from Trinity."

"Yes, we know they have been altered to be more addictive, and stay in people's systems longer." Alison said.

Erin shook her head, looking more worried, "No, that's not it." She looked at Gabriel again, "I'm so sorry Gabriel; with the focus being on weapons, I have been putting all of my time into helping James with any enchanted objects that might hurt people, and getting ready for injured people ..."

"Erin, what is wrong with the drugs?" Gabriel asked firmly. Erin didn't normally panic; Gabriel wanted to keep her on topic.

She looked hopeless, "There was a bunch of filler content in them we thought was just failed alterations, but I was looking at them, and ... they've changed."

"What's changed; the drugs?" Sean asked.

Erin nodded, "Yes, about an hour ago the samples started to change. Not all of them, just some. There were compounds and enchanted elements in them that activated ... it was like they were on a timer or something. We didn't detect them before now ..." she said.

"What do they do?" Alison asked.

Erin shook her head, "I don't know yet."

A uniformed officer came in the room, "You guys seeing this?"

He didn't wait for an answer. Running over to the TV, he turned off the recording and turned to CNN. They were playing footage of several men being tackled by police. The men were trying to bite and claw at the cops.

"Whoa. Bath salts," Sean said, "They make some people crazy as Hell," Sean looked at the caption, "Sucks for Dallas PD."

"Just them?" the uniformed officer asked, turning to FOX News who had similar footage, but from LA. Then MSNBC with the same from New York. "It started happening about an hour ago, the news said."

"Erin, how long ago did the drugs change?" Gabriel asked her urgently.

She looked at the TV in horror, "About an hour ago."

From outside the room, Gabriel heard someone start to scream.

SAMPLE OF ARK

TRACY HOPE woke, her eyes blinking in bright sunlight. Above her was a high, cream-painted ceiling. She was dreaming. She rose up in bed to look around the room. She knew this dream. At the moment, Tracy was in control of her body and emotions, but it wouldn't stay that way. It never stayed that way. The dream was a memory from ten years ago. Tracy looked to her left, gazing out of a large window that looked into the heart of Hiems. The City Lord had returned two weeks prior, his forces pushed out of Domum, a Vis town somewhere in the States. The war would end in six months' time, but Tracy's eleven-year-old self didn't know that. None of the Nobilis did. That was what made this dream so horrible. Tracy was inside her eleven-year-old dream, reliving the last day of Hiems.

Tracy lost control of her body as the dream moved of its own accord. She left her room to go have breakfast. At the kitchen table was her teacher, Johanna. Johanna's normally expressionless face looked concerned. She sat at the table contemplating her eggs as if they were a complex math problem. Tracy sat across from her. Her name wasn't Tracy yet. Marcus had recommended that name. Her real name was Kajsa, and she had been living in Hiems for two years.

Johanna didn't say anything to Tracy as she sat.

"Is everything ok?" Tracy asked.

"No," Johanna said after a moment, "I think it might be time to send you away from Hiems."

Tracy felt a pang in her gut. Why didn't Johanna want her around anymore?

"Johanna, I will try harder; I promise!" Tracy said, desperate to stay, "I can learn faster, you will see … I I I," she spluttered. She couldn't be alone again.

Johanna looked sad, "I am not sending you away because you have done something wrong or because you do not train enough. Hiems very well might be attacked soon. I do not want you to get hurt."

Hiems might be attacked? That didn't make sense at all. Not with the City Lord here.

"But the City Lord is home; the Arks won't come here," Tracy protested.

Johanna's expression became concerned, "His presence here is why Hiems will be attacked." She said, "You know he lost the battle in America. The Arks will strike while his forces are weak."

"But he will beat the Arks," Tracy said defiantly, "He killed an Ark in Domum didn't he?"

Johanna nodded, "Yes, he did. From my understanding; as Stella Beldame's army recaptured Domum, the City Lord was able to fight and defeat her."

Tracy knew that the Nobilis had taken heavy losses in Domum, but the bulk of the City Lord's army made it home to Hiems. They would be safe.

Before Johanna could say anything else, there was a siren outside. Johanna turned pale and muttered to herself, "They attack so soon?"

Johanna stood, as did Tracy. "Go to the basement," Johanna ordered.

"What's happening?" Tracy asked, worried.

"We are under attack. Now go to the basement until I come and get you."

"No!" Tracy said, "I will fight the Arks with you!"

"You will do no such thing," Johanna said firmly, "you have learned much of the sword, but you have no control over your Vis. Now go!"

Just then Tracy saw something off in the distance. What was it? The light coming from the windows was red. Tracy looked out the window as did Johanna. Tracy could see a wall of red above the town. It was town wards. They wouldn't hold long against an assault. They were better suited to keeping Humans from finding Hiems and to repel small forces than to shield a town the size of Hiems from a large attack. The town's wards faltered under the unseen force. Then they vanished, and all was calm. Where were the Ark troops?

The sky turned dark above the town.

"Tracy, go now!" Johanna barked.

Tracy had never heard that tone from Johanna before. She obeyed, running from the room. In the hall she looked out a window as she passed it, and stopped. There were clouds above the center of the city. The house she was in was atop a hill; Tracy looked down on the town where people were running about. Trolls and wolves were in their full forms. Tracy enhanced her eyes. It was one of the few augmenting Vis skills she'd mastered.

The people looked terrified. It was obvious who were the City Lord's troops. They wore uniforms and jackets of purple; the City Lord's crest embroidered on their backs.

There was a clap of thunder making Tracy jump, her gaze moving to the dark sky. Parts of the clouds almost seemed to glow. She gasped as bolts of lightning shot from the clouds, striking the center of town. She refocused on the people, some of whom now lay on the ground dead, smoke rising from their bodies. Tracy turned away in horror, running for the basement.

She was in the corner of the room, her practice sword clutched in her hand. Would she need to defend herself? She stayed in the corner for hours as she listened to muted crashes and booms from outside. A large boom shook the house, followed by the sound of splintering wood and glass. Above her, she heard the house coming down. Miraculously, the basement wasn't affected. Tracy huddled in the corner, shaking in fear. The rational part of her mind told her the city had been breached. *Are we winning?* She wondered. No, she decided, they weren't.

Johanna's teaching came into her mind. She started thinking about battle tactics Johanna had taught her. *The high ground will be important.* Tracy thought. Tracy lived on a hill, putting her house on the high ground. That must have been why Johanna hadn't told Tracy to try to make it to some short of shelter. The City Lord and his army would try to hold the hill that Tracy and Johanna lived on, wouldn't he? That would have made staying in the house dangerous, though. It would be the center of the battle.

Tracy was confused. There were no sounds coming from outside, but she was too frightened to go look for Johanna. *She told you to wait,* Tracy remembered. So she waited, and waited, and waited, until finally sleep took her.

The next day, Johanna didn't come for her. On the third day, driven by hunger, Tracy ventured out of the basement. The house was gone. As she reached the main level, she was greeted by blackened wood and open sky. On either side of her house, other homes were burned, smoke coming from larger buildings in town still on fire.

Tracy couldn't believe her eyes. Bodies were everywhere. Mutari and Mage alike littered the streets. Tracy made her way downtown, hoping to find Johanna. All she found was blood and rubble. Her once-beautiful home was now a mound of bodies, burned building, and rocks.

"Who are you?" A voice asked.

Tracy spun to see several Mutari in black coats. With a start, she realized they were Ark troops. Tracy spun, running down what was left of Main Street.

"Hey come back!" They cried after her.

Tracy hid in some debris, surprised that the Mutari didn't chase her.

She didn't find anyone she knew. Well, she didn't find anyone alive that she knew. She did, however, find where the main battle must have taken place. It was around the City Lords home in the center of town. Bodies in purple and black covered the ground, blood oozing from wounds.

Tracy stayed in the shadows to avoid the notice of Ark troops in the area. They were ordering around some Trolls in purple. *Prisoners*, Tracy figured. The Trolls were gathering bodies to be burned. Tracy couldn't stand the sight of it. She looked away, noticing something she hadn't before.

It was an arm. Tracy crawled to the body, wondering if she knew the person. It was a woman, her face under some wood. Tracy's heart began to pick up. She looked like Johanna, but that wasn't possible; Johanna was one of the top Paladins in town. She wouldn't have lost. *No, Johanna had been captured by the Arks*, Tracy tried to tell herself. She moved the wood off the woman's face.

She tried to scream, but no sound escaped her. The left half of Johanna's head was gone, blood soaking her clothes. Tracy reached out to touch Johanna's face and found the skin was cold beneath her touch. Tracy's vision swam as tears filled her eyes. How had this happened? Tracy moved more debris off Johanna's body. Next to her was her sword, Dolor. Tracy looked down on the blade. *Didn't you defend your master?* She thought accusingly at it. Then she heard the sound of people coming. *The body crew,* she realized.

Prior to being taken in by Johanna, Tracy had spent a year living on the streets in Stockholm. As she heard the sound of boots on pavement, a part of her that had been asleep for several years awoke. It was the part of her that had kept her alive during her time on the street. Tracy reached out, gripping Dolor in her hand, hefting the familiar blade. She was only able to spare one more glance for Johanna before she darted away from the sound of approaching people, her instincts pushing her onward.

Tracy woke with a start. She looked up to the heavy metal door of her cell. Her breath was heavy, her eyes sore. How long had she been crying? She wasn't in Hiems. She was in a cell owned by the Decor family.

Tracy shook her head trying to rid herself of her dream. *It wasn't a dream; it was a memory,* she told herself. It was the worst time of her life, and she had been replaying it every night for a week. Or at least she thought it had been a week. A few years after Hiems, Tracy met Marcus and he'd taken her in, told her about how he hadn't ordered the attack of her town. That he was appalled by the death of those in Hiems. Marcus told her he'd known of Johanna, and would have never wanted her to be killed. Part of Tracy knew those were lies. Before she could think about anything else, the door to her cell opened.

About the Author

Nicholas was born and raised in Denver, Colorado. He didn't want to write until October of 2007. While he was driving around with a friend and said "hey, I wonder if I can write a book." So he thought he would try and write outline and see what happens.

www.NicholasTaylor.co

www.ingramcontent.com/pod-product-compliance
Lightning Source LLC
LaVergne TN
LVHW050928080826
845145LV00001B/250

* 9 7 8 1 9 3 8 3 8 7 0 7 4 *